A matter of Fate

heather lyons

http://www.heatherlyons.net

A Matter of Fate
Cerulean Books
ISBN: 978-0-9858653-3-7
First Edition

Cover Photograph and Design by Carly Stevens.

To Jon, with love.

a matter of fate

part I

chapter 1

I am a chronic daydreamer.

Not so much because school bores me—in fact, a number of my classes are pretty interesting. No, I tend to daydream about escape routes. Places to run to when the inevitable, predetermined outcomes of my rigid life leave me no other choice. If it's possible, even in the tiniest way, just how would I break away from what Fate and family has set before me?

Florence is currently my favorite spot to imagine disappearing in. It's a city of impossible beauty and history, one I've longed to explore. Maybe I'd become an artist there— not that I'm artistic by any means, but maybe I'd be inspired to be something new. Different.

There's also the possibility of New England. My parents took me there once when I was little, the only time I've ever been outside of California. My father went for work, and while he was busy, my mother drove me to a number of little towns running up and down the coastline. One particular small city in New Hampshire is rooted in my memory, where flowers practically raced in bursts of color straight to the ocean's edge. It was incredibly charming, the perfect sort of place to go and be someone—anyone, really—who isn't me.

Are you kidding? snorts a little voice in the back of my mind. *C'mon, why pick these places, when there is a much better place for you, and you know it?*

Inwardly, I groan at the thought. My conscience has always been far too opinionated.

I move on, wondering what sheer anonymity would be like—to simply be a girl in a nondescript place, serving pancakes and mugs of coffee to weary travelers on long journeys. The land would be flat and golden as far as the eye could see, and driving through it, with the windows down, I'd be able to smell sweet grass in warm air.

And there's the far north, where the Northern Lights illuminate the sky. I'd be speechless upon seeing them for the first time, standing in snow while gazing upon ribbons of color streaking across the stars. I wouldn't have to be anyone there, either. I'd be just another person, in another small town, making my own choices.

I don't bother looking up when the classroom door creaks open, because I'm still imagining those Northern Lights, still wondering how liberating it'd be to feel so small and insignificant for once. For as long as I want.

A voice breaks through, though. One impossible to ignore. "Excuse me," it says, "I'm new to the class."

My entire body freezes, all except my heart, which goes berserk. Because I know this voice, and this can't be real.

He's not real.

The ground under me shifts. It's like an earthquake—not the rolling kind, but the jarring sort that comes out of nowhere, hits you hard, and then disappears just as quickly. The kind that leaves you stunned and wondering if it happened at all, it moved so fast. All I can do is reach out and grip the edges of my desk and pray I don't fall out of my seat.

Because it's not an earthquake. It's a shift, and I'm the only one in the room who can feel it. A quick glance once the ground settles confirms this. Everyone is working, talking quietly to one another, or watching the front of the room. There are no signs from anyone that anything had just happened.

But something did.

And he's standing in front of the classroom next to Mr. Snook.

I blink a few times as I stare at him, trying to determine if I'm actually awake. Every time I open my eyes, though, he's still here. Oh my gods. He's *here*.

The guy I'm staring at is tall, athletic, and quite tan, with blackish hair and eyes so clear, so blue, they replicate a cloudless sky. I should know—I've stared into them often enough.

A shy smile creeps across his gorgeous face, creating a dimple in his left cheek as he hands Snook a piece of paper. A textbook is passed over and he's pointed off towards an empty seat. The class explodes in whispers when he sits down; everyone blatantly stares at him. It's obvious he hears it all, because a faint pink stain tinges his cheeks. His longish hair shields part of his face, but it doesn't matter. We've all seen enough of him to continue ogling.

From behind me comes, "Hot. So hot!" Several girls nearby giggle in agreement.

"Math, people." Snook taps the board in irritation. "Gossip on your own time." The reprimand quiets the majority of the class, but the girls behind me text furiously back and forth, their fingers flying across keyboards.

It's hard, but I tear my eyes away from the boy, shocked. I stare blankly at my book, unsure what to do.

How many times had I imagined this scenario before? Too many to keep track of, that's for sure. How can this be real?

Snook's voice resumes its familiar drone at the front of the classroom, but in the confusion of what's happened, I'm unable to put meaning to any of his words. They blur together in low sounds, like the teachers in *Peanuts* cartoons. I ought to pay attention, what with a test coming up, but I can't.

Not with *him* here.

When I look over at the new boy again, the ground shifts for a second time. He's working on some equation Snook put on the board, one I haven't attempted, thanks to being shell-shocked and all. But then he reaches out and grabs the sides of his desk, like he's steadying himself. Like he somehow feels the shift, too. Black hair spills down across his eyes as he takes a deep breath, hiding everything but a small, knowing smile.

He's sitting by the windows, doing math—in my classroom! He's no daydream, no figment of my imagination—although for many years he'd been exactly that.

I realize I'm staring when his blue eyes lift to meet my green ones. A jolt of electricity zaps through my body, all tingly, with promises of familiarity and excitement rolled into one. We stare intently at one another for a good fifteen seconds until a girl next to me asks to borrow a pencil. My eyes jerk back towards my desk and I mumble an incoherent apology. It's just long enough of a reprieve for me to begin hyperventilating.

Get a grip on yourself! the little voice barks. *You're going to pass out!*

The pencil in my hand snaps, driving a splinter deep into my palm.

"Chloe?" Oops. Snook is talking to me. When I merely stare back, he tries, "Your answer, Miss Lilywhite?"

Unable to do anything else, as I have no idea what problem we're even on, I surge, stretching my mind out to someone nearby to find the answer. I land on some guy who's in the thralls of remembering a hot and heavy make-out session with his girlfriend rather than focusing on math, so I'm forced to flip through a number of graphic images before finding what I need.

I *hate* cheating, hate using anything other than my intelligence for schoolwork. This explains why I'm sitting in basic math, rather than AP Calculus like the Cousins.

The moment I find the answer, I pull myself out of the guy's mind, feeling dirty just having his thoughts mingling with mine. *Eww.* "It's X = 2y + 79z."

Snook moves on to the next problem and victim, as if there'd never been any pause at all.

Ugh! I'd gone nine months without cheating, something I was exceedingly proud of. The Cousins heckle me mercilessly about it, saying it's stupid to not use my gifts while in class. But I've held steadfast in my belief that school is a place for intelligence, not Magic.

Also, my hand is throbbing. Picking doesn't help—the splinter is driven even deeper by my efforts. And now I'm bleeding. Great.

When the class bell rings, most everyone packs up quickly so they can get to lunch, but the girls behind me are back to discussing *him*, clearly infatuated with his looks.

As for me, I'm still dazed with disbelief before realizing I should pack up, too. The pause is just long enough to notice Snook motion the new guy up for a quick conference. He walks to the podium with smooth, graceful motions that exude confidence.

I can't hear what Snook is asking, and this only exacerbates my curiosity. I try listening as long as possible until it's grossly apparent I'm sticking around out of nosiness. At least I'm not alone. All the girls behind me are doing the same.

I force myself to go to the door, but before I can walk through it, the urge to look back at him is irresistible. Despite Snook still talking, he looks directly at me. That dimpled smile I've always adored crosses his face, and I go lightheaded. When our eyes connect, a flood of memories rush through my mind, vivid as they were on the nights they were created.

He raises a hand and rakes it through his dark hair. A silver ring glints on his right thumb.

Not silver, reminds the little voice. *Titanium.*

I used to love playing with that ring, twisting it round and round on my thumb. There was an engraving on the inside, but in the haziness that often comes with memories, I can't remember the words. Completely freaked out now, I hurl myself into the hallway, smack into Cora.

"Hey!" She grabs my arm to steady me. "What's the rush?"

I can't help but look over. He's regarding me with an oddly frustrated expression. Blushing, I shove my Cousin out of the door's line of sight. "I'm just glad math is over."

Before she calls me out on my obvious lie, I stick my hand out. When she gently touches my hand, the splinter slides out along with the pain.

She eyes me critically. "Those shifts last period. You have anything to do with them? I'm thinking yes, as you're the only big fish in this small pond."

I nearly stagger, forcing her to detour us toward the nearest set of lockers. Concerned, she surges into my mind, flipping through the last period's events. She finds the shifts easily, but doesn't recognize the reason behind them. A squeeze to my shoulder indicates a need for better info, so I reluctantly push forward a memory a little over a year old to the forefront of my mind. Cora watches it silently, her fingers twisting her magenta-dyed hair. When she signals for more, I tentatively release a couple of incomplete memories from various time periods over the last decade.

"Did you see him? In my classroom?" I whisper, pressing myself up against a locker. My long hair feels sticky against my neck. "Was he real? I've gone insane, haven't I?"

"Yeah, I saw him. He was definitely hard to miss."

I don't know what to say. I'm so freaked out she puts her hand on my shoulder to calm me down. Thank goodness Cora is such a talented Shaman. Her Magical healing abilities have always been able to soothe me like no pill ever could. She's also the closest thing I have to a sister, despite the fact we're only loosely related at best and refer to one another as Cousins.

"Tell me everything," she demands. Cora's like that. She's always demanding one thing or another. "Start with why this is the first I've ever heard of this dude."

I'm not ready yet to share the true beginning. No, those memories are mine. So I began where I can—with the impossibility of the situation. "He's real!"

She gets the look on her face that means she's trying not to shake me. "Okay, but just exactly who *is* he?" When I don't answer, she presses, "Let's try something simpler. What's his name?"

I say it out loud, for the first time, in a really long time. "Jonah."

Jonah is here.

"Alright," she says, shooting the guy whose locker I'm pressed up against a dirty look and an order to get moving. "Where's he from?"

I want to laugh at the absurdity of her question. Where's he *from*? I can just imagine her response if I told her the truth.

"Chloe, how can I help you if you don't actually tell me anything? So far, all I know is that some guy in your math class triggered two shifts *and* caused you to go into shock. I don't recognize him, and you're making things considerably more confusing by repeating things like, 'Is he real? Did you see him?' after very clearly showing me memories you have of the two of you together."

"He's not real," I whisper.

She looks at me like I'm insane.

"I always wished he was, but even I couldn't make him real."

"Babe, I saw him. He's real."

But I shake my head over and over again, forcing my brown hair to go flying. Because Magic is real. Dreams are not.

And I've learned that one the hard way.

chapter 2

Cora and I navigate our way past the crowded food lines in the cafeteria to our normal table, finding all of the usual suspects already present. Meg and Lizzie scoot over to make room for us. Alex barely glances up from his book, murmuring, "Ladies," as if using our names is a chore.

These three are considered Cousins, too, although we share no blood relation. The endearment is more of an honorary one. And the other students at the table aren't relatives. They're people we hang out with while hiding from them who we really are. Because what none of the others know is that we *Cousins* are part of a race of people called Magicals. Our kind is responsible for influencing the course of events within our world and beyond. According to legend, Magicals have been around since the beginning of time, charting courses for the civilizations they populated. All of the major events which have occurred over the history of the Earth can be traced back to Magicals. That's not to say Magicals rule the world, though. We're merely the *cause* of an event. The *effect* is what society and the people within choose to do with it once it's begun.

While our existences have been mostly kept secret, there've been a number of legends created around us. Early peoples thought of us as gods and built temples to worship us, others called us angels. During other time periods, our kind were targeted as witches, demons, and sorcerers. The need for secrecy only compounded over the millennia, until a few hundred years ago when it became expressly forbidden to reveal our existences to any non-Magical.

Even more guarded is the fact that there is more than one plane of existence. Faerie tales and legends over the years have hinted at what is really truth, but Magicals work hard to keep the nons, or non-Magicals, of the various planes believing the stories are simply by-products of fantastical imaginations.

I haven't yet been to any other plane of existence other than my own, which my father taught me early on to know simply as the Human plane, as that's the species in the majority. There are seven planes in all, filled with nons and Magicals alike—Elvin, Goblin, Dwarven, Gnomish, Faerie, and Human, all linked to a central plane which functions as the Magicals' home base.

I'll be going there in the summer, perhaps never to return back here again.

There aren't a lot of us, fewer every year despite our kind being found in every species from every plane. There are probably 250–300 Magicals currently spread permanently across this plane for work, clustered in different pockets—others come and go thanks to more transient jobs, being based in the aforementioned central plane. Magicals blend in with the nons on their planes—you'd be hard pressed to tell if someone is a Magical or a non without surging or witnessing their craft in motion.

One time, when he'd been feeling particularly generous with his knowledge, my father explained, "Our family is comprised entirely of Magicals. That's how we manage to survive. We only live with our own kind—and by kind, I do not merely mean Human Magicals. That's why there are some of the other species here, even if in hiding."

I'd marveled at this and pressed for more information. My father denied me, thinking he'd perhaps already said too much. As a consolation, he reminded me that someday, when I was eighteen, I'd learn everything.

That's the age when we fully Ascend into our powers, the time in which all Magicals remove themselves from their current planes of existence in order to hone their crafts. Many return after years of training to their home worlds, to be sent off on missions dictated to them from a faraway Council.

Everything about being a Magical is preordained, set in stone. From the moment of birth, a Magical learns of their craft from a Seer and whether or not they'll join the governing Council. There's no room to maneuver, no room to change course. Everything is dictated by the nebulous yet all-important Fate.

I hate this. The idea that I'm not able to choose my own college, pick a major, try to find my own job, or live my life on my own terms chafes against my sensibilities.

Meg's giggling brings my attention back to the table. She's super effervescent, always finding the happiness present in every situation and reveling in it. She's a Joy, the epitome of friendliness, school spirit and peppiness. She's destined to help foster and maintain hope within society. People can't help but adore being around her.

Meg, though, adores being around Alex, although he never seems to notice. He's an Intellectual, and that means any matters worth his attention are normally scholastic in nature. This doesn't mean he isn't fun, because he can be, but he's typically more analytical and self-absorbed than the others. I'm not sure what Alex's specialty will be; he won't find out until Ascension. I envy this last bit of freedom he has, that the majority of the Cousins have. They can still dream about the possibilities ahead.

Not me. I'd been told early on about the road I'm to walk on. I'll never be assigned a specific group of people to influence, nor will I ever be tasked with maintaining certain cultural sectors. I'm a Creator, and that means someday, when I Ascend and learn how to master my craft, I'll have the power to build up and destroy civilizations at will. Or, at the very least, at the recommendation of the Council.

I'm labeled a Creator, but in reality I'm more like a two-headed monster from ancient legends, both a Creator and a Destroyer. I'm also slated to join the Magicals' governing Council. Refusal is absolutely forbidden. No one is ever asked to join the Council. You're told you're going to be a member, and when the time comes, you simply sit down in a seat that's been waiting for you.

This is my future. There's an office waiting for me and a group of people expecting my input and abilities. There is absolutely no way I can say *no thank you.* All my daydreaming about escaping to other parts of this world is just that: daydreams. None will ever come true. No matter where I run, I'll be found. If necessary, I'd be dragged kicking and screaming back onto my path until I fall in line.

I used to imagine creating my own world and escaping into it, but that sort of power won't be available to me until it's too late. A child's powers are limited—while we can technically carry out a number of our duties, we don't have the full extent of our range until we Ascend.

So, up until now, I've tinkered with creating small objects, drawing energy and resources from the natural world. When I was little, back when I liked being a Creator, I'd create tiny little planets to circle round my ceiling fan, alongside a field of stars I could gaze upon long into the night. I'd even create my own constellations, making up stories to go with them. But mostly, I'd create things I'd want, like dolls or tea sets or even princess dresses.

And this disappointed my mother to no end. "What would people think," she'd mutter as she'd collect up my supposed contraband to throw away—as if I couldn't just whip up more in the blink of an eye—"if they knew a Creator was wasting her gifts on dolls?"

But the kicker was, I didn't know then, and even still don't know, what exactly it is I'm supposed to be making, and the adults in my life don't seem to think I warrant an explanation, despite previous lines of questioning. I don't know if this is because I'm supposed to inherently know what I'm meant for, or if they just think I'm not worth the effort it takes to explain to me. And it's not like I get to go to a special high school for Magicals to get these answers. I really only have my parents and the other local Magicals to teach me, and that hasn't gone the way I'd like over the years.

So, I don't ask many questions anymore.

Lizzie's sharp elbow jars me out of the pity party I'm throwing myself. She's a Muse. Someday soon, she'll manipulate the creative course arts will take in society. She'd been told she'll be tasked with overseeing a new post-contemporary phase in painting. She's the only one of the Cousins who's as locked into her current destiny as I am. But where I resent what lies ahead—and it is unknown to me—Lizzie relishes it—and *knows* it.

I know what she's silently asking me, what a self-absorbed Alex has failed to address, and what a lovesick Meg is avoiding. Lizzie wants to know about the shifts.

I don't blame her. I mean, the ground shifted below me, and that's something that none in the Magical world can take lightly. I never thought it'd happen to me, though. Shifts always seemed to be for important people, for important events. Not for seventeen year-olds, and definitely not in high school.

Oh, stop, the little voice says. *You know Creators are a big deal, seventeen or one hundred and seventeen.*

I dutifully trail after Lizzie when she heads over to the soda machine to get a bottle of water. Refusal of Lizzie is like refusal of the Council. You just don't do it.

Without bothering to ask permission, Lizzie surges into my mind. Knowing it's pointless to withhold, I release the same information I did with Cora. She mulls the memories over before grabbing a drink. "Let's go outside," she orders, already heading toward the door. I throw a glance over to Cora, pleading for support. She's busy arguing with Alex, so I take a deep breath and follow Lizzie out.

We sit down on a bench near a shady tree, a quiet place no nons are near. Most everyone is lounging in the sun, reveling in the last few days of semi-warm weather before the chill of autumn hits Northern California.

She pulls no punches. "Tell me about this guy." But before I can answer, she says, staring across the courtyard, "He's a twin! Why didn't you show me that?"

Um . . . WHAT?

I follow Lizzie's line of vision and find the boy I know as Jonah talking with someone who looks exactly like him. Things shift again, not so momentously this time, but enough that Lizzie reaches out to steady herself on the bench.

I . . . I had no idea he was a twin. . . .

"You two okay?"

We look up to find Graham Parker watching us. Ever since he laid eyes on her in sixth grade, Graham's been in love with Lizzie. It saddens me to know that there's no hope for such a reciprocation of feelings. He's a great guy—athletic, handsome, intelligent and warm-hearted, the sort of boy mothers dream their daughters will find. All mothers, that is, except Lizzie's, who uttered one small sentence to her daughter a few years back effectively forbidding a match with a non.

Poor Graham. He, of course, has no idea about this. I scoot over to make space for him between me and Lizzie. "We're fine."

He sits down. "You two look a little shaken."

I resist the urge to laugh.

He takes off his letterman jacket and folds it into a neat square. "You girls ready for tonight?" Graham's captain of the football team and star quarterback of the region. Lizzie and I are both on the cheerleading squad—her voluntarily and me not-so-voluntarily.

My mother had been a cheerleader in high school and insisted on me carrying on the tradition. Lizzie naturally gravitated to such a role, as did Meg, who happens to be the squad's captain. Cora, smart girl, avoided joining the team. It's not that I hate cheerleading—I really don't. It's just . . . it's not me. And it's yet another thing I'm forced to do that I didn't get to pick. I'd rather be on the tennis team or taking art classes, like Lizzie. Or working on the newspaper, since I like writing and taking pictures. But no—I'm a cheerleader.

Lizzie answers for both of us. "Of course." I don't bother attempting to answer. Graham knows how I feel. "Think we'll win?"

Although he shrugs, his confidence is palpable. In my mind, Graham's got the world ahead of him—a lock on an athletic scholarship to whatever school he likes, choices of whatever subject he wants to pursue, and the ability to move to any place he fancies.

"You're too modest," Lizzie coos. "I'm sure you guys will do great."

Graham smiles shyly at her praise. I turn my head so they can't see me rolling my eyes at the saccharine exchange. While they continue to discuss football/cheerleading drivel, I tune them out and find Jonah and his brother sitting at a picnic table across the courtyard, surrounded by a group of girls.

Jonah is aware of my staring right away. Our eyes connect across the distance, and I am overcome by another rush that leaves me woozy. And then his brother notices the change of attention and turns to find me.

I very nearly pass out.

Graham elbows my arm, effectively breaking all eye contact. I blink and swing my focus back toward my friends.

"Go, team, go!" I weakly pump a fist into the air, because I really have no idea what the two next to me are talking about.

"Yes—go, history homework, go," Graham teases.

Busted. I shrug unapologetically and glance back at Jonah. He's here, at my school, sitting across the courtyard, with a twin, no less.

He's still staring at me while saying something to his brother. The twin nods, and I shove my eyes towards the ground.

How is this possible? More importantly, what should I do? Does he know who I am? Is it really him? Am I crazy?

Lizzie excuses herself to go get something in her locker, leaving me and Graham to sit in silence. He breaks it first by asking tentatively, "There's really no chance for me, is there?"

Whoa. In all the years he's loved Lizzie, he's never talked about it. It's been implied by his every move around her, every glance of longing, every gentle touch. But never in words—at least never to me.

I don't want to hurt his feelings, but I, of all people, know how cruel false hope is. Even still, I take the coward's way. "I don't know."

He nods, as if this is the answer he expected. And then, "How's math going?"

I don't fight him on the subject change. "Thanks to math, I'll never get into a school as good as you will."

"Whatever." He laughs. "You'll get into whatever school you want, Miss Honor Roll."

I beam, thinking how awesome it'd be if I could go to a regular college rather than just claim I would. "Nah, I'll probably end up around here so I can help out at my mom's nursery." He'll know soon enough that I'll be off, never to be heard from again.

"You're meant for far more important things than just potting flowers."

"Flowers are important, too," I joke. "It takes a special touch."

"Yeah, I know. But, Chloe—you could be anything you want. I know you're somebody important, something big."

I try not to show my surprise. Or my resentment.

When the bell rings, I give one last look toward the picnic table across the quad, but no one is sitting on it any longer.

chapter 3

Jonah's twin is in my history class. As I stare at him, I realize that, other than a small, smooth mole on the side of his left cheek, it would be nearly impossible to tell the difference between him and his brother.

But I can tell. Instantly. I knew it the moment I came into class. I'd even been able to tell the difference across the distance of the courtyard at lunch.

He's sitting next to Graham, legs sprawled out as he reads a book. When he momentarily closes it over a hand so he can reach into his messenger bag, I read the title. *On the Road,* by Jack Kerouac.

Interesting, the little voice murmurs.

Indeed.

When Graham leans over to introduce himself, I eavesdrop, paying close attention when the twin tells my friend his name. It's Kellan.

Why didn't I know that? Why didn't I know Jonah had a twin? Something in me feels like it's something I should've known.

Jonah's twin doodles absentmindedly instead of taking notes during the lecture. I'm mesmerized by just how much he can look like his brother and still seem so completely different at the same time. Kellan's extraordinarily gorgeous, just like Jonah. But there's something different about his demeanor. I can't quite put my finger on just what it is, though. It's like . . . night and day—like this one's whole aura radiates differently, as if his is a dark purple, whereas Jonah's is more of a cerulean blue.

The curiosity over their existences is so overwhelming that I decide to surge with Kellan. I know I shouldn't—it's wrong and sort of creepy, especially with nons who don't know they're being surged upon. It's an invasion of privacy, one they're not able to control.

The moment I enter his mind, though, he raises a hand and rubs his forehead.

There is no way he can feel me. Nons never can.

But then, curiosity turns into frustration. Kellan's nearly impossible to read, his thoughts zealously guarded. It sounds crazy, but his mind is a room filled with locked file cabinets.

I've never seen anything like it before. He absolutely fascinates me.

When I ease out of his mind, Kellan's pencil pauses above his notebook. His head swings around, narrowed eyes surveying the entire room suspiciously.

I'm stunned. *Could* he feel me surging?

Ridiculous. Absolutely impossible.

But why, then, are his thoughts so closely guarded? Most nons have no such protections in place. The average person's thoughts are scattered and freely available, unless it's a deeply repressed memory. Sometimes it can be difficult to surge with nons because it takes a lot of sorting to find what's being looked for.

Magicals, on the other hand, tend to only release what's necessary during a surge, and that's usually only done with permission, as it's considered rude to do so without it. Plus, only Magicals can feel another person surging. Not to be snobby or anything, but nons' minds just aren't as evolved as Magicals' are. So, how is it that this non-Magical boy has such a mind?

Why do you want two mysteries? Isn't one enough? admonishes the little voice.

But I can't help myself. When the bell rings, I dart over to Graham. "What a great lecture, huh?"

My tone's completely forced. I can't believe Graham doesn't pick up on it right away. But, I'm not here for a history recap. I've got a different goal in mind, and he's standing two feet away.

I stick out my hand, blocking his path when he moves to leave. In my peppiest cheerleader voice, I practically shout, "Hi! I'm Chloe! You're new to school, right!"

Graham's startled by my enthusiasm, as is Kellan. He shrinks back some before hesitantly sticking out his own hand. "Uh, Kellan. And yeah, it's my first day here."

His voice is moderately soft and rich, reminding me of hot chocolate on a really cold night. An overwhelming rush of goose bumps race up and down my arms, and my insides nearly melt in excitement.

And there's my hand. It's warm and tingly, like it's fallen asleep in the most pleasant of ways. He stares down at our joined hands before removing his, brows furrowed. Out of nowhere, a whole herd of butterflies beat inside my chest.

"So, you're new here!" I enthuse again lamely, silently cursing myself for becoming verbally stunted at his mere touch.

Kellan's furrowed brows give way to a bemusement. "Apparently."

Graham pats me on the shoulder like I'm his kid sister or something. "Chloe's one of our best cheerleaders."

"Is that so?" Kellan asks, raising one eyebrow ever so noticeably. The level of amusement in his eyes doubles. My cheeks burn.

I feel more than a little ridiculous. "Weelll . . ."

Lizzie joins us and Graham adds, "Lizzie's also on the cheerleading team." She fixes her gaze on Kellan and smiles warily.

When he greets her, I can tell, without a doubt, he's not a victim of instant Muse-worship. He's the first guy I've seen to not fall prey to Lizzie's charms upon contact. My fascination with him grows.

Then Kellan gives me a mysterious smile. I have no idea how to respond, so I merely stare back, my heart racing a million miles a minute. His smile evolves into a sly, knowing one as he turns to leave, reminding me of the one Jonah had right after the second shift.

In the hallway, Lizzie says, "It's interesting how he wasn't affected by me."

"Maybe you're losing your touch," I joke. "Maybe when the Ascension rolls around, you won't be a Muse. Maybe you're actually an Intellectual."

She laughs. "Maybe *you're* the Muse. I couldn't believe how his feelings jolted around when your hands touched."

I stop in my tracks. "How do you know that?"

She tugs me forward. "It's a little known fact, but some Muses can attune themselves to a tiny bit of emotions from those around them, if they're strong enough. It allows us to . . ."—and here she has the decency to look embarrassed— ". . . feed off of those feelings to help create a . . . uh . . . bond."

"And what kind of bond would *that* be?"

Lizzie sticks her tongue out. "I'd bet good money Kellan's thinking about you right now. You know, you ought to probably talk it over with a Seer."

"Why in the worlds would I do that?" I snap. Sooner or later, I know I'll have to, as all Magicals tend to go to see one at some point. But, the idea of once again being told by someone about my predetermined destiny pisses me off big time. My mother's been bugging me for over a year now to see one, citing my continued *"abhorrent stubbornness and spiraling, petulant behavior"* as the reason. My vehement refusals had been taken to my father, and in his perpetual state of not giving a rat's ass about anything other than his work, he'd failed to listen to any of my mom's arguments.

It didn't stop my mother, though, from continuing to pressure me. And out of freely admitted spite, I've continued to refuse to go.

But now . . .

Maybe Lizzie has a point. And not just about Kellan. Because Jonah was in my math class today, and he was real. My curiosity about him . . . about *them* . . . is nearly incapacitating.

How will I be able to focus on anything else?

chapter 4

Today, like most days after school, the Cousins and I head over to the diner on the outskirts of town. It's called The Hollow Deer and has stuffed animal heads all over the walls. They're dusty and gross, so I tend to only eat salads when I'm there.

Alex watches me as I squish cherry tomatoes with my fork.

"What?" I demand.

"There were three shifts today while we were at school."

Cora coughs while drinking her tea. Her pointed *ahem* toward Lizzie prompts Meg to ask, "What am I missing?"

"So?" I stab at the tomatoes, popping them. Seeds and goo seep onto the cabbage.

He huffs, something he does when he gets all Intellectual on us. "I'm not stupid, Chloe. They were yours. *So,* I'm wondering what they're about."

I put my fork down. "What makes you think they're mine?"

He laughs and leans back in the booth. "I don't think. I know."

"Ohmigods," Meg squeaks. "That's so cool, Chloe!"

"Shifts," Alex continues, "tend to only occur during truly significant events in a Magical's life. They're pretty rare and should be taken seriously. Some Magicals never even experience them, and here you are, with multiples in one day. The first one was very strong. What precipitated it?"

If he wasn't being so sanctimonious and bossy, I might've asked him what he thinks about all of this. But Alex has a way of rubbing me the wrong way when he demands information. It's like he thinks, because he's an Intellectual, all information is his by default.

We girls have long learned to not talk to him about secrets, relationships, and sensitive feelings. Talking to Alex is like talking to the most non-empathetic shrink ever. Everything is textbook, analyzed within an inch of its life. There's precious little feeling behind his advice or conclusions. Why Meg adores him is beyond me.

I tell him, "It's none of your business."

"I think shifts like those deserve an explan—"

"Back off," Cora snarls. "She doesn't want to talk about it. If she did, she'd already have done so, Alex."

This doesn't faze him in the slightest, I can tell.

"Am I always the last person to know anything?" Meg accuses. "How do you know those shifts belong to Chloe, Alex?"

He shrugs. "Intellectuals know these things. It's written all over her."

I have no idea what he's talking about, but I don't like the thought of something so personal being broadcast all over my person without my knowledge.

Cora points her spoon at him. "If you can read what's written all over her, then you should know to shut your trap."

He sighs, frustrated. "When was the last time any of you felt a shift? It's been years. And today there are three, and they belong to Chloe. I can't believe none of you are curious—"

"I am!" Meg pipes up.

"—about what they mean," Alex continues. "Chloe, let's face it. You're a Creator. That in itself is a big deal. But now you have three shifts connected with you. Aren't you curious about what they symbolize? You must have an idea. If it's something big, then we have a right to know."

"No, you don't," Cora says. "Whatever this is, it's her business."

"She's a Creator," he repeats. "Creators don't get to keep their business to themselves."

I pick my fork up and stab at the ruined tomatoes some more, pretending they're his brains. But he's right, of course. My life is pretty much an open book. Chloe the Creator. Everyone knows what I'm capable of and where I'm headed.

But they don't know about *him.* Jonah's always been *my* secret, someone and something that no one else has a say over or an opinion about. Mine and mine alone.

I get what Alex is saying. Had three shifts happened to any other person at this table, I'd be pressing hard core to find out what it was about. And he's right. Shifts are a big deal. They're pretty much the equivalent of a bell ringing, heralding the arrival of something—people or events—majorly important.

But old habits die hard. And since it's bad enough I gave up a few memories to Cora and Lizzie, I'm done with show and tell.

Okay. I lied. There's one person I'm willing to talk with, but it's not Alex.

"You look like crap," Caleb says when he finds me sitting on a fallen log. We're in the woods on the outskirts of town, somewhere peaceful and far from anyone or anything I like to avoid on a regular basis.

"Nice. Remind me why I came here again?"

It's amazing he's able to keep a straight face when he says, "Because I'm awesome and you can't do without me."

I grin at the Faerie in front of me and think, once again, how amusing it is that he looks and acts nothing like how most people assume a Faerie would. For instance, he isn't wearing a little leather or gossamer outfit like Disney tells us Faeries do. Instead, he's got on a hooded sweatshirt, jeans, and tennis shoes. His hair is dreadlocked, with one side tucked behind a pointy ear. His eyes are wide set and deep hazel, his mouth perpetually curved in amusement.

I met him as a kid at the first annual get together for all the Magicals of our region that I'd gotten to go to. We'd instantly clicked as friends. I also discovered at that meeting that there were more than just Human Magicals living here. In fact, we had a number of Faeries and Gnomes living in homes shielded by Magic in the woods.

Caleb sits down on a low-hanging branch nearby my log. "Actually, I've been waiting for you."

I've always been impressed with his sense of intuition. He unfailingly anticipates my needs, even when I'm not sure of myself. Over the years, I've come to rely on him as a sounding board, even more so than Cora or Lizzie.

But what's up with the disapproving look he's giving me? "Really?" I ask.

"Do you want the truth?"

This is what Caleb is like. Somehow or other, he always seems to know what I need to hear. Sometimes it's so eerie, so uncanny, I don't know what to make of him. But talking to Caleb is nothing like talking to Alex, or even Cora or Lizzie. (I don't include Meg in the sharing circle because Meg, inevitably, will turn a conversation back to Alex. You could be talking about the fall of the Berlin Wall and she'll somehow tie it to Alex.)

I say hesitantly, "Sure?"

"It's really him."

This is what I'm talking about. How he can even guess at something like this is beyond me. Am I really such an open book? "How do you know about him?"

Caleb stares into the distance. "I'm a Faerie. We know things."

Uh-huh. I'm not buying it. Faeries, even Magical ones, aren't all-knowing. "There's no way you could have known."

He shrugs, drumming his fingers against a knee. "I've got a revolutionary idea. You should talk to him."

"What?" I sputter, laughing.

"Why not? You want to, right?"

I do, of course. If he really is the Jonah I know, then I desperately want to talk to him. Touch him. Hold him. Kiss him. Do anything, really, as long as it's with him. But I also don't want to go through this last year again.

"You're hesitating, Chloe. Why?"

I don't know quite how to explain it. So I offer lamely, "I don't want to sound stupid."

He flies down from the tree and sits down next to me on the log. "You know what's stupid? That reason."

I tear a brown leaf apart carefully at the veins until all that's left is a skeleton. "I've dreamed about him since I was a little girl," I admit out loud, the first time to anyone. Cora and Lizzie might've guessed this, but I didn't actually tell them. "Lucid dreams, pretty much every night. I've watched him grow up until just recently."

"How recently?"

The pain over this last memory still rubs at me like a shoe rubs against a healing blister. "Up until about a year ago. He just . . . disappeared."

Caleb frowns. "One would think that you'd be happy about him being here, then. Why aren't you over-the-moon happy?"

It's a good question, and surprisingly, one I hadn't asked myself yet. I should be happy. If this is Jonah, I should be so happy I shouldn't be able to think straight. Why am I not happy?

Because . . . I'm *terrified.*

What I don't tell Caleb is that Jonah's disappearance out of my life and dreams a year ago is the most painful experience I've ever gone through.

Pain like that isn't easy to get over.

Pain like that changes a person.

Pain like that changed me.

chapter 5

On the surface, my home appears extremely comfortable—rich wooden furniture covered in leather, plush cushions and blankets. There are stained-glass lamps and windows alongside lush artwork everywhere.

It's a really beautiful house. Too bad it always feels so cold inside.

I find my mother in the kitchen chopping vegetables she's grown in her garden. "Big game tonight, huh?" she asks. Idle chit-chat is not my mother's forte. We rarely engage in full conversations anymore, so it's interesting to watch her attempt to ease into what she really wants to know.

I shrug noncommittally.

When she reminisces about her high-school glory days, I fade out quickly. It's frustrating how she'll open up about irrelevant things like high school, but mostly refuse to talk to me about anything to do with being a Magical. I don't care about her being Homecoming Queen. I'd rather know what the Ascension will be like, if she knows any Elves, if the University I'm set to go to is fun, or if she's ever had to do something the Council ordered that she personally didn't approve of.

These are all questions I've asked in the past. I've never gotten an answer to any of them, and for the life of me, I'm not sure if it's because answering my questions takes too much time and effort on her behalf, or if it's because I'm not supposed to know. I've learned to just stop asking.

I wish we were close. I really do. But my mom just isn't warm with anyone—not my dad, not her friends, and certainly not me. As a Nymph, she loves her plants the way my Intellectual father loves his books.

My mother shoves a head of lettuce my way to chop. "Tell me about the shifts today. I've already gotten a number of phone calls from up and down the coast from Magicals wondering if they stemmed from you."

Fabulous. Everyone is in on my business now. It's bad enough that the Magicals in town seem to know the shifts were mine, but the entire West Coast? I am even more resentful now.

I give my mother the bare bones of the situation, referring to the first shift only, since I don't really have any concrete answers to share. She's no dummy, though. She calls me out on the other shifts right away.

I can't evade her as easily as I can Alex. I have to live with her, after all. So I vaguely describe the second shift.

She sets her knife down and stares at me, hard. "Who is this boy?"

"You won't believe me."

"Try."

It surprises me that she doesn't try to surge, even without permission. *"I'm your mother,"* she's told me in the past. *"I'm allowed to surge when I like."* "Fine," I say. "I met him in my dreams as a little kid."

Her eyebrows shoot up, but before she can respond, my father strolls into the kitchen. "How are my girls doing?"

Like he cares. Like he ever thinks of me when I'm outside of his eyesight.

As is the case with most Intellectuals, my father is hopelessly myopic in his vision towards life. Pursuit of knowledge is key, and while he's considered one of the finest Intellectuals in all the worlds, and a distinguished Council member to boot, he's been an absentee father, both physically and emotionally.

He proves this point by saying, "The Seer has agreed to meet with you," while awkwardly patting me on the shoulder. "What a treat for you. Astrid Lotus is the lead Seer on the Council. You'll be going to Annar to talk to her."

The victorious grin my mother's wearing makes me want to scream. Even still, a sliver of excitement runs through me.

Annar—the plane of existence reserved solely for Magicals. I've never been there, and it's not for want of trying.

"Now," he continues, "did your mother ask about the shifts we felt today?"

The urge to scream intensifies.

It takes a good five minutes of grilling before I can escape. In the quiet of my bedroom, I finally get a chance to get my bearings. Someone I'd always believed to be simply a creation of my imagination stepped out of my head and into my math class.

The first time I discovered Jonah in my dreams, I'd been four. Up until that point, my dreams were like, well, dreams: unicorns, flying, stuff like that. But then, one night, I saw him and my dreams changed. They became very lucid, so much so that I remember them more like true memories rather than dreams.

He'd been little then, too. He was sitting near a riverbank, reading a book. There was a break in the tree canopy, and the sun shone off of his glossy hair, nearly blinding me.

I was a goner right from the start.

We didn't talk for several nights, although I faithfully watched him from a distance. He'd catch me and reward me with a dimpled smile that caused my heart, even back then, to do back flips. But after awhile, my curiosity grew so much that I had no choice but to join him on the river's edge.

When we spoke, it was like I already knew him.

There was a deep connection between us, stronger than any I had with anyone else. Stronger than the bonds I had with the Cousins. Stronger than what I had with my parents. It seemed crazy, since he was someone from my dreams. But I didn't care. Real or imaginary, he became the most important person I knew.

Our secret rendezvous were something I impatiently looked forward to every night. No topic was off limits. I often caught myself storing information in the back of my mind just to share with him.

There was no other person who could make me so happy. And then, sometime around the age of eleven, he kissed me. We were sitting in a tree, high above the river, laughing so hard my sides hurt. That dimple of his had appeared, and I just loved it so much I touched it. The laughter faded away and he looked at me intently before he brushed his lips against mine.

I fell irrevocably in love with him. No—I'd *always* loved him. The kiss just permanently cemented this fact. Our feelings for one another only intensified with every year that passed—we began to see each other by more than simple words and emotions. I coveted my time with him, even though when I woke up I'd remind myself that what I believed to be memories were only dreams, made up in my head.

In the end, it didn't really matter what the reasons were for his existence—as long as I had him, life was good. And then it became harder and harder to find each other.

Approximately one year ago, a day when we were standing knee deep in a purple ocean, Jonah told me in the most heartbreaking way, "Know that I love you. That I always will."

It was like he was saying goodbye.

And the weird thing was I had known that same night that I'd needed to say the same thing, too. Because there was this inherent knowledge, just like I knew my hair was light brown or that I was a girl, that I was going to lose Jonah and had absolutely no control over it.

When I woke the next morning, I could smell him on my clothes and in my hair. I sat in bed for hours, hugging my knees to my chest, breathing in his smell, replaying our farewell over and over until I shattered.

He was gone. I knew he was gone. I felt his absence plain as day. Something crucial to my existence was missing, and it hollowed me.

I cried a lot that day and many days after, refusing to explain to anyone where my outbursts were coming from. I fell into a deep depression, one I didn't really care to get out of. The misery became a companion of sorts, something that told me, dreams or no, he'd been mine. That my heart hadn't lied.

Things went downhill fast. It was then that the resentment toward my destiny and my surroundings intensified, and I lashed out at everyone and everything.

That was at the end of last summer, and while I continued to search for him in my dreams, I didn't see him again until today.

I have no idea what to do. And since I'd never told anyone about him, I don't really have anyone to go to for concrete advice.

I dreamed about Jonah. For years. And dreams aren't real. They'd felt real, and I'd prayed for so long that they could be real, but they weren't. They couldn't be. No one ever told me that their dreams came true. That's movie stuff, not Magic.

How do you explain him then? the little voice asks. *Cora and Lizzie both saw him, so he isn't a delusion. You need to figure this out. Go and talk to him. Get answers. No matter what.*

No matter what . . .

But what if Jonah disappears again?

A year after I lost him, I'm still bitter, miserable, and unsettled. If we were to reconnect, and he left me again . . .

I have no doubt. Being hollow would be the least of my problems.

chapter 6

Later that night during our football game's halftime, I spot Jonah and Kellan. They're standing near the exit closest to the parking lot, directly in my line of sight. I surreptitiously stare to my heart's content instead of listening to the Cousins talk, until a couple of girls descend upon the two boys. To my relief, Jonah takes a cell phone from his brother and heads out into the parking lot just before the girls reach them.

Kellan looks, for the briefest moment, like an annoyed deer caught in the headlights of these girls. As I study him, a slew of questions hit me: Where did Jonah go? Why did he leave? Is he really the Jonah I know? Did he dream about me, too? Does he remember me? Had he seen me on the field? Does he want to talk to me? Should I ignore Kellan? Should I talk to him? Speaking of, why didn't I ever know Jonah had a twin? I should've known, right?

I swear, the little voice sighs, *sometimes you give me a headache.*

I decide to live in the moment. I lurch forward, one foot in front of another. I block out the questioning looks on Cora's and Lizzie's faces, as well as Alex's suggestion to find him ice cream. I just keep walking until I reach Kellan.

Have you thought this through?

But I'm tired of overanalyzing everything. This feels like the right thing to do. Still, my insides are quaking, forcing me to take a deep breath to steady myself. I'm not sure if it's because Kellan looks so much like Jonah. Maybe it's because of the way my hand tingled long after we ceased touching this afternoon.

Then again, maybe it's because I'm acting like a crazy person. I stop directly in front of him. "Hi there!"

He grins, somewhat surprised but definitely amused. The pretty girl standing closest to him is annoyed, though. I know why, but she can flirt with Kellan later. I need answers.

"So." He focuses on me. "Nice cheering tonight."

And then, I can smell him. It's a warm smell, a little spicy, and definitely not what I remember Jonah smelling like. It's rather intoxicating, which is . . .

NOT A GOOD THING.

Focus! "Yes, well, that's what we cheerleaders do best! Go, team, go!" I pump my fist up lamely.

Kellan doesn't seem to notice when the girls leave. "Can I be honest, Chloe?"

He remembers my name! An almost uncontrollable desire to touch his hair rushes through me. Does it feel anything like his brother's? Because if it does—

Do NOT go there! the little voice demands.

I Velcro my hands to my sides. What was he saying? I can't remember, so I merely smile wider and do a multi-purpose head bobble.

"You don't really seem like the cheerleader type. What's up with you being on the team?"

Wait. What? "Excuse me?"

"The perky voice, either. Can you really tell me that you enjoy sounding like that?"

So not what I thought he'd say. My cheeks burn, but then he smiles this insanely alluring half-grin and my heart jolts unexpectedly.

What the hell is going on?

I desperately attempt to bring the focus back on the information I've come over for. "So, uh, I noticed Jonah left. He's not enjoying the game?"

Apparently, it's my turn to surprise him. "You know my brother?"

And . . . this tells me that, while I never knew about Kellan, he never knew about me either. This throws me even more off balance. "Um . . ."

"To answer your question, though," Kellan says, "no."

I'm lightheaded when his smile returns. "And . . . what about you?" I ask.

He leans against the fence, stuffing his hands in his coat pockets. "The same."

"Why didn't you leave with him?"

"I was trying to gracefully find a way to escape from the group you found me in. Thanks to you, I don't have to work so hard now."

I'm still dazed at that half-smile. Damn, it's gorgeous.

Why aren't you scanning the parking lot for Jonah? the little voice demands. *Focus! If you're going to hang out here, at least ask questions that will help!*

And then Kellan reaches forward, and I hold my breath as he brushes something off my cheek. His touch is light, but there's no mistaking how strongly I feel it. My skin tingles furiously. "Was there something on my face?"

When he says, "Just a stray eyelash," I feel like lightning strikes me.

Which leads me to mumble something lame like, "You should have saved it for me, so I could've made a wish."

More of the grin. "What would you have wished for?"

"Don't you wish you knew?" I'm flirting, and this is crazy. And wrong. Because I am in love with his brother, and all my wishes have been about him. So, despite still being dazzled by Kellan's fabulous smile, I finally ask a question about the person I should be focusing on. "So, your brother just left you here?"

He smirks and rubs at his hair in this charming, unassuming way. "That's sort of how it is with us—one usually takes the fall while the other escapes. It isn't like I haven't stuck him in the same situation before."

"It must be nice to have a brother like that," I say, and it's sincere. I've always wanted a sibling, but Magical families only produce one pregnancy. "Sadly, I'm an only child."

He motions towards the concession stands, where the Cousins are still standing. "What about those girls over there? You seem to be tight with them, and one even kind of looks like you."

It's surprising that he's noticed who I hang out with, even more so how he was able to pick up on the distant familial bond between me and Cora when no one else does. So I find myself telling him the truth, or, something close to the truth. "They're sort of like my . . . adopted family. I guess you could say that Cora and Lizzie are the closest people I have to sisters, especially Cora."

"Which one is she?"

I point Cora out, adding, "You met Lizzie today in history, remember?"

He turns his gaze back towards me. "Did I?"

"You cannot tell me you don't remember her," I laugh. I mean, it was *Lizzie*. He shrugs, and I can't stand it anymore. "Why are you here?"

Kellan looks as if he's holding back a laugh. "Define 'here.'"

Oh, to really ask for the truth. I settle for the easiest *here.* "At the game. You know, since you two hate football and all."

"We sort of promised our dad that we would come and make an effort to, and I quote, *'blend in'* at our new school."

"Do you always do what your father says?"

He shrugs again. "We like to throw him these little bones every so often."

And then I remember that Jonah's mother died when he was little, which is probably why Kellan is only talking about his dad. Speaking of Jonah . . .

I allow myself to scan the parking lot for him. He still hasn't come back, and it's making me antsy. Where could he be? But then the buzzer sounds, indicating half-time is over.

"Isn't that your cue?" Kellan asks.

I'm hesitating, and I don't know why. I want to say it's because I'm hoping Jonah will come back, but something in me says, while that's true, it's not the entire reason. We stand and stare at each other in silence. A rush of butterflies nearly crash out of my chest, which is weird because Jonah's been the only guy I've ever felt butterflies for. Even though it was irrational, no other guy I've dated could live up to him. All the boys I knew at school paled in comparison in every way possible.

So how is it that I'm so attracted to Kellan? Because I think I am, and I definitely know he's not his brother. And this makes me feel guilty, and confused, and finally forces me to take an awkward step back.

I tell him I do indeed have to go, but I still don't leave.

“One would almost assume,” he says lightly, “that you aren’t eager to get back to cheering.”

I nearly jump out of my skin when Lizzie lays a hand on my shoulder. At least she has the grace to look sorry for interrupting.

“Right. *Right*.” I take another step back. “Well, I guess I’ll see you later, then. At school, I mean. I mean, in class. In history. You know what I mean.”

OH MY GODS. WHAT IS WRONG WITH ME?

Kellan looks like he’s having a hard time keeping the corners of his mouth from tugging upwards.

Lizzie smiles apologetically. “Sorry to have to steal her away. I should introduce myself. I’m Lizzie.”

“According to Chloe, we’ve already met,” he says, matching her apologetic smile, “so introductions are unnecessary.”

A weird look crosses her face. She turns to me. “You’re talking to Kellan.”

My face warms. “Yes?”

Now she looks pissed off. “Kellan.”

The guy in question tilts his head to the side and studies Lizzie thoughtfully. And yet, she repeats it for a third time through gritted teeth. He must think we’re lunatics.

“So,” Kellan says to me. “I’ll see you later, C. In school. Possibly even in class. Maybe it’ll be in history. Who knows?”

Why does he have to keep smiling at me like that? Does every girl fall prey to . . . Wait. What did he just call me? “C?”

"Yeah. C. For *cheer*. You know, your very favorite thing to do." And with that, I watch him go, nearly burning a hole in his head with my staring.

"Kellan?" Lizzie repeats for a fourth time.

I turn toward her. "Why are you repeating his name so much? You probably freaked him out."

"I assumed you were talking to his brother," she snaps. "Cora and I were certain about that. You were flirting, for crying out loud!"

I deny it, but I was. We both know I was. I shouldn't have been, but I was. And I don't know why.

chapter 7

"You should know I'm being called back to Annar to deal with some . . . challenging situations."

Trips to Annar are extremely common, but since my father rarely explains ahead of time why he goes, I'm intrigued. "What situations?"

His eyes ferret around the kitchen before he beckons me to sit next to him on a barstool. My mother sits down opposite us, knitting silently. "I need you to pay close attention," he tells me, "so you can take care of yourself if need be."

Make that *very* intrigued.

His voice is low and steady. "Over the last decade, there has been a rash of Magical murders. Cora's father, for one—you know about that one already."

I nod. Cora's dad died five years back in Washington D.C.

"Lizzie's father, as well—"

Hold on here. Lizzie's dad disappeared three years ago. It'd been assumed he ran away with another woman, or so Lizzie's drunk mother often insists while screaming at the top of her lungs.

When he sees my confusion, my father says, "Well, it's not like young children need to be told about these things." He waves a dismissive hand. "Focus on what's important, as it's critical you understand what's at stake. Over the last decade, there have been eleven murders we know about on our plane. I won't bore you with the statistics of the other planes, but there have been murders there, too. During the last year alone, there've been three murders here. The Council believes that whatever is going on is escalating rapidly."

A chill races down my spine. "Are you sure they're all murders?"

"Yes. Trackers are on the hunt for the culprit, or culprits, but the truth is, we aren't even sure how many sentient creatures are involved. Chloe, I tell you this because you are a very powerful, important Magical nearing her Ascension. Every single Magical murdered so far has been one of importance. Prior to the last month, all victims had Ascended. The most recently attacked, though, were not."

I swallow hard. "You're saying I could be a target."

My father pauses, kneading his hands back and forth across the counter top. My mother sets her knitting needles down and answers for him. "Yes."

My mind sort of flatlines.

"You must be vigilant," my father urges. I've never seen him so concerned about me before. If it wasn't in such a scary context, I might actually cry. "As of right now, you are no longer allowed to go anywhere without another Magical present."

And . . . there go my fuzzy feelings. "Are you serious?"

"You are a Creator. Your price to the Council is incalculable. It has been decided that you must be guarded at all costs."

"My *price?*"

"We have no idea who is doing this. It could be a Magical, taking out the competition. It could be one of the species after discovering the presence of Magicals. We just don't know anything, despite our best efforts. Whoever it is, they are strong enough to take out powerful

Magicals who normally would have nothing to fear from the nons of their plane." He stands up, sighing. "The Council must always have a Creator. Kleeshawnall Rushfire is old and is nearing the end of his life span. You are the only other Creator in existence. Whether you like it or not, you will be guarded. And you'll follow the Council's orders to the letter. My daughter will not embarrass our family or risk her life because she's seventeen and unhappy with a lack of freedom. It's a small price to pay to ensure our kind keeps evolving."

"There's another Creator?" I whisper. They've never told me this before.

My father has the audacity to look bewildered by my bewilderment. "Of course there is."

"Do not focus on Rushfire," my mother snaps. "Are you listening to your father? You will do as you're told, Chloe." She then escorts me up to my bedroom. This is not a good sign. "Someone will be here soon to watch over you," she says as I sit down on my bed. "I wanted him here tonight, but he's currently out on a mission." The windows are then checked to make sure they're latched. She's never checked them before, not even when I was little. This drives home the severity of the situation.

My hands are shaking. "Who is this guy? Are the others getting babysitters?"

"No. There is no need. You're the only one Council bound." She pulls the curtains shut. "You'll be watched over by Karl Graystone. He is young, only twenty . . . but your father assures me that the Council insisted on Karl and Karl alone."

Only twenty . . . "What is he?"

She knows what I mean. "A Quake."

An earth mover, another rarity in the Magical world. "Why would the Council send someone so valuable to look after me?"

"As I explained, he is the best. He does not fail at his missions. But, I need to stress something to you. If . . . gods forbid, someone actually ever *does* manage to get through Karl, you must protect yourself at all costs. I do not care if it happens in front of two thousand nons, you do whatever is necessary to protect yourself. The Council cannot lose you."

The sad thing is that my parents' concern seems only to be what is best for the Council, not for their daughter. How I wish my mom was hugging me right now, telling me it was going to be okay. That she was going to make sure that nobody hurt her little girl. But no—I get a lecture on how I can't embarrass the family by getting myself killed. Gods.

"When does this Karl arrive?"

"Soon." She pins me with a long look. "You should know that Karl is recently married and his wife is pregnant. So, no hanky panky."

I gape in outrage. "Are you *serious?* I mean, Mother, if there are things out to kill me, do you really think my first thought would be how to sex this guy up?"

She ignores this. "Caleb should be here any minute. We've asked him to come and stay until Karl arrives."

"Caleb? He's a Faerie. And small. What can he do if we're attacked?"

"Hey," says an indignant voice. "I'm a Magical, too, you know. And, besides, I have a cell phone."

Sure enough, Caleb is hovering in my doorway. And for once, he's not smirking.

"Good. You're here," my mother says. "I expect you to hold to our bargain, Caleb."

He flies into the room and lands on my desk. “Of course.”

When she leaves, I ask, “Bargain?”

He drops a small duffle bag next to him. “I’m supposed to go with you everywhere until this guy gets here.”

“Everywhere?”

“Everywhere.”

“You’re not going to the bathroom with me,” I tell him, and he just laughs.

chapter 8

Graham is throwing a barbeque today at the beach. Well, it's really more like the football team is throwing the party, but it's mostly due to Graham. He's a people pleaser and loves getting everyone together in one place to make sure they're all having fun.

I didn't feel like getting the fifth degree from Cora, so I neglected to tell her when she picked me up about what my parents had said the night before. And when it came time to leave, Caleb gave her some line about wanting to sketch the shoreline rather than ratting me out. He even insisted on staying in the car, as long as we cracked the windows and left water and food, like he was some kind of dog rather than a person.

"Where's Graham?" Cora asks Lizzie as soon as we find her. There are already a ton of people at the beach—playing volleyball, laying out despite the cool temperatures, playing board games, or just milling about, talking.

Lizzie points at the water. "Out surfing."

My eyes follow Lizzie's finger. I scan the group of surfers bobbing up and down on their boards for Graham. He loves to surf, but it's the one sport he doesn't excel at. He keeps trying, though, bless his heart.

"The red wetsuit," Lizzie clarifies. And then, a tad defensively, "He's been doing great today."

Cora snorts, but manages innocence when Lizzie glares at her. I continue scanning the waves, seeing if I recognize anyone else.

And . . . there they are. Clad in dark wetsuits that match their hair, Jonah and his twin are out in the water. I marvel at how skillful Jonah is when he catches one of the larger waves. I don't know much about surfing, but I do know this: he's good. Like, *really* good. Way better than any of the guys I know at school. It's like being at an art gallery and seeing a masterpiece hung next to a stick figure. He's so amazing he takes my breath away.

And then another large wave swells, and Kellan catches it. He's just as talented as Jonah is, and the two of them on back-to-back waves are quite a sight. But I'm not the only one who's blown away. Nearly everyone on the beach has stopped to watch their sets.

"Did you know he surfed?" Lizzie asks me.

Yeah, I did. He loves surfing. He's been doing it since he was little. I just had no idea he was so good at it.

Graham comes to shore and joins us, shoving his board into the sand. The salt water on him smells tangy and sharp when he hugs me. "If it isn't my favorite trio of ladies. How's everyone today?"

Cora grins. "I see you return victorious."

He laughs, embarrassed. "If wiping out five times today still qualifies as victorious, I'll take it."

Lizzie immediately jumps to his defense. "I thought you did a great job out there!"

He can't hide his pleasure, even when he evades. "Man, did the new guys put us all to shame, though."

"Hmm, yes," Cora says. "We most certainly did notice that."

I discreetly stomp on her foot. She stomps right back on mine.

Graham shakes the water out of his hair. "I guess they've been surfing a long time."

Cora nudges me slyly. "Are they here for the barbeque?"

He looks out at them. "Nope, just for the surfing. I invited them to join us, but I guess they already have plans for the afternoon."

"That's too bad," Lizzie says, eyeing me meaningfully. I try to downplay this by yawning.

It doesn't take a mind reader, though, to realize that Graham's wondering if Lizzie has an interest in either of the twins. He looks so dejected I want to say something to clarify things to him, but he beats me to the punch. "Yeah, it is too bad."

Cora and I just stand there lamely as Lizzie blushes straight to her roots. "Well, I mean . . . they're new, and it's . . ."

"I get it," Graham says.

Desperate to change the subject, Lizzie laces her arm through Graham's. "Think you could show me how to work a barbeque?"

His smile is bittersweet but acquiescent. After they've walked away, Cora leads me towards our blanket nearby. "Talk to me, babe. What's going on in that pretty noggin of yours?"

I stare back out in the water. Vulnerable with Jonah so close, and yet so far away, I admit, "I miss him."

She digs in her straw tote for a pair of sunglasses. "He's right there, you know."

Is he, though? I mean . . . is it *really* him? The Jonah I know?

She sighs at my silence. "Let's start with the easy questions. Just how long have you known him, anyway? I know from surging that it's been awhile. But just how long?"

I tell her the truth. It takes a lot to surprise Cora, but she's surprised now. "Point him out to me." After I do so, she says, "You should go talk to him."

I slide my own sunglasses on, self-conscious about possibly being caught staring. Because I can't help *but* stare. "It's not that simple, Cora."

"It really is."

Ahem, the little voice mutters. *Even Cora thinks it's a good idea!*

Jonah's caught another wave, one even bigger than before. "Look," she says. "Do you love him? Because that's sure how it felt when I surged."

I rub some sand in between my fingers. "Yes."

She's surprised again. "Wow. I didn't expect you to answer that question so quickly."

"You said you were going to ask easy questions. That's an easy question."

"Then why are you so unwilling to go talk to him?"

The night before, I'd dreamed about him. It wasn't like the old dreams, though. This one starred a copy of Jonah who told me he had no idea who I was, that I was crazy for approaching him, and that I needed to stay away.

It wasn't really him, but it was terrifying enough to remind me of what I stand to lose.

Cora motions towards the shallow water, where Jonah waits for Kellan to finish his ride. "He's standing right there. Here's your chance. Go."

Just as my hands grip the towel to push myself up, Kellan joins his brother and they leave. A dull ache in me expands with every step Jonah takes toward the stairs that lead up to the parking lot.

Look at me, I want to yell. *I'm right here! Can't you see me? Don't you know who I am?* But he doesn't look. He and his brother disappear into the parking lot and out of view.

"That's what you get for inaction," Cora flatly declares. The little voice viciously agrees.

A football whizzes by our heads, landing about twenty feet away. Someone calls out for one of us to throw it back. When Cora pretends she didn't hear anything, I reluctantly go over to get it. As I reach down for the ball, I notice a key ring lying in the sand. I pick it up and turn the keys over in my hand—three keys next to a small, wooden surfboard. I'm just about to do a general surge to find a panicky person sans keys when I become aware of someone standing behind me.

"It appears you're quite helpful, aren't you, C? Dismissing unwanted people, finding lost keys . . ."

I whirl around and nearly smack into Kellan. His hair is wet and disheveled, dark sunglasses sitting up on top of his head. He's wearing a gray hooded sweatshirt, his wetsuit peeled down low on his hips.

Heavens.

My mouth goes dry again. "These yours?"

His fingers brush mine when they remove the keys, and my skin tingles deliciously. The butterflies beat against my rib cage, loud and strong.

A smug smile slowly breaks out across his face, like he can hear just how hard my heart is pounding. Before I can pass out from shame, one of the boys on the football team appears and side checks me hard enough that I lose my balance. Kellan reaches out and saves me from falling.

"Yo, Chlo!" the jock says, grabbing the football. "We're in the middle of a game, babe! You're holding things up."

Once I'm steady, Kellan lets go. Now my whole body is buzzing from his touch, and I nearly fall over again. Much to my pleasure, Kellan appears disoriented, too.

"Sorry," I murmur to the jock, and thankfully he quickly leaves. After a moment of the two of us simply staring at one another, I clear my throat. "You guys aren't staying?"

Kellan's crazy half-grin reappears, twisting my stomach into nervous, excited knots. "Nope."

I can't believe I'm going to do this, but I want him to stay. I mean, I want *them* to stay. "Why not? Don't you guys like barbeques?"

The keys twirl around his index finger. "Sure, but we already have plans."

"Change them." And then I slap a hand over my mouth. What is *wrong* with me? Why can't I censor myself around him?

He removes my hand slowly. Oh, my. The tingling returns full force.

I'm completely flustered now and babbling like an idiot. "Um, I mean, you guys are new here, and it'd be a good opportunity to meet new people . . . since you're new. So, you should . . . stay . . . if you . . . want?" I try laughing, but it only makes me sound worse and sort of like a hyena.

His hand drops from mine. "As nice as it would be to meet new people, since we're new and all, I'm afraid we're going to have to pass."

My cheeks are on fire. "Oh. Well, sure."

"Really, C. Who could I possibly meet who would be more interesting than you?"

Oh, lords, is this guy charming. I need air. Stat. Which is ridiculous since we're outside, on the beach, for crying out loud, in sixty-degree weather. I fear I'm about to swoon when he jingles the keys in his sweatshirt pocket. "Thanks for finding these. Jonah would have my head if I came back empty handed."

And . . . that'll do it. Swoon over. "They're his?"

He looks confused, but quickly teases, "Your powers of observation know no match."

I break into nervous giggles. "Oh, you know me!"

"Actually, I don't." Kellan leans in, close enough to my ear that I feel his breath on my neck. I'm helpless at suppressing the excited shiver that overtakes my whole body. "But maybe there'll be a future opportunity to get to know new people, such as yourself. At least, I can hope so. See you later, C."

When Kellan walks up the stairs, Jonah stares down toward me with an unreadable expression, thanks to a pair of dark sunglasses. I stare back, transfixed, before he turns to finish mounting the surfboards on the rack on top of his SUV.

And then the spell is broken, and I stumble back to Cora, even more confused than before.

chapter 9

What every daughter longs to hear her mother say at breakfast is what mine just announced: *"You look awful."*

I'd had nightmares all night. I'm utterly exhausted, mentally and physically, and wishing today was Sunday and not Monday. I do not want to go to school.

"Thanks," I mutter, nursing a cup of tea.

"Did you have trouble sleeping?" my mother asks, and when she reaches out a hand, I hold my breath, because it looks like she's about to take mine in hers. But she doesn't. She picks up a pencil near my bowl instead.

I crush down my disappointment. "Yeah. Bad dreams."

She opens up the newspaper to the crossword. "Dreams are mostly irrelevant. Just shake it off."

Sympathy is an alien creature to my mother. Why I should've expected it from her is beyond me. "But, obviously," I point out, "sometimes dreams are valid."

"That's wishful thinking, Chloe. Usually they're nothing but images your brain cooks up while resting."

"I think you're wrong."

She looks up from the paper, face scrunched in consternation. "Are you referring to the boy you think caused the shifts on Friday?"

Irked, I insist, “He’s real.”

“I have no doubt whatever boy you’re talking about is real.” Eyes drifting back to her crossword, she taps her pencil against the paper. “But I highly doubt you’ve seen him in your dreams before.”

“Why?”

“Because if you had, we’d have known about it by now.”

What does *that* mean?

Caleb straggles in, refusing to eat, and looking just as tired as I feel. I cannot believe my parents have requested he escort me to and from school until the Quake shows up. Caleb doesn’t seem to mind, but I’m sure he’s got better things to do than babysit me all day.

I’ve just moved my bowl and mug to the sink when my mother says, “You’re to visit the Seer tomorrow.”

I look up, surprised.

“Your father and I feel you could really use some guidance and insight, especially with the news you were given over the weekend. Don’t think that we haven’t noticed the turmoil you’ve been in during the last year.”

Seriously? This how she’s going to play it? I mean, she’s virtually ignored me for the last year, not to mention most of my life, never bothering to even *ask* what was wrong. So, rather than being grateful she’s now noticing, I become angry. “If you’ve noticed, then why haven’t you tried to talk to me? Or help?”

Caleb instantly busies himself with a section of the newspaper.

“I’m mentioning it now, aren’t I?”

That does it. “Too little, too late, Mother.” I stand up and stuff my backpack with notebooks, resentful at her hollow attempt at caring. It’s like, because Caleb is here, she’s putting on a show of motherly concern.

But she isn't fooling anyone. I've told him everything over the years. She'll never get a shiny Mother of the Year award.

Caleb's smile is of supreme sympathy, but instead of making me feel better, I only become angrier. Her silence and distance is far preferred than this façade of caring.

"Why do you think we're sending you to a Seer, Chloe? This is us helping you."

"Wow, that's excellent, Mother," I snap. "Sending someone else in to do your dirty work. Am I really such a bother you can't take five, ten minutes out of your busy day to take care of me? Or spend time with me? Is it really so wrong to expect you to occasionally ask me how I'm doing, maybe guide me through some of these difficult changes?" I'm gripping the island now, knuckles turning white under pressure.

"Chloe," Caleb says in a low voice. "Let's just go."

My mother ignores him. "Every Magical has to go through Ascension. What makes you so special that you need extra attention to do so?"

She might as well have slapped me.

Worse yet, she's clearly bored, like she can't even be bothered to get worked up over this, either. "What do you want from me, Chloe? Should I hold your hand through the process? For gods' sakes, you're a Creator, and you will be sitting on the Council in a few years. Act like it. People will be looking to you for guidance and action. How do you think they'll feel, finding out you're an insecure little girl?"

Even Caleb is appalled.

She ruthlessly continues. "I will not tolerate my daughter acting like this. Pull yourself together and stop embarrassing yourself. You have many obligations ahead of you, Chloe, and we will not tolerate you tarnishing the Lilywhite legacy."

I can barely think, I'm so angry. This is how she sees me? "When were you ever asked to destroy a civilization? When were you ever asked to take life away from hundreds or thousands, or gods, even *millions* of souls? Would you be ready to do so, if asked?"

"Stop being so maudlin," she shoots back, her eyes like glittering marbles. "You may never be asked to do those things. And if you are, it'll be your job." My mother practically taunts me to counter her. When I don't, she says flatly, "Sometimes I wonder if Fate made a mistake when it gave you the powers of Creation."

It's a kick in the stomach.

"Abigail," Caleb snaps, angry himself now, "enough!"

She ignores him just as easily as she does me. He and I leave her behind without even saying goodbye.

The school bell rings the second I turn off the car's engine, and within a minute, the parking lot transforms into a ghost town. I stay in the safety of my car, gripping the wheel while reliving the conversation with my mother over how I'm a great big disappointment to her. To everyone.

What's really sad is how I can't remember the last time either parent said *I love you* to me. Truth be told, I don't think they ever have.

I beat my forehead against the steering wheel.

"That's going to be pretty," Caleb says quietly.

"Like it matters."

"Your mother is who she is. Expecting her to be anything else only hurts you."

"How stupid of me. I expected her to act like a *mother*."

"She loves you," he says, but I cut him off.

"She doesn't, and you and I both know it."

"I think she does. But in her own way."

I try so hard not to cry. "Whatever. I don't want to talk about it anymore."

Caleb tries to argue with me, get me to continue talking, but I all I want to do is go to class and pretend none of this happened. He reluctantly lets me go, reminding me he'll meet me after school.

I'm walking across the parking lot when I spot the twins standing next to a rather expensive looking yellow sports car. I try not to stare, but it's a lost cause. Both turn at the same time to look at me, and as luck would have it, I stumble over the curb.

FANTASTIC. I'm contemplating creating a hole to sink into, when Kellan gives me a worried, sympathetic smile. And Jonah is watching me with what appears to be genuine concern. He moves forward, like he's going to come over to help me, but then Kellan calls out, asking if I'm okay.

"Fine, thanks," I croak. And then I rush away as fast as I can, because I can't deal with this on top of everything else this morning.

By the time I get to the office, I'm nearly out of breath, humiliated, still angry at what's happened with my mother and rubbing at a very sore forehead. So I'm not exactly in the best of moods when the ancient attendance clerk levels a stern look at me. "Miss Lilywhite," she says in her steely voice, and I'm momentarily taken aback, because someone her age ought to sound frail and not like a battlefield general. "Tardy by twenty minutes. What would your mother think?"

"Ex-excuse me?" I stutter.

She points a gnarled finger at me. "I said, what would your mother think? She was an excellent student, never late once. I remember, missy. I was here when she was, and she was a really top-notch pupil. It would do you a world of good if you tried to be more like her."

I gape at her for a couple of incredulous seconds before something in me snaps. "Are you kidding?"

Her back yanks straight in outrage. "What was that, young lady?"

"I *said,* are you *kidding*?" It isn't my finest hour. But, man—I can't deal with the comparison, not after what happened earlier.

The clerk narrows her eyes at me. Then in clear, crisp words, she says, "Too bad you're not more like her."

Everything in my mind sort of short circuits. How dare she! The little voice in my head urges me to calm down, but I'm seeing red. I lean my palms against the counter and hiss, "Shut your mouth! You have *no* idea what she's like! I couldn't be happier that I'm nothing like her!"

The clerk opens her mouth to speak, but I cut her off. "What's the big deal, anyway? It's a *tardy*. Give me my slip already and back off!"

The little voice is shouting at the top of its lungs: *Are you INSANE? Do you want to get SUSPENDED? Shut. Up. NOW!*

"HOW DARE YOU!" the clerk shrieks, her eyes bugging out.

"I said—"

"ARE YOU THREATENING ME?"

The counter below me shudders, and for one small, irresponsible moment, I contemplate blowing it up just to see what she'd do. But then I remove my hands and curl them into fists at my sides. *She's not your mother,* the little voice whispers. *She's just a school clerk. Her opinion of you means nothing. Taking your anger out on her isn't worth it.* So I take a deep breath and say through gritted teeth, "Of course not, Ms.

Applebaum. It would be unwise for a student to even think of doing that during their senior year."

"That's a poor excuse for an apology if I've ever heard one. Who knew what a mouth you have on you? You have everyone so fooled, thinking you are just a delightful girl, but *I* know better. I've always seen you for what you are." The gnarled finger is pointing at me again. "Don't think I won't call your mother!"

There is a stifled laugh from the back of the room. I turn to find, much to my utter dismay and chagrin, the twins sitting on the wooden bench against the wall near the door.

How long have they been in here?

Kellan mock-whispers, "I've got my money on you." Jonah, though, looks beyond shocked. Eyes wide and concerned. Angry, even. For the briefest of moments, I wonder if he's going to stand up and say something. Defend me. Maybe it's wishful thinking, but he appears just as upset as I am. Our eyes meet, and he actually does stand up, but, appalled at how he and Kellan have just witnessed me melt down and lash out at a clerk, I whip my head back towards Applebaum. My insides are churning, my hands trembling. Why do I let my mother get to me like this?

Much to my utter shock, the clerk is scratching out a tardy slip for me. And all I want to do is run, because Jonah just saw me do that. They both did. Gods. What must they think? That I'm a lunatic with rage issues?

She holds the slip out and I snatch it out of her hand. Unable to help myself, I choke out, "Go ahead and call her. I don't care. What's the worst you can do to me? Suspend me? It doesn't matter. None of *this* matters."

And then, because my confidence finally fails me, I flee the room.

chapter 10

During passing period, I shove my head into my locker, wishing for a way to cram my entire body in. Then I could shut the door behind me, leaving all of the events of the morning to fade into the darkness.

"Tough day?"

I yank my head out and find Kellan standing next to my locker. My breath catches in the back of my throat, because he's so unbearably sexy. And I'm not alone, because every girl walking by drools unabashedly. I can't believe he's here. Next to my locker. Talking to me after watching me yell at the attendance clerk! I blush, ruining any effort at playing it cool. "Sort of."

He raises a hand and scratches his forehead—there's a wide black leather cuff on his left wrist in place of a watch. I like it. It seems so him. "That was some show you put on in the office."

I'm about to say something witty, like, "Ugh, don't remind me," but then I decide to tell him the truth. "Everybody has their breaking point. I guess I reached mine today."

Stupidly, I'd expected (hoped for?) a phone call or a text from my mother expressing her disappointment in my actions, but true to form, nothing appeared. Because to call me would have required that little bit of effort a loving mom would put out for her daughter.

"Yeah?"

I chew on my bottom lip and study him. He seems genuinely interested in my answer. "I don't like being compared to someone else, you know?"

"No one does, C."

"I guess you'd know that pretty well, huh?" He gives me a questioning look, so I lamely add, "What with you being a twin and all."

I can almost read his mind: *Ah, let the twin jokes commence.*

I try for damage control. "Does that happen to you a lot? Comparisons, I mean?"

He gives a small laugh. "Every day."

"Huh. You seem so different from one another. You even look totally different."

Surprise softens his features. "You think? Most people have a very difficult time telling us apart."

I blush again, realizing my slip. "It's just, uh, from what I could tell so far, you seem different from one another."

Kellan studies me intently for a moment. I try not to squirm. "I wouldn't have pegged you for the tardy sort."

"And you are?"

He chuckles. "Occasionally."

I laugh, and all of the crummy feelings plaguing me since waking up this morning evaporate.

He grins at me mischievously. "So. Here we are. At school."

"Yes, but not in class," I offer, remembering my foolish words from Friday night.

"Hmm . . ." He crosses his arms across his chest, tilting his head to the side. "You're right."

Out of the blue, I become aware of a very strong, distinctive pull toward him, almost as if there's a cord connected between the two of us. It tugs at me in strong, mouth-watering ways. Okay, Chloe. *Breathe*. "So, what class do you have next?" I ask, trying to sound casual.

His lips curve upwards. "What would you say if I told you I don't have any more classes today?"

"Surely you're not planning on ditching!" And then I want to groan, because HELLO. Do I sound like the ultimate goody-goody or what?

"Why not?" And then, after a short pause, much more seriously—"Come with me."

Positive I misheard him, I offer a sophisticated, "Huh?"

He doesn't repeat anything. Instead, he holds out a hand.

And I take it.

When his fingers curve over mine, it strikes me how right his hand in mine feels. Like our fingers are meant to fit together.

Rather than discussing destinations or the insanity of our actions, I lean back into the warm leather seat of his car and ask, "This yours?"

With a completely straight face, he says, "It's stolen."

"Just this morning, or late last night?"

An eyebrow quirks up. "Yesterday afternoon."

I laugh as he fiddles with the stereo. "So. Why yellow?"

"Why not?"

"They say that a car's color says a lot about its owner."

"Is that so?" He glances over at me, amused as he shifts gears. "What do you think yellow says about me?"

"Hmm. I would say that yellow indicates a need for . . . being recognized."

He laughs out loud at that. "Is that what I'm doing?"

"Maybe," I smile, although it's obvious he doesn't have to seek attention. The last few days have shown me that attention follows him whether he wants it or not.

He surprises me when he asks, "Your car is blue, right?"

"How did you know that?"

He ignores the question and asks instead, "What does blue say about you?"

"Maybe it means I'm looking for peace."

"Really." He's quiet for a moment. "Well, since you think we're so different, what do you think my brother's car's color means? His is white."

I picture the SUV I've seen several times already. Grappling for something that won't shriek, *I love your brother,* I offer, "White means . . . a need to blend in."

Kellan glances at me, somewhat surprised for a second, before snorting. "He'd find that interesting."

"Is it accurate?"

"I guess you'd have to ask him, wouldn't you?"

I wish I could. Yet, here I am instead with Jonah's twin, heading to parts unknown, and my tightly leashed life suddenly feels less restrained than it has in a long time. And I know it has a lot to do with the guy sitting in the seat next to me. Which is crazy, crazy, CRAZY, because it ought to be Jonah, yet it's not.

A quick glance at the speedometer tells me Kellan's driving fast for rain. But rather than being alarmed, I'm not bothered in the least because, for some bizarre reason, I completely trust his instincts. I don't know when it appeared, but it's here all the same—a very distinct feeling of safety with him. An inherent knowledge that this guy would do everything and anything to make sure I stay safe.

So I lean my head back and savor the scenes whipping by us, green-and-brown watercolors of blurred trees mixing with the rain streaking on the windshield.

Kellan leans against a guardrail overlooking the ocean and tells me, "I like this place."

It's still raining, so I allow myself the opportunity to move close enough to feel the lovely warmth radiating from him. "Why?"

"I feel connected to the ocean, like I'm part of a larger picture. Part of a whole. But at the same time, very singular."

"How very poetic."

He laughs, cheeks pink. On him, it's amazingly disarming and tempting at the same time.

"Is that why you enjoy surfing so much?"

"Yeah," he admits. "It helps me think."

"Deep thoughts?"

He pretends to consider about this. "Occasionally shallow."

"I watched you surfing on Saturday," I confess with a sheepish smile. "You're very good. It seems to suit your personality."

"More than the yellow car?"

I laugh. "More than the car."

"How's that?"

"Well, it sort of goes back to what I was talking about earlier. Everyone was talking about you. You were impossible not to notice out there."

He puts a hand against his chest, pretending to be wounded. "So what you're saying is that I'm some sort of attention whore?"

"No! I mean . . . that came out wrong." I fumble for the right words. "I don't think you do it on purpose. I think you're the sort of person who is impossible to ignore."

He taps a finger against his chin. "Impossible?"

"You know what I mean." A flush creeps up my neck.

"Let's say you're right about this attention thing," he says, generously pretending to ignore my foot in my mouth. "How does this explain my brother? He's just as good as me at surfing. If he wants to . . . how'd you put it? Blend in? What does it say about him?"

Now I'm completely flustered. "Oh. Um . . . he likes to hide out in the waves?"

"You can do better than that, or I'll start to think you're just grasping at straws," he teases. And then he tucks a strand of misty hair behind my ear and my knees weaken. I am excruciatingly aware of every inch of him, of how fabulous he smells, and of how each accidental graze against me makes my heart feels like it's going to smash out of my chest. "Do you surf?"

I struggle to find a level voice. "No, but I wish I did. My parents never would let me. They told me such activities don't suit my personality."

"But cheering does?"

I roll my eyes. "According to my mother, who I should point out barely knows me, it does." And then—"I want to quit."

"What?" he gasps, pretending to be shocked. "You aren't a perky cheerleader?"

"Definitely not."

"I thought not," he says rather smugly. "You don't have the temperament for it."

I stare at him, perplexed.

He clarifies, "You hide your true feelings a lot from people."

I blink a few times, surprised by this assessment. "And you know this . . . how?"

He shrugs. "I have a knack for this sort of stuff."

"This sort of stuff," I repeat.

He doesn't say anything further, just smiles knowingly. I'm flustered again and rather breathless at the same time. "So," I say, still wanting to hear his voice, "how long have you been surfing?"

He thinks about this. "Since we were six. We had an uncle who surfed, and he'd take us out to help us deal with things."

Deal with things? I shift through my memories for anything Jonah might've told me over the years that Kellan might be referencing. Maybe . . . their mom's death, since it occurred around the same time?

Kellan's quiet for a moment. "You know, if you really want to try surfing, I'd be more than happy to show you how. We've got some extra boards at the house."

I let him change the conversation. "Really?"

"Sure." A wicked smile forms. "We won't tell your mom, though."

Imagining him teaching me to surf makes the goose bumps come back. "I would love that."

"Then it's a date."

I literally have to will myself not to swoon. As I pick at peeling paint off the railing, I ask, "Why the extra boards? I was under the impression surfers get attached to a specific board and tend to use it religiously. At least, that's what Graham tells me."

"Well, if Graham says it, then it must be so." I give him a mock-stern finger, and he laughs. "Sorry. He's right, though. I do have a favorite board."

"What makes it special?"

"My uncle took us to a surfboard maker in Hawaii several years ago for boards made to our exact specifications. We got to hang around the shop and watch the process, even help. It was pretty amazing."

"It must mean a lot to you, then."

"Yeah," he admits, smiling a little. "To answer your other question, the extras were my uncle's; he passed away recently, and we inherited them."

"I'm so sorry." I place a hand on his arm. The tingling that comes with our touches is becoming addictive.

Kellan stares at my hand, confusion flashing across his face. I begin to pull my hand back, worried I'd misread things, but then he places his over mine. And then, while we're both staring at our hands, they slide and link together.

All I can stupidly think about is how much I want this guy to kiss me, which is WRONG, because I love his brother. At least, if his brother and the guy from my dreams are the same, which I *think* is the case, no—*know* so—

I have got to get a handle on myself. Ask non-kissing kinds of questions. "How do you like California so far?"

His cocky smile returns. "I'd say it's growing on me."

Okay, so I'm back to the whole kissing thing again. Must. Focus. On other. Things. "Why did you move here?"

"The Old Man decreed it so."

"Who?"

He smirks. “My dad.”

“Why would he do that, at the beginning of your senior year?”

“I have to admit, I questioned the logic behind suddenly moving three thousand miles away myself.”

I think about this. “You’re from the East Coast.”

He nods. “Maine.”

“When I think of Maine, I think of blueberries and lobsters, not surfing.”

“Well, it’s not like living in Hawaii full time,” he says. “But it was tolerable for our local needs when we weren’t able to travel to better breaks.”

“On the East Coast?”

“Anywhere,” he shrugs.

“Let me get this right,” I say, trying to ignore how good his thumb running up and down my hand feels, but it’s a losing battle. “You go places just to surf?”

His head tilts to the side, puzzled. “Yes?”

“You’re lucky,” I say quietly. “I’ve hardly ever had the chance to travel. I’ve been trapped here my whole life.”

“That’s too bad,” he murmurs, and then I hold my breath as his other hand carefully pushes wet strands away from my eyes. “There are a lot of places that help expand one’s horizons out there.”

The butterflies in my stomach take off, making me dizzy. Or maybe they’re not butterflies—because butterflies are so delicate. These are strong feelings. Maybe they’re more like dragonflies with incandescent wings.

We're staring at each other now, eyes locked together, and all of those butterflies or dragonflies are insane with need. I'm tingling and nervous and giddy and terrified all at the same time.

Is he feeling the same things I am? He's so calm and collected, so outwardly opposite of what's going on in me. My hands are itching, desperate to touch him, bring him closer. My heart's racing, chanting words I'm terrified of: *kissmekissmekissme.*

As if he can hear this, Kellan gently takes my face in his hands. Then he leans forward and his lips touch mine, so softly, really, but at the massive jolt it sends into my system, the dragonflies explode into a full-fledged frenzy.

And then we're really kissing, and he's like a drug or fine wine or any of those things that people say make them lightheaded and delirious. My body moves with a mind of its own, close as possible to his, because I want him, need him so much that it's almost painful. Thunder cracks overhead and the rain falls harder. But I don't care, because the only thing that matters is this connection between the two of us and the way it makes me feel.

Eventually, when the rain gets to be too distracting, we climb into the backseat of his car. And there, he kisses me senseless. After we come up for air, he murmurs, "You were not in the plans."

I think of the unbending and stressful path before me. "What sort of plans do you have?"

He looks out of the fogged up window and says quietly, "The sort that are difficult to go into detail over."

I reach over to hold his hand. "Believe it or not, I can relate."

His beautiful blue eyes stay fixed on the window. And then, hesitantly, "I like spontaneity—prefer it, even—but my life is pretty much a mapped-out thing. Not a lot of room for variation."

Those two sentences pretty much sum up my future, too.

Then he turns back toward me and presses his forehead against mine. "I know this is going to sound completely crazy, but the very first time I saw you last week, it was almost like I already knew you."

Words to keep forever.

He laughs, embarrassed. "The truth is I've never been so instantly attracted to someone in my entire life as I've been to you. It was a crazy weekend, because you were all I really could think about."

Thank goodness I'm already sitting down, because I just might swoon.

"Too much, too soon?" he asks me.

"No," I whisper, unable in the slightest to explain or understand all of the wonderful and confusing feelings streaking through me. And while I can't say it's the first time I've ever been so attracted to someone, it's been the only other time.

I should be thinking about Jonah, I know I should—I even *want* to—but it's almost impossible to in Kellan's presence. I'm utterly overwhelmed, like I've jumped off a cliff, exhilarated and terrified at the same time. There isn't room to think about anything else except for the fall.

I'd fallen for his brother the very first night I'd seen him. I'd been a little girl and loved him instantaneously. And here I am, one-hundred-percent sure I'm falling for Kellan, too. Here, in his car, damp and hot and barely able to breathe, I know it. But because I can't say it, can't formulate those words or any others I probably ought to be saying, I finish answering by kissing him again.

Kellan's phone beeping finally breaks us apart. He groans and kind of laughs as he reads a text. "Unfortunately, it appears I'm late for an appointment."

I try not to read into the situation, that the text had come from Jonah. But it's no good— my stomach is doing queasy flip-flops. "Will you get into trouble?"

He gives me a cocky grin. "I'm good at convincing people to not be angry with me."

I can totally believe this.

On the way home, I motion at the dashboard clock. It's half past four. "School let out a while ago." At his confused look, I add, "Didn't you come to school with your brother?"

"He found a way home," Kellan tells me. "He's very resourceful."

Confusion floods me, of how I can sit here with Kellan, wanting so much more from him while at the same time be so utterly concerned about and aching for his brother. And wondering just how in the hell he got home. And if it was with a girl.

Please, for the love of all that's good in the worlds, don't let Jonah have gotten a ride home from a girl, especially a cute one.

Kellan's eyes flick over at me. "Are you worried *you'll* get in trouble?"

With Jonah, oh yes. Very worried. I scratch my scalp viciously. "It'll take a miracle for my parents to notice."

He murmurs softly, "Don't I know that feeling."

Because I'll die if I don't know, I ask, "Did your brother know you ditched today?"

"He knew."

A fifty-ton boulder nearly rips a hole in the bottom of my stomach. "What did he, uh, think of that?"

His eyes slide back over toward me in a silent question. Finally, after an excruciating silence that I refuse to fill, Kellan says carefully, "I don't think he really had an opinion."

WHAT DOES THAT MEAN? I might as well dig my own grave. "Did he know you were . . . with me?"

Kellan doesn't look over this time. "Nope."

Sweet relief. "Do you ditch with girls often?"

He'd laughs. "No." And then, after thinking about it, "Actually—this is a first."

The uneasiness of the last minute slips by. "What do you normally do when you ditch?"

"It depends, of course. But I go surfing a lot." He turns off the radio. "What about you?"

I grin. "I don't ditch, remember?"

"But if you did, what would you do?"

I look out the window, at the streaking colors, now muted with growing shadows. And then I find myself telling him the truth. "I'd want to go somewhere and be anyone who wasn't me."

For a long moment, the only sounds are that of tires on blacktop. Rather than saying something unhelpful like, *Why would you want to do that*? Kellan merely says, "You and me both."

chapter 11

"What in the hell were you thinking?" Caleb shouts as we huddle under the overhang of my front porch.

Oops. I'd forgotten that Caleb was going to meet me after school. "I'm sorry," I say for what feels like the fiftieth time.

"Do you know how worried I was?" Caleb snaps, his wings beating so hard they manage to fan my soaking hair. "I waited at your car for hours!"

In an effort to deflect blame, I feebly attempt, "Why is everyone else allowed to ditch, but not me?"

"Because you are a Creator!" Caleb shouts.

Ah, yes. All those lovely expectations that apparently I didn't get the note on. I practically snarl, "So sorry to disappoint, *Mom.* Or should I call you Dad?"

Caleb winces hard, but he's unrepentant. "That was really irresponsible of you, Chloe. You could have at least called me."

And when would I have done that? In between kisses?

YES. Is kissing a boy really more important than your safety? the little voice barks.

I let the door slam behind us. Upstairs, a note from my mother waits for me on my bed. It instructs me to get to Annar in the next few hours in preparation for my appointment with the Seer. Cora is to come with.

I crumple the paper and throw it away.

Once changed and dry, I call Cora. "WHERE HAVE YOU BEEN?" she explodes right out of the gate.

You'd think I'd murdered someone by the reactions I'm getting, rather than simply ditching class. "I was with Kellan—"

"Kellan?" Cora shouts. *"Kellan!?"*

Whoa. Where is this coming from? "Calm down," I tell her, "or hang up."

She takes a number of audible deep breaths. "*Talk.*"

I'm so not digging where this is heading so far. "We decided to go hang out at the beach."

"Hang out."

Nor do I like the stark disapproval in her voice. "Yes. Do you have a problem with this?"

"You two ditched school to go to the beach, in a storm, to *hang out*."

Every part of me is bristling. First Caleb, now Cora? "I can do what I want, you know."

"Even if it's stupid?"

"Gods, Cora, what's your problem?" I snap. "And by the way, it's not like I have to ask your permission if I want to go somewhere with someone!"

"Someone," she bites out. "Oh yes, we're talking about just a random boy at school now, aren't we?"

"You don't know him, so I don't see why you're acting like—"

"But I do know Jonah now."

The phone nearly slips from my fingers. "What?"

"While you were off hanging out with his brother, Lizzie and I met Jonah."

Just like that, all of the happiness built up over the afternoon disappears in a torrent of confusion and longing. My heart is beating hard. Too hard.

"What happened with Kellan today?" she asks.

I'm so off balance at the moment, I actually tell her. "We kissed. It was . . . I don't even know how to explain it. It felt *right*." Two fingers touch my mouth; I'm still able to visualize how wonderful his lips felt on mine.

"WHAT?" And then—"I'm coming over."

"That's not necessary," I say, sitting up, but it's too late. I'm talking to a dial tone.

Cora shows up fifteen minutes later. She walks in without knocking. Lizzie arrives not one minute later, her lithe body stiff with worry.

"What is this?" I accuse. "Are you guys staging an intervention over me ditching school?"

"We should be," Caleb mutters from the other side of the room. He's still so pissed off he won't make eye contact. Instead, he's spent the entire time we've been inside surfing the net on his phone.

Lizzie sits down next to me. "Sweetie, we're worried about you."

This is unbelievable. "It's not like I'm the first person to ditch school, you know!"

"It's not that," she says. "It's because of the Whitecombs."

"The *who*?" I ask.

Lizzie looks to Cora and then to me. "Didn't you even ask Kellan his last name?"

Cora snorts, "Figures," and ceases pacing. She throws herself in the chair opposite the couch and says, "You'd think she'd at least learn his last name before sticking her tongue in his mouth."

"Jesus, Cora!" I explode, blushing furiously.

"Not helping the cause," Lizzie mutters to an unruffled Cora. Caleb tosses his cell phone down and sighs loudly.

My Spanish Inquisitors both fold their arms and wait for my answer. "I didn't know his last name," I finally admit, grappling with the growing discontent in my stomach. "It doesn't change anything, though."

Cora laughs outright. "Oh, really? Think about the importance the Lilywhite name carries in the worlds. Or Pinksten. Or Carregreen."

I am so tired, all I want to do is go upstairs and crawl into bed. "If you have something to say, then just say it. I'm not in the mood to play games." Lizzie opens her mouth to speak, but I cut her off, despite what I've just said. "Look—I *connected* with someone today, and I'm not quite understanding why this has got you all bent out of shape! And, besides, it's none of your business, anyways!"

Cora jerks back onto her feet. "Seriously, Chloe? This is how you're going to play this?"

I jut a finger out at her. "I'm not the one playing games right now, Cora."

She closes her eyes and takes a deep breath, like she's counting to ten or something. Then she opens her eyes and says, fairly calmly, "You may have only shown me a little bit of your memories of Jonah, but I clearly saw the depth of your feelings for him. Are you telling us those are gone, after just one afternoon with his brother?"

Of course they're not. There's never been anything that's been able to dull my feelings for Jonah. Not even when I believed I was insane for falling in love with someone in my dreams. Not even when I was kissing his brother today, as wrong as it sounds.

But I feel trapped. Cornered. Confused. Guilty. So I lash out at the people in front of me. "For all I know, *he* has no idea who I am! It's not like he's made any effort to talk to me. If he's really the same person, he'd have talked to me, *come* to me. But he hasn't!"

"To be fair, you haven't made any efforts yourself," Lizzie offers.

I hold back the impulse to smack her. "That's different!"

"Do you hear this crap?" Cora asks Lizzie and Caleb. "The girl has not one, not two, but three separate shifts over this guy's presence after dreaming about him her whole life, and now she's acting like a baby." She swivels her focus back to me. "Is this some kind of punishment? *He didn't talk to me, so I'm going to make out with his brother. That'll show him.* Because if that's what you're doing, it's a really shitty thing to do, Chloe."

I have never been so angry at her in my entire life. "Shut your mouth, Cora, before I shut it for you. You don't know anything about any of this!"

She actually laughs at that.

"Way to finesse the situation, Cora," Caleb mutters. But he knows this is just like her.

So does Lizzie. She steps in between us. "Everyone, let's discuss this rationally."

It's my turn to count to ten—then to twenty—before being able to continue. "What are we talking about?" I demand. "How is any of this your business? Why are you so put out that I like Kellan?"

But of course, Lizzie sidesteps these questions. "In a situation like this, with these boys . . . it's totally understandable how you would be confused. They're identical twins. You're probably just transferring your feelings from one to the other."

Anger flares once more. What do they know about my feelings toward Jonah? *Nothing*. But what's worse is the terrible surge of jealousy that pumps through me.

They know him. They talked to him. He's always been mine. My secret. My love.

And now they know.

"What did you think you were accomplishing today when you hooked up with his brother?" Cora yells around Lizzie.

"I'd like the answer to that one myself," Caleb murmurs.

How do I even go about answering that when I don't fully understand it myself? "I don't know!" I yell in return. "For once, I just ran with what I was feeling. What's wrong with that?"

"People like us," Lizzie says flatly, still positioned between me and Cora, "do not run with our feelings. We do not have that luxury."

The irony of that is too much to pass up. "Oh, that's choice, coming from you of all people!" I snarl, and Lizzie steps away, wounded.

"Nice, Chloe," Cora snarks, but I'm done with all of this.

So I unleash some words of judgment, too. "Wouldn't you know that best, Lizzie, since you're a master of bottling up those feelings, even if it means hurting those they're intended for."

"Chloe, this is beneath you!" Caleb growls, but Lizzie waves him off.

"I know what's expected of me," she counters. "I don't delude myself into thinking or feeling things that cannot be."

I laugh bitterly. "Well, forgive me, but I felt something today, and I went with it. It was nice for once to do something for *me,* not because it's expected or because I had to."

"Way to be responsible," Cora snaps.

There's a roar in my ears, so loud I can't even hear my own heartbeat. "How *dare* you."

Cora blinks, surprised.

Take a breath, the little voice quickly urges.

"Chloe," Lizzie says, her eyes just as wide. "I don't think Cora meant—"

But the words keep coming. "I'm *so sorry* that I'm such a disappointment to you all. I fully realize what a pathetic excuse of a Magical I am, and how I embarrass the crap out of you all over how I don't manage to fulfill my expectations—"

"Chloe," Caleb says, flying closer. "You need to calm down—"

"Why? So yet another person can tell me how I'm an utter failure?"

"That's not what I meant, and you know it," Cora says quickly.

I snarl. "Isn't it, though?"

A lamp in the room explodes and light bulbs in two others flicker and then shatter themselves. Things go blurry and all I can feel is such rage I don't know if I can hold it all in anymore.

Not responsible. Letting them down. Not fulfilling expectations. Not living up to potential. Always doing the wrong things, making the wrong choices.

I am an utter failure in the eyes of everyone I know.

"Calm down," Caleb soothes again, but I don't see him.

All I can think of is how, yet again, I'm not doing what I *should* be doing. I wish somebody had given me a manual, so I could get something right once in awhile.

"Just listen," Cora says, more calmly. She comes back into focus when she approaches me like I'm a rabid dog—warily, hands up. Caleb blocks her from coming too close. "I surged with Jonah."

"You didn't ask permission?" Caleb yells, strangely aghast.

"I didn't know," she stresses. To me—"I mean, this guy literally steps out of your dreams and shows up a year later. You, of all people . . . I would've thought you'd want to figure it out immediately! Chloe, I *saw* your feelings for him, *felt* them. I just don't get why you . . . I don't know, ignored him! Went off and kissed his brother! Why did you? What happened?"

They're all waiting, but I don't know how to answer them. Jonah's disappearance last year had broken me. The fear over that event, and the pain that still lingered, was excruciating.

I can't live through it again.

Cora sighs through her nose, frustrated. Caleb barks out another warning, but she doesn't back down this time. "You're being supremely stupid, Chloe."

"Cora," Caleb says in a dangerously low voice, "enough. She doesn't have all the facts yet, and may I point out, neither do *you*."

Throat constricting, I manage to whisper, "What don't I know?"

She glares at him before saying to me, "When I surged, I learned something." She pauses, licks her lips in a weirdly defiant way. "Jonah knows you."

"Tell us something that we don't know," my Faerie friend mutters.

"I'm not finished," she says testily. And then, "I only got to see a brief flash before he locked me out, but it was there. Jonah's here because of you, Chloe. *For* you."

Jonah *knows?*

He's here, for me? Just like I'd always—

I stagger back, straight into Lizzie. She wraps her arms around me, like she's shielding me from something.

What had I just done? How can I *ever* begin to explain what I'd done with his brother? What I felt, still feel . . . ?

There's nothing to say. What could I possibly? Nothing. Nothing at all. Because my world has just turned upside down.

chapter 12

"It's pretty amazing, isn't it?"

I don't bother to turn around when I answer Cora. "Yeah, it is."

She leans against the windowsill next to me. "I can't believe we're finally in Annar."

Both of us have wanted to visit the Magical city-state plane for as long as I can remember. And now that I'm finally here, the view in front of me surpasses anything that I've ever imagined. The architecture throughout the city is all done in gray sandstone flecked with quartz crystals that sparkle all day long. The streets are paved in small, smooth stones, the sidewalks in brick. Large trees provide generous shade over the roads, and everywhere I look, there is beautiful landscaping.

It's like no city I've ever seen before.

Cora points into the distance. "That must be Karnach."

She's referring to a rotunda, the most prominent feature as far as the eye can see. Its dome looms wide and large, a central focus that all other buildings lean in toward. Karnach is the Council's domain. Every single Council member has an office there, and from what my father tells me, it's also where they conduct all of their meetings.

When I don't acknowledge her, she says rather grudgingly, "Look, I'm sorry. I know that I sort of threw you for a loop yesterday, but I honestly felt like you needed a reality check."

I simply stare at her. To say I'm still annoyed by yesterday's fight is an understatement.

She's genuinely flustered, which isn't something she tends to be often. "Obviously you don't want to talk about this with me right now."

"You're right about that," I say flatly.

"But," she continues, "I told you that Jonah and Kellan's last name is Whitecomb."

All of a sudden, I'm reminded of a time when I was little. Caleb, ten years my senior, was trying to explain things my parents frequently neglected to teach me about. "Each species of Magicals have similar names," he'd pointed out as I gathered up colorful leaves to make a collage back home. "Chloe, are you listening?"

"Yep." But as I was probably seven, I wasn't really.

"For example, Magical Faeries all have names that are things found in nature. For example, my last name is Windbrook. Caleb Windbrook. Get it? A brook is something found in nature."

A beautiful red leaf distracted me. I went to go get it.

"All Magical Elves have surnames that are plants."

"Plants," I'd repeated as I carefully placed my new find in a basket. He'd mentioned Goblins, Dwarves, and Gnomes, too, but I totally ignored him until he came to Humans. "Your kind all have similar names, too. Colors. Your last name is Lilywhite. What's the color there?"

"White?"

He'd been relieved. "Exactly!"

"My friend Greenlee has a color name!" I'd exclaimed. "Is she a Magical, too?"

"No. That's her first name. Human Magicals always have a variation of a color in their *last* name. That's not to say that everyone with a color name is a Magical, though."

I can't believe I didn't catch it last night. I smack my forehead. "They're Magicals."

"Yeah," she says, smiling a little. "After he forcibly ejected me from his mind when I surged, I made a call to one of my dad's old friends here in Annar, asked if they'd ever heard of any Whitecombs before, possibly a set of twins? And he had. Said they're well known and that their father is on the Council."

You'd think that after all the surprises I've gone through in the last few days, another one wouldn't affect me. But this does. "Magicals," I repeat quietly. "But, they're twins."

Cora lays a hand on my arm. "My friend said that, though they're rare, there can still be Magical twins. I guess Jonah and Kellan are currently the only pair running around."

HELLO! I feel so incredibly stupid. It all makes so much sense now. Of *course* Jonah is a Magical. I dreamed about him most of my life! How could he have ever been anything *but* a Magical?

The better question is, why had we never discussed this? And, had he ever suspected I was one, too?

Forty minutes later, on our way to Karnach, my father is saying, "I expect you to be on your best behavior today when you meet the Seer."

I ignore the slight and instead focus on everything going on around us as. "Are these all Magicals?" I ask, motioning toward the throngs of people on the streets. A Goblin walks by, chatting on her cell phone, the first one I've ever seen up close. She's tall and slender, with a pallid green complexion that reminds me of the Witch of the West, except she's very beautiful, with short, wavy black hair. It surprises me because I'd always assumed Goblins to be short, fat, and ugly, like the stories tell us they are.

"The majority of Annar is populated by Magicals of all the species," my father says, sounding a bit bored. "But there is a small non population who works here who've primarily been recruited. Of course, they're required to abide to a confidentiality contract to prevent them from ever revealing the secrets of Annar to their respective worlds."

He holds me back at a street corner as a group of Gnomes go bicycling by, all wearing tiny cycling spandex outfits. I am inappropriately amused by this.

He pushes me forward once the bikes have cleared. "It's a blood oath. You'll be doing it later this afternoon. All Magicals perform the oath on their first visit to Annar."

"I have so many questions about this place," I admit, warming to the idea that he might be in a sharing mood for once.

"You have about ten minutes to ask away before we arrive at Karnach."

I'm a little girl in a toy store, not knowing which object to pick. I have to think about it for a moment. "Why are there no Muses on the Council?" This is something I'd learned from Lizzie, a fact that bugs her to no end.

"They once were. For much of history, Muses took their jobs seriously, and the art world flourished in ways civilizations had never seen before. As an example, for our plane, look at the glorious Renaissance, or the Baroque period of music. Such advancements; the Council was so proud." He pauses to clear his throat. "But art is a fickle place, filled with capricious people. It's no wonder that the Muses followed suit."

A Faerie snarls at me to watch where I'm going as I almost run into him.

"Think about many of today's artists, Chloe," my dad continues. "So many are incredibly vain. Shallow. That's not to say they all are. There are many talented artists out there, enriching lives and cultures. But for every barrel of beautiful apples, there must always be a number of spoiled ones. It's just how these things go."

"What does this have to do with the lack of Muses on the Council?"

He says, "Over the last hundred years or so, artists have progressively become more and more self-important. Some of this is very well warranted. But many artists find themselves with egos filled with superiority and entitlement when it's not truly warranted."

"And this is being blamed on the Muses?"

"Yes, and rightly so. They've become bloated with feelings of self-importance. It seems as if all the years being around artists have altered who they are. Now, don't get me wrong. We still have a good number of Muses doing their jobs properly. But there are many making a mockery of the arts. Roughly a hundred years ago, the Council had enough." He pauses thoughtfully. "Several Muses were stripped of their crafts for not carrying out their duties properly."

I stop walking. "Magicals can lose their powers?"

"Yes, although it's not done often, and only after a unanimous Council decision." He urges me forward.

Even though I instinctually know the answer, I still ask, "Who has the power to do such a thing?"

"Who else? Creators."

My stomach sinks. Of course.

And yet, my father smiles, oblivious to my turmoil. Motioning to the beautiful building in front of us, he says reverently, "There it is. Karnach. Come now, it's time for you to finally cross its threshold. After all, soon you will call this place home."

Karnach reminds me somewhat of the Pantheon in Rome. Intricately carved statues and gargoyles surround the marble building, as do curved stained-glass windows. Under a good number of these windows are ledges filled with flowers.

It's beyond lovely.

My father abandons me at a map of the building off to one side of the front doors, an etched copper sheet hammered onto a large wooden stand, so he can chat with a colleague. The first floor houses the main Assembly Room, as well as business offices, a couple of museum-type rooms, and a library. Floors two through eight are reserved solely for Council office use. Scanning the directory next to the map, I note that there are two Creators' offices on the fourth floor. One of the offices already shows my name.

I wander alone into the museum rooms, which are filled with art from all of the planes. Some pieces look familiar, others so foreign in nature that they don't make sense to me. But all are equally captivating.

It's something, though, to be finally standing in front of so much Magical history. I'm wandering around the library when someone asks, "May I help you?"

I turn to find an extremely pale Goblin, his hair wiry gray. "Just looking," I say, smiling.

"You are the Creator, correct?"

I blush. How'd he know? I stick out my hand. "That's me. Chloe Lilywhite."

"Fraank Moutainhold," he says. "I'm the current head Librarian."

He can tell I've never heard of his craft, because he adds with a small chuckle, "It's like a cross between Intellectuals and Storytellers. We deal in books, inspire authors and such. But my job here at Karnach is to tend to the books, make sure Council members have what they need for research."

I look around. "Are there Magical histories here?"

He gives me a rueful smile. "No, child. Only the Storytellers have that privilege."

My father finally makes his way over to where we're standing. The Librarian says to him, "What a delight, finally meeting your daughter, Noel. So many people are eager to have the new Creator take her rightful place in the Council."

"Yes, well," my father murmurs, studying me thoughtfully. "We have hopes for her yet."

He doesn't notice the look of confusion on the Librarian's face. I simply batten down the squalls of disappointment forming in my chest.

In my father's office, I'm forced to sit silently, either reading or staring into the distance as he works at his desk. I have my doubts he even remembers I'm in the room.

Some things never change.

I let approximately a half-hour go by until I clear my throat to remind him of my presence. His startled jerk tells me I was probably right in my assessment.

I fumble for something to say. Anything, really, has to be better than this awful silence. "When does the Council meet next?"

"This afternoon," he murmurs, eyes drifting back to his text.

"What are you guys talking about?"

He frowns, as if this is none of my business. It's frustrating, considering someday soon I'll be on the Council, too. "There are no pressing matters for this particular agenda. It's expected to be short, as there is a party tonight that all Council are expected to attend."

"A party for what?"

He pushes at his glasses. "I don't remember off-hand. Maybe it's Elvin in nature. They like to throw parties."

"What kind of parties?"

"Really, Chloe." He plunks his book down. "I don't know. Why is this so important? I have work to do, you know. I can't entertain you all day."

My fingernails dig into my palms. "I'm sorry . . . I just thought, this being my first time to Annar, and to Karnach, that I—"

"Yes, well, you will have more than enough time later this summer to acquaint yourself with Annar, daughter. But for now, I need to finalize some plans that need to be sent off to a team of Intellectuals on the Human plane before the end of the week. Show a little restraint, will you?"

If he'd slapped my face, it couldn't have hurt worse.

A half-hour later, a Gnome enters after knocking briefly yet not waiting for my father to answer. She's young, quite cute, with a small, pert nose and wide brown eyes and wearing clothes which could have come straight off a Paris runway. "Noel? You wanted to be reminded of your daughter's appointment with Astrid?"

“Thank you, Hilda. How was your . . . your . . .” My father flounders for a moment, idly fiddling with his glasses.

She smoothes one of her long, white-blonde braids. “My meeting was fine, thank you. No new developments on any front you need to be bothered with.”

“Excellent,” he mutters, already back to his book.

“Would you like me to show you to the Seer?” Hilda asks me.

Grateful to finally escape my father’s office, I follow her out. Once the office door is shut behind us, Hilda says, “The Seer’s name is Astrid Lotus. Have you met her before?”

“I haven’t really met anyone,” I admit as we head to the stairs.

She briefly looks surprised. “Really? I would have thought that you, being the incumbent Creator, would know most of the Council already.”

I snort at the absurdity of her assumptions. “Don’t you know my father at all?”

“You father is a very great Intellectual,” she says defensively.

Perhaps so, I sigh to myself. *But he’s also a really lousy dad.* But Hilda doesn’t need to know this. She doesn’t need to know anything about how much my parents ignore me or find me lacking. “This Astrid,” I ask instead. “What’s she like?”

“She’s lead Seer, the best we have. She tends to work mostly with Council families, the upper echelons of Magical society.”

“Have you seen her before?”

“No,” she says. “As I’m in the lowest Council tier, I’m not in her sphere of influence.”

I nearly trip on a stair. “What does that mean?”

Hilda squints at me, confused. “I’m not sure what you’re asking.”

“Are there, I don’t know, social caste systems here? In Annar?”

She looks at me like I'm crazy.

"I know very little about Magical society except for the people living near me on the Human plane," I say, keeping two steps below so I don't tower over her. "I'm curious about what things will be like here for me, that's all."

She squares her shoulders. "Things will be fine for you here. As Creator, you will be first tier. Annar and the worlds will be oysters at your feet."

I want to scream, because even this girl isn't willing to really talk to me about the things I don't know. "Look—"

"Your father would be upset if I we discussed things that aren't my business," she says curtly. "And, being an Intellectual, I work for him. Please understand I don't want to cause trouble where trouble isn't needed."

Trouble? Talking to me will cause *trouble*?

It hurts, but I dig my heels in. "Will you at least tell me what tier this Astrid is in?"

"Astrid is second tier." She pauses, then says, "Tiers one through three are considered upper class here in Annar. It's not about money, though—not like back on our planes. Here, it's all about power and how strong you are. Alliances are beneficial. Certain families—old, respected family lines—help, too, especially for those non-Council Magicals."

"Do you know if Cora Carregreen got to see Astrid today?"

She stops in front of a door on the fourth floor. "I believe she saw somebody else. One of the lower-ranking Seers agreed to meet with her as a favor to your father."

I say, probably more sarcastically than needed, "Let me guess. Cora is middle class here."

“She isn’t Council bound,” Hilda says almost clinically. “But she is technically related to you.” And then, nodding her head once, she leaves.

chapter 13

Much to my surprise, Astrid Lotus is an Elf: beautiful, willowy, and pale. Her light-blonde hair is braided to the side and knotted under, her eyes a washed-out violet. She has a large number of chunky necklaces with various semi-precious stones around her neck, and both arms are stacked heavy with bangles.

"You do not want to be here," is the first thing she says to me.

The little voice urges me to be honest with her. "I guess that's true."

"Why?"

I tell her, "Because this was my mother's idea."

"I see. You and your mother do not have a close relationship."

One of my eyebrows quirks up. "Is that your guess, or your professional evaluation?"

"Both." Her bracelets clink together as she shifts her arms. "I see that quite clearly in you. But, I can also hear it in your voice."

I snort. "She thinks I need guidance."

"Do you?"

I look down at my hands, folded in my lap. What I need is a mom who gives a damn. "Are you like a shrink? Do I tell you how I'm feeling? Stuff like that?"

"If you like," she says. Her voice is incredibly soothing. "It helps to know, sort of like puzzle pieces that help me create a whole picture.

What I normally do is read your paths, see what's going on in your life. Have a peek at things that you're meant to do. Then we'll discuss these things, alongside your emotions, so you may make informed decisions on your future."

"Are you telling me I have choices?"

"There are always some choices available to us, Chloe. Not as many as we may like, but they are there all the same. But much of your destiny, as you well know, is already mapped out. I'm merely a conduit for knowledge about that route."

She holds out her hands, and after a brief pause, I reach out mine, too. And then we sit in silence for a really long time, maybe five, ten minutes, my hands in hers, her eyes closed, while she sees whatever it is she sees.

When her eyes open, she lets go of me. For the briefest of moments, confusion flickers across her face. Sadness.

"Is . . . everything okay?" I ask.

But the serene face she'd shown me when I'd first come in is back. "Of course. Now, I see you are quite conflicted about being a Creator. You're hesitant about that path."

I let my eyes drop again. "It's a lot of pressure," I admit.

"It is," she agrees. "You have one of the most challenging crafts of all. I would be worried, really, if you were completely at ease with everything."

I look up, surprised.

"A lot will be asked of you in the coming years. Someday you may be required to do awful, destructive things. A person unbothered by such actions is someone I don't think I'd like entrusting civilizations with."

Something in me squeezes painfully. It's almost alien to have somebody to talk to about this stuff who isn't so judgmental. "I've always been told to just suck it up," I say quietly. "Like there's something wrong with me because I'm conflicted."

Astrid is silent, her lips pursed tightly.

"I'm sorry," I say quickly. "I don't mean to—"

She holds up a hand. "No. Don't apologize. And don't 'suck it up,' either. The Council doesn't need a Creator who bottles everything up and suffers in silence over the course of her craft. What the Council needs, and deserves, is someone who understands the implications of her actions. Who has the mettle to think things out and not act like a mindless drone. You are first tier, Chloe. Magicals of your caliber should never *suck it up*."

I'm stunned. This is a total one-eighty from what my mother claims.

"These worries, your doubts—they're there for a reason," she continues. "They, along with your conscience, will help guide you through your work. There will be many battles you face on the Council. There are always those out there who have agendas, who work in coalitions that may or may not have the planes' best interests in their hearts. As a Creator, and first tier, you will need to make sure that you're there for the billions of people we oversee, and not just Magical society. So please know that there is nothing wrong with you for feeling how you do about being a Creator. Embrace those worries. Cultivate those doubts. Let them guide you, allow you to be a moral compass when others might want to head in other directions."

I'm speechless.

She tents her fingers together, her bracelets clacking together. "Your ties to your parents are very weak. This is troubling. Would you mind telling me what your life at home is like?"

"We, uh, don't get along well. I mean—I suppose it's civil, to a degree. But we don't talk much."

She frowns.

It's hard to admit out loud. In fact, it's downright humiliating. But the little voice urges me to continue with honesty. "They don't have time for me. I . . . disappoint them. Embarrass them." I stare down at my hands again. "I don't know a lot about what it means to be a Magical. They won't talk to me about it. I'm told I have expectations, which they are shamed I don't live up to, but they won't let me know what they are. This trip . . ." I clear my throat. "It's the first time I've been to Annar. I don't know even really know what the Council does."

"Your father is an Intellectual," Astrid says slowly. "He doesn't talk to you about the Council?"

I shake my head. Has she met the guy before? Hello!

"Do none of the Magicals in your region talk to you?"

She's got to be kidding, right? The Cousins are like me—latchkey kids with workaholic parents. This is why we've banded together as a family, why we really can only count on one another. "No. The other teenagers nearby and I have pretty much been left to fend for ourselves. We share what we learn with each other, though. And sometimes some of the Gnomes and Faeries living the woods nearby tell us stuff."

"I am astonished." She leans back in her chair, shaking her head. The bracelets clack against each other. "Not all Magical parents are like this, Chloe," she says after a long, uncomfortable pause.

Lucky me, I guess. I feel worse than ever.

"Karl Graystone will be coming to guard you. I advise you to talk to him. Ask him questions. You need to come to Annar prepared, Chloe. The Council needs your wisdom, not your ignorance."

I nod, wiping at my nose with my sleeve. I'm on the verge of tears.

"Now then," she says gently. "Shall we talk about other things?"

I feel raw. Exposed. Like someone has been picking at my skin, peering underneath. All I want to do is run and hide. This Seer now knows what I am, of how I'm ignorant, scared. Unloved. But I tell her, "Sure," anyway.

"Is there something you want to ask me?"

I look up at her, confused.

"There are relationship paths that some Magicals have, special ones. Ones that typically most people want to know about. I'm not sure if you are one of those people, though."

I have no idea what she's talking about. Magical paths are always about crafts, right?

She bites her lip, glancing briefly at the ceiling, then back at me. "Tell me about your dreams, Chloe."

"Dreams?"

"As a child. What kind of dreams did you have?"

I blink at her a few times, confused, until it hits me. She knows. Somehow or other, she *knows*. And because she's been so kind, so nonjudgmental, I tell her. "I dreamed about someone. Since I was three or four. The same person, all my life, until last year."

Her face is perfectly calm with the exception of one small muscle twitching by her mouth. "Do you mind telling me a little bit about that?"

I tuck my legs under me and pick at the frayed hem of my jeans. "We grew up together. I thought he was a figment of my imagination, someone who loved me when my parents didn't. Someone who listened, who cared. I know it sounds crazy, but . . ."

"Not crazy," Astrid interjects.

"Um, okay," I say, surprised yet again. "Well, he was my friend. My best friend." I pause. "I fell in love with him, which was totally bonkers, considering he was in my dreams . . . but it was like I didn't have a choice."

She smiles faintly.

Keep going, the little voice urges.

"And now, he's at my school," I whisper. "Since Friday."

Now her eyebrows lift up. "What?"

"The guy in my dreams. He disappeared a year ago, but on Friday, he showed up in my math class. There were some shifts—"

Astrid says quickly, "Those were yours?"

I let go of the frayed ends, embarrassed. "You felt them here in Annar?"

"I wasn't in Annar," she admits after a brief pause. "I live on your plane, as we Elves can blend in if we wish to. And those shifts were particularly . . . strong; I believe much of States felt them."

Fantastic. As if I wasn't already embarrassed enough.

She prods softly, "Please continue."

I take a breath. "And then, it turns out he has a brother. A twin."

Astrid nods, her lips thinning.

"And . . . I don't even know how to say this. Explain it. But something happened with *him*—"

"The one from your dreams, or the twin?"

"The twin," I say, resuming the destruction of my jeans' hem. "Yesterday. Then, when I got home, my Cousin Cora told me that . . .

that the twins are Magicals. And that she surged with the one from my dreams and saw that he . . . he . . .” I close my eyes, trying so hard not to cry. And Astrid waits for me. Her bracelets don’t even clack. “He’s real,” I finally whisper. “The guy I’ve been in love with my entire life is real. And he’s come for me, and now I’m so confused, because it’s everything I’ve ever wanted. *Everything*. But something happened with his brother, and I don’t know what to do anymore. Because that felt so real, too. I don’t . . . I don’t know what it means. I don’t know how it’s possible. I mean, I dreamed about him. That’s crazy, right? Dreams aren’t real.”

“Well, dreams are sometimes real.” She pinches the bridge of her nose. “In fact, there are Dreamers who work all over the different planes.”

Why don’t I *know* this stuff? Why couldn’t my parents bother to tell me things like this?

“Remember how I said that Magicals sometimes have paths, relationship paths?” I nod and she continues. “It’s very rare, but some Magicals are linked together in a way that allows them to meet early on through their dreams. It appears this has happened to you.”

I go still.

“Everything that happened with him over the years, it’s all real, Chloe. It wasn’t your mind playing tricks on you.”

Sweet validation.

“You have a very strong, very distinctive relationship path. One that is . . .” She shakes her head, taps her lips with a finger. “Your path is very important but also very . . . conflicted.”

“Conflicted?”

She shakes her head again and stares out the windows. “I have to tread a very fine line here, Chloe. There are a lot of factors that need to be taken into consideration, things that people like me have no business intruding in whether we want to or not."

Huh?

"You are loved very much. But sometimes love isn't always . . ." The bracelets clack again as she shifts. "Gods. I'm doing this badly. I'm sorry, Chloe. I know you want answers. You deserve them. But I don't think I'm the best person to help you."

"I . . . I don't understand . . ."

"I know," she says sympathetically. She taps her lip again. "Love can be very complicated. And I'm afraid that this is the case for you."

"Because I met this guy in my dreams?"

She sighs. "I can't talk about it anymore, Chloe. I'm sorry. I'm not the person who can help you with this."

"But . . . you're a Seer, the lead Seer. If not you, then who . . . ?"

She stands up and comes close, laying a soft hand against my cheek. "You are a dear girl, one I have much hope for. I wish you the best, darling. I truly do. All I can do is urge you to be careful—careful with your heart and of those you love."

"But—"

"Think about what I've said," she says, helping me off the couch. "I have faith that you will be a good Creator for us."

"But—"

"As for the other thing, go to your regional Seer, someone who isn't connected to the Council. Someone who would be there for you, and you alone. Someone who isn't invested in the outcome, who . . ." Astrid looks away. "The path you're on, it's . . . well, you should ask questions. But the outcome is something only you and those involved can determine."

“I don’t understand—”

“I know,” she says, walking me to the door. “And I’m truly sorry about that.” She blinks, her eyes glassy.

She has tears in her eyes.

And then she hugs me tightly. She’s warm and smells good, like honey. She feels exactly what I want a mother to feel like. “You are a good girl. A smart girl. No one could ask for someone better, not really. I’m so glad for that. Truly.”

When she lets go, I’m left with more questions than I had before seeing her.

chapter 14

I really should be enjoying the party more—there are hundreds of people, all seemingly having a great time as they mingle, but the room feels empty to me. Lonely even.

I watch my parents at a distance. As always, my mother is cool. Aloof. This is how I'd always assumed all Magicals to be, but at this party, I see differently.

It's just my mother. She, herself, is dispassionate.

I think about Astrid and how, even when she was confusing and pulling away, she was still caring enough to hug me. Tell me I mattered. That she believed in me.

What I wouldn't give to have my own mother act like that.

"Wanna talk about it yet?" Cora asks, tugging on my sleeve.

I didn't tell her about Astrid, other than saying it was a tough interview. I blow out a long breath. "And say what?"

"Start with how you're feeling about things and we'll go from there."

She's trying, the little voice says. *Cut her some slack.*

I shove my hair out of my face. "I'm pretty confused right now, Cora."

"Why confused?" she asks, genuinely puzzled herself. "Because, from my point of view, you're in a pretty good position right now. You've got a gorgeous guy, a Magical no less, madly in love with you."

She knows this, how?

"Okay," she says, rolling her eyes. "I got that from the surge, too. The point I'm trying to make, though, is I don't see a downside. You. Jonah. In love. Have been for a long time. What's the problem?"

"Are you serious? Haven't you been listening?"

She considers this. "Are you talking about his brother? Because that's no problem at all. Admit it was a mistake and move on. Jonah will understand. Tell him you were confused because they look alike."

I don't know why I bother talking to her about anything like this in the first place.

"Excuse me—are you Chloe Lilywhite?" I whirl around and stare up at an exceedingly tall and well-built man who appears to be in his early twenties. He says, clearly amused as I gape up at him, "Cat got your tongue?"

"Who's asking?"

A hand is stuck out for me to shake. I fear bones are being crushed as he pumps mine up and down. "My name is Karl Graystone. I'm the Guard who's been assigned to watch over you until you Ascend later in the summer." He mercifully lets go of my aching hand.

Cora leans forward and introduces herself. Once that's out of the way, she asks him, "A Guard? Like a bodyguard?"

His hazel eyes peer down at her in suspicion. "You don't know what the Guard is?"

"Obviously. If I did, I wouldn't have asked."

"The Guard is a branch of the Council, comprised of about seventy members of all the different species," he says, frowning. "In addition to maintaining law and order within our society, it's both an offensive and defensive team used to protect Magicals and our way of life."

This gets both of our attentions. I ask, "You mean, you guys do things like fighting? Like the military?"

"I suppose you could see it that way," Karl says, scratching at his short brown hair. "I guess the military comparison is fair."

"Why is some military guy assigned to my Cousin?" Cora demands.

He addresses me. "Didn't your parents tell you of the arrangements the Council has made for me to come to stay with you?"

I nod. "She said you're to be a babysitter of sorts."

The word *babysitter* obviously doesn't sit well with Karl, because both his eyebrows raise high into his forehead before snapping down in irritation. "I'm nobody's babysitter," he practically growls. "I'll be there to protect you, and will be expecting your full cooperation."

Cora turns to me. "Protection from *what?"*

Ugh. I so don't want to get into this at a party. "Um . . . I guess there have been some Magicals hurt over the last few years . . ."

"Killed," Karl points out flatly. "There have been injuries, yes, but also a fair number of murders."

Okay, that sends Cora over the edge. "Whaaaat? Why am I just now hearing about this?"

I become defensive. "Well, my mind has sort of been on some other things."

She stares at me like I'm an idiot. And I guess I can see why—worrying about boys should not take precedence over worrying about whether or not I'll be killed.

"As of now, I hope your focus will be on what's important, Chloe." Karl's voice is deep and rumbly, making me wonder if he ever laughs. "Anyhow, I wanted to come over and introduce myself tonight and let you know I'll be by your parents' apartment late tomorrow morning to discuss with you a few things before we head back to the Human plane."

A very tall, handsome gentleman in an elegant suit approaches Karl. I do a double take, because other than silvery-blonde hair, he looks like an older version of Jonah. "Karl, if it's possible, a few of us need to talk to you before you leave tonight," the man says.

"Of course," Karl replies. Then he turns towards me and Cora. "Ewan, this is Chloe Lilywhite and Cora Carregreen. Ladies, this is Ewan Whitecomb, one of the senior Faiths on the Council."

And . . . that's why. The reason he looks like Jonah is because he's his *dad*.

"Ah yes, the Creator," Ewan says, smiling faintly. His voice is cultured with the smallest hint of an accent I can't place. "It's a pleasure to meet you. The Council is anticipating your arrival."

Does he know about me and Jonah?

Ewan Whitecomb turns backs to Karl, his polite interest in me obviously over, which leads me to believe the answer is no.

Karl arrives at exactly eleven the next day, suitcase in hand. My parents have gone out for the morning, leaving a note behind for me and Cora. We're to go back home with Karl since they'll be staying in Annar.

This is nothing new or even surprising. They've been leaving me alone with Caleb as a babysitter since I was seven. Sometimes I prefer it this way. The silence in the house is less painful.

I've decided to at least try to be pleasant to Karl, considering he'll be living with me for who knows how many months. So I greet him cheerfully at the door, only to be met with a curt, "Good morning."

I lead him into the apartment to where Cora's already sitting on a couch. "I'm glad you're both here," he says as I plop down next to Cora. He remains standing in front of us, arms laced behind his back. "Let's go through the rules."

Should I get something to write them down with? "Rules?"

This guy is dead serious. "All good missions follow pre-determined rules."

"Mission?" Cora cuts in.

He motions at me. "This is a Guard mission. Protecting the Creator is a mission."

"Her name's *Chloe*."

"It's okay," I assure her. "Let's let him finish."

"Are you the only person on this mission?" Cora asks, ignoring me.

He blinks. "No."

"Who else, then?" she asks before I can say anything.

It's obvious he's annoyed with her questions. "There are a number of people assigned to the Creator—"

"Chloe," Cora says fiercely. "She's more than just a Creator. She's a seventeen-year-old girl named Chloe."

"Cora," I say quietly, but she waves me off.

"He's making it sound like you're a vase in a museum instead of a person with thoughts and feelings. He'd do well to remember it."

His cheeks flush dark red. "Now, listen here—"

"You may continue," Cora says, waving a hand.

His mouth clamps shut; the veins in his neck bulge. "First off—"

"Why rules?" Cora interrupts. "I thought you were merely coming to watch over Chloe."

"Do you want me to do this or not?" he grinds out.

Cora smiles like a beauty pageant queen. "Of course. Continue."

He sighs loudly through his nose. "These rules, in case you're wondering, are to ensure that the Creat— uh, Chloe stays safe. Please understand that we are not trying to be punitive—"

"We?" Cora asks.

"Oh, for gods' sakes!" he explodes. "Will you let me talk here or what?"

"How old are you?" Cora asks, undeterred.

I legitimately worry he's going to strangle her. "Nearly twenty-one."

"Damn." She whistles. "You're like a baby Guard. They're sending a kid out to protect my Cousin?"

"Age is irrelevant when it comes to the Guard."

"He's also on the Council," I tell her.

She eyes him with a new interest. "You can be both on the Guard and Council?"

"Yes," he says, his neck flushing, "it's not common, but there are about ten of us who do double duty. But that's not the point here—"

"You were in the process of telling me who is on Chloe's team."

"Gods almighty," he barks. "Are you serious?"

"Why wouldn't I be? Chloe's my Cousin. I have a vested interest in her, other than how she's a Creator. I actually care about her *life* and *safety,* as opposed to what she can do for the Council. I just want to know she's in good hands."

He presses his palms against his eyes. “She’s in excellent hands, Carregreen. There is a Guard team set up to oversee her case.”

“Case?”

Okay, now he’s had enough. He holds out a hand and when she tries to speak. “Shut up and listen, will you? I need to get these rules out so we can get back to California.”

Cora doesn’t need him to strangle her. She’s doing a pretty good job of looking like she’s being strangled herself.

“As I was saying, the first rule will be that you, Chloe, will no longer be allowed to drive yourself anywhere without me present.”

I stare up at him, agog.

“The majority of the attacks have occurred while a Magical was alone. A car does not offer protection. I’ll be taking you to and from school. You will be no longer allowed to participate in after-school activities. I’m told you’re involved in cheerleading—sorry, that’s no longer allowed.”

Rainbows explode around me. “Are you saying I’m off the cheer team?”

“I’m sorry,” he says, but I stand up and scream as loud as I can.

“Is this not the BEST DAY EVER?”

“I guess there’s a perk to death threats after all,” Cora muses.

Karl’s righteousness deflates some. “You’re not upset?”

“Hell no.” I happily drop back on the couch. “This is awesome.”

“Okaaay,” he drawls slowly. “Um, well . . . you’ll be expected to meet me within a reasonable time after the last school bell on a daily basis. I’ll need you to keep your cell phone on at all times in order for me to reach you and vice versa.”

Still focused on how I no longer have to cheer, I cheerfully accept this as Karl turns to Cora.

"Carregreen, we're still working out whether or not I'll be taking you to and from school."

"Whatever for?" she demands.

"Because it was ordered, that's why. And because you're under my watch, too—albeit in a much-reduced capacity."

"Why?" she asks, jerking her back straight. "I get Chloe needing the cover and all, but I'm small fish, not even Council bound!"

"Because it was ordered," he repeats through clenched teeth. And then, before she can argue, he adds, "Many extracurricular activities will no longer be allowed. This includes parties I cannot get into—"

Wait—

"Going out to restaurants without me—"

Wait a—

"Dates I can't follow along on—"

"You'd go on a *date* with her?" Cora asks. "What are you, a voyeur?"

His mouth snaps shut as his eyes begin to bug out.

"It's creepy," she continues, unperturbed. "How'd you like to go out on a date with some beefy bodyguard watching you?"

As if he didn't know which part to be insulted by, he manages to say, "I'm . . . I'm *married*."

"Even creepier," she points out.

"Cora, stop," I hiss when Karl turns a really ugly shade of red.

"I'm just saying," she whispers back, as if Karl can't hear her easily, "how are you going to get things resolved with—"

“AHEM.” Karl’s fists clench at his sides. “May I finish?” When we nod, he says, “If you need to go somewhere after school, it’ll be with me. I’ll drive you wherever you need to go and stay with you. This includes shopping, eating, going to the beach . . . If anyone non asks you who I am, you’re to tell them that I’m a relative who’s staying with you. Under no circumstances are you to tell people that I’m there to watch you.”

“This shouldn’t be a problem, considering she won’t ever be allowed to see anyone again,” Cora mutters.

“Cora, please!” I yell. “This isn’t helping!” They both stare at me. “I get the situation sucks,” I continue. “And it does. I’m not looking forward to being babysat. I can take care of myself, despite what most people think. But I’m also not keen on dying.”

“I know you can take care of yourself,” Cora says softly. “Even if this jackass doesn’t.”

“Hey now,” Karl says, but I hold out a hand.

“I get why the Council is worried, so I want to work with you. I just I can’t let you smother me, though.”

He sighs. “If it’s any consolation, I’m not overly thrilled about being away from my wife for so long, either.”

“She a cougar?” Cora asks.

Karl stares at her, mouth open.

“I’m just saying,” she says defensively. “He looks like the sort to snag a cougar.”

She did *not* just say that. “Cora!”

“My wife is off limits to you.” He shakes a finger at her. And then, after a moment, “She’s not a cougar.”

Cora cackles brightly.

His focus returns to me. "I know this seems unfair in many ways. But, you need to understand the seriousness of the situation. The Council feels very . . . certain, if you will, that you could be a target."

"Yeah, yeah," I murmur. "Creator. Council bound. Got it."

"And Cora, as for why you'll be watched," he continues, "sometimes the people closest to the targets have become victims. You won't be as guarded nearly as closely as Chloe, but anytime you're with her, you'll be expected to follow all the aforementioned rules. Is that clear?"

"Fine," she grumbles.

"What about my other Cousins?" I ask.

"Cousins? You mean . . . the other Magicals you associate with?" I nod, and he continues, "No one sees them as questionable targets." Karl digs a piece of paper out of his pocket. "You have . . . three additional Magical friends in the area?"

"You are well-informed, sir," Cora answers.

A thin band of gold on his left hand catches my eye. "Do you need to go say goodbye to your wife?"

"No," he says quietly. "We already did that this morning."

"Can't they get someone else?"

"I'm more than capable of ensuring your safety, Chloe."

"That's not what I'm saying," I quickly correct. "It's just . . . my mother mentioned your wife is pregnant. I can't imagine it'll be fun for you to be watching me on another plane when she's expecting your baby."

"Dude," Cora says, whistling. "Daddy Karl? Bust out the shotguns and white wife-beater already, why don't you?"

He ignores her. “I was chosen for this mission, and the Guard always follow through with their orders. My wife is on the Guard, too. She understands the mission and accepts it. It won’t be a problem. Don’t worry yourself over it.”

I tell him I won’t, but can’t help but feel sympathetic toward him, even while I figure I ought to be resentful.

chapter 15

Over the last day and a half, I haven't yet come to any real conclusions over what to do about Jonah and Kellan Whitecomb. For one, I haven't talked to Jonah yet, but ache to. Need to. But on the other hand, I'd connected with Kellan in a way that, despite Cora's beliefs, can't easily be dismissed.

Speaking of, Kellan texted me yesterday, while I was in Annar: *So. Today, I didn't see you at school. In class. In History, even.*

I'd been amazed to discover that apparently my cell phone coverage included Annar.

I hadn't written back because I didn't know what to say. There'd been no message today from either of them. Not that I'd expected Jonah to text me, but I suppose it'd be fair to say I'd had some hope he would. That because I now know he's a Magical, it makes a difference. That maybe he knows it, too.

I don't know his phone number or where he lives, so it's not like I can go over and talk to him myself.

So, maybe that's the answer then. I go to the one I can talk to first. *Meet me early tomorrow morning? Parking lot?*

It takes twenty seconds to get a response. *You okay?*

A warm, fuzzy feeling blooms over the fact that he cares. *Yeah. You?*

It expands with Kellan's next text: *Better now. See you @ 7.*

Karl is in the guest bedroom, watching something on a food channel. I sort of hover in the doorway until he notices me. He clicks off the TV and says, "Is there something I can help you with?"

I clear my throat and glance around the room. In the four hours he's been here, I happen to know he's made five phone calls and received seven, including, if I'm not mistaken, several with his wife. He'd checked the perimeter of the house, conferred with Caleb over logistics, and has pretty much left me alone, which I'm thinking was purposeful after my small speech on how I'm used to fending for myself.

But now I find myself wanting to maybe give Astrid's suggestion a try. "You all settled?"

"Yep, thanks for asking."

"Um . . . where are you from?"

He motions for me to sit down, but I remain standing. "I've split the bulk of my life split between Annar and the East Coast."

"Oh." It's weird that he hasn't put any pictures or personal items up yet. "Do you like it like that?"

He's confused. "Meaning?"

"Living in Annar. Do you like it there?"

"Sure," he says. And then, "I live full-time there, now, though. Most Guard do."

I lean against the dresser. "It's interesting you're on both the Council and the Guard. I didn't know people could do that."

He gives me a questioning look, like he's trying to determine if I'm teasing him or not.

I clear my throat. "Do you like one more than the other?"

“I prefer the Guard, to tell you the truth. I have a bit more Guard mentality than a Council one.”

I wipe a finger across the top of the dresser. It’s spotless. My mother can’t bother to take care of me, but damn if she doesn’t ensure there isn’t one speck of dust in the house. “Did you grow up, always knowing about . . . this sort of stuff?”

“Stuff?”

I wave my hand between us. “You know.”

“I really don’t,” he says, brows furrowed.

I look toward the door, even though I know my parents aren’t at home. “I didn’t.”

He scratches at his head. “Chloe, I feel like we’re speaking two different languages here. What are you referring to?”

It’s uncomfortable talking about this with him. More than confusion—I think it’s the entire concept that me, as a Creator, and apparently someone the Magical worlds are looking forward to, knows squat is humiliating.

All I’d heard at the party in Annar the night before was how excited everyone was that I’m coming of age. How they expect great things of me. How they can hardly wait until I hit the ground running.

So many expectations. So many hopes. So much pressure amongst my ignorance that I feel like running.

I can’t look at him when I admit, “I’m talking about the whole being-a-Magical thing.” I sit down next to him. “No one talks to me about it. I don’t know jack about . . .” He prompts me to finish. “Anything,” I say in a small voice.

“I’m sorry,” Karl says, “but I’m still confused here.”

"Me too. That's why . . . I need your help." I square my shoulders and decide, good or bad, I've got to take a chance here. So I break down and tell him the truth, of how ignorant I am, of how my parents hoard their information, of how terrified I am, even more so than being attacked, of continuously failing people and their expectations of me.

When I'm done, he doesn't judge. He doesn't berate me for asking for help. He doesn't belittle me for not being someone I'm not. Instead, he agrees to help me. And then we begin to talk.

"What do you know about the University in Annar?"

Karl is driving me to school the next morning. I'd sort of lied and said I'd already promised a friend I'd get there early before I knew about the rules. I'm not sure why I didn't tell him about meeting Kellan. I suppose it's because I'm not sure what I'm going to say myself.

I've got several choices, all uncomfortable:

1. I'm a Magical, too. Did you know?
2. I know your brother and have been in love with him my whole life. Did you know?
3. What we did together on Monday was amazing. I feel connected to you more than I do with any other person save your brother. Oh. Did I tell you about your brother?

"Not much," I admit to Karl. It's easier to talk about this than my love life. "Just that I have to go there in the fall."

"In some ways, it's like a traditional college. You'll go to classes, have professors, assignments. Only, you don't get to pick your schedule. Based on your craft, the U picks your classes for you. Puts you on a track that will help cultivate the knowledge base you need to put your skills to good use in the field."

“Let me get this straight,” I say as he breaks at a stop sign. “I don’t get to pick my job. I don’t get to pick my college. I don’t get to even pick my classes. It’s all done for me?”

Karl’s smile is rueful. “You have the choice whether or not to complete the assignments.”

“And if I fail?”

He snorts. “No one fails at the U. It’s just not done.”

“Someone must fail,” I insist. “Not all Magicals can be geniuses. There have to be a fair share of dumb bricks out there, too.”

His second snort indicates he’s trying hard not to laugh. “Intelligence isn’t a requirement to be a Magical, that much is true. I suppose the U is more for practicality’s sake. You learn what you can so you can be successful. Failure in the field is looked down upon and may have consequences.”

“Like jail? Is there a Magical jail?”

“Yes, but that’s not what I mean. The Council doesn’t accept failure. If you do so, you can get censured.”

“So, you do badly and they . . . what? Call you names? Slap you on the wrist?”

We pull into the parking lot. “You don’t have to worry about that, Chloe.”

“Why not?”

“You’re a Creator. You’ll get a free pass.”

I stare at him as he parks. “You mean, I can screw up and nobody will hold me accountable?”

“No. I didn’t say that. What I said is, as first tier, there aren’t a lot of people who will have the power to rebuke you.”

I rub at my eyes. "Can I at least trust that you'll always rebuke me when necessary?"

He laughs for the first time since we've met. "Sure."

Kellan is waiting for me on a bench partially shielded by a large tree. He's reading a book, but notices me when I get within ten feet. At the same moment he realizes I'm nearby, there's this weird tugging sensation in the pit of my stomach, the same pull I'd felt around him a few days ago.

I still don't know which discussion option to choose.

This morning, when I woke up, I came to the conclusion that everything that happened with him must've been a fluke. My mind had been playing tricks on me, pretending on some level that Kellan had been Jonah.

But the closer I get to Kellan, the hotter my cheeks burn. The more my insides flip and twist in agonizingly yummy ways.

He stands up when I reach him, a half-smile forming charmingly on his lips. The butterflies in my stomach explode into a full-fledged frenzy. Like he can sense this, his smile turns radiant.

"Hi," we say at the same time. My mouth is so dry I end up licking my lips. He watches this, of course.

"Thanks for meeting me so early," I say. It comes out like a breathy giggle a femme fatal might use. So, so awful.

"Is everything okay?"

I'm so anxious, it's ridiculous. "Sure. Um . . ."

"You're nervous," he says, reaching out to touch my face. I go lightheaded. "You don't need to be nervous around me." His fingers slide against my cheek after tucking a strand of hair back, and it takes every last brain cell to attempt to focus on the task at hand. After all, it's a little hard to try to have a rational conversation when all you want to do is lose yourself in someone.

"I . . . uh . . . want to talk to you about something."

"Good or bad?"

Telling him about Jonah would be . . . bad? Telling him I'm a Magical, too, would be . . . good?

Start with the good. Definitely.

"I was absent for the last two days because I took a trip."

His half-smile quirks. Damn, it's attractive. "You want to talk about your trip?"

I nod.

His hand drops to mine and tugs me towards the bench. "I thought you said you don't travel."

He actually listened to me? "I don't. Not normally. This was the first time I've gotten to go to this particular place." And then, practically whispering, "And . . . you've been there, too."

He thinks about this for a moment. "I've been a lot of places."

A quick glance around shows a group of girls standing roughly fifty feet away, but they're gossiping so loudly I doubt they'd ever be able to hear anything I have to say. "I saw your dad there."

He stares at me for a long moment. Then he stands up, scratches his forehead and stares some more. After what feels like forever, he leans forward and cups my face with his hands. "Your last name is Lilywhite."

And here I was, feeling lame that Cora had to practically smash a brick over my head to get me to figure out the whole last name thing. Kellan hadn't gotten it, either!

“I can’t believe that went right by me,” he grins, something between awe and surprise in his voice.

I match his grin. “I didn’t figure it out myself until Tuesday.”

“In Annar,” he clarifies, and a zing races through me. He knows now. He knows about me, he knows about Annar.

“So, what are you?”

I’m a bit drunk on giddiness right now, so I showboat a bit by holding out my palm. Kellan peers down at it, but then I close my fist. When I open it, there is a tiny Karnach snow globe.

I sneak a peek at Kellan to see what he’s thinking. His face is totally calm, as if there’s nothing in my hand at all.

Unnerved, I smack my hands together and the snow globe disappears. I try to shrug it off with feigned nonchalance. “I’m a—”

“Creator,” he finishes for me. My eyes fly back up to his face. He’s smiling again. “We knew that there was one our age floating around, but . . . wow.”

Terribly pleased that he seems impressed, I ask, “You’ve heard of me?”

“Well, not specifically *you*, no. No one ever mentioned a name, or that the Creator was going to be this gorgeous, sexy girl, just that there was one getting ready to Ascend shortly.” Man, does he know the right things to say. “Had I known who you really were . . .”

“What would you have done?” I ask, eager for him to finish his sentence.

“Maybe have gone to Annar to see you these last two days?”

Good gods, he is too charming for words. I grin like a fool. “Yeah?”

“Yeah,” he admits, moving closer.

Logic flees me. I know I ought to tell him the truth, right here and now, about me and his brother, but inexplicably, what I want to do instead is feel his lips on mine once more. In a sultry voice that doesn't resemble my own, I murmur, "I wish you had." And then I place my hands against his chest. There's no softness below my fingers, just hard, lean muscles and warmth seeping through his shirt. He feels amazing.

What are you DOING? the little voice barks. *Are you mad? This is Jonah's BROTHER!*

My hands fall back to my sides and I take a step back. Attempting to sound flirty rather than shaken, I smile and ask, "What about you?"

Kellan blinks a few times, as if he'd just snapped out of a trance. "Me?"

Do I affect him just as much as he affects me? I point at him, rather than touch this time. "Your craft?"

He blinks one last time and his whole demeanor shifts back into a casual stance. "We're Emotionals, both me and Jonah."

"Emotionals," I murmur, and then go still, staring at him with wide eyes. Oh. My. GODS. "Does this mean . . . have you ever done anything?"

"No," he says quickly. "I've always made it a policy to never use my craft on people I want to be around without permission. I certainly don't want to ever question why a person is with me, if you catch my drift."

I wrack my mind for what I know about Emotionals. They are able to make anyone feel anything they want, whenever they want. They also—OH NO. "Are you able to . . . know what I'm . . . feeling . . . ?"

He manages to look both amused and guilty when he nods, because Emotionals can pick out the smallest, most nuanced emotions in every single person within their vicinity. They don't need to surge to get an idea of what a person's up to. They can sense it without even needing to look.

Horrified, I take another step back, which he counters with a step forward. "Don't be embarrassed."

"You . . . you've known this whole time . . . how I *feel* around you?"

"Yes," he says, trying to grab my hand. But I evade, so embarrassed I want to die. "Chloe, wait."

"You *know*?"

"Yes." He catches my hand. "It's a good thing, C. Knowing how you feel is . . . it's amazing. A gift. So wonderful it nearly blows my mind."

"Embarrassing," I whisper.

"No," he insists, tugging me closer. "Wonderful." And then, with his lips pressed up against my ear, "Just because you can't sense it, doesn't mean I'm not feeling all of these very same things, too."

I pull away so I can look into his eyes. I don't know why, but I'm surprised to see how sincere they are. How much he already cares for me, too.

"So . . . you've never worked, what, your mojo? On me?"

He shakes his head solemnly.

"Do you use it here at school?"

Squeezing my hand reassuringly, he says, "Sometimes. If warranted."

"And . . . your brother?" My heart stumbles at the mere thought of Jonah.

Kellan studies me for a long moment, our hands still clasped, before he says, "Jonah has the same policy as me when it comes to people he wants to be around. Although, he . . ."

The stumbling worsens. The suspense is killing me. "He what?"

"He did something for you. On Monday. The attendance clerk was pissing us both off, yelling at you like that. He made her give you a pass. She wasn't going to, you know."

You wanted Jonah to stand up for you, to help, right? the little voice murmurs. *Well, he* did. *Maybe now you'll start focusing on him rather than Kellan. Where is Jonah, anyway? Why aren't you finding this out?*

I clear my throat, but before I can ask Kellan, he says, "I knew there had to be a reason I'm so attracted to you, why you've become all I can really focus on. These last few days were pretty tough—I have to admit, I think I failed a test in physics because I was daydreaming about you."

A flower blooms inside my chest. No, an entire garden of lovely, precious feelings forms. I am lightheaded, deliriously happy.

And he knows it, because his gorgeous smile mirrors the sun before he kisses me.

chapter 16

By the time I get to math, I'm a disoriented wreck.

How can I be attracted to Kellan? How can I want him so much? Crave his kisses? It's ludicrous—I should be doing the Snoopy dance of joy because Jonah is here. Jonah, who I've loved my entire life. Jonah, who I've measured all other men against.

Everyone's always failed my standards because they aren't him. But now, his brother waltzes into my life and somehow, I'm rendered into a mindless idiot, consumed with need for someone who *isn't* Jonah.

It doesn't make sense, especially since the tug that I feel with Kellan is here with Jonah, too, the moment he comes into the classroom. It's strong. Distinct. Inescapable. I'm drawn to him like a moth to flame.

Jonah is here. *My* Jonah.

We stare at each other for a long moment. I'm about to say something, anything, but the bell rings.

My concentration fails me during class. I am so excruciatingly aware of Jonah and every movement he makes that it's almost painful. According to Cora, he's here for *me.*

I want to cry, I'm so happy. Things suddenly seem so clear. That I'd even considered being with his brother is insane. I made a mistake, because Jonah's the one for me. He's always been the one. For crying out loud, we'd met in our *dreams.* That's something, isn't it?

I try not to stare the entire period at him, but it's futile. Every time I sneak a look, he knows, because he looks right back. And each time, I nearly hyperventilate.

Toward the end of the class, he gives me one of his smiles, the one that shows his dimple. I nearly die.

Today. Today we'll talk and then I'll have my Jonah back.

Are you even remembering that just a couple hours ago you were kissing his brother? How do you think that's going to go down with Jonah, huh? Because I'm thinking it isn't going to fly with him.

An entire brick wall rains down on me, pounding me back into reality. The little voice is right. How in the worlds am I going to explain that one?

I'm frantically trying to come up with a solution when the door opens. Karl walks into the room, his lips tight, his body radiating tension. Snook jolts up out of his desk. "Can I help you?"

Karl holds out a pink slip of paper. "I'm here to take Chloe Lilywhite out of school."

The bells rings and the room begins to empty, but I don't move. Karl scans the classroom with narrowed eyes as he walks over towards me. "Get up. We need to leave."

"What's going on?" I ask. He grabs my book and stuffs it into my backpack.

"I'll tell you—" Karl stops, straightening up. "Jonah. What are you doing here?"

I swing my head around and stare at Jonah, who in return is staring at Karl with equal astonishment. These two know each other?

"We moved here," Jonah says, and I nearly melt at how wonderful it is to hear his voice again. It's him. Really and truly *him*.

"When?" Karl asks, yanking me up to my feet. I complain, but he doesn't hear me. Over at his desk, Snook raises his eyebrows, but I throw a smile over to smooth things out.

Jonah takes a couple steps closer. The tug is intense now. "Last week."

"Who's here with you?" Karl asks, still gripping onto my arm.

"If you mean the Old Man," Jonah says, "he's at work."

"Crap," Karl says quietly. And then—"Kel nearby?"

"Down the hall. Karl—"

The Guard swears under his breath. "I didn't know you were here!" Karl picks up my backpack. "And if I don't know, Zthane must not know. He's going to have a fucking conniption fit when he hears about this."

"Language, sir!" Snook calls out. Karl glares and Snook quickly goes back to grading tests. The few remaining students stare curiously.

Jonah looks at Karl and then to me. "Is there something I should know?"

"Yes," Karl says, dragging me with him as he steps closer to Jonah. "There's a shitload you should know right now. Unfortunately, I can't explain it this second. I need to get Chloe out of here—"

"Did something happen?" I demand at the same time Jonah asks, alarmed, "Is she in danger?"

"Get your brother, tell him he can't let you out of his sight," Karl says. "I'll have someone out here ASAP for you—"

I try again, "What happened?"

But Karl is already pulling us towards the door. "J, I want you out of this school and in hiding within fifteen minutes. Do you understand?"

Jonah stares at me now, worry obvious in his eyes. "I'm coming with you."

"Get Kel," Karl growls. "Now."

And then Karl and I are off.

We find Cora in the hallway, and, like me, she's practically dragged to Karl's hulking gray Hummer. "Buckle in," he orders, throwing himself behind the wheel. "I tell you what, though. I'm glad to see J is in at least one class of yours. That's assuring."

"Who?" Cora demands, leaning forward.

"Seatbelt, Cora," Karl says. He revs the engine. "I'm talking about Jonah Whitecomb."

"You know Jonah?" she asks, surprised.

"I've known the Whitecombs for most of my life." He slides a high-tech-looking cell phone into a special holder on the dashboard and dials a number. "They're like brothers to me. Now, be quiet for once." The call goes through. "Zthane?"

The gravelly voice that answers is crystal clear despite being on a cell speakerphone. "I would have thought you'd be taking Lilywhite into hiding by now—"

"In the process as we speak. Who's Jonah Whitecomb's assigned Guard?"

The voice answers, "Giuliana."

Karl grinds out, "Why isn't she with him right now?"

"There haven't been any sightings in his area in the last month."

"They're here, Zthane. In California. Unprotected!" Karl swings the Hummer around a corner, forcing Cora and I to slide across our seats despite being buckled in.

“WHAT?” this Zthane roars. “Are they with you now?”

“No. My mission is Lilywhite, and by association Carregreen, only.”

“I know, I know,” Zthane mutters. “Okay. They can take care of themselves.” He yells at length to somebody on his side of the phone. “Giules is on her way. Dammit, Karl! Some idiot just handed me the change of address form Kellan dropped off a couple weeks ago when I was off on a mission.”

Karl sighs, scrubs at his face before jackknifing around another curve. “They’ll be fine, bro. This is Kellan we’re talking about. Jonah.”

But I am not willing, unlike these two, to simply assume that Jonah and his brother can take care of themselves, especially if they’re in some kind of danger. “Karl,” I interrupt, “go back for him.”

“Is that Lilywhite?” Zthane asks. But before Karl can answer, he says, “Get the Creator to safety. She’s our number-one priority.” And then he hangs up.

I try again, more forcefully. “Go back for him. *Now*.”

Karl doesn’t even bother looking at me. “No. There’s been an attack nearby. You aren’t safe.”

“What kind of attack?”

“I’ll tell you later, Chloe. Once we’re safely hidden.”

Panic tightens my chest. “Why would Jonah need a Guard?”

“Council bound, second tier. Only other person the Council deems crucial, next to you.”

“Why?” Cora asks—no, *yells*—over the sound of the Hummer roaring through the streets.

“How well do you know them?” Karl asks me, braking hard then gunning around another car.

“It’s—” I say, but he cuts me off.

“The Whitecombs are the most powerful Emotionals ever to be born.” He hits a button on speed dial on his phone. “One for the Council, one for the Guard. What they’ll do for us is . . .” He shakes his head. “Let’s just say they’re VIPs and leave it at that. Look, girls. I need to talk to them and explain some things. So, stay silent, please. I can’t concentrate on getting us out of here and talk to them if I’m fielding dumb questions the whole time.”

“Dumb questions?” Cora explodes, but Karl gives her a meaningful look in the rearview mirror.

“We’ll be quiet,” I assure him, wincing at Cora’s death grip on my shoulder.

He flips the call to speakerphone again, mumbling to me, “Dwarven technology is the best,” in an effort to explain how crystal clear the reception is.

Kellan answers after three rings. “Karl, Jonah says you’ve taken Chloe Lilywhite out of school?”

“Yes,” Karl says, pulling the Hummer out onto the highway.

“Want to explain why? And what you’re doing here?”

“I’ve been assigned to protect her. Hasn’t your dad told you anything about what’s going on lately?”

There’s a brief pause. “You think the Old Man’s changed his policy on parenting?”

Karl swerves around another car. “Good point. What about Zthane?”

Another pause for a brief discussion between the brothers, who are also on speakerphone. “Are you referring to the serial killings?”

They know. Of course they do. Everyone knew except me.

“Yes. The Council ruled last week to send out Guard to two Council-bound members—”

“Let me guess,” Kellan says flatly. “J and Chloe.”

“Yep.”

“If that’s the case, where’s my brother’s Guard?” Kellan snaps at the same time Jonah insists, “I don’t need one, Karl.”

“Council ruled, buddy. Take it up with them if you disagree.” Karl nearly hits two cars he tries to pass. “Just talked to Zthane. Giuliana is on her way as we speak. Are you doing what I said, Jonah?”

“We’re en route now,” Jonah answers.

“Kellan,” Karl says, “you’re under an order of protection, too.”

“Oh, for gods’ sakes,” Kellan mutters. “What a waste of Guard resources.”

“We can take care of ourselves,” Jonah adds, also annoyed, and I would giggle if I wasn’t so terrified at the moment, because he sounds so much like me.

“There’s been an attack nearby, forty minutes ago. One Magical hurt, three nons killed.”

Cora and I stare at each other in terror.

“Details?” Kellan asks.

“Giules will fill you in when she arrives,” Karl says, driving on the wrong side of the road and nearly killing us in the process. His eyes flick to the dashboard clock. “Portal from Annar is, what? Fifteen minutes from the school? Depending on your location, she should be there within a half-hour. Find a spot she can access without having to rip the city apart.”

Cora and I clutch onto the handlebars above us to stop from screaming as Karl skids into the proper lane.

“Texting her our location now,” Jonah says.

Cora leans forward and whispers into my ear, “Are we the only ones who don’t seem to know what in the hell is going on?”

I nod, eyes glued on the road.

“FYI,” Karl says, nearly hitting a semi, “the Guard have been authorized to use any force necessary on these missions.”

My mouth drops open. *Any force necessary?*

“Giules will like that,” Kellan says, and all three men laugh.

“Who is this Jewel they’re talking about?” Cora whispers.

Out of the corner of my eye, I notice a couple of black shapes streaking next to the road. When I turn to fully look at them, my heart sputters. “Karl,” I say, tapping on the glass and frantically trying to not freak out and mistakenly set off an atomic bomb of fear, “look . . . look there . . . those, I don’t know what those are . . .”

His eyes follow my finger. The black shapes, misty and shifting, mass, break apart and then splinter into the road.

“Holy mother-effing *shit*.” He slams on the breaks. All the cars around begin swerving and skidding to halts. Several smash into each other.

“What’s going on?” both Kellan and Jonah demand, but we’re all staring at the shapes shifting in the road in front of us.

And then the screaming begins. Ear-piercing, agonizingly horrible screaming sounding like it’s coming from a million souls.

My feet scramble below me, searching for a non-existent gas pedal. “Do something. Do something now, Karl.”

I should be doing something, too. Gods, what? What can I do?

Karl throws the Hummer into reverse, gunning the engine. Jonah is yelling, “Where are you? What’s your location?”

“Get into hiding and wait for Giules!” Karl barks before hanging up, and the Hummer three-sixties as the black shapes surround us, still screaming. Then, to me and Cora, “Hang on, ladies!”

A couple of black shapes streak out in front of us, moving so fast I can’t fully determine their constitutions. One strikes the car hard, forcing Karl to slam on the brakes again; the Hummer skids as it rotates direction, nearly missing an overturned minivan.

“Tell me what to do!” I shout. What good are my powers if I’m only to sit like a lame duck, ready to get picked off?

Another black shape smashes into the back, busting tail lights. Karl swerves past a downed motorcycle. “I don’t know, Chloe! Right now, we’re just going to run!”

The black streaks multiply faster than we’re able to outrace them. Karl’s driving at almost a hundred miles per hour, but these things are easily keeping pace.

“What are they?” I scream.

“I’m assuming,” he yells, dodging an attack, “these are the things that are killing our kind.”

Cars everywhere are out of control, but in this game of chicken, all manage to move out of Karl’s way. “Hold on,” he orders. Cora and I grab the handrails above us as he does a one-eighty, tires squealing against the blacktop. Behind us, an explosion ricochets, thrusting us into the air.

As I watch a wall of fire shoot sky high, the Hummer hits the ground. My head, on the other hand, hits glass.

Karl’s massive hands struggle against the wheel to steady us. “Earn your keep, Cora. She’s got a head injury.”

Everything tilts to the left when a touch to my head leaves my hand red and sticky.

"Lean back, baby," Cora's saying. "Let me see." Cool hands press against my head. My skin stings as it pulls back together, but it's a distant pain. The kind which ought to make me scream but oddly doesn't. "Get us the hell out of here!" my Cousin yells. Her words are barely discernible over the screaming outside. "I need to have a better look at her to assess the situation!"

"What do you think I'm trying to do?" he barks back. A few black shapes dart dangerously close. Karl sends the Hummer across the traffic lanes, cutting off a big rig. It slams on its breaks, skidding until it takes up all lanes of traffic. This small action is just what we need, though. It's enough to help us escape. Within minutes, the screaming subsides.

Black spots appear before my eyes. Residual blood trickles down, landing on my nose. I wipe it off, staring at it against my fingers. All red and black and polka-dotty. Like ladybugs. "Are these things . . . coming af . . . after him, too?"

"What?" Karl asks.

"Canna lose 'im." But my own voice begins to fade in my head. "Not 'gain . . ."

"Are you okay?" I can barely hear the worry in his voice, even though I know it's there. "What are you talking about?"

"I'm fiiiiiiine," I say slowly, each word feeling like it's stretching out forever. "Don . . . donya let 'em get 'im. Seeeeeee?"

"What . . . ? Cora. What's wrong with her?" The words float above me as I sink into the pool below.

“She’s got a concussion, Karl,” Cora says. Her voice is no more than a whisper. “And I can’t do much about it while you’re driving like a madman!”

My head drops below the water line, ending my ability to hear anything else they might have to say about me.

chapter 17

The room I'm in is sterile, beige, fairly dark, and screams crappy motel. "Karl? Cora?"

"I'm here," Cora says, coming out of the bathroom nearby. "Karl's making a phone call outside."

"Where are we?"

"Some motel about fifty miles up the coastline. That man drives like a maniac. How in the hell he got his license, I'll never know." I fumble for her hand. She slips it into mine, squeezing soothing comfort. "You had a pretty wicked concussion, but I fixed it while you slept."

Karl flicks on a light near the door. He smiles tightly and waves his phone around. "Had to call the wife, tell her the details. She's disappointed she didn't get to come out and play."

"Are you serious?" Cora asks, eyes wide.

He shrugs. "My girl likes action." But he seems happy about this. Proud, even.

"So, those things . . ." I struggle to sit up. "What happened to them?"

"Don't know," he says, setting the phone on the table. "They disappeared after awhile."

I'm groggy, but I remember what he'd said before. "You said there'd been an attack. What happened? Who was it?"

Karl looks distinctly uncomfortable as he spins his phone around on the table. "Maybe we ought to save this for later."

I bite my lip so I don't scream in frustration. "Karl, please! You know how I hate being constantly kept in the dark. Just tell me."

He takes a breath and straightens in the chair. "Okay, then. It was your father. He was on the way home to pick up some books before heading back to Annar. These . . . things, whatever they are, tried to kill him, but two Faeries and a Gnome found him mid-attack. They were able to distract the black things long enough for your father to get away. I'm sorry to say the rest didn't make it."

My father may be a lousy parent, but he's still my father. I grip the bedsheets. "Is he okay?"

"Yeah. He's good. He made it to the portal—hurt, but still functioning. People at the Transit Station found him and took him to the hospital right away."

"Here?" Cora asks, shifting into Shaman mode.

"No. In Annar. The Shamans there have him all fixed up and knocked out comfortably for the night."

Her eyes are wide, scared. "Do you think this might have something to do with Chloe?"

"It's the Guard's theory. Chloe is a big target. If someone is taking out Magicals, and lately targeting powerful ones, she's the coup, you know?"

"I haven't even Ascended," I protest, as if this will somehow make me less attractive as a victim.

"Doesn't matter. Right now, you've got to be ten times more powerful than the majority of the seated Council. Thus, the need for protection."

I ask, "Can I talk to my dad?"

"He's asleep," Karl says, but it's done kindly. "It's best to let him rest."

"Listen," Cora says, pointing at the television set playing in the background.

"Sam Reigns is here to present today's weather forecast. Sam?"

"Yes, thank you, Dick. It's being advised for everyone to stay indoors for the next couple of hours, as we've just had a freak lightning storm over our area. We are cautioning people traveling just south of the Bay Area to watch out, as there have been numerous reports of multiple strikes in that region."

"Is that her?" Cora asks excitedly.

When Karl says yes, I ask, "Is that who?"

Cora bounces on the bed. "The other Guard! She's an Elemental. How cool is that? She manipulates the weather!" The weatherman is now showing photos of some of the lightning strikes. "What's her name again?"

Karl flips the television off. "Giuliana Arancionestella. She's a good girl, great at her job."

"So . . . she found them?" I ask.

Karl tilts his head, studying me carefully. "You mean Kellan and Jonah?"

I nod, completely embarrassed.

"Yeah, she found them."

I cannot look at him when I ask, "And . . . are they okay?"

"For the most part," he says casually. He leans forward, resting his arms against his knees. "Want to tell me why the interest in them? Other than the fact that they're, in general, babe magnets?"

"What's that supposed to mean?" Cora demands.

His smile is sly and unsettling, like he knows something already. "I'm just curious. Chloe's asking a lot of questions. She wanted me to go back and get them. Or was it singular? Him?" He pretends to search his memory.

I chew on my lower lip, wondering how to address this. "Well, *they* are . . . Magicals, too . . . and if one . . . I mean, both are targets, then it'd only be . . . logical? To ask? To make sure he's . . . *they're* okay . . ."

He laughs. "Sure. Right. Want to tell me why I got separate phone calls from each of them, asking how you are, ordering me around on how important it is to keep you safe?"

"They did?"

"So I have to ask, is there something I should know about you and the Whitecombs?"

Cora snorts loudly, giving me a pointed look.

I'm floating in happiness, knowing that they both cared enough to check up on me. "Um . . . Well. See . . . it's like this . . ."

As I fumble for something to say—anything, really, that might explain the absurd situation I'm finding myself in—Karl's cell phone rings.

He holds out a finger, tells me to hold my thought, and then answers. "Giules! Talk to me. The Shaman make it out to you yet?"

Whoa—a Shaman?

Karl sighs. "You're the one assigned to them. It's not my fault if you can't rein them in." He pauses, laughs. "Don't even try to pin the blame on them working their wares on you. You've known them almost all their lives. You've got to stop looking into their pretty blue eyes and . . .” He pauses again, laughs some more. “Did you tell Jonah that this is what comes from disobeying orders? He’s lucky he only came away with a broken arm.”

A BROKEN ARM? I leap off the bed, sick to my stomach. “Is Jonah okay? In pain?”

Inappropriately amused, Karl winks at me. “Well, Kellan’s not alone with his concussion. Lilywhite got one, too. Granted, it was from smacking her head against the car window, not from rolling off a cliff.”

THIS JUST KEEPS GETTING WORSE. “Off a CLIFF?!”

“By the way,” Karl continues, ignoring me, “don’t go telling the boys about Chloe’s injuries. As far as they know, she’s fine.” He rolls his eyes. “I know. It’s rather entertaining, isn’t it? Considering they’ve only been here in California . . . what? A week?”

“Man,” Cora whistles. “Who knew that the Guard were gossipmongers?”

“Oh, fine. I’ll talk to him.” Karl sighs. “How’s the arm, J?” He nods, making noncommittal noises for a good minute before saying, “For the ninetieth time, Jonah, no one will get through me. Lilywhite is safe as a kitten tonight.” He hm-hm’s. “No, you may not come here tonight. Why do I have to keep repeating this? Did you smack your head, too? ” He then groans. “Oh, for gods’ sakes. I refuse to argue this point with you any further. Let the poor girl sleep, she’s had a rough day. Put Giules back on, why don’t you.”

I’m buzzing despite the head pain. Jonah’s asking about me. He’s concerned. Worried! He wants to see me! But wait—his arm . . . I hope he’s not in pain. Is he in pain? I should be there. How can I get there?

“Let me talk to him,” I squeak, reaching for the phone. Karl merely shoves me back toward the bed and waves his hand. He chats another minute with the Elemental before saying, "Put him on. . . . Kellan? What is this, tag-team bullying?" He drums his fingers against the table. "I swear to— Listen. How many times do I have to say it? She's *fine.* Safe as a puppy—"

"Kitten," Cora corrects, way too invested in his conversation. "You told Jonah she's like a kitten."

Karl gives her the evil eye. "Yes, she's awake. No—she needs her rest. She doesn't need to be interrogated right now, Kel. Why don't you go rest, huh? Considering your concussion?"

My phone beeps. Cora slides it toward me, rolling her eyes.

Is Karl being nice to you? Are you really okay?

I smile, the tingly bit blossoming in my stomach again. I tell Kellan: *Other than putting me in a motel that I believe might rent by the hour, I'm good. You? Is your head okay?*

A moment goes by before Karl stands up, outraged. "It's not like I had a lot of choices, Kellan! This place is safe! It's got a good, strategic location!"

Cora gives me a disapproving look. "You're playing with fire, Chloe."

I'm well aware of it.

My father is in the hospital.

I try calling him when I finally get home, early the next morning, despite Karl's warnings. I don't get through on the first two attempts, but my mother answers on the third. She: a) reprimands me for interrupting my father's recuperation, b) assures me that he's fine and resting comfortably, and c) doesn't bother to ask me how I am, despite my also having been attacked.

I suppose I'd called in an effort to make sure my father's doing okay, but I feel worse off when I hang up. This, on top of still having to go to school, makes for a bleak morning.

Lizzie nearly chokes me when she delivers a two-punch of hugging and lecturing before school starts.

"Geez," I tell her once I free myself, "it's not like I was maimed or anything." But the truth is I'm warmed by her concern, coming on the heels of my mother's apathy. All of the Cousins cluster around in various states of concern and outrage.

Alex cuts to the chase. "Talk."

"This isn't the time or place." Cora motions to the students milling about. "How about we meet at Chloe's tonight to discuss?"

This doesn't deter him in the slightest. "We had no idea what was going on, other than the gossip mill at school yesterday claiming Chloe had been yanked out of class and that you two had been seen with some guy practically running off campus."

Cora muses, "That about sums it up."

"Who was the guy?" Meg demands. "Everyone said you were with some giant."

"I wouldn't call him a giant," I say, but Lizzie smacks me. "Fine. His name is Karl Graystone. He's a Guard—"

"Why would you need a Guard?" Meg shrills loudly before Cora shushes her.

"And," I murmur, "Cora has a point. Let's talk about this tonight, okay?"

It isn't what they want to hear, but all reluctantly agree.

A few minutes later, I'm in the middle of trying to sound sufficiently sad about resigning from the cheer team with Meg when

Cora tugs on my sleeve and hisses, "You better start thinking straight, Cousin."

She points into the parking lot. Jonah and Kellan Whitecomb are standing outside of another ugly Hummer, talking to someone through the passenger-side window. As far as I can tell, Jonah is fine; there's no cast or any evidence that his arm had been broken.

I have never felt more relieved in my life.

"What's this?" Alex asks, following our attention.

"It's the new guys," Meg whispers loudly. "Aren't they cute? Ohmigods, I forgot to tell you guys—rumor had them leaving campus yesterday around the same time as you guys!"

Cora mutters something under her breath.

"They don't know," I remind her.

"Know what?" Meg asks.

"They're Magicals," Cora explains. "Emotionals, to be specific."

"What?" Meg squeals, alternately gaping at us and at the twins.

"Why didn't someone tells us?" Alex barks. "How long have you known?"

Lizzie shrugs and smiles faintly while Kellan makes a beeline for me the moment he spots me. Jonah, on the other hand, stays at the car, in deep conversation with whoever is driving.

"Thank gods you're okay," Kellan says when he reaches me. "Where's Karl?" And the next thing I know, I'm in his arms and being kissed.

I can barely breathe, but I love the sublime sense of protection I feel in his arms. And that kiss . . . Wow. Just, wow. It takes me a good ten seconds before I can tell Kellan, "He's gone home for now."

The Cousins rubberneck, especially Cora and Lizzie. Cora goes as far to mouth: *What are you doing?*

And . . . she's right. Because Jonah is here . . .

He's stopped about halfway toward where we're standing, looking utterly shell-shocked. A riot of confusion and guilt slam around me alongside the beautiful things Kellan's presence is triggering.

There's no doubt in my mind that I've just hurt Jonah more than I ever thought I could. I don't know what to do. Oh my gods. What should I do? What should—

Alex coughs politely behind me, demanding an introduction. I barely manage to tear my eyes away from Jonah. "Guys, this is Kellan."

"Indeed," Alex says rather coolly.

Kellan ignores this unnecessary posturing, flashes a smile that appears to weaken both Meg and Lizzie's knees, and turns his focus back on me. "Karl wouldn't tell me anything last night, which leads me to wonder exactly what happened. And I can tell you're disoriented today. Mind filling me in?"

Disoriented, the little voice snorts. *That's a good way to put it.*

"She's fine," Cora snaps. "You neglect to remember she was with a Shaman when she scrambled her brains."

He gives her a brief, annoyed look before asking, over the same question the Cousins are asking, "Scrambled?"

It is wrong, so wrong, but I am deliriously delighted to know just how concerned Kellan is about me, especially in light of what I've just done to Jonah. Oh, gods, Jonah. He's right over there, still as a statue. And the look on his face—it's like I've kicked him in the stomach. "It was a concussion," I murmur, nauseated. Then I remember, "And you? How are you feeling?"

He dismisses this, insists he's fine. Behind him, Jonah is finally moving past us with long, purposeful strides. His expression is now unreadable, and the panic in me wells up significantly. Should I go talk to him?

Yes, yes, you should.

"It's okay," Kellan murmurs in my ear. "You don't have to panic. They're long gone."

I am worse than nauseous now. Kellan is an Emotional; he can sense all this in me!

Cora nearly snarls at Kellan, "Shouldn't you go with your brother?"

He glances after Jonah and frowns. "He definitely doesn't want to be hovered over right now."

"How do you know?" she presses, making me want to kick her.

Kellan simply looks at her, eyes narrowed. Then, to me, he says, "Let me walk you to your class."

Cora starts to say something, but Meg manages to do the kicking for me.

"That's weird," Kellan says when we're out of earshot.

"What?"

"Cora's hostility."

I chew on my lip. "She's sort of overprotective sometimes—"

"No," he corrects quickly. "Not toward me, toward you. Have you two been fighting?"

Realizing it's going to take me awhile to get used to Kellan's craft prompts another round of panic, because how in the worlds am I going to be able to hide the mass of tangled emotions I'm feeling toward both him and his brother?

"Sort of." He takes my hand in his, our fingers knotting together, and the anxiety eases. "Let's not talk about her. I want to hear about what happened to you yesterday. Karl said you went over a cliff, which is . . ." I fumble for a worthy enough word. "Terrifying, really."

He laughs, flushing. "I didn't have a seatbelt on, thus a concussion. Stupid, right?"

"Don't do that again." I stop, surprised at how vehement the feeling is. How territorial I already feel toward Kellan. How important his safety is to me. How much I genuinely, truly care. It's frightening how strong all these feelings are, considering I only met him a week before.

And that I'm in love with his brother.

Kellan squeezes my hand. "I won't."

Because I can't help myself, I ask, "Was that how Jonah broke his arm? From the fall?"

We lean against the lockers by my class. "No." And then, very quietly, so no one around us can hear, "One of those things . . . those black things, it broke his arm when he was trying to keep them away from the car." His lips twist ruefully. "I was already out at that point."

My brain sort of short-circuits.

"It's okay," Kellan says, his voice as soothing as his hand in mine. And then, as if he knows I need to hear it, "He's fine now."

I gasp, "Why would he confront them?"

Kellan brushes a few strands of hair away from my eyes. "Because it gave us something to work with. Turns out these things have feelings. We both were able to manipulate them."

I think about this, trying to push away the awful images of those things going after my guys. And then I try to not think about how messed up it is that I've already classified both twins so quickly in my mind as *mine.* "How so?"

"If you find the right mixture, they can be subdued. J had a mass of them on the ground, controlled, until one came shooting out of the woods."

"And the lightning storm?"

"Giuliana's attempt to get them away from Jonah." The warning bell rings, and, even though it's the worst possible thing to do, I'm the one to kiss Kellan goodbye.

And I like it.

A lot.

chapter 18

Just the thought of Jonah hurt, or angry—or worse, both—nearly brings me to my knees over the course of the next couple classes. Seeing the shock, the pain in his eyes before school was unbearable. Had Kellan not been there holding me, I would've dropped straight to the ground, sobbing.

But then—that's the thing. I was there with Kellan, and he *was* holding me. And insane as it is, I liked him there. I more than liked him there. I wanted him there. I don't understand. How can I feel so strongly about both of them?

Any hope of an easy out is gone. Someone, one of them, but more likely *me*, will end up hurt.

By the time math rolls around, I'm beyond a wreck. I want a chance to talk to Jonah. He's got to be furious, and I understand that. But I also know him. There's a bond between us that is impossible to ignore. Talking to him is the key. If we talk, things will make sense.

But Jonah never shows up to class.

Why isn't he here? Has something happened to him? Have those black things infiltrated the school and somehow tracked him down? My mind is racing with so many horrible scenarios that the lockers around me shudder uncontrollably after class, freaking out the students nearby. It isn't until Kellan arrives that everything around me stills. He explains as we head toward the cafeteria that Giuliana came to get Jonah, since the Shaman who fixed his arm asked to have one more look at it before heading back to Annar.

There goes your chance to clear the air, the little voice grumbles. And then, *Would it even matter to warn you to stay away from this guy until you CAN go talk to Jonah?*

Kellan's hand finds mine and, as a potent mixture of contentment and excitement sweeps away my anxiety, I realize there's no way I can stay away from him.

But the little voice isn't the only naysayer. When Kellan dismisses himself to go to the vending machine, I'm left behind at our lunch table with two rather pissy girls and one blissfully ignorant non-Magical.

"Explain," Cora and Lizzie say in union. Graham looks up from his sandwich, startled by the vehemence in their voices.

I feign innocence in an effort to mask my irritation. "About?"

Lizzie leans in. "What was with that show you put on this morning?"

Before I can say anything, Cora mutters, "Typical Chloe."

"What's that mean?" I ask at the same time Graham says, "Ladies."

"Graham, stay out of this," Lizzie snaps. And then, to me, "Has something else happened that I'm not aware of?"

Why are they doing this? "Whatever happens in my life is none of your damn business. I thought we established this on Friday."

Both girls flush bright red, then quickly shut up when Kellan sits down next to me. He gives them a look, one with narrowed, knowing eyes before turning to me. "You okay?"

"I'm fine," I murmur, absurdly pleased that he cares.

"So, Kellan," Graham says, obviously trying to broker peace between me and the girls by changing the subject, "how're you liking it here?"

Kellan smirks a little. "It's a typical high school."

"I'm assuming you were popular in your old school," Cora says, but it's without much malice. No—she's saving all her pointed looks for me.

It may be disgruntled with me, but the little voice sides with me when I wonder what her problem is.

"Popularity is a subjective thing," Kellan says casually.

I nearly choke on my orange juice when Cora snipes, "You must have dated a lot."

But Kellan clearly is ready to give tit for tat. "Why would you think that?"

She flushes again and shoots me yet another dirty look.

Lizzie picks up where Cora's left off. "We were just asking Chloe about an interesting rumor going around school right now concerning you two."

Graham says, confused, "I don't remem—" but is stopped with what I assume to be a swift kick under the table.

I totally want to disown both girls.

Kellan, though, is totally amused. "I'm not much for the rumor mill."

"Word is," Lizzie doggedly continues, "that you two are dating, of course."

The half-grin settles on his lips as he pretends to think about this. "Is that what's being said?"

Graham chuckles under his breath until Lizzie (or Cora) kicks him under the table again. And rather than verbally confirm the "rumor" she's conveniently just created, Lizzie just nods. Graham quickly excuses himself to go buy a soda.

Frustrated, I lean in and hiss, "Idiots. He knows you're lying. He's an Emotional, remember?"

"It's okay, Chloe," Kellan says when both girls blanch. "They're just trying to be protective."

"Don't be reading my emotions," Cora snaps, but it's done nervously.

He is still clearly amused. "Then don't broadcast them so loudly."

She drums her fingers against the table. "Look, a friend of mine in Annar told me about you, about your reputation."

I want to crawl under the table. "Cora, *stop*."

"I could mention the things I've already heard about you here at school, Cora," Kellan says evenly, "but that'd be pointless, wouldn't it? Since I barely know you?"

She sits back, lips clamped shut.

"Anything else you want clarified?" he asks after a moment of tense silence.

Lizzie gives me one last meaningful look and then turns to Kellan. And then she surprises me by asking him about what being an Emotional entails.

"I'm sorry about my friends," I say as Kellan pulls a book out of his locker.

"Don't be," he says. "It's sweet."

I laugh. "Right. Sweet."

He laughs, too. "Okay, it was annoying."

"You don't have to put up with them, you know."

He shuts the locker door. "I think I do." Then he tugs me closer. "They mean a lot to you. Being around you means being around them. And since I want to be around you, I will learn to put up with them."

My heart flip-flops so hard I forget to breathe.

"And as for my reputation—"

"I don't care," I say, and I mean it. "It doesn't matter."

It's the first time I've ever been reprimanded by a teacher in the hallway to stop kissing.

Karl is already waiting for us after school, standing outside his Hummer wearing dark sunglasses that make him look like a Secret Service agent. When he sees Kellan, though, a smile breaks out on his face.

I listen to them chitchat for a few minutes while we wait for Cora. It's obvious that they are good friends who have a long history with one another.

"Have you talked to Jonah yet today?" Kellan asks Karl as he hands me my backpack.

Karl, sunglasses on top of his head now, observes this action with no comment. "I was just over at your house, conferring with him and Giules. He is in the worst of moods, bro. I thought he was going to take a baseball bat to the furniture."

My heart sinks, but Kellan merely laughs. "He's being babysat. Can you blame him?"

Kellan doesn't know, the little voice marvels. *How fascinating.*

It really hits me then, how Kellan really does know nothing about me and Jonah. He'd never be here with me if he did. He'd never have kissed me. He never would have hurt his brother like that this morning.

Jonah never told his twin about me. And that stings.

“Absolutely,” Karl is saying, grinning. “He held back. I would’ve definitely smashed the furniture.”

“That’s such a typical thing for a guy to say,” Cora snarks as she walks up. “Machismo bullshit is *so* attractive.”

“Ah,” Kellan says mildly. “I see that I’m not her only target.”

“My singular goal in life is to be attractive for you, Cora,” Karl mutters.

She gives me a very pointed look when I snort in laughter.

“It’s just, Giules is totally babying him right now,” Kellan continues with Karl. “I honestly thought J was going to jump off the balcony last night when she offered to spoon-feed him soup.”

Karl grins, shaking his head. “You know Giules. She can’t help herself.” He pauses. “By the way, her soup is excellent.”

“Karl. It was canned.”

“Oh, well, that makes a difference.”

“Do you hear this?” Cora says to me. “Poor babies. I wish someone offered to feed me some soup.”

“You didn’t break your arm, Cora,” Karl says.

“Chloe smashed in her head and I didn’t see *you* babying her,” she snipes back.

Karl grinds his teeth together but doesn’t say anything. For the millionth time that day, I find myself telling her to knock it off.

She grabs onto my arm. “I just think—” But after a serious frown from me, she backs down, muttering a terse apology for being bitchy.

“The fact is,” Kellan is saying, “Guard brass knew we moved. I notified them before we left.”

Karl rubs at his jaw. “Zthane wasn’t given your note. He’s all sorts of pissed off right now.”

"And another thing—why wasn't I told ahead of time what's going on?"

"Believe me, I had a similar conversation last night with the higher-ups."

Cora is silent the entire ride to the Whitecombs' house. But I know my Cousin—she's watching and listening. Judging. She insisted I sit in the backseat with her, so in order to talk to Kellan or Karl in the front, I need to lean forward. Every time Kellan turns to speak to me, she tenses. Every time he touches me, she practically flinches.

It's beginning to piss me off.

When we get to his house, Kellan tells Karl he expects to be briefed that evening about the current situation. Cora finally speaks. "Aren't you a little young to be giving orders like that?"

Kellan and Karl ignore her. Kellan comes round the car to my side and opens the door. "Call me if you need anything."

I don't want to let him go. It's crazy, especially since I know Jonah's in the house in front of us, just behind the door somewhere, but I'm already sad to see Kellan go. Then he leans in, kisses me, and leaves.

Karl pulls away from the curb and clears his throat. "Now, *that* was interesting."

Cora jumps on this, eager for whatever dirt she may think Karl can throw her. "Oh?"

"Remember, I love those guys. But Chloe, I hope you know what you're getting into with Kellan Whitecomb."

"Do tell," Cora gleefully insists.

"He's always been quite . . . popular, if you will, with the girls. If you catch my drift."

"And Jonah?" Cora continues relentlessly.

"J's not like that," Karl says. "That's not to say he didn't have his fair share of chasers, but he certainly hasn't . . . um . . . dated as much as Kel has. Don't get me wrong—you'll have a lot of fun with Kellan. I just want you to be aware that no one has managed to keep his attention for long. Sorry, but it's true."

Cora chortles unattractively.

"Whatever you're thinking about him, though, Cora," he tells her, "is probably wrong. He's a great guy, extremely smart, and loyal to those who earn his trust."

"Ah, yes," Cora say derisively. "A saint who sleeps around."

Karl nearly chokes on this. I end up smacking her. "I have to admit, Chloe," Karl continues, "I'm a little surprised it's Kellan you're . . . with? Dating? Friendly with?"

"Yes, Chloe," Cora says. "Tell us exactly how you categorize your relationship with Kellan Whitecomb."

"It's none of your business," I hiss to my Cousin.

"I've *made* it my business," she replies calmly. "Just the way you would if the situation was reversed."

"I would've placed good money that it was Jonah you were interested in," Karl says. "I mean, I knew something was up with you and those two. But . . . I don't know. The vibe I got was that there was something between you and J. I'm not usually wrong about these things."

Cora doesn't smile. Neither do I. The rest of the ride is done in silence.

Later that night, Lizzie's standing in front of the bay windows, looking out. The sun's begun to set, casting long, dark shadows across the grass, which eerily resemble the things that attacked us yesterday. I am unsettled enough to lay my hand against the wall, solidifying the wood until it's virtually indestructible.

She's clearly upset. "I'm sorry we weren't there to help you guys yesterday. It makes me mad that we didn't even know what was going on until everything was over."

Hell, if there wasn't anything *I* could've done, there sure wasn't anything a Muse, Intellectual, or a Joy could've accomplished. But I thank her for her concern.

Karl, who has so far been listening to my Cousins in silence since telling them the basics of the situation, frowns. "Technically, this doesn't concern any of you."

"Bullshit," Alex says from his chair nearby. "First off, she's considered family, and we protect our own. Secondly, if I'm not mistaken, this sort of thing concerns the Magical worlds in general. We may be young and ignorant, but we're still part of that population."

"The Council and the Guard are taking care of matters."

Alex rolls his eyes. "Great job you're doing. Because from what we've just heard, until yesterday, you didn't even have enough eyewitness accounts to accurately describe these things, let alone have someone actually attempt to fight back. While you Council members have been yapping, people have been dying. No one knows who these things are. No one knows where they're from. No one knows what they want. So, by my book, that's a big fat fail coming from Annar."

Karl doesn't say anything, but he's definitely glowering.

Cora picks at a few of the brighter pink strands in her hair. "Guys. I was there. I can safely say that there's nothing that anyone in this room could have done to counter these things, save perhaps Chloe. Sorry, Karl—I can't see how an earthquake would have stopped them, either."

"You'd be surprised," Karl says through clenched teeth.

Lizzie squats down next to Alex. "I agree with you on the grounds that none of us possess the powers to be able to really stop these things, based on what Karl's said. But that doesn't mean we can't *do* anything. What's to say that, gods forbid, they get past Karl to Chloe? Are any of you willing to take that risk?"

"They're not getting past me," Karl insists. When Alex questions this, his eyes flash. "You think you can protect her better?"

"No," Alex admits. "I have no defensive skills that would serve in the heat of an attack. But I've got other skills, man. Skills that can help in other ways."

"Meaning?"

Alex takes off his glasses and polishes them on his shirt. "I'm damn good at what I do, even if I'm not Council bound."

"Are you talking about research?" Karl asks skeptically.

The Intellectual side of Alex kicks in. "Obviously, they're Magical beings of some sorts with extreme speed and the ability to attack while not fully corporeal. You yourself admitted they have emotions that can be triggered, which leads to the assumption that they're beings. They coordinated an attack—they moved in teams and yet were able to break apart and strike in different locations if necessary. This leads me to assume there's intelligence."

Karl simply stares at him.

"They've been active for a certain amount of time. Such a timeline could help pinpoint facts. And they're moving in between the worlds, unless there are teams on each plane. They have to have come from somewhere."

Warily, Karl asks, "What are you saying?"

"I'm saying I'm going to find out what they are."

"Alex," Meg interjects for the first time this afternoon, "don't do anything that will make you a target!"

"How can that make me a target? I'll be researching. If they can sense me reading books, then they're far more powerful and worrisome than we've been lead to believe, because at that point, they'll be close to omnipotent."

"Knowing someone is reading a book has nothing to do with omnipotence," Cora snorts.

"Sure, we can figure that out by surging," Alex says. "And we can do it by sight. But no Magical, as far as I know, can actually tell if someone is doing something. Am I wrong, Karl?"

"Mostly," my Guard friend murmurs.

"I'm with Alex," Lizzie says. "We may not be strong enough to physically protect Chloe—"

How many times do I have to say it? "I can take care of myself!"

She ignores me. "But we can do other things. We can aide Alex in research."

"Yes," Cora says, grinning wickedly. "I like this line of thought."

"Oh good lords," Karl mutters.

One of Alex's eyebrows quirks up. "Do you have the authority to stop us?"

"Yes, actually," Karl says. "I'm on the Council and act, at all times, as a representative."

"Chloe outranks you," Cora smirks.

"Chloe *will* outrank me. But as she's not officially seated—she hasn't gone through the induction ceremony. She can't yet act in the Council's stead."

Cora waves a hand dismissively. "Are you going to help us or not?"

"I *am* helping. I'm assigned to watch over Chloe until she moves to Annar."

"Yeah, but that's not really *helping*," Cora says.

As Karl looks like he's about to strangle her, I interject, "Don't you remember how he's here instead of back in Annar, with his wife? Think about how long pregnancies last. You think that's not a sacrifice right there?"

Cora finally shuts her mouth and has the grace to look sheepish.

"I'm glad you're here, Karl." Meg wrings her hands. "I'm so scared something will hurt Chloe."

"Nothing's going to hurt her. Look. I know you guys are apparently a bit sheltered around here, and I'm sorry for that. I really don't get why your folks aren't teaching you guys what you need to know, like how the Guard works. But Chloe's a top priority to the Council and the Guard. There's nothing we won't do to ensure her safety, which is why *I've* been sent here."

"But you're the only Guard around," Lizzie points out.

"No," Karl says. "Giuliana is here, too. And if Giules and I fail, then you still have Kellan and Jonah Whitecomb."

"Really," Cora sneers. "You'd put Chloe's safety in the hands of two teenage Emotionals."

It's enough to push Karl to his limit. "I'm going to ignore the insult you've just issued, because you're obviously ignorant about the different crafts out there. You have no idea what those two are capable of. Put it this way: there have always been Emotionals on the Guard. They're always involved in the most difficult missions, because they can get things done that no one else can. You think they're just all anti-war sentiments and community-building efforts? Think again. Yeah, they can make you happy. They can even make you fall in love. But they can also take you to the worst, darkest places a soul can go. When we want someone stopped, we unleash an Emotional on them."

Everyone stares at him, mouths open. Including me.

He points a finger at her. "I told you before. Those two just happen to be the most powerful Emotionals ever born, and that's even before Ascending. If Giules and I both fail, then you can count on them."

Alex clears his throat. "Girls. If we want to keep Chloe safe, then we've got to trust Karl. We've got to trust the others to do what we can't."

"Since when?" Cora says, arms folded tightly across her chest, "When have we ever been able to count on anyone other than ourselves? See, Karl, I figure you've been raised as a good Magical. You have a support system. You have knowledge. We don't. We only have each other to rely on."

"No," he says firmly. "You don't. You have me."

chapter 19

The next few days are probably the most stressful I've had in forever. Jonah is . . . angry. Wounded. He won't even look at me.

Every day in math, I struggle to find a way to talk to him. Every day I believe I'm going to, but then something comes up and we end up not speaking. Yet, I keep telling myself that some kind of mistake has been made, that whatever's going on with Kellan is a fluke. That somehow, I'm not really dating him.

But I am. Because when I'm with Kellan, something in me switches on. A sense of rightness, contentedness. And love, as impossible as it sounds. These are all familiar feelings I've felt with Jonah. *Still* feel for Jonah.

I bring this up to Karl in a roundabout way one afternoon while he and I play video games. "Is there such a thing as true love?"

He hoots unattractively as he wins a round. "Sure."

"Magically," I clarify. "A Magical sort of love."

He pauses the game and turns towards me. "Yes."

"Yes? That's it?"

"It's a little more complicated than that, but yes. It's rare, but some Magicals have what's called a Connection. It's a tie between two people, making them soul mates. It can never be broken."

"How do you know if you have one?"

He thinks about this. "Well, there's a pull to the other person, like you're magnets. You can't resist them. Love is pretty much instantaneous, passionate, and only builds, never dulls. There's a sense of . . . safety, I guess. Belonging."

Holy crap. He could be describing what I feel toward both Jonah *and* Kellan.

"Nobody else does it for you." Karl shrugs. "Best way to really know, though, is for a Seer to confirm it. It's typically the first question a Seer gets. Most people desperately want one."

A bit of what Astrid was hinting at makes sense now. Could I possibly have a Connection? "You said it's rare?"

"Yeah," he says, smiling a little. "Not everyone is lucky enough to be assured of a soul mate. Doesn't mean you won't find love, it just won't be the same."

"You know anyone who has a Connection?"

Now he grins. "Sure. You're looking at one."

"I'm assuming it's with your wife?"

His scowl could wither plants. "Obviously."

"And . . . only one Connection per person?"

"Yep. That's the way it works."

This isn't the answer I'm looking for.

Karl is leaving for the weekend, which is good, because I think he's missing his wife a lot lately. I'd bugged him a little more about what it's like to be away from your Connection. He'd said that if the separation is done in anger, pain, or is forced, it's unbearable. But when it's on a mission, and done in understanding, it's tough but doable. He still refuses to consider getting someone else in to permanently watch me, citing the need for the best. Which is him, of course.

Kellan is over as Karl packs sporting a faint black eye. He shrugged off my concern earlier, claiming he smacked his face with his surfboard, but I saw look that got passed between him and Karl. And I definitely noticed when Kellan quickly changed the subject.

I get a little jealous when I hang out with both Kellan and Karl, and it's not so much their friendship I envy. It's the fact that they've grown up how Magicals ought to grow up: knowledgeable, part of the worlds, and fully understanding what's expected of them.

"Who's coming in your stead?" Kellan asks Karl. I am snuggled in close to him in the oversized chair in Karl's room.

"Raul's on his way as we speak."

When Kellan groans, I ask, "Who's Raul?"

"Raul Mesaverde is possibly the biggest flirt you'll ever meet," Karl says with a sly grin.

"You know him?" I ask Kellan.

"Sure. I know most of the Guard."

Another reason to feel jealous. "What's his craft?"

"Raul's a Cyclone," Karl answers. When I patiently make no comment, he continues, "He's sort of like Giules, but specializes in tornados, hurricanes, windstorms. That sort of thing."

Frankly, that sounds awful. "I guess I've never really thought about how many horrible jobs are out there," I admit, twisting one of Kellan's belt loops on his jeans in my fingers. It's hard to keep my hands off him for extended periods of time, even when I'm constantly wondering where his brother is, what he's doing, is he thinking about me?

Yes, I'm completely messed up.

"Not horrible," Karl says, appearing offended. "Necessary."

"I didn't mean you," I quickly say, but he winks.

"Earthquakes are horrible, too."

Kellan plays with my long hair. "We all have to do things we don't like. It's just how things are."

"Yin and yang," Karl offers.

"Two sides of a coin," Kellan counters.

"Butter and toast," Karl says, and I laugh.

"Okay, okay. I get it. Are there any natural disasters that aren't caused by Magicals?"

"Nope," Karl says. "All of them are Council ordered."

Kellan motions to a nearby newspaper. "Speaking of, Iolani did a great job."

Karl nods. "Ever expanding her growing island fleet."

I hold my hands in time-out formation. "Who's Iolani?"

"A Volcanic," Kellan answers, as if it's obvious.

"Iolani Popolohua is a descendant of Pele," Karl adds. "Anytime a major volcano goes off, she's the one triggering it."

I've asked Karl a thousand questions about the Guard so far, but now the most basic one comes to me. "How does someone go about joining the Guard?"

Karl gives me a weird look. "Chloe. Are you serious?"

"Uh . . . yes?"

"The Seer at your birth tells your parents, just like they would about a Council placement."

"Oh. Well, that makes sense. So you two have always known?"

"Chloe," Karl says again. Both he and Kellan look surprised. "You do know, don't you?"

"Know what?"

"You're on the Guard, too," Kellan says.

I sit up, startled. "I'm not on the Guard. I'm on the Council."

"Well, yeah, that's true," Karl says. "But you're also Guard. You're like me. Didn't your parents tell you this?"

Are they pulling my leg? My voice is shrill when I say, "No, no they did not!"

There's an uncomfortable silence before Karl carefully explains, "All Creators serve both the Council and the Guard. It's always been like this. Creators have the sort of job that requires the Guards' protection."

I leap from the chair, furious. This is so typical of my parents! Yet another thing they didn't bother telling me about. I'm going to be on the Guard, and somehow, that was too much for me to know?

"Whoa," Kellan says, standing up now, too. I feel like running again, but this time, Kellan grounds me with his presence and his arms.

Muffled against his shirt, I whine softly, "I'm so tired of being in the dark. I feel so dumb."

Karl quietly leaves the room.

"You're not dumb," Kellan assures me, his words soft and sweet as his lips against my temple, but it doesn't matter. How am I supposed to live up to my parents' expectations, anyone's expectations, really, when I don't even have a clue what they are in the first place?

Raul Mesaverde is several things. First off, he is possibly the most exuberant person I've ever met. He simply oozes charm and delight. A smile perpetually shines on his face, laughter follows almost everything said or heard. He hugs both Karl and Kellan at least two times (although it would've been three had Karl not told him to knock it off) and me and

Cora four times apiece. After he kisses both my cheeks twice, Kellan steps in and tells him to quit, which does nothing to dampen Raul's good mood in the slightest.

Secondly, he's flashy. He drove up in a cherry-red Lamborghini (explanation: *"What's the point in driving if you don't have fun doing it?"*), wears a diamond-encrusted Rolex (*"A simple gift from* mi abuela *when I Ascended."*), and favors silk T-shirts as opposed to any other kind (*"Jersey is itchy and* muy bourgeoisie, *don't you think?"*). He finds it hilarious when Karl and Kellan refer to him as a Spanish gigolo.

Third, he's mind-blowingly gorgeous: tall and lanky, with stylish dark-brown hair and warm hazel eyes which twinkle more on the green side. His teeth are so white he nearly blinds me with every smile.

I'm beginning to wonder if the Guard only employs good-looking Magicals.

He is grossly disappointed when Karl informs him we can't go to San Francisco for the weekend or anywhere else except the small town we're already in. "This is a hamlet," Raul complains as Karl gets into Kellan's car. "What are we to do for fun around here?"

"Chloe has three close friends," Karl says, nodding towards an outraged Cora who is hissing under her breath about sexist pigs. "And one of them is a Muse. Figure it out."

Raul shifts back into radiant joy. "Is this true?"

"Keep your hands off my girl this weekend," Kellan tells Raul before kissing me goodbye. Cora predictably huffs, irritated at the action.

"You are no fun." Raul says, feigning hurt. "I swear. You steal all the girls in Annar and now you steal this gorgeous woman here, too. Where is your sense of sharing, Kellan?"

I try not to laugh.

“I’ll send my brother over here if you don’t follow my rules.” But it’s a tight smile Kellan offers when he says this.

My laughter dies pretty quickly. Cora’s interest perks right up.

“And why won’t you be here to watch my progress seducing your lovely?” Raul teases. I turn beet red and attempt to stammer some kind of *In your dreams, buddy* protest.

Kellan gets into his car. “Zthane wants to see me.”

Raul and Karl smirk at one another. “Ah yes. Such is the life of the golden boy.”

I shoot Kellan a questioning look, but he doesn’t offer any clarification. “I’ll call you later tonight,” he says instead. And then they leave.

Lizzie and Meg do not come over that night. Instead, Raul spends a good deal of time on the phone with Giuliana as he cooks us paella, discussing what’s been going on back at Guard headquarters plus what’s going on here locally.

I still haven’t officially met Giuliana, but I’ve caught glimpses of her in the mornings when she drops off Jonah and Kellan. I wait for those small windows of time in which I can wear dark sunglasses and watch Jonah walk straight from the car to the building without anyone knowing I’m blatantly staring.

He never talks to any of us. Alex once asked Kellan about this, but all Kellan would say was that Jonah has a lot on his mind lately. I can’t help but wonder what Jonah’s telling his brother, what explanation he gives for his distance.

While Raul is talking to Giules, I surreptitiously type in Jonah’s number over and over on my cell as Cora watches a movie. Kellan’s given it to me, just in case. It’s not that he doesn’t trust Raul or Giules, he'd said. It's just that if I was in trouble, and he was still in Annar, he trusted his brother best to keep me safe. How's that for irony?

I come close to calling Jonah several times. Each time I press *call,* I end up just as quickly pressing *end call.* Because . . . what would I say? How do I even start this conversation?

Oblivious to my internal struggles, Cora leans in and whispers, "What's the deal with this guy?"

Raul is animatedly gesturing with a spatula, like Giules can see him over the phone. "You mean Raul?"

"Shhh!" she hisses. And then, "Spill the beans, why don't you?"

I glance back again at Raul, a European model resplendent in a frilly apron. And then I look back at my punk-rock Cousin and her magenta hair. "He's a member of the Guard."

"I know that," she says. "What else?" I briefly relate the facts I've learned about Raul so far. She waves a hand at me. "That's biography stuff! I want the dirt."

Before I can ask what she means, she shushes me again, and I'm thankfully saved by Raul cheerfully announcing that dinner is ready.

Giuliana shows up Sunday morning, Jonah in tow. He doesn't get out of the car, but then, I don't leave the house. I watch him from my bedroom window upstairs. At one point he looks up and catches me staring, since I have no sunglasses to protect me. He's the one hiding behind sunglasses now.

My heart slams around so hard my chest hurts.

I ought to run downstairs and out the door, straight to the car. Beg his forgiveness, declare my love. But I don't. Fear keeps me rooted to my spot. Fear of his rejection, fear of his anger, fear of possible hatred.

I don't think I can live with him hating me. Ignorance is better than actually knowing. If he hates me, at least I don't have concrete proof of it yet.

As Raul and Giuliana talk to each other in my front yard, Jonah and I stare at each other through our respective windows. I raise my hand and press it against the glass, wishing it's his hand I'm touching.

I expect him to turn away, to pretend my motion means nothing. But he surprises me. After an excruciating minute, he lifts his hand up, too. And places it exactly in my line of sight.

The moment is broken when Giuliana gets into the car. His hand drops and his head turns so they can speak. I pound on the window, desperate for his attention, but it does no good.

"Interesting," Cora murmurs, studying me over the top of the books she's reading.

I hold back tears of frustration.

She sets her book down and comes to hug me, telling me for the millionth time that Kellan's not for me. That Jonah is. I simply cry on her shoulder.

For the rest of the day, Cora baits Raul with various taunts or giggles hopelessly at his poor excuses for jokes. I'm baffled by her behavior, because Cora's not the sort to flirt. Men, she's repeatedly told us Cousins, are good for only one thing: furthering the continuation of the species. Alex, oddly, has never taken issue with this concept.

But it seriously appears as if she's flirting now.

"You must be very good, to be on the Guard," she practically coos as we stroll around Old Town. I feel a bit like a third wheel as I trail several paces behind the two of them.

“I do my best,” he says modestly, but there is no blushing. I don’t think Raul even knows how to blush.

“Tell us what it’s like to be on the Guard,” she says, and then she shocks the hell out of me by looping her arm through his. “Karl tells us nothing.”

I beg to differ, as Karl tells me plenty, but I keep quiet, wanting to hear what Raul has to say. “I know of nothing else,” he says. “I suppose you could say it’s in my blood. My parents were both Guard, as were my grandparents. And the Guard, of course, is like a family itself. We are all very dedicated to our work and to each other.”

“Is that how it works, then?” I ask, jogging a few steps to catch up with them. Raul loops his free arm through mine so we became a merry, linked trio. “Are people on the Council or Guard typically there due to bloodlines?”

“As a matter of fact, yes,” Raul says, flashing one of his most beguiling smiles. “Heredity always plays a big part in a Magical’s life.”

“Neither of my parents were Council or Guard,” Cora says quietly.

“While I certainly am grateful that I am on the Guard,” Raul says, leaning toward her, “I must admit it is not the lifestyle for just anyone. Being on the Council and/or the Guard is a lifetime commitment. You are . . . not a slave, per se, but certainly beholden to the responsibilities of the job. There are times I envy those who do not have to carry these weights on their shoulders, who get to practice their crafts without being under a constant microscope. Like you, *mi guapita*. You will get assignments, yes, but you will also have a much freer life than, say, Chloe or I.”

“You think?” she asks in a weird, breathy, vulnerable voice.

“I know,” he says, his smile and eyes soft. I don’t think he even notices when I pull my arm out of his so I can wander to a nearby window to check out pair of shoes.

part II

chapter 20

Over the last few weeks, I've spent most of my free time with Kellan. Alex spends most of his in my father's study, poring over books. He's got free rein of the space, considering my father and mother only come back from Annar for shorts visits since the attack. Communication between my mother and me is at the bare minimum, consisting mostly of questions about school, homework, and whether or not I'm behaving appropriately for Karl.

Lizzie and Meg have taken it upon themselves to help Alex with the research. Personally, I think Alex sees this as more of a bother than a help, but as he rarely ever tells any of us no, they're put to work doing what he figures they can do.

As for myself, when I'm not hanging out with Kellan—or rather, making out with him, because we seem to have a hard time keeping our hands off of one another—I work with Karl on weapons. I've never considered making them before, but he feels that, if necessary, I ought to be able to defend myself.

"We're all going to do our best to keep you safe," he tells me in my backyard one evening. Caleb has joined us, serving mostly as color commentary on my burgeoning career as a weapons manufacturer. "But no one is invincible. You've got to have tricks ready in your arsenal to use."

"I'm not comfortable with the Destroyer aspect of my craft," I admit. Caleb gives me a sympathetic smile.

Karl sets down a knife I've created on a picnic table. "Don't think of it like that. Think of it as a means for survival. Our society requires a Creator to function. The Council is like a machine built of multiple parts. Each part has a function necessary to keep the machine running. There are no extraneous parts. Each member of the Council is one of those parts, Chloe; each one necessary to keep the worlds functioning. Now—many of those parts are replaceable if they break down or fail. For example, I'm not the only Quake up and running nowadays. There are two Quakes per plane; each plane is represented on the Council. If I die, another Quake will take my place."

I touch the tip of the knife. "Even if they aren't meant for the Council or the Guard?"

"Even then. Fate will change their paths for them. This is the case with most of the Council. It's not the case with you, though. There are two Creators in existence, and the other is very old and not very useful anymore. Throughout history, Creators are typically solitary creatures. They have a lot of power, more than most Magicals, and Fate doesn't want too many über-powerful beings running around. You and Rushfire will overlap each other for only a very small slice of time. After he dies, if you were to die, we'd be up shit creek. The Council would begin to fall apart, because the machine wouldn't have all of its parts."

I set a crossbow down next to a knife. Caleb pipes up with, "Jeez. No pressure there."

"Embrace the pressure, Chloe. It'll keep you alive." Karl runs his hands across the battalion of weapons I've created spread out on the table. "These are good, but they're typical. Let's work on something better. Something only a Creator can do." He squats down and curls his fist. "I can use a gun, a knife; but my greatest weapon is my hand." The fingers uncurl as he places his hand against the grass. A small shudder jars the weapons on the table. "I'm a Magical, Chloe. Just like you. Show me something that only you can do."

I stare at his hand, now twisting a few strands of grass. They snap easily in his fingers. His hand can move the earth. It can break it apart.

My hands . . .

I hold them out, flipping them up so the palms face the sky. All around me, atoms bump and buzz against each other, invisible to the eye—to anyone, really, but me. I am constantly aware of them. I can draw upon them, use them, build with them.

I call out to them. And then, as if I'm shaping pottery with clay, I round a ball of light between my hands. It crackles, the energy humming against my skin. I cup the ball in one hand and use the other to gesture in front of me. A large wooden crate appears twenty feet away. Then, I wind the ball back and heave it at the crate.

Light explodes in front of us in a rain of splinters and fire. A gust of heat throws all three of us to the ground before sucking backward towards the epicenter. Karl rolls to his side. "Are you—"

But his words are lost as the explosion begins anew. A firestorm rips high into the air, like a pillar of light straight into the clouds, heat pulsing all around us. And then everything stills as the pillar evaporates right before our eyes.

Small gray flicks of ash rain down, whisper soft against my hot skin. I stare into the sky—it's so blue and clear that I wonder if I've just destroyed the clouds that were there mere minutes before.

Karl's laughter starts small and grows rumbly, until he's gasping for breath. Caleb joins in, his guffaws just as loud as Karl's. The two of them are nearly crying, they're laughing so hard.

My own laughter surprises me. The three of us laugh together for a long time. Later, as he helps me to my feet, I catch the distinct look of awe in Karl's eyes. A bit of envy, too. Because I've just bested a Quake, and it's a tough thing to do.

And that's a really good feeling.

I am in the kitchen, feeling domestic as I make coffee for Kellan and Karl. Although today was tough, with another painful snub by Jonah again in math where he refused to even acknowledge my presence but found the time to gift some red-haired bimbo his dimpled smile, I'm in a fairly good mood. Of course, this is solely due to Kellan.

In the last month and a half, there've been a lot of changes to my life. I'm slowly but surely getting a foothold on my Magical powers with Karl as a guide. He works with me every day, both strategically and defensively. But perhaps the best gift he's given me is his counsel. He listens to my questions and never teases or berates me for daring to ask them. He answers to the best of his ability, and the times he doesn't know what to say, he finds someone who will. I've talked on the phone now with a number of Guards—including his wife, Moira—and rather than being condescending about my woefully ignorant ways, people genuinely seem to want to help.

Karl isn't the only one to help me. Kellan does his fair share, too. He is the epitome of the perfect boyfriend: attentive, loving, nonjudgmental, and tolerant. He's taken the time to get to know *me*—the things that make me tick, make me happy, make me sad. We spend hours talking, getting to know these things about each other. Each piece of knowledge makes the feelings we have for one another stronger, the bond we have tighter. When I'm with him, I'm walking on air. When he's out of my sight, though, my thoughts head straight back toward Jonah.

A month and a half has gone by and somehow or other, Jonah and I haven't spoken a single word to one another. The more time I spend with Kellan, the less I see Jonah. Karl and I tend to pick Kellan up in the mornings now before school; Giuliana drops Jonah off mere minutes before the bells rings. I never see him at lunch or in the hallways during passing periods, nor do I see him after school. Math is my only chance, yet those are the most stressful fifty minutes of each day. He comes in at the last moment and refuses to look at me, like I don't even exist, and leaves the very second the bell rings. His anger is palpable. And the times that Giules comes around my house, Jonah stays in the car, forcing the stunning Italian and Karl to talk outside, even in the rain.

I've slowly gotten to know Giuliana Arancionestella over the course of these visits. She is, as are the majority of Guard I've met so far, beautiful. She's got a thick Italian accent and is prone to breaking into her native language at the drop of a hat. She's warm, though, and funny, and it's obvious she adores Jonah and Kellan and would do anything to keep them safe. She's taken a shine to me, too, often calling in the evenings to discuss with me a variety of topics, ranging from different missions she's been on to the latest fashions she's coveting from Milan.

But Jonah . . .

He's the one I want to talk to. He's the one I ache for so much that it literally hurts. And when he ignores me, it's the same as a blow to my stomach. I completely realize that the situation, complex and murky at best, is one of my own doing. I need to fix it, make things better for him, but I'm not sure how.

I'm thinking about these things as I measure the coffee grounds into the filter. Karl and Kellan are in the living room, talking. They spend a lot of time together, considering that where I go, Karl goes. Their friendship runs deep, and it makes me happy to see it in motion.

"So," Karl is saying, almost hesitantly, "I've got to ask, bro—what's up with Jonah lately?"

There's a prolonged silence, one that I don't shatter by moving. "I'm assuming you're asking why he's there and I'm here so much."

"Partly. I'm also referring to how he nearly bites off anyone's head when they try talking to him. And how when Giules comes over here, he won't get out of the car. And how he goes to Annar most afternoons when you and I both know he'd rather gouge out his eyes than spend quality time with your dad."

The good mood I'd been precariously clinging to evaporates.

"Jonah is not acting like Jonah," Karl continues. "What gives?"

Another bit of silence. "He's mad at me."

"Why?" Karl asks, sounding stunned.

Kellan answers slowly. "I don't know really what to say other than I know he's so pissed off he can barely be in the same room with me anymore."

"You tried talking to him about it?"

"Of course," Kellan sighs. "For weeks, I tried asking him what was wrong. But it only made him madder. He blocks me at every turn, so there's nothing I can get from him. So . . . I've stopped asking."

I peek around the corner; Karl is absolutely boggled by this. "You think it could be the move?"

"I don't think so. Believe it or not, he was happy about it. No—he was beyond happy. He tried to block me from knowing it, but I got bits and pieces. I was the one who was pissed to move to this hellhole of a town. But then, right after you and Giules came to town, he began to shut down. He barely speaks to Giules unless she specifically asks him a question. And he's taken a few swings at me when I've dared to demand any explanations." He laughs under his breath and touches the skin under his left eye. "Caught me off guard once."

I knew that surfboard story was a lie, the little voice snorts.

Karl is shaking his head. "That's not your brother."

"Tell me about it." Kellan slumps down on the couch. "I wish there was something I could do, but anytime I reach out, it makes things worse. It's like . . . he hates me."

"Kel, I don't think . . ."

"I feel it when he lets me."

My stomach churns violently. "Do you think it could be that he's being watched?" Karl asks after a long moment.

"I used to think so. But, he never had a problem with Giuliana before. In fact, he's always rather liked her. I mean . . ." Kellan blows out a hard breath. "Karl, Jonah is shutting down right before my eyes and there's nothing I can do about it. He's the reasonable one of the two of us. I can't believe that the Guard sending someone out would piss him off this badly. It's got to be something more." He pauses, pulls at his hair. It's a nervous tick I've noticed of his. "Would you be willing to talk to him?"

"Dude. Last time I tried to even ask how school is going, he threatened to put me in a coma."

"I know . . . but . . ."

More silence. The only sounds in the house are those of coffee dripping into the pot. Finally, after what feels like forever, Karl says, "I'll try."

"Thanks," Kellan murmurs quietly.

I turn back toward the kitchen and busy myself with getting cups down from the cupboard and creamer from the fridge. When Kellan appears next to me, my heart nearly breaks at the look on his face. I wrap my arms around him tightly and he buries his head in my hair. We don't say anything.

Because how can I tell him the reason his brother is so angry at him is because of me?

That night, the pressure inside builds up so strongly that I have no other choice than to do something to help relieve it. Yet, this isn't an easy task. Cora and Lizzie have made their positions clear—Kellan is a mistake. Cora's outright hostile to him in some perverted sense of indignation, which he ignores the best he can. Lizzie, on the other hand, has made an effort to get to know him—she and Graham think he's great, but privately, she still tells me she thinks I'm meant to be with Jonah.

Meg and Alex are useless to even attempt to talk to. Alex is so wrapped up in his research that he can't be bothered with anything other than schoolwork. And Meg . . . well, Meg is Meg. Talking to her about such an emotionally fraught topic would be like kicking a puppy. Joys don't do depression. When Meg is sad, a kind of malaise settles over the school. It's just not worth it.

A mother-daughter chat is out of the question. Caleb is in Annar for work. That leaves Karl.

Even though it's well past midnight, I still creak down the hall to his door. The TV's on, which isn't unusual—Karl often falls asleep with it on. So I knock softly, just in case he's already gone to bed.

But he's not. He's awake, albeit rubbing his eyes, and surprised to see me at his door. "Why are you still up?"

Suddenly it doesn't seem like such a good idea to talk to him anymore. "Never mind. It can wait . . ."

But he reaches out, placing a comforting hand on my shoulder. "If something's wrong, let's talk."

We head downstairs to the kitchen. Karl makes me hot chocolate—not the kind from a packet, but the real kind. A mixture of three different melted chocolates and thick milk, the kind of hot chocolate that could warm the cruelest of hearts. Being a diehard chocoholic, I can safely attest his version is the best I've ever had.

"What's on your mind?"

I've been imagining what to say to Karl for several hours tonight, but all my words fail me. I simply stare at the mug of hot chocolate as embarrassing tears drip down my cheeks. This alarms him, of course.

"Did something happen?" he asks, shifting into defensive-big-brother mode. "Did someone hurt you? Did you talk to your parents tonight?"

I want to laugh over how he correlates my parents and hurt together. Karl's been around long enough to know that I am the least of their concerns as long as I toe the line they've drawn for me. I sniff, wiping at the tears with my robe's sleeve. "I'm really confused, Karl. I don't know what . . . who to turn to."

"You can turn to me. You know that."

Ironically, Karl's been the best gift my parents ever forced on me. I try not to break down in front of him. "I hope you know that, even though I've only known you a short time, you've . . . well, I'm very grateful for you."

He waves this off dismissively, but I know he cares a lot about me, too. "Does this have to do with your craft?"

I wipe my nose with my sleeve again. "Actually . . . it's about Jonah."

He repeats slowly, "Jonah."

It's funny what you notice when you're upset. There's a crack in one of the island's tiles which looks like a winking cat. There's also a stain in the grout resembling New Zealand. I focus on these small details as I say, "I overheard you and Kellan talking about him today. I . . . I know why Jonah's upset."

"Oh?"

My eyes shift to the mug. I'd made it in first grade—it says *#1 Mom!* It's bizarre that she's kept it all these years, considering I've never seen her use it once. I nod, tracing the words I used to hope would prove true. How nice it would be to sit here with my mother, pouring my heart out to her and getting advice, not because she feels it's necessary to give, but because she loves me enough to want to help. Instead, I'm sitting here with a surrogate brother/father figure barely three years older than me who I've only known a couple months. Not that I'm ungrateful or anything, it's just part of me really would like that mother-daughter experience.

Karl, unlike my mother, does seem to care enough to help, even though he's clearly confused and a bit uncomfortable. "He's talked to you about it?"

"No." I clear my throat. "We haven't spoken to one another in over a year now."

Slowly, "I wasn't aware that you two have known each other that long."

I finish the cocoa and push the mug away. "Longer."

Karl's clearly surprised.

"He's upset," I tell my friend, "because of me."

"Upset."

"Hurt," I clarify quietly.

Jonah's never specifically told me this, of course. All I have to go on is our shared history, the feelings I have for him and the ones I am confident he has for me, even now, even still, and the knowledge that he'd come to California for me only to be slapped in the face with me inexplicably dating his brother.

And then there's Karl. His loyalty to Jonah and Kellan has long superseded what he feels toward me. I know I'm more to Karl than simply an assignment, but I also know that they are two of his oldest, dearest friends. But rather than judging me like I figure he would, or even should, Karl says instead, "What's really going on, Chloe?"

The words pour out. "I'm confused. Scared. Unsure of what to do. Unsure of what's going on."

He drums his fingers silently against the tile. "Exactly how long have you and Jonah known each other?"

I look back down at the cat, still winking at me in mocking judgment. "All my life."

"How long have you known Kellan?"

"Two months."

"Did you meet Jonah in your dreams?"

My eyes fly up to meet his. He's serious. Oh my goodness, he's absolutely serious. How does he know?

"I'll take that as a yes," he says calmly. Then he pulls out his cell phone. "I'm going to call a friend of mine in the Guard and ask her to come and have a visit with us."

"Um . . . okay?"

"While I have my opinions and ideas about this," he waves a hand at me, as if painting a picture of my troubles, "I think you might want to talk to Kiah Redrock first."

"Who?"

"The best Dreamer I know," he says as he scrolls through his contacts list.

chapter 21

Lizzie's called the Cousins together, saying she has something important to share. Alex is annoyed to be pulled away from my father's library; Meg is annoyed in solidarity with Alex, even though it's obvious she's dying of curiosity. Cora and I proceed with caution when Lizzie ushers us into my bedroom.

She's atypically nervous and excited at the same time after shutting the door, talking fast while pacing restlessly from one end of the room to the other. "First off, I want you to all keep an open mind about what I'm about to say."

Cora and I exchange an amused glance. Lizzie is so rarely rattled that it's always fun to watch her when she is.

She blows out a breath that makes her wispy bangs float around. "I . . . uh . . . finally hooked up with Graham."

Meg snaps to attention—Joy or no, she adores gossip. She squeals, "When?"

Cora sticks a finger in one ear. "Damn, Meg. Calm down." To Lizzie, she says, "This is why we're behind a locked door? Because you and the Quarterback King finally gave into six years' worth of sexual tension and flirting?"

“What’s this about sex?” Alex’s expression is hilariously thunderous. He likes to see himself, gangly and nerdy as he is, as our protector.

“There’s no sex,” Lizzie says. “We’re not talking about sex.”

“Pity,” Cora murmurs, stretching out on my bed. “It’d be nicer if we were.”

Lizzie ignores this. “As I was saying, Graham and I went to the movies last week, and . . . things happened. It was really good—nice, you know?”

“Nice?” Meg demands. “You make out with Graham, and it’s only *nice*?”

“The Joy has a point,” Cora says.

This gets more of Alex’s attention. “You two were making out at the movies?”

“Oh, for gods’ sakes!” Meg snaps. “If you want to know the details, listen the first time so we don’t have to keep repeating things!”

Lizzie, Cora, and I all stare at her. Meg never snaps at Alex, because snapping would be counterproductive to her never-ending attempt at seduction.

“Anyways,” Lizzie finally continues, “I realized that I really, really like him.”

“No shit, Sherlock,” Cora mutters.

“And, I know he’s not a Magical, but . . . I really think it shouldn’t matter. It, in fact, *doesn’t* matter to me anymore. It’s stupid that we’re expected to only fall in love with another Magical.”

“Er,” Alex begins, but Meg shushes him.

Lizzie is near tears. “I love him. He’s a good guy. Smart, caring . . .”

"No need to list Graham's qualities to us," Cora says. "All of us dig the big lug, too." This is surprisingly sweet and supportive coming from Cora.

Lizzie smiles gratefully. "And I think, that sometimes you can just *tell* if someone is right for you. In their kiss, you know? When it touches you in the heart and the toes and the tips of your fingers. Where you can feel it in every strand of hair and heartbeat."

"Whoa," Meg whispers, eyes wide.

"It's all there with him. He's it. He's the one."

Alex frowns. "You mean the one right now."

But Lizzie shakes her head. "*The* one."

He rolls his eyes. "Seventeen is too young to know about forever, unless you have a Connection."

Alex knows about Connections? Since when?

"I know, Alex. I want to be with him. Without secrets." Lizzie puts her hands out, as if she's pleading some sort of case with us.

Secrets. Wait—what?

Meg beats me to the punch. "I'm so very glad that you're finally with Graham, but when you say secrets, you can't possibly mean telling him about us, right?"

Lizzie smoothes out imaginary wrinkles in her skirt. "I already have."

There's a moment in which all sound in the room dies, in which there's no motion other than Lizzie's elegant hands moving over the blue cotton of her skirt. And then, all four of us stand up, as if on cue.

"You told Graham?" The thunderous look Alex had earlier transforms into a murderous one. "Dammit, Lizzie, it's forbidden!"

Her chin juts out. "It's a stupid rule."

"But a necessary one!" Cora exclaims, grabbing onto my arm like I'll somehow keep her upright over the strain of surprise. "Think about what's happened in the past to our kind, when it gets out what we are. Think about how many Magicals have been hunted, murdered!"

"This is Graham we're talking about," Lizzie insists, as if this is enough of an explanation.

Alex's face turns dark red. "I don't care if it's the flipping Queen of England! If it's discovered that you've blabbed, Lizzie, you will be disciplined. Do you understand that?"

Her lower lip trembles as her confidence fails. "I love him."

"Did you even stop to think what will happen to Graham if it's discovered he knows?" Alex persists. "You think the Council or Guard will let him be? Think again, Lizzie. Dammit! I thought you were the sensible one of this group!"

"Hey now," Cora protests.

I go over to Lizzie and put my arm around her slender shoulders. Her eyes are glassy. "Everyone calm down for a moment. Does he know only about you?"

My heart drops out of my chest when she shakes her head.

"You told him about *all* of us?" Meg screeches.

Lizzie flinches against my arm. "I don't want there to be secrets between us."

Alex is shaking now. "You . . . I can't . . ." And then he storms out of the room, slamming the door behind him. Meg looks at the door and then at Lizzie, her eyes filled with accusations of betrayal. She turns on her heels and rushes out after Alex.

That leaves me and Cora behind. And Cora isn't happy in the slightest. "He's just a guy, Lizzie. A non we go to high school with.

When you move to Annar at the end of summer, he'll be gone. I don't give a rat's ass if you want to have something with him until then. Go for it, I say. But you telling him about us? That's bullshit! You've betrayed our kind over a *guy*. Worse, you betrayed the people who've always been here for you. You just sold us out. And if things go south with him, what then? You ever think of those consequences?"

The tears finally begin to fall. "I'm sorry, Cora. I really thought this was the right thing to do."

"It was the very opposite of right." And then Cora leaves, too.

Lizzie turns to me, lower lip still trembling, tears streaking her alabaster cheeks. Remembering my horrible choices lately, and of how I am in no place to judge, and how love is a difficult thing to control at times, I simply fold her into my arms.

As she sobs, I debate what to do about Graham. On one hand, he's a good guy, and I've always been able to trust him in the past. On the other hand . . . well, who could blame him if he freaked out over learning about Magicals? For all I know, he could be secretly plotting to turn us over to the government for experimentation.

"Lizzie," I say softly, stroking her hair, "I really think it's important to talk to Graham and hear what he has to say about all of this."

She wipes her nose. "Okay. If you think it'll assure everyone."

I know no one else will be willing to speak to him. Just minutes ago, they'd all been talking about Graham like he's now the enemy. "It'll be just me. But . . . if it's okay, I'd like to ask Kellan to come over, too."

Her eyes ask a silent question.

"I'm a Creator, and while I can build pretty much anything, I'm no good at sensing lies. Kellan can, though. He'll be able to tell right away if Graham accepts what you've told him. And if he doesn't . . . then . . .

Lizzie ends up crying even harder.

An hour later, Kellan and I discuss this in the backyard, outside of Karl and Lizzie's earshot. I give him permission to take the memory through surging, so he can see exactly what Lizzie's told me. He's thoughtful for a long time before speaking. "The truth?"

"Of course."

"I'm pretty pissed off myself that she did such a stupid thing." He says this, but you'd never know it by looking at him. He's still ridiculously calm.

"That's fair. But what's done is done. We can only try to make the best of the situation."

"I like Graham," he says. "I even consider him to be a friend. But this is a lot for a non to handle. Even someone as easygoing as Graham."

"I agree. That's why I want you with me when I talk to him." The implication, of course, is that Graham will either assume that Kellan also knows about Magicals or that he, too, is one. Either way, I'm asking a lot of Kellan, asking him to risk his, and Jonah's, safety. It's not something I'm doing lightly—because I've come to realize their safety and welfare are paramount to me. But I owe this to Lizzie. She's stood by me over the years and has offered her support time and time again when my parents didn't.

"Chloe, if I'm to be there—and I agree I should be—I need you to understand that if I sense even the smallest inclination toward Graham spilling what he knows, I will neutralize him. And I'll do it in a way that'll ensure he never talks to or comes near any of us again."

I dislike the thought of this happening, but I completely understand the reasoning. “Alex said something about Lizzie being punished if it’s discovered?”

He pulls me over to the picnic bench so we can sit down. “I’ve seen this happen twice before, and both times the punishment was the same. The non’s mind was wiped clean and the Magical ordered to never see them again. One followed the rules. The other didn’t and was forced to remain in Annar, under house arrest, and never go back to his home plane.”

I look up toward my bedroom window. Lizzie’s still up there, probably alternating between crying and sleep.

“I’m assuming you haven’t told Karl yet.”

“I considered it,” I admit, “but I wanted to come to you first.” And the reason for that is surprisingly clear. Two months for some couples is barely enough time to know each other’s likes and dislikes. Nearly two months with Kellan is like two years for me. I know him. I trust him. I love him.

I’m in love with him, just like I’m in love with his brother.

I batten down the guilt and longing, sadness, and regret as I sit there, holding hands with Jonah’s brother. I often wonder if Kellan senses these conflicting emotions in me whenever I think of Jonah or see him. I wonder what he thinks they come from, and if he can tell or know they’re directly related to his brother.

“Are you okay?” he asks, much concern in his voice.

I look away from my bedroom window and back at Kellan. I don’t necessarily lie to him, but I say, “I feel bad for Lizzie. She loves Graham . . . and love sometimes makes people do unexplainable things.”

"I agree," he murmurs, and then he kisses me. There is sweetness on his lips, and promises. "Because, even though I'm supposed to report her to the Guard right away, I'm going to help you instead."

Graham is clearly nervous as he sits down. We're back in my bedroom—just me, Kellan, Lizzie, and Graham. The Cousins have already left, and Karl is in the kitchen downstairs, talking to Moira. Every night they webcam each other for at least an hour, so we figure we have enough time to deal with Graham without being discovered.

Lizzie sits next to him, clutching his hand. Her eyes are red, her lips tight. For his part, Graham doesn't seem to be nervous around Lizzie. He's holding onto her hand just as tightly as she's holding onto his. I wonder what Lizzie's told him about me, about what I can do. If he knows that I'm capable of destruction as well as beauty. If he knows Cora can save a life and yet kill millions after unleashing viruses. If he's aware that Lizzie will inspire artists to brilliance yet at the same time have the ability to damn them to madness over their art. Or what he'd think if he knew Kellan can inspire the greatest of loves and yet make some men the cruelest of murderers.

"I told Chloe that I explained everything to you," Lizzie says—and it surprises me that her voice is firm, not hesitant. Not like she'd been with the Cousins. "But she wanted to talk to you to make sure that . . ."

The corners of Graham's lips curl up. "That I don't squeal?"

I stay on my side of the room, afraid to scare him too much. "Do you mind if I ask what you know about me?"

At least he's not outwardly regarding me as a freak. "She said that you're something called a Magical. And that you can make things—anything you want."

"Well, not *anything*," I murmur, thinking of the three things I know I am absolutely unable to make. Through experimentation over the years, I've discovered I can't create food, water, or money, which I guess is Fate's way of ensuring I'm not omnipotent. "How do you feel about all of this?"

Graham thinks about this, scratching his chin. "I won't lie—I was freaked out at first. I think anyone would feel . . . *surprised* . . . if they discovered that fairy tales are real."

Lizzie flushes guiltily. "I may have told him quite a bit."

I turn back to Kellan, who looks rather bored, but I know better. He's carefully studying Graham. "Like what?" I ask.

She sighs. "I told him *everything.*"

I briefly close my eyes. "Everything."

"Yes," she says defensively. "About Magicals, the different species, the different planes, Ascension, Annar, going to school there, assignments—*everything*."

I don't know what to say. I'm so bowled over all I can do is gape at her first, then at Graham, and then turn to Kellan. I ask quietly, "Did the other two you told me about go this far?"

"No," Kellan tells me.

Fabulous. "Will the punishment be the same or worse?"

He doesn't say anything, but I can see the answer plain as day in his eyes. I reach up and rub my own. "Is there anything else that we ought to know, Lizzie?" he asks.

Her eyes flick briefly toward Kellan. "It's like I said. I told him everything. About everyone."

A wave of crushing disappointment and anger washes over me. "You didn't have that right! It's one thing to risk yourself, another thing to risk your family. But you had *no* right to risk anyone else."

"But—"

I am unmoved. "How dare you!"

"Chloe," Kellan says calmly from behind me, "you don't have to worry about me."

"I don't like the secrets anymore," she snaps, giving me a meaningful look that is easy to interpret: *Unlike* your *secrets.*

Before I unleash a basketful of anger on her, Kellan's arm slides around my shoulders. Graham stands up next to Lizzie, assuming the same position. "Kellan," he says, trying to sound cool, but it's no use—he's obviously nervous. "Is there any way for me to . . . I don't know . . . deflect what you're going to do to me?"

Lizzie must finally realize why I've really called Kellan over, because she starts crying again.

"If there was, do you think I'd tell?" Kellan asks, amused.

"Is anyone immune?" Graham asks.

Kellan shakes his head.

"Any way to reverse it?"

"If another Emotional were to influence you, then yes. But it's not a potion, Graham. It doesn't wear off over time. If I influence you, that's how it'll be until I decide differently."

Graham nods, biting his lip. Lizzie grips his arm. "Chloe," she says, low and urgent, "I know you're upset, and . . . and . . . I get that what I've done isn't allowed . . ."

"It's illegal," I say hotly. "And for good reason."

"I know. But . . . you know Graham!" She turns to her boyfriend. "She knows you! You wouldn't tell, would you? You'd never tell, right?"

"Of course not," he insists. Then he takes a deep breath. "Look. If it'll make things easier for Lizzie, could you maybe . . . do something to make me not talk?"

"Don't say that!" Lizzie rotates in his embrace. "You don't mean that!"

"I don't plan on telling," he says to her. "But sometimes stupid things happen—like talking in your sleep, or in anger . . . or . . . I don't know. Anything. I don't want to betray you, but how can someone make that promise? When so many things can so easily go wrong?" He looks at Kellan. "She's told me about you, about what you can do. You can manipulate people to do exactly what you want by reprogramming their feelings. If it makes you and Chloe feel better, if it reassures everyone that I won't betray you, do something now. Make it so I'll never have the ability to let this secret go."

"No," Lizzie interjects quickly. "You don't want that. It'll change you—"

"But doesn't your kind do that anyway? Isn't that what you're going to do to some artist in Spain in a few years? Change him so he can change art? What's the difference?"

"It's different," Lizzie wails.

Graham shakes his head. "It's not, though. All it'll do is make sure I never tell. And that's what I want anyway." He looks back at Kellan. "Can you do it?"

"It's done," Kellan says, looking bored once more.

"Did you really do something to Graham?"

We're in the kitchen, making tea. Kellan is standing at the counter, dipping my tea bag over and over again in the cup. "Yes."

"Do you mind me asking what?"

"I did exactly as he asked."

"I figured that part out," I say, sliding up behind him and wrapping my arms around his waist. "But what'd you do?"

He turns around to face me. "I did it the moment he walked into the room. I didn't want to take a chance. I like Graham, and . . . he's freaked out, yeah—but he truly loves Lizzie and wants what's best. He loves you, too, and doesn't want to risk anyone. So I simply heightened his senses of protectiveness and guilt toward the whole situation. He'll do anything to protect the secret. And there's dormant guilt that will spring at the first hint of him attempting to tell anyone, consciously or unconsciously. It'll be so overwhelming that he won't be able to get three words out."

"So nuanced," I marvel.

He shrugs and reaches for my tea. "You love your friend. I made sure that she's safe for the time being."

I'm overcome with love for this person. It rocks me to my core and then explodes until every last nook and cranny is filled with it. I want to tell him this, want to explain what he's come to mean to me, but I can't. Because it's so much, so overwhelming, that speech isn't necessary.

chapter 22

"Have you missed me, *mi amiga?*" Raul is standing in the doorway, a sly smile on his face.

I leap off the couch and receive a huge, albeit far too friendly, hug. "What are you doing here?"

He motions behind him. "I come bearing gifts." A short girl with dark skin, curly, dark hair, and dark eyes appears. Everything about her is so darn adorable and friendly that I'm instantly drawn to her.

"I was wondering if you'd show up!" Karl says from behind me.

"And miss out on meeting the Creator? I think not, mate," the girl says. She's got an accent . . . Australian, maybe?

"Let them in, Chloe," Karl says. I step aside and Raul and the girl come into the living room. Karl motions to her. "Kiah, this is Chloe Lilywhite. Chloe, this is the Dreamer I told you about. Kiah Redrock."

It turns out Kiah is Aborigine, hence the accent, and extremely bubbly. She talks a mile a minute, is whip smart, and cracks so many jokes that she's got the guys laughing the entire time. She insists on cooking us dinner but, missing some ingredients, sends the guys to the store. When Raul protests, she quickly reminds him that she's a Guard, too—and one that can alter any being's perceived reality, and wouldn't learning from her technically serve me better than someone who can create a tornado or shake the earth?

Humbled, the guys leave for the store.

She gives me a wink. "Now then. I figured it'd be nice to have a bit of privacy without those boys listening."

I lean against the counter as she begins preparations for making vegetarian lasagna. "What does a Dreamer do?"

Of course, this confuses Kiah, so I lamely offer the truth of how my parents have kept me pretty much in the dark.

"Wow." She sets a wooden spoon down. "Well. Let's see. I can infiltrate someone's mind asleep or awake, causing them to see and believe things that may not necessarily be true. Much like an Emotional, I suppose—but rather than causing an actual feeling, I alter the reality of the mind."

"Is that your main purpose as a Magical?"

"Oh, no," she says, smiling. "It's just one aspect. Not all Dreamers are on the Guard, you know. I do a lot of that because it's necessary for my job. Mostly, a Dreamer deals with just what you'd expect—dreams. Let me explain it from the Aboriginal viewpoint, since that's what I was raised to understand. There are two parallel planes of consciousness, if you will. The time you are awake, and the time during which you are dreaming. Some people believe dreams are just images we make in our heads. But there's also the belief that during some dreams, whatever happens affects the events of the opposite plane of consciousness. We call this Dreamtime."

I nod, urging her to continue.

"We Dreamers help manipulate that sort of stuff for our constituents," she continues. "But we also can tinker with other Magicals, too. Like you. You've walked Dreamtime most of your life, right?"

Surprised, I ask, "You can tell?"

She's quiet for a moment as she puts wide noodles into a pot of water. "There's no real easy way to tell you this other than just to say it. When you were an infant, my mum erected a door to your dreams, to the place where you walked. You were on her caseload."

"She built . . . a door?"

"It's gone now," Kiah says, stirring the pasta. "But yeah, you had a doorway. The closer you've gotten to Ascension, the more unstable the door became. I'd be gobsmacked if it was still functioning nowadays."

"Why would a Dreamer build a door for me?"

"*Think*, Chloe."

Astrid Lotus had told me that some Magicals meet through their dreams. And Karl had asked if I dreamed about Jonah . . . "Are you saying that we were *meant* to find each other?"

She knows exactly what I mean, no clarification necessary. "Of course. Fate wants you two together."

Like you didn't always know, deep down, the little voice murmurs.

"Lucky girl, having a Connection and all! So many of my mates are always trying to buy me off, find ways to connect them off with doorways to some bloke they fancy."

I grab hold of the counter to steady myself. I'd assumed I had one, but now . . . Now I know for sure. And I am inexplicably blown away by this.

She stops stirring and looks up at me. "You didn't know you have one?"

I think back to what Karl's told me about Connections. How it's true love. "I . . . uh . . ." I drag a stool over and sit down on it. "How do *you* know?"

"Dreamers know," she says, grinning while tapping the side of her nose. "When we're in Dreamtime, we find out if a person needs a doorway, if they're meant for a Connection. And then we go build one. My mum knew you had a Connection, so she built you a doorway to find him. I'm taking it you did?"

My mind races so fast that it's a miracle I can grab onto any coherent thoughts at all. I already knew I was in love with Jonah, have been since day one, because . . . he's my *Connection*. It's so obvious! Why didn't I see this before? Does Jonah know we're Connected? Is this why he's so angry all the time? And—he sees me with his brother. He knows I'm dating . . . kissing . . . doing gods know what with his brother, and if he knows, then he knows it's his true love, his soul mate doing these things. What kind of monster am I?

"Does . . . uh . . . Fate ever make a mistake?" I croak.

She gets me a glass of water. "Never. Are you telling me you didn't fall in love?"

I drink it all in four huge gulps. "I fell in love."

"Well, that's good," she says brightly. "That's the way it's supposed to work."

"Is it real?"

"Pardon?"

"My feelings. Are they real? Are Connections—I don't know—byproducts of Magic? Did someone *make* us fall in love?"

"No, Chloe. Connections just *are.* You fall in love because that person was created to be yours." She pulls a stool over and sits down across from me. "My mum once told me that it was like identical twins. You know how they start? As one? And then they split and become two? Connections are like that. Puzzle pieces that fit perfectly together. Two halves which make a whole. Sounds rather co-dependent, doesn't it? But all the people I know with Connections—and it's not many, because it's a rare gift from Fate—say it's not like that. It's hard to explain, which is why you should talk to Karl about it all."

"You know Karl has a Connection?"

"Yeah," she says quietly, grimacing. "I know." She sighs and looks off to the side.

I'm intrigued by her reaction, but smart enough to not put my nose where it doesn't belong. I swallow hard and ask, "Do people with Connections ever fall in love with other people?"

"Nope. Not possible."

"Never?"

"Oh, sure—you can love someone, but you can't ever be *in* love with another person." She stands up and stirs the noodles again. "Trust me. I know."

"Do you have a Connection?"

"No, mate. I'm not one of the lucky ones."

The front door slams and Karl and Raul's voices fill the air. Kiah closes her eyes and takes a deep breath. When she opens her eyes, her face is relaxed, happy even. All of the pain I'd just seen has disappeared. "It's about time!" she says when the men come into the kitchen with their bags. "The noodles are just about to go soggy. Get to work, boys. I want a sauce."

"Giules is so jealous of us right now," Raul says once the sauce is on the stove. "She's having Top Ramen tonight."

"She loves my lasagna," Kiah says. "Calls me an honorary Italian."

Raul steals a taste, ducking when Kiah swats at him. "We invited her over, but apparently she'd promised Jonah he could go surfing."

I look out the windows into the dark sky. "At night?"

"No one said it'd be here," Raul winks. "Kellan was tempted to stay, wanting to come see his girl here, but I guess Jonah insisted he come with."

Kiah looks up sharply from the dish she's laying noodles in. "You're dating Kellan Whitecomb?"

Raul cuts himself a piece of mozzarella. "They are disgusting together. You won't recognize our Kellan. He's gone soft around her. Even threatened me once, saying I had to keep my hands off Chloe or else."

"He was just joking," I mumble.

Kiah's eyes are wide in surprise. She knows, I realize. She knows it should be Jonah. "I can hardly believe it," she says carefully, going back to her noodles.

"Me too," Raul says, elbowing Karl. "Who'd have thought—"

And . . . Karl comes to my rescue, cutting Raul's words off. "You should talk, what with your horrible dating track record and all."

"We can't all be Connected like you and Moira," Raul laughs, but a burst of awkwardness explodes in the room. He quickly changes the subject, but I witness a brief, agonizingly uncomfortable glance between Kiah and Karl.

When we're setting the table, Kiah brushes up against me as she lays down a napkin. "Kellan Whitecomb doesn't have a doorway."

I plead with her silently for answers, but she has none to give.

Kiah may not have any answers to give, but Alex does a few days later. His victory yell fills the house as he runs from the office into the living room. "I'VE DONE IT! I'VE FIGURED IT OUT!"

"Whoa," Karl says, turning off the TV. "What are you talking about?"

Alex doubles over, panting even though it's a short distance down the hallway. "I know what . . . *who* have been attacking our kind."

"Well?" I demand. "Are you going to tell us or what?"

"Oh, I'm going to tell you, little Cousin. I'm going to tell everyone." He turns to Karl. "Can we set up a meeting?"

"Between you and Guard brass?" Karl asks. "Sure."

"No. I want to do it here. If the Guard wants to know, they can come here."

This so doesn't fly with Karl. "Excuse me?"

"Well," Alex says, looking a bit flustered at Karl's scowl, "I'd rather do a dry run here, maybe with all the Cousins and the parents . . . and then, if it goes well, I'll do it for the Guard."

"How about you just tell me now," Karl says firmly.

Alex literally puts his foot down. "No. I'm confident in my results, but if it's all the same, I'd like to . . ."

"Practice," I offer. He's an Intellectual—this is his sort of thing. But he's young, hasn't Ascended, and is terrified of looking like a fool in Annar without the backing of acceptance. I get it.

He nods gratefully at me. "Can we do it or not, Karl?"

"Remember," I say to my Guard friend, "none of us are as seasoned as the rest of you."

He shakes his head in disgust, but Karl pulls out his phone and calls Annar anyway.

Once word got out amongst the different species that there was going to be a quorum, local representatives began clamoring to come. Caleb explains this to me one night as I'm doing homework. "You're going to get a ton of Faerie and Gnomes at this shindig. They don't want to be left out."

"No pressure on Alex," I joke, setting my pencil down.

"No kidding," he laughs. "Kid better have his ducks in a row, know what I mean? But Alex has always been a bit cocky. I just hope this doesn't come back to bite him on the ass."

"Meaning?"

"Well, rumor is Karl got *his* ass majorly chewed out for not forcing Alex for the intel. It took a lot of favors being called in for the Guard to agree to this meeting. And even then, there'll be a contingent of Guard present—more than just Karl, Giuliana, and Kellan. At least six big guns are coming, including a Hider. They want no chances being taken with this information being disseminated on the Human plane."

"What do you know about Karl?" I ask, glancing at my shut bedroom door.

"Karl Graystone is one of said big guns," Caleb tells me. "He's well liked, very smart, and very influential. It's widely believed that he'll be Guard brass sooner rather than later."

"Seriously? But he's so young."

"Think about military units, how there are regular soldiers and then there are special teams? Like Navy SEALS and whatnot? Well, the Guard is sort of like that, too. Everyone in the Guard is good—the best, really. A lot of people believe the Council is made up of the most powerful beings, but really they're sort of split between the Council and Guard. But the Guard has its elite, and they're, well, *revered*, actually, in Annar. Karl is one of those people. And he managed, for you, to pull together a meeting that technically shouldn't be allowed. Which should tell you that, despite your parents, you're starting to make the right allies you'll need to navigate Annar."

Kiah and Raul return the next day, accompanied by two other Guards. The woman is tall, exotic and clearly Hawaiian. Karl introduces her as Iolani Popolohua, the Volcanic he'd mentioned awhile back. I am in awe of her the moment she comes into my house. She moves with an alluring sense of self-confidence that I desperately wish to possess.

The man is introduced as Kopano Melesi-Yellowbird. He's a Hider—the Guard's best, apparently. He's extremely tall and so dark that his skin nearly matches the black leather coat he's wearing. He's to build a shield around the venue we're using for the quorum.

I am humbled and excited at the same time to be around these Magicals. And unlike my parents, they don't send me from the room so they can discuss matters. It's simply assumed I'm part of the group, that as a Creator, and thereby soon a first-tier Council member, my input is just as valid as everyone else's.

But then, they also feel the same way towards the Whitecombs. A call is placed to Giuliana on speakerphone. "Everyone's present but you three," Iolani says to her. "Get your butt over here."

"I want to," Giuliana grumbles. "But I am afraid it is not possible."

"Oh?" Kopano asks. He has a soft, attractive accent. "Why not?"

"It is a long story," Giules sighs. "Hold on. Let me put you on speakerphone on this side so Kellan and Jonah can hear you, too."

Kiah gives me a pointed look that makes me squirm on the couch.

Karl gets right down to business. "To review the basics, Alexander Himura, an Intellectual, claims he has determined the identity of the beings involved in the September attacks. These are the same beings suspected of the many attacks and murders on six planes. Scant eyewitness reports we have from survivors corroborate this."

Iolani flips through a folder on her lap. "This says that he's refused to tell anyone his findings so far. Why weren't they taken?"

"This is a very good point," Giuliana says. "I'd suggested that either Kellan or Jonah compel him, but Zthane asked us to wait due to not wanting to possibly anger certain Magicals."

Everyone in the room looks at me.

"I wouldn't have been mad," I offer weakly once I realize by *certain Magicals* they mean *me*.

Raul rolls his eyes. "Himura is typical of most Intellectuals. He's grandstanding, and Zthane's humoring him because of his associations. That's all."

I lean close to Kiah. "Does this happen often?"

"Politics are a messy business," she whispers back. "And the Guard doesn't want to get off on a bad foot with you."

"The site chosen," Kopano is saying, "is a high-school gymnasium. There are five entrances that will need to monitored." He looks at me. "Are you able to take care of the doors?"

Somebody finally asks for my help, and what do I do? I manage only a quick squeak of a confirmation.

"There is a field to the west," Kopano continues, "which has lighting. To the south is a parking lot, the east a courtyard, and to the north another school building. It is not the ideal location to defend, but it should not pose too big of a problem."

"Recent sightings?" Kellan asks over the phone.

Iolani answers him. "Two over the last week. One in Europe five days ago, and one here in the States two days ago."

“Location?” Jonah prompts. I feel a burst of pleasure at the sound of his voice, as it’s been too long since he’d put himself into self-imposed exile.

Iolani flips through her notes again. “Colorado.”

“The meeting should be in Annar,” Giuliana says. “I do not like these odds.”

“Agreed,” Kiah says. “But as it’s already decided, we’ll make do with what we have here. Now, we also have to take into consideration that two additional Council members will be here—”

“Oh, shit,” Kellan says suddenly.

“Are you talking about the Old Man?” Jonah asks.

All of the Guard laugh, save me.

“Of course,” Karl says. “Jens went and snitched like a good kiss-ass.”

“Jens?” I whisper to Kiah.

“Jens Belladonna is the head of Guard,” she whispers back.

“Noel Lilywhite will be coming, too. He’s . . . uh . . . perturbed that Himura has been using his office,” Karl adds, giving me a sympathetic smile.

“No offense, Chloe,” Raul says, “but sometimes your dad has a giant stick in his ass.”

“None taken,” I say cheerfully.

Karl shoots Raul a warning to shut up. “And, a Storyteller has been requested.”

The entire group, on both sides of the phone, goes silent for a good five seconds. Kopano speaks first. “Storytellers never leave Annar once Ascended.”

Karl scratches his jaw. “This is true.”

I can't help but ask why.

Kopano tells me, "Well, if a Storyteller was to be captured by a non and interrogated under torture, just imagine the damage that could happen to our kind. Storytellers hold our histories." He pauses. "All of our histories—from every single species. It's just safer they never leave Annar. That way, they're never a risk."

Iolani looks to her notes and then back at Karl. "Uh . . . which one is coming?"

"Oliver Crocus," Karl says, and the silence returns for another five seconds.

"*Fuori di testa!*" Giules exclaims. "This cannot be."

Crocus . . . Crocus . . . that's a plant name. So, the Storyteller is an Elf?

"The Council is desperate," Karl offers. "And since Lilywhite's—er, not you, Chloe—your dad's team can't seem to figure this out, they're willing right now to do what it takes to find an answer, including sending Crocus out."

"Obviously he'll be guarded," Kiah muses.

Karl nods. "Zthane will be accompanying him."

"I thought the team was supposed to be entirely Human, considering the terrain," Kopano says, surprised.

This pricks my interest. So far, all I know about this Zthane is that he is pretty high ranking in the Guard and one of Karl's best friends. So, this means he's a different species? But which one?

"Yes, well, things changed once Crocus agreed to come," Karl says.

"ETA?" Iolani inquires.

Karl looks at his watch. "The meeting is scheduled for seven tonight, meaning Zthane will be at the site with Crocus five minutes prior. The Storyteller will be present only long enough to hear what's necessary and answer any questions Himura may have for him." He rubs at his hair. "Please, gods, let this go smoothly."

chapter 23

Kopano is already on the gym's roof when we arrive. Kiah is nice enough to explain to me how a Hider's shield works. "He's built an illusion around the gymnasium, something like a replica. He takes a period of time into his memory, so when he projects the shield, it'll look like it did before. It's sort of like a movie, playing scenes from the past. He'll be replaying them in his head, projecting them outwards."

It's cool outside already, so I wrap my arms around myself. "Are these the only kinds of shields he can build?"

She laughs. "Not even close. Kopano can manipulate just about anything. Quite handy on missions when people, objects, and places need to be hidden or distorted." She steers me off to the side of the building. "You should know I asked Giules about Jonah recently, after you and I had our talk. She says you two don't hang out at all, or—as far as she knows— interact. Am I missing something?"

I sag against the bricks. "So you know Jonah's my Connection?"

She fingers her multiple earrings. "I'm aware of who has doorways and who doesn't. And as Connections are always built between people of the same age, and you two are the only ones currently seventeen who had doorways on the Human plane, it wasn't hard to connect the dots." She pauses. "Do you love him? Do you feel the Connection?"

I turn and look into the parking lot, where Jonah and Kellan are talking to Raul and Karl. "You said people with Connections can't fall in love with other people, right?"

She nods.

"Then why am I in love with his brother? How can I be in love with two people at the same time?"

This takes her by surprise. "Are you sure? Because sometimes, people can confuse—"

"I'm not confusing anything."

She turns to look at the twins as well. "I don't know, Chloe. I've never heard about anything like this before. I don't think it's possible. It's just not how these things work."

Both the physical and emotional distance between the brothers is starkly apparent, even from a distance. And once again, I am at a loss over what to do. One thing is becoming apparent, though: I need to talk to Jonah, as soon as possible. Not just to attempt to straighten out this mess I've managed to get myself in, but because I miss him and want him so much that I can barely think straight anymore.

And . . . I need to talk to Kellan, too. Tell him the truth, because it no longer seems fair to keep such a huge thing from someone I love. I am terrified over hurting him like I'm hurting his brother, but I know sooner or later, the situation is going to explode unless I get a grip on matters.

Alex had me create a special machine for him earlier in the week. He requested something that would be multifunctional, projecting not only books and maps he can put up without transparencies, but also memories. It'd been tricky to do, but after three tries, I managed to give him exactly what he wanted.

He's fiddling with the device when Kiah and I finally come into the building, fresh from me sealing shut all the doorways save one. All of the Cousins' families are present, including my own. My parents are talking to Ewan Whitecomb—my mother gives me a tight smile and a small wave when she notices me.

In addition to all of the families, there are easily thirty Faeries and Gnomes present, including Caleb.

Karl makes his way over to me and Kiah. He rubs at his eyes with the heels of his palms. "There's been a black shape shifter sighting roughly a hundred miles north of here."

Kiah's body tenses. "When?"

"Three hours ago."

"Son of a bitch," she swears under her breath. "We should cancel this, now."

"I agree," he murmurs. "But the brass says no. They think we have enough Guard here to outweigh the risk."

Her eyes rove around the gym. "Your opinion?"

"I don't like it. But Zthane and Crocus are three minutes out. Getting another meeting time is impossible."

She grimaces. "Do the others know?"

He crosses his arms and nods. "Zthane, Raul, Kopano, and Kellan will stay outside. You, me, Giules, Iolani, and Jonah will stay inside. The directives are clear. Chloe is still our number-one priority; Oliver Crocus is next. Then Ewan Whitecomb and Noel Lilywhite."

"What about everyone else?" I ask, looking around the room.

A guilty flush steals up his neck. "Those are the only orders, Chloe."

"What about Jonah?" I ask hotly. "And Kellan? I thought they were also under orders of protection. Jonah's going to be on the Council, too—"

"Of course Karl meant to say their names," Kiah says, giving Karl a pointed look. "He forgot because they work with us so often, it's naturally assumed."

As if on cue, Jonah enters the gym with Iolani. They're talking quietly to each other, heads far too close together for my comfort. My eyes must bug out or something, because Kiah says soothingly, while rubbing a hand up and down my arm, "She's just a flirt, and an old friend. You have nothing to worry about there."

Karl looks over at Jonah and Iolani and then back at me and Kiah. With all of the chaotic plans going on lately, he and I haven't gotten to finish our talk. I can tell he wants to say something, but at this moment, Giuliana comes in with a very old, distinguished Elf.

"Ah," Kiah says. "Crocus has arrived."

Oliver Crocus is wearing a dark suit, a long black trench coat, a wide-brimmed hat, and uses a walking cane. His hair is nearly black and long to his shoulders, but his goatee is pewter gray. He is regal and elegant, and obviously, from the murmur going throughout the room, very well respected.

"Well, well," he says to Karl when he makes his way over to where we're standing. "This must be the Creator I've been hearing so much about." He turns to me and holds out a smooth, alabaster hand; when I place mine in his, he lifts it up and kisses it lightly. "You are just as charming as I imagined, Chloe Lilywhite." He's got serious charisma leaking from every pore. I find myself blushing furiously. "How delightful," he says, reaching out to pat my cheek. Then to Karl, "I'm afraid we must begin straight away. Nightstorm is not allowing me more than an hour." Then he extends his arm to Kiah, and she leads him over to Alex, leaving me alone with Karl.

He's not smiling. "You and me, we're like glue tonight. Understand?"

I try not to roll my eyes.

Cora claps her hands, attempting to get everyone's attention. She's emceeing for Alex, which makes sense considering she's got the loudest voice of anyone present.

While everyone is quieting down, I sneak a look over at Jonah, who's still standing with Iolani. As always, he senses me right away, shifting his eyes over reluctantly to meet mine.

In all the times we've ever connected this way, I always remain so stunned that I either keep a straight face or one of astonishment. But here's my chance, small as it is—how many more will I get before he completely washes his hands of me? So this time, I purposely, suggestively smile. He's confused, cautious, before the corners of his mouth tug upwards.

When his dimple appears, my heart soars. And then Iolani leans over and says something to him, forcing his attention back toward her.

It's something, though. Small as it was, it's a victory.

"I know this is somewhat unorthodox," Cora is saying, hands on her hips, "having you all come here like this. But Alex has some important things to share, making all of this worth your time. First though, Meg will share with you some background info."

Meg pulls out a sheet of paper and lays it down on the projector. "I've divided the chart into the six planes, here," she says, pointing to the different headings. "I'll start with the Human plane. Over the last ten years, there have been eleven murders and forty attacks, including the most recent." The room is eerily quiet. She points to the next column. "On the Faerie plane, there've been twenty-one murders and sixty-five attacks."

The Faeries all murmur their outrage.

Meg clears her throat. She's so atypically serious it's like she's been muted. "The Gnome plane has seen eighteen murders and fifty-seven attacks."

The Gnomes at the top of the bleachers bellow in anger, forcing Cora to yell at them to quiet down.

Meg continues, "On the Elvin plane, there have been sixteen murders, eighty-one attacks."

I look over at Oliver; he's merely nodding, stone-faced.

Meg points to the last column. "And finally, the Goblin plane has seen a total of nine murders, with nineteen attacks."

"Why so few?" Alex's mother wonders loudly.

One of the Gnomes snorts. "Don't you know any Goblins? They wouldn't stand for such nonsense! None of us should!" He pumps a tiny fist in the air, riling the rest of the Gnomes up again.

Cora grabs a nearby bullhorn. "Calm down and *listen*." The Gnomes mostly do so, allowing her to talk. "Clearly, based on these statistics, something major is going on. What you don't see is that the majority of the deaths have been of Council members, or future Council members. Of course, we didn't know any of this until Chloe was attacked." She pointedly glares at our parents. "Since this was unacceptable, we decided to do something about it. And Alex has, unlike the so-called 'experts' in Annar."

My dad doesn't even blink.

Alex is up next. When he thanks everyone for coming, the room once more falls silent. “Searching for these things was like searching for a needle in a haystack at first,” he says, shifting nervously next to the projector. “But I had a few things going for me. For starters, I knew they were Magicals. Or, at the very least, were similar to our kind. This was due to their speed, ability to move between the planes, and tendency to act in corporeal ways even though they appear non-corporeal.

“I asked myself several questions: Why are these things targeting Magicals? What is their goal? Do they gain something from our deaths? Occam’s Razor tells us that the simplest answer is usually the correct one. Why do most murders occur? Revenge, of course. Think about it—revenge for being abused, revenge for drug deals gone wrong, revenge for being the wrong sort of person. The hate and heat associated with murder usually can be tied somehow back to revenge. So I began looking for those who might want revenge against our kind.

“I’m sure everybody in this room—from the Human plane, at least—is quite familiar with Greek legends: stories of our ancestors, who, because they were different, were worshipped as gods.

“I spent a lot of time rereading these stories. And then I came across one that fits in every single way.” He picks up a book and places it on the projector. An image appears on a screen behind him, much to my pleasure: a perfect replica of the book he’s looking at. He taps the picture below, of Zeus standing over a hole, lightning bolt in hand. “This is the chapter I found most interesting. It tells of how Zeus, being leader of a new pantheon of gods, decided to overthrow the Titans, the elder gods of Greece.”

A Faerie whose name I don't know calls out, "In our stories, he is not called Zeus. His name was Thaniel, but the story is pretty much the same."

"The same for the Gnomes," someone else adds. "Ours was named Jurgen."

Alex nods. "Yes, there are versions of this story on every plane, I imagine. Since we know that most of these stories are based on facts—as distorted as they've become over the millennia—I couldn't help but wonder, exactly who or what had the Titans been?" He flips a few pages and points to another picture. "According to Human texts, the Titans were the first group of rulers. They were a small group—powerful, and less nuanced than the later gods and goddesses. Zeus was, in fact, the son of one of the Titans—Cronus—who was the son of the first god, Uranus. It was a familial battle that pitted Zeus and his brothers against his father, grandfather, and elder relatives. In the end, the younger gods and goddesses won, banishing the ancients. And if Zeus—or Thaniel, or Jurgen—was an early Magical, who were Cronus and Uranus? Who were the rest of the Titans? It's my belief they were Magicals, too." He stops to clear his throat. "My theory is that Zeus, or whoever he was, felt threatened by the early Magicals and had a Creator strip them of power and/or their corporal existences. Oliver, this is where I need you to come in. Will you share with us the story of the Titans?"

Oliver stands up and makes his way over to Alex. Once in front of the audience, he takes a deep breath before raising his hands. A ball of light grows, shimmering between his fingers. Then he turns and throws it at the projection screen. The ball splatters in a burst of rainbow-hued light, flickering before settling into a moving picture of the Titans.

"Alexander has given you a good start to the story of the so-called Titans," Oliver says. "And I applaud his ingenuity. He in on the road to becoming a very fine Intellectual. But, of course, he has only read the legends left behind by the ancients and does not have the complete story. Only the Storytellers have the true tale."

chapter 24

In the beginning, there was an early group of Magicals. They called themselves the Elders, for they were the alphas. The first of the Elders was a Creator, Enlilkian, and he conjured a mate out of the four elements: equal parts of fire, earth, wind, and water. She was an Elemental in the strongest form, for there were no divisions within a craft as there are today. This Elder, Cailleache, became disillusioned with having only two Magicals to do all the work. She insisted on children, and then grandchildren, until there were a total of forty-three Elders.

Together, they controlled the only plane of existence. All non-Magicals looked to the Elders for everything—for the sun shining over their heads to the food grown in their fields. Nothing was left to chance. Everything was dictated by the Elders.

And then one of Enlilkian's sons, Rudshivar, tired of sharing a singular plane with the rest of the family. He was a Creator, too, and one night while the rest slept, he broke the plane into six pieces. When Enlilkian awoke, he was outraged by the audacity of his protégé.

Rudshivar was banished to the outermost plane, leaving him almost nothing to rule over. But Rudshivar was clever, so he quickly began creating his own people to rule over. Once the first group sprung into existence, he created another, and then another, until all six species—

Elves, Humans, Goblins, Gnomes, Faeries, and Dwarves—were wrought.

Reflecting on his work, he pondered how he ought to make others like him, in order to split the workload of caring for so many sentient beings. While it took a large effort and much time, five of each species were molded into Magicals. They were different from the Elders, for they were now of Rudshivar's making. They did not look like Elders, nor did they act like them.

For when he had created his species, he had built in varying characteristics to make them unique from one another. And these new Magicals took their unique abilities and began to rule their new world.

The sixth plane flourished more so than the other five, still dominated by the Elders. At first, Enlilkian tolerated Rudshivar's machinations, viewing them as harmless. But once he truly saw what was occurring in that realm, he decided to sever the sixth plane and all that existed within it, for it would not be tolerated to have such sentient creatures. He declared war, wreaking havoc and mayhem in all six planes. In the end, the thirty Magicals, along with Rudshivar, finally outmatched the Elders. But Rudshivar could not kill his father and mother, nor his brothers and sisters. He did not have it within him. So he left their fates to the thirty Magicals. Now, none of the early Magicals delighted in the death of any creature, so they brought forth their Creator, a woman named Eva, to drain the Elders of their corporal existence.

Once they become husks of their former selves, a Quake opened the ground in the fifth plane. The Magicals collected the remains of the Elders and banished them to this abyss, to contemplate what could have been and what was to be for the rest of their existences.

Rudshivar dispersed the Magicals equally to each plane, along with their species. He then willed himself out of existence, leaving behind his children to rule the worlds as they saw fit.

This is where the true changes came about, of how Magicals began leaving the aftermath of events to the peoples they were guiding. Over time, once they had begun to populate and create new crafts and skills, they asked their Creator to forge one last land, that of Annar, so they would have a haven where they could discuss their worlds and the changes necessary to advance their societies.

chapter 25

A picture of the first Council flickers on the wall behind Oliver before fading away. "And that, ladies and gentlemen," he says in his mesmerizing voice, "is the story of the Elders, or as Alexander has called them, the Titans."

No one says anything, but you can hear the wheels beginning to turn in every single head in the room.

Alex pulls out a map of all of the different planes, marked up with red dots. "The first murder occurred on the Elvin plane. Oliver, is this the plane that the Elders were banished on?"

The Storyteller is staring at the map, his brows scrunched. "Yes, in fact, it was."

"They would be long dead by now," my father suddenly calls out. "This happened millennia ago. No Magical is immortal. Pinning the blame on these Elders would be tantamount to blaming King Arthur and his Knights of the Round Table."

A nervous titter moves through the crowd.

"How do you know they weren't immortal?" Alex asks.

My father sniffs in his typical, haughty way.

"Oliver said that Rudshivar had to will himself out of existence," Alex persists. "Why would he do that? Why wouldn't he simply wait his time until death could take him?"

"Perhaps he couldn't live with what he had done," my father argues.

"Perhaps," Alex says stubbornly, "it's because he *couldn't* die."

"Young man," my father tries, but Alex smashes his fist down against the projector.

"These things—these black shape shifters are the Elders, Noel! Everything adds up. They have the perfect motive for revenge against our kind. Oliver himself said they were left as husks—and *that's* what attacked Chloe. A husk of an ancient, immortal being with quasi-functioning powers that no other beings, save Magicals, have." He forcefully taps on the picture of the hole Zeus had created to confine the Titans in. "They were imprisoned on the Elvin plane." He grabs a nearby book, shoving it on to the projector. "There was an earthquake on the Elvin plane ten years ago. It preceded the first Magical murder by five days. Five days! You think it's a coincidence?"

My father is royally pissed off. "Yes!"

"Is this because I'm seventeen?" Alex says hotly. "Or because I haven't Ascended? Or is it because you and your department have failed for *ten years* to figure this out?"

His mother shrieks, "Alexander Himura, you stop this at once!"

But he holds his ground. "I will not! Chloe could've been killed, and even though you Council sorts claim you're trying to protect her, she still was attacked!"

"Not your fault," I whisper quickly to Karl, who appears as if he cannot decide to strangle Alex for the insult or defend his ability to keep me safe.

"Look," Alex yells, tapping the map again. "The murders started here, on the Elvin plane, and then spread to the Faerie plane. It continued, seeping into all the planes one at a time until all but Annar had been touched. The facts don't lie. The dates don't lie!"

Nearly everyone begins murmuring.

"They're moving as a group," Alex says. "I think it's because they're not whole yet, that they're more powerful this way. Haven't any of you listened to any of the memories of the attacks? The screaming is of multiple beings, not one. And they're intelligent—they know how to attack, to coordinate strikes. They're only lacking corporeal forms." He turns to Giuliana. "I was told they split up when they attacked you, like they had a plan of attack. Do you mind showing us?"

She smiles hesitantly. "Show you?"

He clarifies, "May I surge to see?"

Just as with Oliver Crocus's stories, a movie appears on the projector screen behind Alex when he touches the screen. But not any memory—Giuliana's memory of that day.

She, herself, is so stunned that her mouth is hanging open.

Everyone is back to talking at the same time until Cora grabs her bullhorn again. "Do you people want to see what these things do or not?" she hollers. "Because here's your chance to help, rather than sit around and wring your hands!"

"Cora definitely needs some people skills," Karl whispers, flinching as several Gnomes scream down at her.

But I can't deal with any of that. Instead, I'm riveted on watching what happened to Jonah and Kellan that day.

Giuliana's Jeep is traveling at a frightening speed, racing south of the city. She's swung closer to the mountains than we had, leading them up a winding road. Jonah is next to her, silent as he grips the handle above him. Kellan's in the back, watching out the rear window. "They're there—to the left," he says, pointing towards the woods next to them. She watches his hand move, flicking almost imperceptively; the black shapes streaking and weaving through the trees falter and shriek loudly.

*Guiles snarls, "*Basta! *What will it take to get away from these things?"*

"We can take them," Jonah says, sounding extraordinarily calm. Kellan voices his agreement.

"Are you crazy?" she yells. "Absolutely not! I have my orders—you are to be removed to the safest place possible."

Kellan leans toward the window again, watching. Her eyes flick toward him in the rearview mirror—he's doing something to the shapes again, causing them once more to shriek. "Sorry to be the bearer of bad news, but I don't think we can outrun those things, not in this Jeep."

"We will!" she hisses.

A large black mass streaks out in front of them, causing Giuliana to weave first toward the woods and then toward the other side. She sees the swift drop off the side; there's only a small guardrail protecting the road from below. The Jeep three-sixties as she tries to steady it.

"Listen to me," Jonah insists as he angles one of his hands toward one of the black shapes, causing it to retreat. "We can take them."

"He's right," Kellan agrees. "There are three of us. We can do it."

But Giuliana is unmoved. "No—I have my orders. You are not to engage them, do you understand, Jonah Whitecomb?"

She doesn't look back at him when Kellan says, "Fine. Then let me be the one to do the engaging."

"Giuliana, I appreciate the thought," Jonah says wryly, "but you and I both know I'm going to do what I want anyway. Don't force my hand—I'd hate to have to grab the wheel once you fall asleep."

Before Giuliana can reply, a black mass darts in front of them again. She slams on the brakes as the mass rams into the Jeep, splitting apart into ten pieces which scratch across the sides and top.

The Jeep goes spinning, hitting the guardrail. Giuliana reaches out and forces a gust of wind to blow the vehicle back toward the road, but in her panic, she misjudges the pressure necessary. It skids back toward the group of ten shape shifters, which circle it, raising the Jeep up momentarily before crashing back down. Five of the shapes dart toward the side and reformed into one again, smashing against the passenger side. It all happens so fast that no one in the car has time to react.

The Jeep flips and skids down the hill until crashing into the guard rail. The rail snaps, a loud, ugly groaning sound, allowing the Jeep to fall through. Giuliana screams as they drop about forty feet before landing, driver's side down, against a redwood.

Her vision hazes in and out, but she still can hear Jonah saying, "Kellan! Answer me!"

And even though I know he's fine, that they're both fine, *here*, I still tense.

Guiliana tries to unbuckle herself. Her voice is slow and sticky. "Jonah, don't get out of this car . . ."

But Jonah has already climbed into the backseat. "Don't you do this to me, Kel . . . Wake up, wake up . . ."

She drops against the window once her own buckle is released. The screaming surrounds them, shattering the front windshield. "Let me get out."

Jonah pays her no mind. He reaches up and tries to open the door, but it refuses to budge. Then he leans back and kicks it open. "Don't you leave," she orders, blinking rapidly as she tries to focus.

He pulls himself out of the car, not answering. A quick glance at Kellan shows him unresponsive, his temple bleeding heavily. She fumbles for his pulse; once reassured, she lets go and heaves herself out of the car.

Jonah's already ten feet away, the black shapes forming a crescent in front of him. One of his hands is out—each small flick brings about another round of intensified screaming. He winces at the noise, but never backs down.

"Get back here!" she yells at him. "That's an order!"

She might as well be talking to herself. Whatever he's doing, he multiplies the effort, and the black shapes constrict, drifting toward the ground in oily pools as he, himself, crouches lower. And then, a strong wind blows past Giules as one of the black shapes shoots directly at Jonah. It hits him full on, knocking him to the ground.

Giuliana reaches up toward the sky; clouds build up quickly, like one of those nature documentaries using time-lapse photography. "Come on, come on," she chants, watching the black shape push down against Jonah. He tries desperately to connect with it, but his hand moves through it as if it was smoke. Then it twists around his arm, leaving a small tail behind; the tail cracks, like a whip—the noise the only sound as the rest of the shape shifters had fallen silent. She hears Jonah's arm break in a number of places, but Jonah makes no sound himself. He simply winces, hard, and yanks his mangled arm away.

The clouds finally build up enough that she's able to pull down lightning bolt after lightning bolt, striking the area surrounding Jonah. The black shapes he'd downed earlier have begun reforming, some enough that they are edging toward where he's lying. She races toward him, throwing more lightning down until they relent and race off into the distance.

The screen goes blank when Alex lifts his hand. My heart is beating hard, so hard that I wonder if Karl can hear it. I want to scream and throw up at the same time, or better yet, do something—anything—to these beings that think they can attack people I love.

"Damn," Karl whispers. "We got off easy, didn't we?"

I don't answer because I'm staring at Jonah. He's listening to something Iolani is whispering, completely unfazed by the memory, which boggles my mind.

"Karl?" Alex is asking. "Is there anything you guys saw that varied from the behavior we saw here?"

"Don't you dare," I hiss, suddenly aware that my inabilities and lack of decisive action might be up on a screen for all to see. With my unforgiving, easily embarrassed parents in the room, no less.

Karl ignores my warning. "Only that they were able to cause an explosion."

"Do you mind if we have a look?" Alex asks.

Karl gives it to him, offering me some half-assed "It's for the good of the group" spiel. Alex's eyes unfocus once more as he touches the projector, allowing Karl's memory to be seen by all.

It's like watching a car wreck, no pun intended. I know what's going to happen, and as much as I want to look away, I can't. It's almost as if I *have* to see just how ineffective I was in Karl's Hummer that day.

Thank gods Karl is more selective than Giules with what he allows the others to see. He starts at the moment he'd began weaving toward the other side of traffic, leading up to the Hummer spinning and gunning in the opposite direction.

Karl looks at me, and I'm surprised by appearing much calmer than I remember being. And then an explosion rips through the air behind us—Karl sees the entire thing in the rearview mirror. The black shapes mass into one giant entity, stretching out like a rubber band and then snapping back in. The moment they constrict inward, a fire bomb goes off, exploding in every direction. The shape shifters follow the explosion lines, streaking hot and fast towards the Hummer.

We lift off the ground, lurching toward the left before slamming hard into the pavement. Karl watches my head smash against the glass and even reaches out to brace me a split second too late.

I don't remember him doing that.

There's a lot more blood everywhere, more than I remember. Cora's babbling hysterically—I don't remember that, either—*before grabbing my head. Karl yells at her to get it together* (good gods, do I remember *any* of this correctly?), *and she does, masking her panic with soothing words I can tell are hard for her to say.*

Karl's eyes flick back to the rearview mirror; he's putting enough distance between us and the black shapes so he's able to turn some focus back to me. I'm white as a sheet, my eyes unfocused and nearly black. Cora screams at him about concussions and a cracked skull.

Thankfully, Karl cuts the memory off here, right before I pass out.

I am dying of shame.

Gods. Jonah had gotten out of the car, had *fought* those things. What had I done? I'd been frozen, unable to think of a single thing to do. My mother is shaking her head, not in a *I can't believe my daughter almost died* sympathetic way, but more in a *Gods, can't that girl get it together and stop shaming our family* way.

I do not allow myself to look at anyone else, even though I can feel Jonah's eyes burning a hole into me. I want to turn around, hide behind Karl even, but I simply stand still as can be, counting the cracks in the parquet floor.

"That is most interesting," Oliver Crocus says, breaking the uncomfortable silence in the room. "They have the ability to create fire and explosions, which leads one to believe an early form of an Elemental is present."

Meg's father says, "I thought only Blazes do that."

"Indeed," Oliver says mildly. "Today. But not with the Elders—their Elementals would have had control over the four elements."

"And the deaths?" Lizzie's mother calls out. "What are they gaining by the deaths? Why mostly Council members?"

"Are not our Council members most potent?" Oliver queries.

The room explodes in an angry, scared frenzy, with almost every single person talking at the same time. Just as Cora grabs her bullhorn, Raul races in.

"They're on the move, spotted within thirty miles of here," he says. "Meeting over!"

Chaos erupts. Everyone frantically clambers down off the bleachers.

Karl grabs my arm so tightly I can feel bruises being born. "Is Kopano still on the roof?"

Raul nods. "The shield is still functioning. But they're moving fast, brother!"

Karl swears under his breath. "Where's Zthane?"

"He and Kellan have taken off toward the direction they're moving in." Raul searches the room until he finds Kiah. "Redrock, you're needed out there!"

"On it!" she yells, sprinting to the door.

Karl turns to Iolani and Jonah. "This room is getting locked down in," he looks at his watch, "five minutes. You have your orders."

Orders?

I grab at Jonah's attention. He gives me a very calm, very measured look that tells me not to panic, but I am.

Holy cow, am I panicking.

Karl tells Raul that he needs to get back outside to help defend the building if Kopano's shields fail. But, I need to do something. I can't just sit back this time and do nothing.

Iolani and Jonah are now standing with us, debating whether or not to have the entire building sealed. I can do this, I know I can. It's easy—takes little to no effort. But if the building is sealed, and Kopano is inside, then it's still at risk.

I can . . . I can . . . make the shield permanent, right? I can do that easily, too. I will just make the atoms in the shield hold still.

"Let me solidify the shield," I say, interrupting what Karl is saying.

They all stop talking and look at me. And then, every single one of them, Jonah included, say, "No."

Raul dismisses himself and heads back outside.

"I can do it," I tell Karl. "You know I can."

He lets go of my arm and gives me a toe-curling frown of disapproval. "I know you can. But letting you outside would be idiotic, considering you're our number-one concern."

"The building will be at risk if there's no shield," I argue. "And we don't know enough about these Elders to know whether or not they can sense us through walls. So, let me go outside and solidify the shield. That way, everyone outside can come inside, and no one has to risk anything."

Again, every single person standing by me says, "No."

"Chloe," Iolani tries, "you must realize that our number-one priority is to protect *you.*"

I look up at Karl, whose arms are now crossed. He will not budge; of this I am sure. *Don't do it,* the little voice warns, sounding far too panicky when I feel so bloody calm for once.

But I do. I turn on my heels and sprint out the one remaining door as fast as I can. I build a number of barriers between me and the door so anyone following won't be able to get through easily. Then I grab Raul who is standing outside, talking on his phone. "Get me on top of the roof right now."

"Did Karl agree—"

"NOW," I order, trying out my very best Council voice.

"No need to be nasty," he sniffs. Dark clouds suddenly mass above as thunder booms so strongly the ground shakes. And then the winds around us whip furiously into a small, thin tornado.

Karl is screaming from behind the wooden planks I'd thrown up, but thankfully the thunder is so loud, Raul can't hear him.

"Ready for a ride?" Raul asks, grabbing me tightly around the waist. He flicks out a hand and the tornado veers directly toward us.

He's kidding, right?

There are those rides at amusement parks, the ones that move so fast that you can no longer move your limbs easily. And your face sorts of starts moving on its own, all stretched back or to the side because the pressure against you is too much. This is what it's like when the tornado barrels down on us. And rather than being terrified, like I ought to, I feel completely calm. Rationally, I figure I'm about to die, but my mind is razor sharp, clear and focused.

Seal and solidify the shield. Protect those I love.

It doesn't matter that I'll probably be found dead in an hour or so, not killed by the Elders, but because a house or a barn or a car has smashed down on me two counties over. I'm going to be that Witch whose shoes Dorothy stole. Only no one will want to steal my ratty Uggs.

Raul grips me tighter and throws us right into the tornado. It's five million times worse than any of those rides that smash your face up and incapacitate you. Raul is saying something to me, something against my ear in this bizarre, intimate way that ought to unnerve me. I have no idea what it is, nor do I care. Because all I know is that I'm not going to fail this time.

When we crash down on the roof, my hands bleed against the gravel. I don't bother checking them out as I tell Raul, "Text the team outside and tell them to get inside right now. I'll seal the building once it's complete."

He nods and pulls out his phone.

Kopano is still seated, ear buds in, hands out in a meditative pose. "I cannot focus if you are going to be doing that around me," he says.

"They're coming," Raul says, fingers flying across the keyboard. Kopano's hands drop; the shimmering around the building begins to fade.

"Wait!" I stumble over to where he's sitting. "Build it up again. I'm gonna make it permanent."

Down below, Karl is screaming my name. Jonah is, too, and it tears at my heart. Raul lowers his phone briefly and asks, "What's this?"

"Ignore them," I say firmly. "Kopano, put the shield back up *now*."

He looks toward the ledge nervously. "I cannot guarantee it will be perfect now that I've lost my build-up."

"Whatever you do will be enough. Now, please, before it's too late."

Kopano and Raul exchange an uneasy glance, but Kopano spreads out his hands and chants something, low and soft. When the shield shimmers and reappears, I surge into his mind to collect the image of the scene replaying over and over. Then I scramble to the side of the building and grip it tight.

SolidifySolidifySolidify

Horrible screams begin to fill the air around the building. Raul sprints across the roof and skids to a halt at the very edge. "Lord Almighty! They are even closer than we thought!"

"Is everyone inside?" I ask quickly.

Raul peers over the side. "Er . . . no."

"Get them in right now. Tell them I'll be done in less than a minute and we'll meet them inside."

He pulls out his phone and calls Karl.

Kopano unfolds himself and leaps to his feet. "Time to go, Chloe."

"Are they inside?" I ask, feeling the last bits of the shield solidifying.

"Yes." Raul stares into the distance. "Gods! Half a mile at the most! Let's go, Chloe! You're in deep shit, by the way."

"You sure everyone is inside? Everyone but the three of us?"

"Yes, yes," he says impatiently.

The calm clarity expands. Everyone I *really* love is safe inside this building. Jonah. Kellan. The Cousins. Karl. Caleb. Even my parents. But it doesn't guarantee anything. The Elders could still figure this out. They could still be at risk.

Because they want me. I'm the big catch, right?

So I do what I have to do. I erase the remaining door to the gym.

chapter 26

"We need to get out of here," I tell Raul and Kopano as a ladder spreads out below us.

"We need to get back into that building, girl," Kopano argues.

I throw my legs over the side of the building and climb down. It's surprisingly faster than tornado travel. "It's me they want, and there are just too many people in there to risk. So let's get going already!"

"You're INSANE!" Raul yells as he scuttles down after me. "Chloe, Karl wants—"

"Yeah, yeah," I mutter as I drop to the ground. "What about what I want?"

"To die?" Kopano asks as he drops to the ground next to Raul. "Because that is what you are asking for if you do not get into the building."

I am not going to stand by and watch anyone else get hurt. I just can't. Jonah and Kellan had not been afraid of the Elders. They'd stood their ground, whereas I'd passed out. Not again.

"What I want is everyone to be safe. So why don't we give those things out there something to chase after? They want me, right? If they follow us, they'll pass this building up with no thought."

"But Karl—" Raul tries again.

"Aren't you two Guard?" I demand. "Can't you defend me just as well as he?"

"Yes, but—"

My fists ball up tightly. "I am leaving with or without you. So, choose."

They stare at me for what feels like forever. The screaming around us intensifies to where it's impossible to hear anything else. But then Raul grabs my arm and we sprint to his rented Corvette. I have to share a cramped seat with Kopano, who holds onto me like he's afraid I'll fly away. I haven't even buckled our seat belt when Raul peels out of the parking lot toward the main drag in town. "Where to?"

I unroll the window and scan the horizon. Sure enough, the Elders are right behind, split into two long tails on either side of the road. "Somewhere crowded, where it'll be nearly impossible to pick out a small group of Magicals."

"I've been wanting to see San Francisco," he yells, swerving around a minivan. "Here's my chance!"

The Corvette's top lowers. I unbuckle my seatbelt and stand up, surprisingly steady due to the death grip Kopano's got on me. He swears as one of the black shapes darts away from the pack and streaks toward us. I gather as much energy as I can from the power lines above and roll it into a miniature sun between my hands. Then I launch it at the shape as hard as I can.

Two summers of softball hell with Cora finally pay off. Just as the shape comes within a foot of the Corvette, the energy ball smashes into it and explodes. The Elder shrieks, shooting high into the air and then to the right.

Damn. They're still alive. Maybe I'm not strong enough to kill them after all? Maybe . . . because I haven't Ascended yet?

Two more black shapes break rank and dart into the road. A number of cars behind us squeal to hasty stops before being knocked over by the shifters. "Hold on," Raul tells us, throwing the car into fifth gear. He reaches an arm out to steady me, despite Kopano's grip.

I quickly yank as much energy down as I can. I'll have to be content with maiming rather than destroying. My little fire bombs strike true, forcing the shape-shifters off the road. But more and more break from the pack, hurtling past and tipping over car after car in their pursuit of us.

They're fighting in the open, the little voice marvels in horror. *Where anyone can see them. This is not good.*

I hesitate as more cars skid to halts behind us. People are fleeing their vehicles and running toward anything nearby that offers safety.

"Hit them!" Raul yells. "Don't worry about the public! Someone will take care of them."

"People are getting hurt!"

His eyes stay steady on the road. "Focus, Chloe! Get those things off of us. This car can only go so fast!"

A cell phone rings in the cup holder below. Sure enough, Karl's name flashes on the screen. But I am not going to lead them here. No way.

I snatch the phone and lob it in an arc. It disappears in a ditch. Kopano's goes off not a second later, prompting me to snatch that one as well. "What the hell?" Raul demands. "We need those!"

I build up another ball. "For what? So they can follow us?"

He grunts, swerving around two cars. Kopano's grip on me is now close to cutting off my circulation. "Stronger, Chloe," the Hider says.

"Do not worry about damage. The Guard will come and clean up any mess." Then, despite still holding onto me, he closes his eyes and chants. The car begins to shimmer.

"What's going on?" I ask Raul.

"He's hiding us. Because this is going to get picked up—and no matter what, *you* cannot be seen."

"So the Elders can't see us?"

"I think it's more that people will not notice who is in this car," Raul says, passing yet another vehicle.

After throwing out a few more mini suns, I decide to try something different. I'd done pretty well in P.E. during archery, so I figure if I need to hit these Elders on a regular basis, it's going to be done with a bow and supercharged arrows, which I get to creating immediately. Each arrow tip is infused with a concentrated bomb meant to explode upon contact.

Raul glances up at me as I cock the string. "Why not a gun? Why not grenades?"

"I'm no good with guns." I aim at the black mass toward our right and then let go. The arrow races directly into the heart of the Elders and explodes. The mass splinters into four different strands, each surging high into the air, all the while screaming so loud that the car vibrates.

"Look at that!" Raul hoots as the four sections falter and hang high in the air. "They're scared!"

Kopano signals me, still chanting: *Again*.

I angle to the left this time, firing two consecutive arrows. A number of Elders fall back or head into the woods as the air around them explodes. And then I continue firing, arrow after arrow, into the dark masses surrounding us.

Most of the Elders retreat, confused by my arrow bombs. A few doggedly follow even though I hit them repeatedly. It isn't until nearly thirty minutes after I began do we seem to be in the clear. But Raul doesn't slow down. He can't afford to.

I eventually slide back down into Kopano's lap. He's still chanting. "Think we're safe?" I ask.

"No." Raul's lips form a thin, hard line. "They're regrouping."

I pan around us. "How can you tell?"

"Because," he says grimly, "no one has been able to kill one of those things yet."

I crack my knuckles, feeling rather than hearing the pops. "There's a first time for everything, isn't there?"

He turns briefly to study me. "Death isn't pretty, Chloe."

"No," I agree quietly. "It most certainly is not."

It isn't until we are halfway across the Bay Bridge leading into San Francisco that the Elders reappear.

Traffic on the bridge is almost always a sure thing, and today is no different. We are slowly crawling across the bridge, buffered on all sides by either steel beams or other cars. Frustrated, Kopano smacks the side of the Corvette. "They're coming. I can sense them crossing the bridge's threshold."

I whip around in my seat and stare. Sure enough, two black shapes are zipping in and out of the cars as they make their way toward us.

"What do we do?" I squeal, fumbling for the bow wedged between my legs.

The Corvette comes to a dead halt alongside all the other vehicles. Raul smashes his fist against the steering wheel. He glances up in the rearview mirror and says, "We run."

I hold still. "Excuse me?"

"Running will be excessively better than sitting like ducks in this car." A tan hand runs wistfully across the dashboard. "It's a shame, really. This car's a beaut."

"You can get another," Kopano says, practically tossing me over the side. Then, as he leaps over himself, "Run, girl!"

It's a tough thing to run on a crowded bridge. Some of the spaces between the cars are tight, making it difficult to squeeze through. This doesn't stop the Guards with me, nor does it seem to slow them down. They jump and skid over hoods when necessary, dragging me behind like a ragdoll when I'm not fast enough.

The Elders are hot on our trail. They aren't screaming, which is somewhat comforting to my nerves, but they're still fast. Fast enough to keep up with Raul's fast Corvette. Fast enough, I'm sure, to overtake us on the bridge.

At one point, I slide into automatic. My mind just sort of goes into overdrive and allows my body to move on its own. Feet slapping on metal, hands sliding across cars, all my body wants to do is to get the hell off that bridge. My lungs are burning but I still push harder. Faster.

They're coming! the little voice calls. *Do something!*

But I don't have to do something. Raul does it for us. "Don't be scared," he yells, grabbing my hand tight. "And don't let go!"

I want ask what he means, but I can't. Because in the next second, Kopano grabs my other hand, orders, "Rip us a hole, Chloe!" and the three of us run directly into the side of the bridge. Metal crumbles beneath my fingers, allowing us to plummet two hundred and twenty feet down into San Francisco Bay.

As I fall, I can't help but think: I'm going to die anyway! People commit suicide off bridges because when they hit the water, it kills them! We're going to die! In the water! Great White sharks have been seen in these waters! OHMYGODSI'MGOINGTODIE!!

But I don't. Something in me snaps moments before impact. Alongside the winds Raul whips up, a life raft appears right under us, making the impact feel like hitting that hard, squishy stuff in playgrounds beneath the equipment rather than the concrete water becomes after a long distance. The wind's knocked right out of me, and this is only exacerbated when Kopano throws his body across mine. Soft words flow from his mouth, over the three of us and the raft.

The Elders streak by, none the wiser. He's hidden us.

I stare up at the bridge. People are hanging over the sides, many screaming and pointing. They're searching, I'm sure, for the three lunatics who threw themselves over the edge. Police sirens blare in the near distance.

"Think I'll get my deposit on the car back?" Raul asks, wiping the sweat off his brow. And I laugh, because, really, what else can I do?

Raul and Kopano are arguing over who to call first an hour later. As my cell phone is back home and Kopano's and Raul's are somewhere in a ditch, we're forced to use the phone in the hotel we've holed up in. Zthane might still be in town, they're saying, and if that's the case, he should be notified first due to seniority. Then again, they fret, perhaps it ought to be Karl, since I'm his assignment. They're a little nervous about calling Karl, though. From what I can tell, Zthane would be their preferred option. Something about being less of a ball buster.

"Calm down," I say as I flip TV channels. "Neither of you were ordered to bring me back into the building, were you? So what's the problem?"

They both stare and then smile like I've given them the shiniest, best birthday presents ever. Raul slaps his hands together. "She's right!"

"She may be right," Kopano admits as he drops onto the second bed. "But I do not think that will smooth any ruffled feathers. Karl is going to blow a fuse."

"Why are we calling again?" I ask. The news is talking about eyewitness reports of three people jumping off the Bay Bridge a couple hours earlier. Some eyewitnesses are actually crying.

"Because," Raul says, "we're alive and they need to know this." He shoves his hands into his pockets. "*Díos mio*, Karl is going to squash me like a bug."

"Once we explain everything, I'm sure he'll be fine."

"Chloe," he sighs, sitting at the edge of my bed. "You need to understand that the Guard has procedures put in place. Going off radar like this is very much frowned upon."

"Fine," I say, rolling over and sitting up. "Pin all of the blame on me. It was my idea to run. And you know what? I'm glad I did. There's a whole building full of people back home that are safe right now because we left. And we're fine, too. So it was a good plan."

Kopano laughs. "It was no plan, girl. You know as well as we do that we all acted on instinct."

True. But I hadn't fainted. I'd done something this time, something good. Something that kept people safe. Well, almost everyone. "Do you think that those people are okay?"

"People?" Raul asks, forehead scrunched.

"The nons whose cars were overturned."

His forehead smoothes out. "The moment Zthane or Karl heard those things screaming outside of the building and discovered you'd sealed the doors shut, a whole herd of Guards were most likely called in to track us. None of those people probably remember anything, Chloe. I'm sure that they are all healthy and wherever they need to be at this moment."

"And . . . our friends?"

"Well," Raul muses, "they are out looking for us. That's a given. Thus our need to call before panic sets them on fire."

I don't know this Zthane they're talking about, so he's not the one I'd call. I don't want to call Karl—he'll rip my head off straightaway. They're right about that. And while I want with all my heart to call Jonah and hear for myself that he's safe, our first contact shouldn't be like this. He deserves more.

"I'll make the call." Both men watch in surprise as I dial a number.

I hope I'm making the right choice over who to contact first.

"Yes?" I hear from the receiver.

"It's me," I say.

"Chloe!" Kellan yells. "Where are you? Are you okay?"

Raul turns off the television set. "I'm in San Francisco—"

"San Francisco!" he repeats. And then, "Please tell me you're all right."

"I'm fine, I swear I'm fine."

“Okay, okay,” he says, and for the first time, I can hear the anxiety below his forced calm. “Where specifically in San Francisco?”

Kellan and Giules show up forty minutes later. There’s a portal in San Francisco, down on Pier 49 in one of those shops that overlook where the sea lions like to hang out. I guess California is one of those rare places on our plane that has a number of portals. Some states, even countries, don’t have a single portal. California alone has four. Some previous Creator must have really liked it here to make so many portals.

Raul doesn’t question me about why I choose to call Kellan. I think he might’ve even been a little glad that I hadn’t called Karl. Giules, both he and Kopano figure, is an acceptable substitute to acquire our location and status. She oversees the Whitecombs and often is tasked with overseeing me. In their minds, that practically makes her Karl.

That doesn’t stop Kopano, however, from telling me right before they showed up, “Expect Kellan to get completely reamed by the brass for not informing them about your location.”

“He’s not in the Guard yet,” I insist. “They can’t punish him if he’s not officially part of the Guard.”

His answer is a set of raised eyebrows and troubled dark eyes.

I’d questioned them earlier on why we needed any more Guard to come and get us. After all, there’s a portal in town—why couldn’t we just use it to go home? But neither felt that was an acceptable option. They figured the Elders would be hot and bothered by this point about our evasion tactics. Four Guard, they insisted, would be a safer bet than two.

I feel this slam of relief at seeing Kellan, like somehow all of the stresses of the day evaporate in his presence. I launch myself at him, almost knocking us both over.

"Well," Giuliana says, shutting the door behind her. "I am relieved to find you three safe and sound. You should have heard the panic alarms sounding when Chloe closed that gym up. You'd have thought that a nuclear war was commencing outside."

"Just how did you guys get out?" Raul asks, ushering his friend to a chair.

I tug Kellan down on the bed next to me. He's thankfully not saying anything—no reprimands for stupid choices. I figure he wants to, though, but he's sweet enough not to do it in front of everyone else.

Giules laughs. "Karl, of course. Split the wall in half. I guess an earthquake isn't unheard of here in Northern California, is it?"

I squeeze Kellan's hand and look into his eyes. Disappointment's there, yes. The strain of worry is evident, too. But he's also relieved, so I figure I can live with the other things.

The guys tell Giules and Kellan all about our race to San Francisco, sparing no details. I progressively lose feeling in my fingers as Kellan's grip grows tighter with each detail. I finally tell him during the bridge story that if he doesn't loosen up, I'll lose the use of my hand permanently.

"We'll stay here tonight," Giules says afterwards. "Maybe the Elders will not suspect we'd remain in the same place they last saw you. But I do need to check in."

"But—" I begin.

"No buts," she insists. "The search must be called off. There are a lot of people vulnerable right now because they are out looking for you. You would not wish them harm just because you do not want to be yelled at by an angry papa bear."

Jonah is still out there, of course. So I relent and don't complain any further.

All of us hear Karl shouting through the phone. Giules holds it out for the majority of the conversation, but man, she does me a favor. She tells Karl that I'm tired, but fine, and he can talk to me all he wants tomorrow when we come home, but he needs to leave me be for the night.

Kellan stays silent until we get to the ice machine down the hall. Once there, and out of earshot of our friends, he leans back against it and crosses his arms. "You will not do that again, Chloe."

His heart is in the right place. Even still, I bristle at the words. "I had to."

"I know you think you did, but I'm telling you that you didn't. Chloe, it's not worth it. You getting hurt is completely unacceptable."

"I'm not hurt," I protest, but he reaches out and turns my palms over gently. Fresh scabs riddle them from falling on the roof earlier. His eyes then track down to my scabbed knees and a good number of bruises blooming from slamming into cars as we raced across the bridge. "Those," I say quietly, "are all circumstantial."

"Notice I'm not injured," he says, and I nod vigorously.

"Exactly my point!" I say.

"I'm not injured," he stresses, "because I was stuck in that building."

"Exactly!"

"I've never been so scared in my life," he admits in a low, husky voice. "I don't know what I would've done if you'd been seriously hurt." Then I'm in his arms, and I can feel his breath in my hair, his heart against my chest. It's comforting. Safe.

I made the right choice.

chapter 27

You'd have thought I'd murdered someone by the reactions I get once home. My mother and Cousins all take turns chastising me during back-to-back strike attacks. Karl reams me during a special one-on-one. I honestly stress that he's going to have a stroke when the veins in his face and neck bulge as he gasps, shouts, and yanks at his hair. Even Iolani has her turn, albeit sounding like a kinder, quieter female Karl.

Coward that he is, my father chooses to ignore the whole affair. It stings, but I can deal with his apathy.

What I can't deal with is Jonah's reaction during a follow-up Guard meeting. I'm twisting my hands in my lap while everyone bickers (hooray for Kiah for seeing the logic in what we did!) like a family reunion on "Jerry Springer" when he catches and holds my attention. He makes no attempts at ignoring me like usual. He's flat out staring, brows furrowed and body stiff with tension. A heavy mix of disapproval, disappointment and worry rolls off of him in dark, thick waves. It's hard not to cringe.

Kellan, on the other hand, defends me as Karl howls over my perceived stupidity. This nearly sends Karl back into seizure mode. While several people try in vain to calm him down, Jonah shakes his head slowly at me, all the while holding my eyes.

His disapproval is the worst. It's beyond painful. I'm not sorry for doing what I did, but I want the chance to explain my logic to him. For the bulk of my life he's been my sounding board. Now he's an angry, silent presence that haunts me.

After the meeting, he refuses to look at me, let alone give me an opportunity to talk. I think about this while Kellan and I sit on my couch, reading for English class a few days after the attack. Well, he's reading. I'm staring at the words, willing them to give me answers.

Fact: I've come to the point where, if I don't talk to Jonah soon, I'll go batshit crazy.

Fact: I miss Jonah; even when he's standing five feet away.

Fact: I'm still in love with Jonah. There's no mistaking this.

Fact: I'm in love with his brother, too.

I peek over my book and watch Kellan. He does this cute thing when he reads, where he gently bites his lower lip and his brows squish down in super concentration. He reads with his knees propped up to balance his book. He loves to read. I love that he loves this.

The weirdest thing is that I want to talk to him about everything. I consider Kellan to be the person whom I trust the most at present. I tell him almost everything. We have no secrets, save one. And that's on me, not him.

It's sick how I want to talk to Kellan about Jonah because, of all the opinions out there, and of all the advice I can seek, I want his. How wrong is that?

"How's the book?" I ask him, taking a deep breath.

He glances up. "Interesting. You?"

The words below me laugh. They know they don't have my attention. "Can I ask you something?"

He lowers his book, sticking his finger in to mark his place. "Of course."

Two words jump out on the page. *Ask him.* I'm not kidding. They're there. "I . . . uh . . . want to ask about . . . your brother."

There's no reaction. I might as well be asking about the weather. "Yeah?"

I stare at the words some more. Words on a page seem safe. Words in the air are temperamental, fragile. You can erase a word on a page. There's no way to erase something once it leaves your lips. Words like that can make or break someone.

I scratch my head. Itchy scalps, my mother once said, are a sure sign of guilt. "Do you . . . No. What I mean is . . . does he, uh, hate me?"

Whatever Kellan might have thought I'd ask, it wasn't that. "Huh?"

"I mean," I say, scratching harder now, "he never talks to me. Why?"

"Sure he does."

"No," I insist quietly. "He doesn't."

The book in his lap slides down some. "He doesn't hate you."

I've drawn blood. Gross. "How do you know?"

His head cocks to the side, searching. I scratch harder. "Chloe," he says slowly, "has Jonah said something to you?"

"No. That's the point! He must hate me. He hates me, doesn't he? You can tell me. Has he told you that? That he hates me?"

He must. I mean, if I was Jonah, I'd hate me, too. He's probably come up with a list of nasty words to refer to me: *bitch, traitor, whore*—no, he wouldn't call me *whore*. He knows me better than that, what with me being a virgin and all. But *bitch* and *traitor*, yeah. And others that I don't want to think about because I'll probably cry.

Kellan reaches out and grabs my hand before I can completely shred my scalp. "Why would he hate you? He barely knows you."

He hates me, I think, because he knows me all too well.

Cora rarely ever sounds apologetic. She does now, though, as I struggle through math homework the next day. "You ought to know that I did something this afternoon that you're going to be super pissed about."

Honestly? This sadly doesn't seem like news. "What now?"

She mumbles incoherently over the phone before asking, "Have you heard from Kellan since school got out?"

"Not yet." And then, suspicion sets in. "Why?"

"I ran into him after school," she rushes out, "before he and Jonah left. We got to talking a little, and, well . . ."

"Well, what?"

"Listen, believe it or not, I actually respect Kellan. But, I know that even though you care about him, he's not Jonah—"

My back straightens like a board. "What did you do, Cora?"

"Ehhhh . . ." she dawdles. "Oh, hell. I told him the truth."

"WHAT?" I shriek, my legs thrusting me upright.

"I told him the truth about you and Jonah!" she says, having the audacity to sound outraged herself. "He didn't believe me, though. I thought maybe he'd go straight to you, but I guess not."

"When was this?" Kellan knows? And if he's confronting Jonah, then Jonah knows, too.

I can barely think straight as my mind explodes. During all the times I've role-played in my head what I'd say to Kellan when I finally admit the truth, I never imagined it would come from another person first.

He absolutely does not deserve that.

"About an hour and a half ago. I didn't want to call you right away, just in case it was you he went to."

"WHY did you do this?"

"Because it was the truth! And I've been thinking about it. Kellan deserves better. He deserves someone who's going to put him first, not pine for his brother constantly!"

"Who says I do that?" I hiss. She doesn't understand the first thing I feel toward Kellan—or Jonah for that matter. Since I'm not able to clearly understand it myself, how can she?

"Me! How Kellan can't tell is beyond me. What kind of Emotional is he, anyway?"

My palms are sweating, I'm so upset. "Did you do this out of spite?"

"No! I told you, I did this for you. To help you."

I pick up a lamp and throw it hard against the wall. It clips a framed picture of Cora and me, shattering the glass. Ceramic shards ricochet into a million directions. It's a satisfying feeling, smashing things.

"I hope whatever that was is going to be fixed by the time your mom comes home," Cora says.

That pisses me off some more, so I pick up what's left of the frame and throw it against the wall so hard that it disintegrates.

"I know you're angry, Chloe. But see, everything just kept staying at the status quo. Was it really that wrong for me to try to help?"

"Who made you judge and jury?" I seethe. "How could you do this?"

"What? Set you free? I did it out of love, babe. You'll thank me someday."

I hang up on her. In an effort to calm down, I rebuild the lamp and photo frame. And then I call Kellan.

I'm sent directly to voicemail. It's a bad sign—Kellan never ignores a call from me.

Why are you calling Kellan? Cora practically handed you Jonah on a silver platter. Why not go for it?

Because no matter what, Kellan doesn't deserve to be blindsided.

I storm downstairs. Karl's sitting on the couch, watching *SportsCenter*. "Just where do you think you're going?" he demands, standing up. He's still somewhat pissed off at me over the whole San Francisco debacle.

"Out."

"Where do you want me to take you?"

"Nowhere!" I snatch my bag from the basket by the door. "I'm going by myself!"

He deftly blocks the door. "If you think I'm going to let you run off by yourself again, think again."

I practically choke on the words. "Cora told Kellan the truth!"

He raises his eyebrows. "Well, well. The shit just hit the fan, didn't it?"

"Oh, thank you, Mr. *State-the-Obvious*," I snap. And then I stop. "You know?"

"Please," he says, rolling his eyes. "Why do you keep underestimating me?"

"Er . . . what exactly do you know?"

He motions toward the couch. "Let me tell you a story."

"I don't have *time* for a story!"

"You have time for this one. Sit." And rather than allow me to do so, he steers me toward the couch and sits down next to me. "Alright. You already know I have a Connection—to my wife Moira."

I nod impatiently.

"Connections are . . . complex. Well—in many regards, they are extremely simple. You and the person you're Connected to are soul mates, bound for life. But Connections are tempestuous things, apt to make people act in ways they might normally not act. Everything is heightened—love, pain, anger, joy. It can be scary and overwhelming because it's so instantaneous and strong. Some people don't know how to deal with that sort of overload on their system." He scrubs at his hair, tired.

"Karl—"

"I was one of those people, Chloe."

I let go of my purse straps and sit a bit straighter. Everything I've ever heard about Karl and Moira is the stuff of legends: they're absolutely, unequivocally in love, perfect together in every, disgusting way. "Pardon?"

"I met Moira when I was really little in my dreams."

Now *this* is interesting.

"And that first look, that first moment we spoke—I was a goner. I adored her. She was the most perfect girl alive. No one else could live up to even half of her standards. But she was a dream, and that made me crazy, right?"

It's like listening to myself talk.

"I spent a lot of time in Annar as a kid. I even did an entire year of high school in Annar. I met someone there, my junior year of high school. And . . . it wasn't Moira. But this girl and I were friends, and . . .

the friendship was good. Better than good, even. And I kept thinking I was insane for being in love with someone not real, so I let things happen with this girl, because I was *fond* of her." He sighs. "Sometimes, I even thought maybe . . . maybe there was something more than just fondness. Love, I guess—I never felt like I was *in* love with her, but yeah . . . there was a kind of love. But I was young, and confused, and completely overwhelmed by my feelings. By my Connection."

My purse slides to the floor. I leave it there.

"I moved to Annar right after high school, and the first day there, I saw Moira in the street. She was talking to another girl, and it was like a bolt of lightning struck me. She was real, she was there, and everything in me became almost too much to bear. I ran straight back to my girlfriend. She knew something was up, but I was freaking out. And then whenever I ran into Moira for another month after that, and when we talked—or, hell, touched—so many things flooded through me that I thought I was going to explode. It was too much, Chloe. Emotionally, I wasn't ready. So I clung onto my girlfriend, refused to talk to Moira much, and . . . even avoided her, much to my shame."

"Oh my gods," I whisper.

"But when push came to shove, I finally realized I couldn't do that to my girlfriend. So I broke up with her. It was awful, so messy that even today it hurts to think about the pain I caused her. But then I found Moira and begged for her forgiveness. She gave it, no strings attached. And once I allowed myself to open up to the Connection, to allow it to work the way it was supposed to, I've never looked back."

Something in my mind clicks. "Kiah."

He nods guiltily.

"But Kiah must have known you had a doorway. She knew I had one.

"She knew. But when people fall in love, sometimes you do stupid, unexplainable things."

"And . . . now?"

He looks away. "We're friends. Coworkers." He clears his throat and scrubs at his hair again. "So. That's my story. Since you happened to tell me that you and Jonah met in your dreams, I know you two have a Connection. And I'll be the first person to say that I get why you might have freaked out over Jonah being here. And . . . I'll even admit that I get why you're dating someone else. But Chloe—it's been a few months now that you've hidden behind Kellan. Frankly, I'm shocked that you aren't running to Jonah right now and begging for his forgiveness, like I did with Moira."

I slump back and close my eyes. "I want to. I really do."

"Then why go to Kellan first?"

Even though my eyes are closed, I still place a hand over them. "I love him, too."

The silence is deafening.

"It's crazy, I know . . ."

"You don't love him," Karl says. "Or, if you do, it's not the same. It's simply not possible."

I choose to ignore this. "He didn't deserve hearing about this from Cora. It should've been from me. Or Jonah."

"I agree," Karl says.

"You're right, though. It's totally overwhelming."

"I know." He hesitates. "I've talked to him, you know."

My hand drops. "Kellan?"

Karl shakes his head.

"You've talked to Jonah . . . about *me*?"

"He's one of my best friends," Karl says, a tad defensively. "And he's been acting . . . well, not like Jonah. Of course I tried to talk to him."

The pins and needles are agonizing.

"He's not dealing with this well. I mean, I get why he's not. He's not only overwhelmed like the rest of us finding our Connections, but he's dealing with the massive blow of seeing you with his brother. It's not uncommon for people to do what I did—to be with someone else in the beginning. That's . . . I hate to say it, *normal*, actually. But still, it's one thing to see your true love with another person. It's entirely different to see your soul mate with your twin."

I jerk back as if he'd slapped me.

"Those two . . ." He shakes his head. "You've never seen what they're like together, not really. They've always been inseparable. They've had a lot of shit thrown at them over the years, and they've only ever had each other to turn to. And now . . . man. They're not talking. The situation is so screwed up. Kellan knows Jonah is mad and hurt, but Jonah won't talk to him. And I get that, because when it comes to your Connection, your mind sort of just short circuits. Jonah's doing everything he can to simply hold it together right now. And he's doing it, absolutely convinced you've picked his brother over him."

The air in my lungs disappears.

"I tried talking to him about it. But Jonah's always been the kind who bottles stuff up, even as a little kid. That sort of self-preservation he'd been forced to adapt to . . ."

I choke out, "What?"

But Karl keeps going. "I asked if he'd confronted Kellan, but he said, 'What's the point? She's made her choice.' I tried to tell him I didn't think that was the case, but he wasn't willing to keep talking."

The air in the room disappears.

"Did you ever wonder why he was so insistent on getting those things, those Elders, away from us during the attacks that day? He didn't want them anywhere near you. He was willing to do whatever it took, even if it meant getting hurt, to distract them from pursuing you. You should've seen Jonah after you took off with Raul and Kopano. He held it together around the others, but when it was just him and me, he was crazed with panic. And then you went and had Kellan come and get you." Karl shakes his head again. "That poor guy."

The air in the *house* disappears.

"Breathe, Chloe," Karl says, startled by the expression on my face. He grabs my arms and yells the order at me.

I burst into tears. Right there in front of him.

Karl is clearly taken aback. It's all well and good to talk to someone about the intricacies of enormous and complex emotions, but it's an entirely different matter to see them in action. It takes him a moment to collect himself before rushing out of the room.

Just when I figure him to be a goner, he returns with a wad of tissues. He passes them over helplessly.

After about five minutes of watching me sob hysterically while awkwardly patting my arm, he tells me that, just this once, he's going to let me go somewhere by myself. He doesn't ask which brother I'll be seeing first, and for that I'm grateful.

chapter 28

Kellan's car is parked exactly where I expect. He's gone to the beach, the place where we first kissed.

He gives no indication he's willing to acknowledge me at first, so I stand next to his car, mustering the courage to speak, as I watch him lie on the hood. "We should talk about what happened today."

I worry he won't answer, but he does. "Now you want to talk?"

There's going to be no easy way out, but then, I don't deserve one. I will myself not to break down into another sobbing, pathetic mess. He's still refusing to look at me, so I reach out to touch him. "Kellan . . ."

He rolls off the car and walks over to the guardrails. The waves are crashing in the distance, loud and heavy in the chilly air. "Fine, let's talk," he snaps. I flinch, because I'm not used to him sounding like this. "What should we start with? The fact you've known my brother for the majority of your life? That you two were . . . are? An item? How I'm the last one to know? You must've had a good laugh at that, right?"

"No!"

"How about what it's like to find out I've been betrayed by the two people I stupidly trust the most?"

"I can explain," I weakly counter, not even remotely knowing how I can.

"Really." But he waits, knuckles white and tight against the rail.

I fumble for any words that can do the situation justice. "He and I . . . we met in our dreams, when we were little. I never thought he was real, not until he showed up in my math class . . . and . . . it was . . . confusing, because I thought maybe I'd gone crazy . . . and then, with the shifts—"

"Shifts!" he explodes. "That was *you?* Because of *him?*"

I cringe. The look on his face is awful, so absolutely awful. I've never seen such pain in his eyes before. I want to break down crying, beg for his forgiveness and mercy, but I know I need to stay strong and finish explaining. My voice is impossibly small: "Yes."

He turns his back on me, leaning forward against the railing. When he speaks, it's flat and unexpressive. "You've known him for thirteen years."

"Yes." Each breath is shuddery now, ready to fall apart. "I got even more confused, because I felt . . . *feel* things toward you, too . . ."

A series of protective walls seem to slam down around him as his face becomes emotionless. It's then I realize he doesn't believe me. He's got to feel it in me, but he's so hurt that his emotions are shutting down and his brain is telling him that I've lied all along.

Kellan tilts his head away, back toward the black ocean. His words are clipped, clinical. "Did you know, that in all the years you and my brother dreamed about each other, he never once mentioned you?"

I'd guessed it, of course, but even still, it hurts to hear this.

"The real kicker is how I never sensed it. Prior to today, I could've sworn I knew everything there is to know about Jonah. Now I feel like I don't know him at all."

“That’s not true,” I whisper.

Kellan pulls at his hair. “He hid you from me.” He laughs bitterly. “We never hide anything from one another. We’d hide a lot from everyone else, but never each other.”

My chest hurts from holding all of the sobs back. “I’m so sorry, so, so sorry . . .”

“I’ve known he’s been angry at me for awhile now, but he’s refused to talk about it. I didn’t know it was because of you. I felt the resentment, but . . .” He stares down at his shoes.

I wait. The air stings as it moves in and out of my tightened lungs.

“He made it difficult for me,” he continues. “I guess I have to admit there was always something I sensed when you two were around each other, but I didn’t know what it was. He scrambled it in a way, to confuse me. And I chose to ignore whatever you projected. I just . . . I guess I was so tired of trying to get him to talk that I gave up and stopped asking.”

I grapple uselessly at the railing.

“We’re twins, Chloe. There’s a bond between us. It’s sort of hard to explain to someone who’s not a twin, but it’s like we’re tethered together. Normally we can feel each other, sense what the other is thinking or feeling. He must’ve compartmentalized you deep within. I never *saw* you, not once in all those years.” Kellan holds out his hands and stares at them, as if he’s surprised they’re empty. “Jonah’s pretty tight with his emotions and thoughts. I mean, we’re Emotionals, so it sort of comes with the territory . . . But hiding things from *me*?”

The tears I’ve been trying so hard to hold in break free and drip down past my nose. I snuffle like a dying cow or something.

"I confronted him today, after talking to Cora. Jonah says you two haven't spoken yet, not once since we moved here. I guess I never really noticed that." He slides a quick glance my way. "You even asked about that the other day. So I guess the question is, why not?"

It's hard to sound coherent when all I want to do is bawl. "I . . . I d-don't know."

"Have you wanted to?"

I give a tiny nod. I lean against the guardrail, as close as possible to Kellan without touching him. I want to, desperately, but it's got to be on his terms, not mine. He grips the rail again tightly, his fingers mere inches from my body. "What are you afraid of?"

His fingers are long and beautiful. I like the way they curve over mine when he holds my hand, how they feel in my hair when we kiss, and how easily they catch my tears when I cry. How do I tell him I've been afraid to talk to Jonah because I'm afraid of becoming hollow if he disappears again? "It's killing him to not be able to talk to you."

The words come out as hiccups. "Did he . . . did he t-tell you that?"

"I know my brother. I know that much at least."

There is a small scab on one of his knuckles. I stare at it in horror. "Did you two . . . f-fight?"

He looks at the scab, too. "We argued, if that's what you're asking."

I want to let go, allow the sobs to fully break through to release the pressure in my chest, but I can't. Not here, not in front of Kellan, not even if he can feel the desperate pain in me. "Oh, oh, g-gods . . . I'm so, so s-sorry . . ."

He bites his lip. "We were once one, you know."

"One?" I manage.

“Identical twins always start out from one egg. We were a singular entity, even if it was for a tiny span of time. And now . . .”

I nod like a bobblehead doll, over and over. I want to ask him if Jonah hates me, or if he, Kellan, hates me. But I don’t. I just keep bobbing my head, chewing my lip, and trying to breathe in a way to keep the sobs at bay.

“We moved here because of you.”

The bobbing slows and then stops.

“We moved here,” he continues, “because my brother influenced my father to do so. So he could be close to you. We left Maine, our family, all our friends, our school, the house my mother designed and had built before she died—all because of *you*. Because of what you mean to him. This all makes sense to me now.”

I feel like throwing up.

He finally turns to face me. “Here’s the thing. I absolutely hate that he’s hurting right now. I hate that there’s this huge wedge between us that’s never been there before.”

What can I even say to that?

“But,” he says, “you’re right. There’s something real between you and me. And he knows it.”

I am a horrible, horrible person. I’ve just hit the grand slam in a game of shitty things a girl can do to the people she loves. “Kellan,” I choke out—but honestly? Nothing I can say is remotely good enough.

He sighs and allows my hand to wrap around his. It’s cold, and he’s tired, so tired that his eyes are shadowed by dark purple-y smudges.

“I’m so mad right now, Chloe. So unbelievably angry at all of this.”

My heart feels too heavy to bear. And then he lets the protective wall around him slip a little. Just enough for me to see the truth of his emotions. His pain, his fears, his anger and sadness, mixed tightly together—and most importantly, the love he impossibly still feels for me.

But still . . . "I need some time away." He says this even while his fingers slide between mine.

"Wh-what do you mean?"

"This is a lot right now. I need time to think about it all." His free hand tugs at his hair again.

A nameless, scary emotion claws at me. "When?"

"I think it's best I go tomorrow. After school."

Breathe, Chloe. Breathe. "Where?"

He hesitates, but tells me. "Maine."

"Oh." The lump in my throat comes right back. I can't believe he's going to leave. Even worse, I don't want him to.

Sometimes I wish he wasn't so good at sensing my feelings. I wish I could just hide my misery, because then he wouldn't feel the need to help me when he should be focusing on himself. "I'm coming back, Chloe. It'll just be for a few days."

"I know," I say, and I'm back to the bobblehead doll action. "How?"

"Airplane. Portals are quick. I want the solo time to think."

I try practicality and hope it'll help me stay calm. "Where will you stay?"

"A friend's. Or even our old house. It's empty."

Our hands have begun to grow warm together. Every other part of my body is freezing and on the verge of numbness. But not that hand. Not in his. "Can I take you to the airport?"

He agrees, and I'm not sure if it's because it's what he wants or because he thinks it's what I want or need.

Kellan is leaving. And it's all because of me.

chapter 29

Jonah doesn't come to school the next day.

Kellan and I have lunch together. It's mostly a silent affair, with the two of us sitting on a bench outside, just sort of staring at random things.

I want to ask him where Jonah is, but that seems cruel. So I ask instead, "The Guard's okay with you going? I mean, I go to San Francisco, and everyone freaks out."

"They know I'm going." *Does Jonah? He must, right?*

"Will you have a babysitter in Maine? Or is it a sentry-free zone?"

He laughs. Just a little. "I'll be fine on my own."

There's never been any tension between us before, but here it is, acting like a freshly diagnosed illness. Even still, the pull toward him is unmistakable, impossible to ignore. I figure he feels it too—even with the anger, betrayal, and hurt—because he still chooses to be with me when he really should've kicked me to the curb.

The sun is shining brightly in the chilly air when we get to the airport. Karl let me drive Kellan by myself, no arguments. I think he knew we needed this small slice of alone time together.

Not really being able to meet his eyes fully for any extended period of time, I ask, "Do you have any idea how long you'll be gone?" A man dragging two suitcases behind him pushes past us, knocking me right into Kellan.

He freezes when we touch, as if he's lost his breath. I quickly right myself and he pulls a hand through his hair, looking towards the airport doors. He ignores my question. "I should go and check in."

My lip starts quivering, and I hate myself for it. "Okay."

He sighs loudly, looking up toward the sky. "I'll miss you."

"Me, too," I say, and it's true.

Kellan pauses for moment, unsure. It's such a rare sight that the guilt in me grows even bigger.

And there I am, standing in front of him, hating that he's leaving, hating it's because of me, loving him so much it hurts while at the same time knowing that the moment he's gone, I'm going to go find Jonah.

Because it's time.

I decided that last night. Good or bad, all the cards need to be laid out on the table. Jonah and Kellan had their talk. Kellan and I had ours. Now it was finally mine and Jonah's turn.

I don't tell Kellan this, though. What I do instead is open up my heart as I wrap my arms around him and let him know how much I care. I can't say those words to him, not when things are so confusing and complicated. Not when I can't promise that when he comes back, there'll still be something between us to come back to.

We stand like that for a long time before he leans down, his lips barely brushing against mine, the tiny butterfly wings fluttering whisper soft against my heart. And then he grabs his bag and walks through the doors without looking back.

Knowing he's leaving tears at my heart.

I wait until I'm back in my car to pull out my phone. If I don't make the call now, I know I'll never have the courage to do it.

Jonah doesn't answer his cell. It immediately goes to voicemail, and it's a good thing I'm already sitting, because his voice makes my knees go weak. I don't leave a message, though. Everything I have to say needs to be done in person. I can't take the easy way out.

So I call Karl next, cutting to the chase. "Where's Jonah?"

"Off to make amends?"

Har-har. "Just tell me where he is, please."

"Actually, I have no idea. Giules gave him the day off despite my protests."

"What?" I snap. "Why does he get a free pass when I don't?"

"What the hell do you think you're getting right now?"

Giules yells out in the background that she doesn't know where Jonah is, either. "You're on your own," Karl says, before ordering me to call within the next hour to check in.

I wrack my head, trying to figure out where Jonah would go. I decide to try the beach, thinking maybe he's like his brother and goes there when he's upset, too. I'm halfway there when I spot his car parked by the side of the road, near a hiking trail leading into the woods. My car skids to a stop in the middle of the street.

He'd come to a forest. Why hadn't I immediately guessed that, considering the bulk of our dreams together happened in forests? And almost all of them by some sort of water, be it lake or river or stream. There are several streams in these woods.

I park next to his SUV. The hood is cold, meaning Jonah's probably been here awhile.

"Well, well," someone says. "Look at what the cat finally drug around."

Caleb's sitting on top of Jonah's SUV. His legs are straight out, his arms propping him up from behind.

I mutter, "Smartass."

He laughs. "Do you want to know where he is?"

I squint at the trail in front of us. "You've seen Jonah?"

"Sure. He's been here all day."

Seriously? I mean, Karl said Giules had given Jonah free rein, but a whole day of no Guard seems implausible. "What's he been doing?"

"It's not like we've been hanging out," Caleb says as he stands up. "But I'll tell you he's not as alone as he thinks." He walks over to the edge of the car, waving me closer. "There's a Guard out there—Faerie, to be exact—watching him right now. You think that big lug babysitting you would ever let you two be unguarded? Please. You've had one on your tail all afternoon. Look," he says, pointing to my car. "He's hiding behind your side mirror. Hey, buddy! How's it going?"

He waves cheerfully, and the Faerie scowls in return.

Caleb leads me down the trail. The Guard follows at a respectable distance, but I still bark out an order for him to stay back, reminding him that just because he's babysitting, it doesn't give him any right to eavesdrop. "Tell that to the other Guard out there, too," I tell him.

The Guard shrugs, but he pulls out his cell phone to make the call.

We hike about a mile before Caleb stops and hovers over the trail. He points toward a particularly large tree shading a stream. "He's down there, hon."

Sure enough, Jonah's sitting under the tree, reading. He's got his knees up to prop up his book, looking so much like Kellan does when reading that my heart squeezes hard. But he's not Kellan. He's Jonah. He's the person I've known and loved my whole life.

I've been so stupid. Why had I tried to fool myself these last few months, thinking that I could ever do without him?

There he is. Within easy reach.

Before he leaves, Caleb tells me where he's going to be, just in case I need him. I'm really hoping I don't, but I'm starting to get panicky, because there's a chance Jonah will reject me outright. There's an excellent chance he'll tell me to go to hell. Even worse, he might continue to pretend I don't exist. No matter what, though, I know I've gotta go over there and give this my best try. I love him. I can't live without him anymore. He needs to hear this even if he can easily live without me.

Wait.

Just why hasn't he talked to me? Why hasn't he approached me even once over the last few months? Why didn't he come to me, fight for me, do anything at all?

He'd told me, time and time again in our dreams, that it was his greatest wish to be with me in real life, that he'd give anything to make it happen. And Kellan even claimed Jonah worked his mojo on their dad to move here. So . . . why hasn't Jonah done anything?

Hot tears spring to my eyes. I'm rooted to this spot, unable to move, unable to talk, helpless and angry, ready to both freeze and explode. Why hasn't he done anything?

Each time I ask myself this question, I lose a little bit of my courage. My heart is on the verge of blowing sky wide. He hasn't done *anything.*

I don't know how long I stand there, fists balled up, silent tears falling like rain. The Guard watching must think I'm a complete lunatic. But then one of my sobs escapes, and Jonah finally notices me.

And then he looks away, scanning the area around me, most likely wanting to see if I've brought an entourage.

So I speak to him, for the first time in well over a year. It's a lame thing to say, but I call out, "It's just me."

There's an uncertainty on his face, a mixture of confusion and wariness clouding those cerulean eyes of his when he stands up. I tremble the entire time it takes for him to walk over to me. He stops a few feet away, just out of hand's reach. We stand there staring at one another, neither blinking, before he says my name.

His voice hits me hard. And the fact that he's finally talking to me? Overwhelming. But I'm an irrational mess, so rather than swoon, I demand, "Why didn't you *do* anything?" Jonah flinches, but I'm in rare form. "All these months," I continue, "you've done *nothing!* Not a word! Not *one!*"

The little voice disapproves, of course. *Hypocrite, thy name is Chloe. He can lay the same claim about you, you know.*

"Chloe," Jonah says again, and the trembling intensifies. He takes a step toward me, and my feet uproot. I stumble backwards, but he reaches out and catches me.

His touch is a massive shock to my system, like when doctors use those paddles to shock a heart back into rhythm. I continue to shake as he pulls me into his arms, and then I cry in earnest.

Because being here with him is like coming home after being gone for so very long. Everything about him is so familiar: his smell, warm and lovely, the way his head feels against mine, the crook in his neck that my forehead fits perfectly into, his fingers spread across my back, and, most importantly, his heartbeat against mine.

I'm finally where I'm supposed to be. I don't have to ask to know he's feeling this, too. His breath is uneven against my neck, his heart racing in tandem with mine.

I'm at a large loss for words—like I'd been when we'd first found each other all those years ago—when I pull myself together. And each time his thumb grazes my skin, shockwaves jolt my system. It's literally taking everything in me to remain standing.

"I'm sorry if I've hurt you," he says quietly, and I shudder hard in his arms. "I thought I was doing you a favor by staying away."

He has no place to apologize, even though I'd just yelled at him for his inaction. But I'm intrigued by what he means. "Favor?"

"That first day, you were so unwilling to even acknowledge me," he says, voice hushed. "I was . . . terrified. I didn't know to do. None of this went down the way I thought . . . *hoped* it would." He pauses. "You weren't the only one who was overwhelmed. I was, too. These last two months, I really haven't had the best grip on my emotions, and that sort of sent me into a tailspin." He pauses again. "I also didn't want to push you into anything you weren't ready for."

I tell him the truth, of how I thought I'd gone nuts that first day.

"I can see why. It's not every day you actually see someone you've only ever dreamed about."

A million questions flood me, so I just randomly grab at one. "Why did you disappear last year?"

He looks so sad. "I don't know why. It just became harder and harder to find you, until one day, I just wasn't able to anymore."

A month before he'd disappeared from my dreams, we'd been standing in a lake, neither of us caring that our clothes were soaking. The sky was a vivid blue, streaked with oranges and reds at the horizon—a sunset that told me sunrise was coming. These were my least favorite moments of the day, knowing my time with him was up.

"I wish I could control time," I'd told him. "Then I'd make sure we could be here forever. Together."

"Yeah?" he'd asked, resting his head against mine. There was a soft breeze blowing across the lake, warm and gentle. His hair, so very like strands of silk, ruffled against my cheek. I loved that feeling. Craved it.

"Most definitely."

"I wish I could cement the door here, so it wouldn't be so hard to find."

That surprised me. "What door?"

He'd laughed. "The one I use to leave my dreams to come to yours."

At the time, I'd chalked that up to wishful thinking. "How did you discover the door?"

"I think the first time, I was dreaming about a playground. A ball I was playing with rolled into some trees nearby. I went to look for it, and found a door instead."

"Did you go through it that night?"

"No. It took me a few nights to dream myself to the door and then to clear away all the plants blocking it. And then the night after I finally had it cleared, I sat and stared at the door for a long time. I was scared at first, I think. But sooner or later, curiosity got the better of me and I went through it." And then the sky had turned orangeish-purple, and a

loud sound pulled me away from him, with everything rushing backwards and forwards at the same time.

But now, Jonah's here with me, and we're both awake. It's almost too much to bear.

"Then, it wasn't by choice?"

"No," he says, startled. "Is that what you thought?"

"I didn't know what to think. I still don't know what to think. How is this possible? Why are you here? How are you real? Oh my gods, you're *real*." I marvel at being able to really, truly touch him. It's heaven.

His hands, warm and strong, cup my cheeks. I stare into his gorgeous eyes while he says, "Chloe don't you know, haven't you always known? My heart belongs with you. I'm here for you."

Joy crashes through me, and I lose my breath as I begin to free-fall. I am beyond giddy.

I am in love.

Karl was so right. When you let go and allow the Connection to take place, it's worth everything.

"Did you miss me at all?" I ask, running my fingers through his hair. Goose bumps race across my skin.

"You'd question that, after everything we've ever meant to one another?" he asks, exasperated. This isn't a new sort of reaction from Jonah. Questions like this, he'd once insisted, should never be asked, because I should always trust in his feelings for me. And I hadn't over the last two months. I'd been so stupid to even doubt him. "Of course. Every moment of every day."

"How did you discover the truth?"

He smiles sheepishly; my heart to skips in delight. "A Seer told me. I sort of had a difficult time after losing you. The Old Man . . . my father . . . made me go to one to see if it'd get me back on track. She saw our Connection, told me you were real. I was shocked. All those years, I'd hoped and prayed you were, but I never really thought you could be. And then, when I learned you were out there, I couldn't rest until I found you. I didn't have much to go on, though. All the Seer could tell me was that you were a Magical, too. So it took me nearly four months to figure out your location."

I consider this. "Why didn't you call me when you first figured it out?"

"I wanted to. I actually had your number. But I thought it'd be better in person, that you might not believe me on the phone. So I manipulated my father into moving here."

I'd known this, but I still laugh, because this seems like such a Jonah thing to do. Over the years, I'd learned that when he gets his mind set on something, he can become very determined.

His fingers trail down my cheek. "When I first saw you—"

"There was a shift," I supply, grinning.

He nods, smiling slyly. "Three. Don't think I didn't count them."

I laugh against his shoulder. "And where were yours?"

"The day I found out you were real," he says, and I squeal because I'm so surprised and pleased by this. "And then on the day I found where you were."

"So why three for me?" He shrugs, unconcerned. So I prompt, "You were saying . . .? When you first saw me?"

"It was like I'd finally come home," he says, and I melt. But then he adds more seriously, "It wasn't easy staying away, not after finding you.

I have to admit, I nearly lost hope recently . . . I began to wonder if maybe I'd been the only one who'd ever felt the Connection."

"No, no, *no*," I insist, holding him tight against me, willing him to feel our bond, strong as always. "Jonah, I am so sorry. To think I could have lost you, due to—"

"Don't." Tiny stress lines cross his forehead. "I don't want to do that conversation right now. I don't want to fight so soon after getting you back."

I desperately want to talk to him about the last few months, to explain myself as best I can. I don't want this to be something that festers between us any longer, but I hold back like he asks. He's not ready to hear it. Or maybe he already knows a lot of it anyway, thanks to his brother. Maybe he doesn't even want to know, ever.

Instead, I tell him, "I've missed you."

"Me, too," he says gently against my neck. And then his lips are there, so soft against my skin. My heart is ready to break through my rib cage. One more kiss grazes where my neck and shoulder meet before I remember we're not alone.

It takes all my focus to tell him we're being watched. He pulls away to look around. "By whom?"

"Two Guard. Both Faerie."

His eyes scan the trees around us as he slides a hand off my back so he can dig his cell out of his pocket. But he doesn't let go of me, and I'm glad for it. "Karl?" he says into the phone. "Chloe and I are going to my house. Let your Guards know that no one is allowed inside for the next several hours. If I find them in there, I'll put them asleep so fast they won't know what hit them."

I laugh against his shoulder.

"I'm talking about you and Giules, too," Jonah continues. He listens to Karl for a moment. "Fine. You two or these Faeries or whomever else it is you expect to watch us can do it from outside, preferably from the inside of a car." Then he turns his phone off and slips it back into his pocket. "Ready?"

"How," I ask, absolutely amazed, "do you get away with ordering him around like that?"

He grins. Gods, I love that dimple. "Maybe it's because we've known each other for a long time. And maybe it's because he knows I don't make idle threats."

"You can do that? Put someone to sleep? Have you put him to sleep before?"

"I can and I have. It's best to deal with Karl Graystone in a way where he's forced to respect your ideas and wishes." He shrugs, and I marvel at his confidence. It's so fricking sexy.

"What's it like living with Giuliana?"

His fingers tighten around mine. "She's a pretty typical Guard, takes her job seriously and all that. She likes to torture me with foreign girly movies all the time. You don't know how often I go to bed early just to escape them. There's a small perk, though—she's a pretty good cook, being Italian and all. But she hovers. It can be annoying, even though I like her a lot."

"I really dig Karl," I admit. "But I hate having a babysitter and being told what to do, when to do it, and how it has to be done."

"I know," he says sympathetically. "But it's necessary, and only for the rest of the school year."

"Why does nobody believe I can take care of myself?"

We reach his car. He takes both of my hands and says in a low voice, "I'm not sorry that Karl is there making sure you stay safe, Chloe. These things, these Elders—they're a threat we need to take seriously." I open my mouth to form a rebuttal, but he plays dirty by touching his fingers against my lips. Oh, my. "But, let's not talk about that; at least, not now. I haven't had you all to myself in a very long time, and I think that needs to be rectified, don't you?"

All I can do is nod and hope that my knees don't give out.

chapter 30

The Whitecombs' house is a large bungalow, dark brown in color and at least three stories. This is my first time inside—for all the months that Kellan and I dated, I'd always insisted we hang out at my house. I'd been afraid to running into Jonah then—which, upon reflection, was the most ridiculous, illogical fear ever.

The house is excessively neat, with precious few knick-knacks and photos. In fact, there's only one photograph in the entire living room, up on the fireplace mantle. I pick it up as Jonah switches on a couple lights. It's of a family of four, smiling for the camera. "Is this your mother?" I ask, pointing to an absurdly beautiful woman.

He takes the picture out of my hand and stares at it for a moment, his face guarded. "Yeah," he says quietly. "I think we were maybe three here."

I wait for him to tell me more, maybe something about his dead mother, but he doesn't. Instead, he leads us to the back of the house and into a whitewashed kitchen. "Wow," I say, looking around at the expansive space, "this is huge, like restaurant-sized. Does your dad like to cook?"

He laughs, at ease once more, and pours us two glasses of water. "Uh, no. If we want to eat anything, we fix it ourselves or beg Giules to work her magic."

I sip my water and give him a flirty smile. “Ugh. I can’t cook at all.”

We stand there smiling at each other, our fingers twiddling together on the countertop. I’m giddy just to be in his presence. And, because I want to see where he spends his time, peek at his CDs, look at his library—get all of the little information that will help solidify my knowledge of him—I ask, “Where’s your room?”

He’s definitely amused. “Upstairs.”

I spy a staircase right outside the kitchen doorway. Without another word, I take off towards it. We race up the second floor, laughing and pushing each other out of the way. I make it through the first door on the right; Jonah follows not a second later, grabbing me around the waist. I hook a foot around his leg and we lose our balance and fall on the nearby bed, collapsing in gasps and giggles. It’s something we’d done dozens of times since we were little. I’d always found ways to slow him down—I never knew if it was because he lets me win or because I genuinely know how to outsmart him.

“You’re such a bad cheat!” Jonah rolls onto his side to prop himself up on an elbow. “First the head start, and then pushing me out of the way. You never change.”

I feel lighter than I have in a very long time. “I never cheat!” He lifts an eyebrow up, regarding me with such an unbelieving look that I crack up. “Like you didn’t know I’d try to slow you down on the way up here. You’re no better, though.”

“You think?”

I lean closer, savoring how my body is buzzing from being so near to his. “You showed up at school, leaving me to worry I was crazy, while you knew all the while exactly everything that was happening. Not to mention your own admission that you used your mojo on your father.”

He pretends to consider this. "I guess you're right about the last one. Although, couldn't we just chalk that up to Fate and not cheats?"

I sit up dramatically, rising to my knees on the bed. "Fate, my foot." I like the easy banter between us, exactly as it's always been. It's like the last year and couple months have been erased.

He also rises up on his knees. "Maybe I cheated a little, especially with how I came to be in this town. Can you blame me?"

There's this rush of intensity pumping throughout my entire body when he skims his hands lightly down my arms. "No," I whisper, the teasing fading as I reach out to feel the softness of his sweater. He pulls me closer, and life as I know it ceases to exist.

Fireworks explode in my head, all intense yellows, reds and oranges. This isn't our first kiss, not by any long shot. It's been way too long since the last, yet the distance makes this one all the better for it.

I give myself over completely to the moment. I can't focus on anything other than him and what he's doing to me. He tastes so amazingly good. The way he kisses me is divine. I want him, in every way possible. And the things he does with his hands . . . It's almost as if we literally can't get enough of each other. I drop down onto the bed, pulling him with me. My hands snake up under his sweater, my fingers tracing patterns across his smooth skin. He shudders in a way that tells me he wants me just as much as I want him.

And I do want him, with an intensity that is awe-inspiring.

I don't even know if I can explain it rationally, but I need to see if it's the same for him. I reach out and hold his face in both of my hands. "Tell me what you're thinking, what you're feeling right now."

The dimple appears. It's Chloe kryptonite. "Look for yourself."

The mere idea of surging with him is exciting. I've never seen the contents of his mind before, as I'd always been too paralyzed to even try in person and it wasn't possible to do in dreams. I surge and am delighted to find a mirror of my own feelings: joy, passion, love and an absolute knowledge of being where he's supposed to be.

With me.

It's almost too much to handle, because I know I'm so damn lucky that he still feels this way about me. Because I love him so much it hurts.

I can't believe I risked losing him.

I'm about to pull out of his mind when he threads his fingers into my hair, twirling ropes around his fingers. "Don't leave yet," he murmurs. And then, "Go farther. Deeper."

I do so, and then he surges, going equally as far in my mind as I'm in his. The intertwining—no, merging of our minds, and to my surprise, our souls, is unlike anything I've ever felt before.

It rocks my entire existence.

There's no flipping through memories, no looking for ideas or events. It's all about our emotions, of how much we love each other and how inexplicably and tightly Connected we are to one another. I'm flying, every single part of my body singing and burning, and it's all because of him. I don't really have any prior experience to compare it to, but I'm pretty sure that whatever this is, it's far, far better than sex ever can be. And this is in addition to the assumption that sex with Jonah would be *amazing*.

We are kissing again, and it's hotter than before. I want to drown in him, in what he makes my body and heart feel.

Afterwards, I am breathless, incapable of words or even coherent thought for several minutes. He's the same, so we end up simply staring into each other's eyes. When my voice returns, I ask, "What was that?"

"Us," he says quietly before kissing me again, so softly. "Us together."

Is it a Connection thing? "My father has always said that it's impossible for Magicals to surge at the same time, that minds and souls can't handle such a thing."

He laughs quietly. "Well, I kind of doubt he would encourage such a thing. I mean, what kind of dad tells their daughter: *Wanna hear about something you can do with your boyfriend that'll literally blow your mind?*"

Did he just say boyfriend? Swoon! "Is that what I did? Did I blow your mind?"

His answer is another soft laugh. He rolls onto his back, bringing me with him so I'm now looking down at his face.

Suddenly, I feel a wild streak of possessiveness. "Have you ever done this with anyone before?"

"And if I said yes?"

I can't even respond to that. I just sort of make a bunch of gasping sounds.

He leans up to kiss me. "Chloe. Don't be ridiculous. Besides, from what I've been told, it's only possible to do with one person, only the absolute right person for you. The one you're Connected to."

So it *is* a Connection thing. His words touch me in a deep, solid way. "Is that how you see me?"

His answer is to kiss me senseless, which is a very good answer, indeed.

Later on, I take a look around. "Is this your room?"

"Yep," he says, and I roll off of him to sit up.

Jonah's room, painted dark green, is much like the rest of the house: minimalist to the extreme. The only thing that sort of looks even remotely teenage-ish is a large print of a surfer hanging over his bed.

I stand up and stretch. "I'm so glad I'm here with you right now. I can't believe I'm in your bedroom."

He props himself up on his elbows. "I remember the first time I saw you, it seemed to take forever before you talked to me. Sort of like now, I guess. I worried for so long back then, too. I just had to keep holding out hope that you'd come to your senses."

I grin at him while randomly picking things up off his desk to look at. "I've never been able to come to my senses around you, Jonah."

He watches me move throughout his bedroom, studying even the smallest objects. Everything has a place in his room. His books and CDs are alphabetized. There are a few pictures sitting on his bookshelf. One is of Jonah, maybe ten years ago. I pick it up and tap the glass. "I remember this shirt you're wearing. It was your favorite."

He comes up behind me and looks at the photo. "Hm. I don't really remember it."

"I do," I insist. He'd worn it a lot in our dreams when we were in first or second grade. "You know," I say softly as I set the picture down, "I cried when you left."

"I'm sorry," he murmurs, eyes crinkled with concern. "I don't ever want to be the reason you cry."

"Crying is in my nature. Good luck trying to change that."

His chin comes to rest on my shoulder. "I would never want to change you."

There's another picture on his bookshelf, a fairly recent one of him and his brother. They're standing on a beach, three surfboards propped up in the sand behind them. Kellan sports his typically sly grin, while Jonah's smile is more even.

My chest grows heavy with guilt and confusion. "I'm not perfect. I think you know that pretty well by now."

"Is anyone?"

And then, because his faith in me is so undeserved, I say in the tiniest voice possible, "What about what happened with your brother?"

He tenses, but he doesn't move away. Silence fills the room, and I hate waiting, hate not knowing what he's thinking. But I won't surge, because if he wants me to know something, he'll tell me.

Eventually, he says in a remarkably calm voice, "It's like I said before. I don't want to talk about that right now."

I'm wondering how in the worlds he can so easily forgive me when he adds, "You have a large heart, and I would've been surprised if you hadn't found much to love in my brother."

Tears threaten to appear. "But . . . what about . . . ?"

"Are you happy right now, being here with me?"

"Of course." I am beyond happy. Ecstatic is a much better word.

"And would you say . . . that *this* is where you want to be?"

It's implied. Here, with *him.* "Absolutely."

"Then what I said earlier stands true—it's enough for me at the moment."

I do as he asks and let it go for now.

chapter 31

Giuliana brings Karl to Jonah's house close to midnight. My Guard friend is insisting he drive me home at such a late hour. Neither of them asks why I'm with Jonah when they come in, nor do they seem surprised.

We stand in the kitchen, discussing recent intel they've received. "There was a special Council meeting yesterday," Karl says as Giuliana rummages around the fridge. "Let me tell you, after Oliver Crocus presented all of Alex's findings, there was a shitstorm of screaming and accusations about why it took a seventeen-year-old to figure this out instead of a whole department of Intellectuals." He gives me a wry smile. "Your dad got his ass chewed out big time."

I try not to laugh.

"Has the Guard come up with a plan on how to deal with these things?" Jonah asks, and I stretch out my fingers and lace them in his. It feels weird to not to be touching him somehow.

"They're working on it," Karl says, eyeing our hands. "They're sending out warnings to all the planes in the meantime."

Giuliana adds, "I'm afraid your days of solo trips are long gone now."

"What solo trips?" I ask sweetly. "If I'm not mistaken, you still sent Guard after us today. Just because they're small, don't think they don't count."

She's totally unfazed by this. "No one guaranteed you'd be left alone. We simply said that *we* wouldn't go with you today."

If Karl has an opinion on this, he doesn't let on. "I'm sure the Guard will find a solution on how to combat these things."

Giuliana pulls out a glass container out of the fridge and shakes it at Jonah. "You have not eaten!"

Jonah shrugs. "I was distracted."

I blush straight to my roots. Giuliana's muttering under her breath in Italian as she shoves the dish into the microwave. "Since Chloe's going home, you will eat it now."

This is Karl's cue. He holds out his hand to me. "Give me your keys. I'll go warm the car up. Be outside in two minutes."

I roll my eyes and hand over the keys without protest. Jonah and I follow Karl out to the living room, stopping at the door when he goes outside. "So," I murmur, "I guess this means I have to go with him, right?"

Jonah takes my hands in his. "It's pretty late, and you've got to be tired."

"Not so much." I don't want let go of Jonah just yet, considering I've gone over a year without him.

He must sense my reluctance, because he says, "I'll be over tomorrow morning around nine, all right?"

It's not a question or a request. He's telling me he'll be there for sure. I like that. "Good. Don't be late."

"Giules is always on time. She's the epitome of a morning person. I haven't gotten to sleep past seven-thirty in months."

"Then why not eight?"

"Because *I* am not a morning person. You won't want me around before I've had enough time to wake up."

"Yes. I do," I insist. I don't care if he's grumpy. Just being with him will be enough.

"You'll get sick of me," he teases.

"Never." I tell him this in his ear. He shivers when my breath hits his skin. "We've lost too much time together as it is. I won't lose out on any more."

His smile borders on smug. "You sure?"

"Absolutely. You?"

"You're kidding, right?" he asks, kissing me to prove his point.

My parents are home and eating breakfast in the kitchen. I try not to be taken aback by their presence. "Jonah Whitecomb is coming over this morning," I say as I fix myself a cup of tea.

This gets my mother's attention. Neither she nor my father has met Jonah yet. "Oh? Where's Kellan?"

Like she cares. In the last two months, she's said, at the most, twenty words to Kellan. Even still, I tell her, while it isn't technically true yet, "We broke up."

"When did this happen?" she asks.

From where he's standing, drinking his coffee, I can see Karl's eyebrows rise. I shoot him a look, warning him to keep his trap shut.

My father saves me by interrupting to ask Karl to drive him to the portal this morning. Surprise, surprise, he's already needed back in Annar, for another round of meetings concerning the Elders.

While they're discussing this, I say quietly to my mom, "I want you to be nice to Jonah, please. And don't embarrass me."

"We never embarrass you, Chloe."

Shocker! Parents *never* think they embarrass their children.

"And do me a favor," I continue. "Don't talk about Kellan, alright?"

"Why would we talk about Kellan?" my father asks, pushing up his glasses as he turns away from Karl. "Wait—who is Kellan?"

I sigh. "Kellan is Jonah's twin brother, Dad."

"Why are we not allowed to discuss him?"

It pisses me off that, in all the months I dated Kellan, my father never bothered to acknowledge him. Thinking about Kellan, even in this small way, though, hurts. I clamp down on the pain and try desperately to push all my happy memories of him into a box. I can't let them distract me anymore, not with Jonah so easily willing to forgive me.

When Jonah and Giules show up, I send Giules Karl's way so I can linger with Jonah alone in the living room before having to introduce him to my parents. He's got this husky, scratchy morning voice that is beyond foxy. The way he says *Good morning* . . . Yum.

"Now that you're here," I say cheerfully, "it's a great morning."

He leans over and kisses me, nice and slow. My insides go crazy, and I have to remind myself that my parents are nearby in the kitchen.

"Mornings," he says softly, "are never anything to get excited about. But I'll admit, this is the first one I've looked forward to in a long time."

My parents are uncharacteristically curious when I bring him into the kitchen. My father studies Jonah like he's one of his books. I think my mother, on the other hand, sees him as a puzzle.

"Your father is a great man," my father finally says, standing up and patting Jonah on the shoulder. "Right. You're one of the twins. Excellent. We expect a lot from you two."

I expect Jonah to tense at the mention of his brother, but he's all ease and charm, not bothered in the slightest. He chats for a few minutes with my mother, answering all of her fake attempts at "Concerned Parent Questions" before Karl and Giuliana come back into the room. Giules announces she'll stay at the house with us while Karl drives my father to the portal.

She also brought breakfast for us, which is a fantastic treat. Karl looks like he's in heaven; I guess he and his wife are big-time foodies who constantly try to outcook one another. Giules regales us with stories of how well the Guard eats when these competitions come up. In fact, she reveals, the pastries she's brought are from Moira. A Guard snuck them in early this morning to surprise her husband. Karl is beyond pleased.

After my dad and Karl leave, Jonah and I escape to my room. We spend the entire day together, kissing and talking and kissing and catching up in every way possible. It's amazing to be able to do these things with him after a too-long absence. He's wrong thinking I could ever get tired of him. It's impossible. Never would happen.

We leave the house when dinner rolls around, and really only because Karl and Giules insist on eating at the diner. They were banned from my room the entire day, and playing video games only held boredom at bay for so long. They want company, they tell us. Company, they add, of people under the age of forty.

I'd always known that Karl was close with Kellan, but until now had never gotten the opportunity to see him interacting much with Jonah. They have an easy shorthand between them, and it's clear that Karl very much respects Jonah's ideas and opinions and vice versa.

Halfway through dinner, Cora and Alex appear next to the table, as if by magic. "Well now," she drawls, eyeing Jonah and I slyly. "Was there a party that I didn't know about?" And I'm surprised that she can tell it's Jonah, not Kellan, right off the bat, as she greets him by name, which only serves to confuse Alex.

The next thing I know, they're joining us at our table. "What are you two up to tonight?" I ask casually, hyper aware of Jonah's arm around my shoulders. He doesn't seem to care or notice that Alex and Cora are blatantly staring at us.

"We're going to the movies," Alex says, dark eyes focused laser sharp on Jonah's arm, "to see some new foreign film Cora's been babbling about. Meg's going to meet us there after cheer practice."

Jonah rolls his eyes as Giuliana squeals. She's so sophisticated, though, that she makes squealing a charming thing. "Is it the French movie?" she presses. "I have tried often to get Jonah here to go and see it, but he refuses me every time." She pouts with puppy-dog eyes that can probably sway just about any man in the vicinity to do anything she asks.

Anyone, apparently, but Jonah.

"Would you turn me down, too?" I attempt to mimic Giuliana's puppy-dog cuteness, but I'm positive I fail miserably.

He asks warily, "Are you saying you want to see it?"

"Maybe," I lie. The truth is I have no idea what movie they're talking about. Besides, I'm more of a romantic comedy kind of girl. "Would you go?"

He sighs and then laughs. "I guess so, if you insisted."

"That is just wrong!" Giuliana gasps. "No fair!"

Jonah shrugs, unconcerned. He's got this great shrug that is so boyish and charming.

Cora laughs outright, prompting Alex to say, clearly unable to stand it anymore, "I know I constantly insist I don't care about dating statistics, but Chloe, c'mon . . . Are you two dating now?"

This makes Cora laugh even harder. Even Karl is snickering. I blush and explain to Jonah, "Being the only guy around for a long time has not made Alex any more sympathetic toward our dating lives."

Alex leans forward against the table. "Yeah, but that still doesn't answer my question."

I must be a mortifying shade of red now. "Fine. Yes."

There. Despite the fact that we'd only reconnected the day before, I've let everyone present know that my feelings for Jonah are serious. Because they are. Very much so.

He squeezes my shoulder and I lean into him a little more. Jonah, for his part, seems utterly at ease with this conversation. Smug, even. But in a good way.

"It's about time," Cora snarks.

"What?" Alex asks, surprised.

She shakes her head, exasperated. "Gods, Alex. Get your head out of a book every so often, will you? Remember those shifts?"

He thinks about it for a moment. "Those were because of these two?"

"Give the boy a prize," Cora says, reaching over and stealing some of my fries. "Now, where's the waitress?"

Karl and I go to Jonah's house the next morning. He's quiet, although clearly making an effort to talk when I know he'd prefer not to. "How do you deal with your first few classes in the morning?" I ask, lounging next to him on his bed.

He yawns. "I don't speak."

"Never?"

"Only if I get called on. And even then, it's rare. I . . . uh . . ." He pauses, laughing in a guilty way.

"You what?"

"I sort of make the teachers leave me alone. It's just best that way."

I laugh and nudge his shoulder. "See? You're a cheat. Just like I said."

He tries to argue the point, but I've got him this time, and he knows it.

We spend all of Sunday together, part of the time at his house, part of the time hanging out in town and having lunch, and then finally ending up at my house. Karl and Giuliana are constantly present, although they try their best to stay out of our way.

We're sitting on my couch, watching a girly sort of movie. It was pretty cute, Jonah protested half-heartedly when I'd picked it. But I tried Giuliana's puppy-dog eyes once more, and this time, without an audience, he totally caved in.

We snuggle under a blanket. It's a delicious feeling, all cozy and happy. Even still . . . "How do you think we're going to explain this?" I murmur.

"What, how you've convinced me to watch this movie?" he asks, jokingly grimacing. "You realize this will only fuel Giules, of course. She'll never accept me saying no again."

"No." I pull his arms even tighter around me. "I mean us."

“I’m assuming that most of your friends already know about us, thanks to Cora and Alex.”

I had, in fact, received texts from both Lizzie and Meg demanding additional info earlier. I’d ignored them, though, knowing Cora could fill everyone in just as well as I could. And Caleb had showed up, acting like a protective big brother, demanding an introduction just a couple hours before.

“I’m not talking about them,” I say. “I meant school. After all, most people assume . . . you know . . . that I’m . . . dating . . . uh . . .”

The silence between us is awkward at best before Jonah says, “Hmm. Yeah, I can see how it’ll be confusing and weird. Maybe you’ll be recommended for a daytime talk show: *Girl Dates Twin Brothers at Same Time.*”

“I am not!”

“Did you let Kel know that when you dropped him off at the airport on Friday?”

Crap. I squirm uncomfortably. “Not exactly.”

He lifts an eyebrow. “Not exactly?”

“Well, *no* then,” I say miserably. “But I plan to as soon as I see him. I’ve thought about calling him, but it would be . . . I dunno, disrespectful. Besides, he asked for space.”

“Fair enough,” Jonah agrees quietly. “He’d appreciate that.”

“Are you mad?” I’m afraid to look at him, worried at what I might see.

He sighs. “Am I disappointed that you two are technically still dating? Yes. Am I mad about it? Yes. But it is what it is.”

We'd gone almost two days without talking about this. Two days too long for me and two days not long enough for him. "I don't want you to be mad," I whisper sadly.

"Do you plan on telling him?"

"Of course. The moment I see him." I chew on my bottom lip, fretting. "Have you talked to him?"

"No." Jonah sounds tired, almost resignedly so.

"Why?"

"What will I say? It's a hard thing, knowing my actions and words will only cause our rift to grow wider. And it will, Chloe. There's no doubt about it."

Guilt hammers at me harder than even before. This is all my fault.

"Look," he says, and I twist around so we're now facing one another, "I'm not sorry you're here with me. I am absolutely not sorry about anything that's happened this weekend. I will never be sorry for loving you, and I hope you feel the same way. I'm only sorry that Kellan is a casualty of the poor choices I made when we first got here. Maybe if I'd insisted on us talking that first day, none of this would be a problem."

He's just said, out loud, outside of our dreams, for the first time that he loves me. I'd be positively gleeful if we weren't discussing how I was about to smash his brother's heart to smithereens. I take a deep breath. "I know you wanted to wait to talk about this, but I'd really like to talk to you about Kellan, about what's happened between us."

He stiffens. I straddle him on the couch so he can see my face as I tell him this. I need him to see, that despite everything, I'm here with *him*. I want him to feel everything in me that will assure him that what I have to say will be okay. It's tense and reluctant, but he agrees to hear me out.

I take a deep breath. I haven't talked about this with anyone. The closest has been with Kellan, but even then, I didn't tell him everything. "For the last year, I've been . . . angry, I guess. I've had a hard time with the lack of choices in my life, of how everything's already mapped out and dictated to me without anyone ever asking what it is *I* want. My parents have a ridiculous number of expectations about who I ought to be, how I ought to act in school, without ever clarifying said expectations. And I'd lost you. It was like the one thing that'd ever been mine, and not Fate's, was gone. It only caused me to act out even more. Things felt as if they were closing in on me from all sides. To know I'm going to be removed from everything I know at eighteen . . ." I pause, swallowing hard. "It sometimes feels like a death sentence. I was close to a breakdown when you first showed up, and when I saw you—like I said before—it was a shock. I mean, there were shifts. I didn't know how to deal with it all. I was completely overwhelmed. Lizzie and Cora tried to talk to me about it, but I just couldn't handle it."

He looks away. "You do realize that we're connected by Fate. It's how we were able to find each other in our dreams. I'm yours because of Fate."

I hadn't thought about it this way. But I do now. And surprisingly, I'm not angry and resentful about it. It's the first time, it feels, that Fate did me a favor. I tell him this before continuing. "The same day you arrived, I met Kellan and he looked just like you. Only he wasn't. It was confusing and fascinating at the same time. And . . . I can't really explain it to you, because I don't understand it myself . . . but . . ." Jonah nods, to encourage me to continue, but he's clearly wary. I muster the courage to continue. "When Kellan and I first met, we connected . . ." It's an unfair word, especially since I've learned I have a legitimate Magical

Connection to Jonah, but it's the only word I can think of to describe whatever it is . . . was between his brother and me. "I can't explain it better than that. There's a pull . . ." I pause, struggling now with the guts to continue.

"Go ahead," he says emotionlessly.

"So I was confused. And . . . other than you . . . I mean, I have reactions to him that . . ."

Jonah says, almost clinically, "I think I understand." Then he slides out from underneath me, stands up, and moves to my father's bookcase, randomly pulling out and shoving in books.

What if these confessions drive him away? I know I've got to be honest with him if we are to make this work, but what if this is all too much for him?

He slides out a book that is upside down and shoves it back in correctly. "He loves you. Did you know that?"

I do, but the words have never been spoken. When I don't answer, Jonah turns and looks at me expectantly. "He's . . . he's never said that to me," I stammer.

"He's never felt that way about anyone before, you know," Jonah says, turning back to the bookcase. Two more books are righted on the shelf. "Will you tell me one thing?"

I pop off the couch. Full disclosure. That's me.

"Do you love him?"

I can barely breathe. I end up stammering some more, completely flustered, "I . . . I . . ."

When I am unable to answer anything coherently, he says flatly, "That's what I thought."

“I love you!” I cry out. I’m on the verge of hand-wringing, like some chick in a historical novel. “I’ve always loved you, for as long as I can remember. I always will.” It’s the absolute truth. He’s got to feel my certainty.

And then my cell phone rings. It’s sitting on the coffee table in front of the couch. I stare at it, refusing to answer, because we both know who it is.

Because the screen shows us both that it’s Kellan.

“You should get that,” Jonah says after I let it ring several times. Then he hands it over.

I have to take a deep breath just to speak. “Hello?”

Kellan’s words are teasing, but I can hear just how stressed he is. “Miss me yet?”

“Of course.” As messed up as it sounds, it’s the truth.

“So, I’m going to stay another couple days. My aunt isn’t doing well. I need to stay and help her out with something.”

“Your aunt isn’t doing well?” I repeat for Jonah’s benefit.

Jonah sinks down on the couch next to me and sighs heavily.

“I can’t really go into it right now, if that’s all right.”

“When do you think you’ll be back?” I ask, my eyes on Jonah. He’s like a statue, he’s so still.

“What’s today, Sunday? Probably mid-week.”

It’ll be best to talk to him as soon as possible in person, even if it’ll kill me to do so. “Can I pick you up from the airport?”

A long pause. “Sure,” he says, but he does not sound sure.

“Kellan,” I begin, but he cuts me off.

“I can’t do this right now, Chloe. I’m sorry. . . But, I just can’t.”

I close my eyes and fight with the lump in my throat. “Okay.”

There is a gulf between us, deeper and farther than simply the miles between California and Maine. But he manages, far too generously, "I've missed you, though. I can tell you that much."

Remorse and sadness fills me up. Jonah senses this, and despite the hurt he must be feeling at the moment, reaches out and takes my hand. It's not enough, not by far, but I say, "Thank you," to both of them.

"Will you do something for me?" Kellan asks quietly.

How can I deny him? "Of course."

"Jonah and I aren't talking, which you've probably figured out. It's just . . . this is all such a mess." I can hear in his voice that this is hard for him to say. "But I was wondering . . . this is tough for me to ask of you, *especially* you, but . . . even still . . ." I wait, tense and sad. "You should go talk to him. I think it's time."

"You want me to talk to Jonah?" I repeat, stunned. Jonah's hand grips mine a little tighter.

"Chloe, I know I'm probably committing suicide here. Don't think I'm not terrified of what may or may not happen. But . . . this is my brother, my twin brother. I love the guy, I . . . I love you . . ." he says, ever so softly, "And things can't keep going like this."

I am beyond queasy. Kellan's finally said, out loud, that he loves me. And it's done while I'm holding hands with his brother, as well as planning on how best to break up with him.

I'm pretty much back to hating Fate at this moment.

"I mean, if you're not willing, if you still don't feel ready, I will understand," he continues. "But sooner or later it's got to happen. All of us need to see where the chips lie."

Trying to blink back the major rush of tears doesn't help at all. They snake out and drip down in salty trails of betrayal.

“Are you crying?” Kellan asks through the static of miles.

“No,” I lie, but I figure he knows I am. I’m snuffling loudly enough.

Kellan clears his throat. “Look, I gotta go. I think I need a little more space, just these last few days, if it’s alright, so no calls, please.” Once I promise to do so, he adds, “I’ll email you my flight itinerary soon. Think about what I said. It won’t be hard to find him.”

I stare at the phone for a long time after he hangs up. Should I have told him that Jonah was here with me already? How did this get so, so messy? “He wants us to talk.” Jonah doesn’t respond, so I ramble on. “He misses you.”

The pain on Jonah’s face is clear as day. He misses his brother, too.

chapter 32

Classes don't start for another fifteen minutes, so Jonah and I, alongside the Cousins, settle down on some benches outside. I try my best to leave some space between me and Jonah, but it's hard. I end up sitting on my hands.

I'd initially argued that since we are a couple, we should act like a couple, but Jonah suggested we lay low until I've had my talk with Kellan. We eventually compromised by agreeing that staying apart at school is unnecessary, but we'd try our hardest to be on our best behavior around others. At home, well, that's a different story.

The Cousins are studying us like we're the main act at the circus. Graham comes over after a few minutes and slouches down next to Lizzie on the bench. He doesn't appear to be surprised to see Jonah sitting next to me, which makes sense when Lizzie says, "FYI, I prepped Graham ahead of time about you two, so . . ."

Judging by Jonah's tense wariness, I'm guessing Kellan never got around to telling Jonah about the Graham debacle.

Flipping fantastic.

Jonah turns slowly and looks at me. Expectantly. I know exactly what he's silently asking, and it's more than whether or not Graham cares about who I'm dating. "Well, Graham sort of knows about . . . us."

"*Us*."

Alex mutters something under his breath and stands up. "Good luck with this, Chloe," he says, saluting me. And then he and Meg leave, arm in arm, which of course makes me want to ask someone about it, but since Jonah is still expecting an answer . . .

Lizzie's totally panicked now. "Didn't Kellan tell you?"

But Jonah doesn't look at her. He's looking at me.

Coward she is, Cora jumps to her feet. "Er, I think I'll go join those two." And then she flees.

Jonah sighs heavily. "What exactly did my brother fail to tell me?"

"Uh," Graham begins, but Jonah holds out a hand.

I scratch at my head. "Just that . . . you know. Graham knows now, since he and Lizzie are dating and all."

Now Jonah turns to look at Graham.

"I'm the one who told," Lizzie offers quickly. "Not Chloe."

Graham attempts to assure Jonah of his loyalties, which goes fine until he mentions the promises he's already given Kellan. This prompts another question to me. "So Kel's in on this?"

"I wouldn't say he's *in* on it. But he knows, yes." But the damage is done. Complicity is assumed.

"To just what extent is Graham's knowledge?"

"Pretty much everything," I admit.

I'm met with heavy, disapproving silence.

"I won't tell," Graham says quietly. "I know the risks."

Jonah's gaze swivels to him, but he remains silent.

Graham continues, "And I had your brother make it so I'll never be able to reveal Lizzie's secrets. So, no worries, man. It's all good."

Jonah grows even stiller. I'm reminded of what an eye in a storm is like. Completely calm. Sunny, even. "You realize this is extremely risky, right? Considering everything that's going on?"

"I know," I say a tad defensively.

"I don't think you do, though." He pinches the bridge of his nose. "If this gets out, no matter how much influence my brother and I have over the Guard, you'll most likely be sent away. Lizzie will be severely punished. And that's only the beginning."

"What's this?" Graham demands.

"Does Karl know?" Jonah asks me, ignoring Graham.

I shake my head. Just once.

"Jonah," Graham tries again, "I won't tell. I swear."

"I know," the love of my life says. "My brother is excellent at what he does."

Jonah's presence in my math class is a fluke. It turns out he's a freaking genius when it comes to math, unlike me, who still struggles desperately over each question.

"You're in here *why*?" I ask as he perches on my desk before class starts.

"It was the only class of yours I could get into. See how I suffer for love?"

I laugh. "You are my new official tutor, Mr. Whitecomb."

"I'll try my best." He pretends to sigh. "But I've seen how easily distracted you are whenever you're doing math."

"It's sort of hard to concentrate when there's a super-hot guy sitting nearby," I grin.

But then, from behind us, several of the girls who have long fancied themselves in love with him begin talking about us. How it's obvious I'm flirting with Jonah, and how disgusting it is since I'm dating his brother. The words they use to describe me are like gunfire—rapid, painful, and almost impossible to dodge.

He doesn't look their way, but I can tell he's listening. "Don't do anything to them," I say quietly.

"Why not?"

"Because what they're saying . . . it's true."

His eyes widen. "No, Chloe. That's not—"

I try to keep my voice steady. "I can't hide behind you to save myself from the consequences of what I've done."

He looks so fiercely protective that I blink a few tears back. "It's nothing for me to stop them from saying something cruel like that."

"I know," I tell him. I want to squeeze his hand, but I can't. Not yet. Not here. "And I appreciate it. But if this is what they think about me, then this is how it is."

He glances back at them. The frenzied whispering hushes. "Their opinions mean nothing, you know."

"I know," I tell him again. And it's mostly true. I just wish that Kellan wasn't going to have to deal with the aftermath of my choices in such a public forum once he comes home.

Giuliana's already waiting for us by the time we walk out the main doors. She's so sophisticated in a black sweater dress, black boots, and black sunglasses that she looks like she ought to be back in Italy sipping cappuccinos rather than chauffeuring high-school kids. A small crowd of boys surround her, clearly flirting, and she's good-naturedly tolerating it.

The moment she sees us, though, she brushes past her paparazzi. "*Ciao, bellas!* Let's get going!"

"What's the rush?" Jonah asks as we climb into her car.

"Karl and I have a fun night planned for you two. But to do it, we must hurry. No more questions. Enjoy the ride."

Twenty minutes later, when Karl pulls the Hummer into one of the parking spots outside of my favorite hiking trail in the woods, it dawns on me where we're going. "Annar?" I exclaim.

Karl turns the car off. "Yep."

"It's about time you see your wife," I tease, but in truth, I'm absolutely giddy over this. I've been to Annar once—and it was under stressful circumstances. Now, to go with Jonah . . .

It'll be perfect.

The portal amazes me just like it did the first time. Some places have portals in buildings, but this one's in a cave behind a series of secret tunnels, accessible only through high-tech handprint and retinal scanners. It's a beautiful, comfortable room filled with couches, artwork, and plants that looks better suited to a mansion than a cave. The actual portal is similar to a large glass phone booth with two doors. Inside, a small panel appears with a single, silver switch.

"You ready for a night on the town?" Giules asks us once the door clicks shut. Karl flicks the switch and white light fills the space around us.

chapter 33

I don't think I'll ever get over just how cool Annar's Transit Station is. It's a high-tech facility, similar to a swank airport. Everything is glossy white except sleek, wooden benches with bright-red cushions and the gorgeous, flowering plants hanging above. It's a massive building, nearly thirty stories high. Countless portals, marked by hammered, copper signs designating destinations, line the hallways. Unlike an actual airport, though, there are no delays, no cancellations. Portals are only closed by a Creator, and only then by Council decree.

Outside, Karl and Giuliana hand over a note and then dismiss themselves. We read the note together:

Guards aren't necessary in Annar, considering it's protected. You've got reservations at 7 tonight at Haven—it's two block south of Karnach on 12th Street. We'll see you two back at the Transit Station by 11.

"What does that mean, Annar is protected?"

Jonah folds the paper and sticks it in his pocket. "Hiders are constantly working on shielding the entire plane. Didn't you notice during Alex's presentation that there'd never been an attack here? The Elders probably don't even know Annar exists, since it didn't exist when they were in power."

It's just beginning to snow, just a light dusting, really—but the small, white flakes glitter like diamonds in the air as they fall around us. And, although there are hundreds of people out and about, rushing all around us, it feels like old times. Where's it just him and me. There are no Guards, no Elders, no Cousins, no hurting Kellan . . . My heart, so incredibly full and content, threatens to burst.

We take our time heading to the restaurant, hand in hand, stopping every so often to window shop or to simply talk. The strain of the last year isn't with us, and it feels so good to have my best friend back. It doesn't matter that a ton of people keep stopping us to say hi to him, it's just enough to be together.

After yet another girl leaves, I tease, "Cora told me you and your brother are rather well-known here in Annar."

"Well, I've spent a lot of time here," he says, completely missing my meaning. "And, if you think about it, despite there being around ten thousand Magicals living in Annar at any particular time, it's really an insular society."

"Did you come here a lot with your dad?"

He hesitates, just a second, really. But it's enough for me to notice a small, fleeting slice of sadness cross his face. "Mostly with my uncle, and a friend of the family. My dad . . . he was here, but I never saw him much."

"Why do you think it's like that?" I ask. "Because my parents are the same. Do you think it's a Magical thing? Are we all cursed to be crappy parents?"

He laughs. "No. I actually don't think they're the norm. There are some Magicals, like our parents, who are so completely focused on their work that they don't see past the end of their noses. There are also a lot of Magicals out there who are great parents, too."

I snort my disbelief. "Do you actually *know* any of these mythical creatures?"

"Yeah. Believe it or not, I do."

I stop and lean against a building. "Really?"

"My Uncle Joey was very involved," he says quietly. "For a long time, he was the only real father figure my brother and I had."

I reach up and twist a strand of his inky hair around my fingers. "You don't talk about him often."

The smile he gives me is so sad it tugs at my heart. "I miss him a lot."

"How did he die?"

"I'm assuming the Elders killed him. But at the time, none of us knew how. He'd gone out for a mission and never came home. His body was found a week afterwards, washed up on shore." When my eyes widen, he adds, "He was a Tide, which is probably why my brother and I love the ocean so much. He's the one who gave it to us. And we're still able to feel him when we're out there."

I want to throw my arms around him and take all the sadness away. "What about your aunt? The one still in Maine?"

"She's . . ." He looks away and sighs. "Let's say that she's never been a very involved sort of person in my life, other than making sure I don't let everyone down. And even that's no longer her concern anymore."

I think back to my phone call with Kellan. "What's wrong with her?"

"Dementia," he says.

"Can't a Shaman do something about that?"

"I think . . . sometimes there are some things a Shaman can't fix."

I don't know a lot about a lot of things, but I do know that a Shaman can pretty much fix anything. "But—"

He stares somewhere off into the distance. "I think Aunt Hannah very much wishes she could be a Creator and will herself out of her existence."

I gasp quietly. "That's horrible."

"She doesn't let anyone help her. She's let herself slide into a place where she's halfway existing—still here in body, but her mind is gone."

Jonah's lost so much for someone so young: his mother, his uncle, his aunt—as distant as she may be. He's been left with a father who can't bother himself to take an interest in his son's life and a twin he's fighting with because of me. My insulated, lonely life seems like heaven next to what he's gone through so far.

I take his face in my hands. "You have me. You'll always have me."

It's not arrogance when he says, "I know."

"I just want you to know that even though your aunt is crazy and your dad sucks, you have me. And I'm not going anywhere."

"I know," he says again, and I wrap my arms around him, because he's here, and he's mine, and I finally can.

The Dwarf at the small jewelry stand near the restaurant has so many facial piercings and tattoos that he looks like a piece of art himself. He nods at us while talking to a group of Faeries, all giggling over a series of bracelets they're looking at.

Jonah nudges my shoulder as I survey the displays. "You don't wear much jewelry, do you?"

I am, as a matter of fact, not wearing a single piece of jewelry at the moment. "True," I say as I pick up a bracelet to look at. "But it's not because I don't like it. I actually like jewelry quite a bit." I pause. "My mother forbade me for a long time from wearing it because she said it *attention*.'"

He looks shocked before bursting out in laughter.

I laugh, too. "And this is the same woman who insisted on me being a cheerleader. Jewelry apparently attracts male attention, whereas a tiny cheerleading skirt does not."

"So I'm taking it that you don't own much jewelry then."

"Not really," I say, fingering a delicate necklace. Then I turn around and hold out my hand. "May I see your ring?"

He slips it off his finger and hands it over. It feels like forever since I last held this ring in my hand. In the waning sunlight, I read the words I hadn't been able to remember that day he first showed up in my class: *To my darling son, life awaits.*

I slide it back onto his thumb. "Obviously from your mother?"

He nods, and I wait for the story behind the ring, perhaps behind the words, but it doesn't come. And it strikes me that Jonah has always been guarded with his stories, with his past. With his mother.

Just then another ring catches my eye, beckoning like a siren's song. It's stacked on a leafless miniature tree's branch along with a number of other rings. I lean in to look at it closely. It's made of a thin rope of knotted wood. The more I stare at it, the more it calls out to me.

Jonah leans in. "Find something interesting?"

"This one," I point out, oddly excited. "It's . . . *beautiful*." My finger, mere millimeters away from the ring, gets a small shock and a humming goes through my body, like recognition. I withdraw my finger and stare at it.

"Are you okay?" Jonah asks.

I nod, dazed. He pulls a stack of rings off the branch, extracting the one I've been admiring.

The Dwarf running the stand appears at our side. "Well, well," he says approvingly, "this is a pleasant way to close shop tonight."

"Pardon?" I ask as Jonah turns to look at him.

"It's always nice to find a match. Seems like it happens less and less nowadays."

When he doesn't offer any clarification, I prod, "Meaning?"

But Jonah is the one to answer, despite appearing dazed himself. "This ring is yours."

"Yours isn't here," the Dwarf says, as if he and Jonah are discussing tomorrow's weather report. "Pairs rarely are mined at the same time."

Jonah simply stares at the ring in his hand.

"No worries, though," the Dwarf continues. "Usually doesn't take too long to find it. Not once the first is, anyway."

"Find what?" I demand, still confused.

The Dwarf leans against the stand. "His ring."

I ask my boyfriend, "You want a wooden ring?"

"It's not wood," the Dwarf says, frowning. "It's Dwarven gold."

I look at the ring in Jonah's fingers and then at the others back on the tree branches. "They look like wood."

The Dwarf stares at me as if I'm dumb. Jonah says, ignoring him, "Dwarven gold is very rare and has certain Magical properties."

"Impossible," I say quickly. Only people have Magic . . . don't they?

"I know it seems like it, but it's true. The thing about Dwarven gold, though, is that it takes on different properties once it touches certain people." Jonah slides the ring onto his pinky. "See, on me, it stays the same." Then he takes my left hand and slides it onto my ring finger. The wood, warm against my skin, tingles before slowly hardening into rose gold. "But on you . . . it changes."

I'm so startled I grab another ring and slip it on. But the new one stays wooden. You'd think, having grown up around Magic, stuff like this wouldn't surprise me, but it does. I look up at Jonah, not asking, but waiting for an explanation.

"It's because we have a Connection," he says softly, moving closer. I ignore the Dwarf's obvious curiosity at our conversation. "The rings are another symbol of how we're meant to be. This one is yours. It'll only ever change for you."

I finger the ring, still warm and perfect against my skin. "And you have one out there somewhere?"

He slides off the second ring and kisses my hand. "Yes."

Several minutes later, after he's bought me my treasure using a credit card exclusive to Annar and we're standing in an enclosed doorway out of the snow, I'm still marveling at the ring. Every time I take it off, it reverts back to wood. But on my finger, against my skin, it changes into something solid and beautiful, something representative of the real feelings and ties I have to Jonah.

"We need to find yours," I say, giddy and drunk over the sheer romance of it all.

There is a long pause where he struggles to find the right words. "Chloe, I need to confess something to you." He holds up my hand, fingering the ring. "I know we've only rediscovered each other recently, but I want . . . *need* you to know that you have been the only girl I've ever truly loved my entire life. I can't remember a time in which I wasn't in love with you."

I seriously feel like swooning. "I feel the same way."

"We're going to be eighteen in just a few months, and living here."

I nod, refusing to break my gaze away from his. My birthday is in three months, his in two.

"And, I want you to know . . ." he says quietly, almost nervously, "that I plan to love you, and only you, for the rest of my existence. The last fourteen months, and most especially the last two, have made that crystal clear to me."

I open my mouth to say something back, but he squeezes my hand, indicating he isn't done. "I want to marry you as soon as we can. I don't ever want to be separated from you again. I know that sounds crazy, with us being so young . . . But like I said, we'll be here soon."

I stand there, my heart frozen, my breath gone, the ring alive on my finger. And if I'd thought I was happy earlier, that my heart had wanted to burst then from simply being with him, well, it's nothing compared to this. "I want that, too."

He lets go of my hand so he can put his behind my head. "There's only ever been you for me, Chloe."

I am so filled with love for this man it's ridiculous. We kiss for a very long time, oblivious to all the people and things going on around us. The first thing I say when we come up for air is, "How soon can we do this?"

He laughs quietly, resting his forehead against mine. "Let's finish high school first, and our first year at the U. But no longer than that, okay?"

But the more I think about it, the better the idea sounds to me. Being with Jonah is fifty times better than being with parents who don't like having me around. "Why not when we first move here?"

He holds his left hand up and wiggles his fingers. "Well, we don't have the ring yet, right? Can't do anything without it."

"Seriously?"

"You heard that guy. Apparently, this is how these things work." When he sees the look of disappointment on my face, he adds, "But isn't it any consolation that, by finding your ring, we're guaranteed Fate wants us together?"

I tug him closer. "I don't need a pair of rings to tell me that."

Despite dinner being in an impossibly romantic location, all I can focus on is the fact that Jonah Whitecomb wants to spend the rest of his existence with me. This person, who I first discovered before I could even read, is telling me that he loves me more than anything. That he's sitting in front of me: real, loving and perfect. And I give thanks to Fate for the first time in a long time. Because it gave me Jonah, and that means everything.

chapter 34

An email from Kellan is waiting for me when I get home. I stare at it for a long time, wondering how things between us have come to two simple sentences telling me about a flight itinerary.

It doesn't require a response, but I send one anyway: Your brother misses you.

That's it, just the one sentence. Any more might destroy everything that's been achieved with Jonah over the last few days. It is a rocky thing, being disheartened and missing one brother while blissfully getting engaged to another.

At a quarter past two in the morning, I call Jonah and tell him about the email. He's unfazed by my late night angst. "Didn't you say he was planning on emailing you his flight info?"

"Yes. You should know I emailed him back. About you."

He sighs sleepily. "I'm sure whatever you wrote was fine."

I close my eyes and burrow under my covers. "I told him you missed him."

"Then that's fine, because it's the truth."

"I know I probably don't have any right to ask this of you—"

"You can always ask me anything. You know this."

I still hesitate, chewing on my lip until it bleeds. "What should I do tomorrow? About the flight?"

There's a pause and what I assume to be another yawn. "Pick him up, just like you promised."

"Maybe . . . you should come, too?"

It's his turn to hesitate. "I don't think that's a good idea."

Panic wells up in my chest. Up until his email, Kellan's arrival home has been intangible, something in the future. But now I have a definitive time for when I'm going to hurt him, and it makes me sick to my stomach. "We could explain things together. Maybe it would be easier for him."

"If it was me," Jonah says, "and I had to watch the two of you reason with me why I was going to lose the only person I've ever fallen in love with, well . . . I don't think I could take it. Kel and I have our differences, but I know he'd feel the same. It'll be better for you to go on your own. But I'll be waiting for you afterwards, like we've planned."

I roll to my side and curl up. "I'm nervous . . ."

"I can understand that."

The tang of blood doesn't stop my lip chewing. "He's going to be angry with me."

"If it's any consolation, he'll be angrier with me."

"No, I don't—"

"Yes," Jonah says firmly.

"Do you think he'll be hurt?"

"Chloe . . ." When I stay silent, he says quietly, "Yeah, he will."

I have to fight off the desperation, so Jonah doesn't hear it. Thank gods he's not next to me feeling it. "I don't want him to hate me, despite everything."

"I highly doubt he'll hate you. He loves you. He'll still love you."

Part me selfishly hopes it'll be true.

"Where were you last night?"

Cora is standing next to my locker, arms crossed. "Annar," I tell her, bending down to stuff a book in my bag.

"Why were you in Annar?"

"For dinner. Why the grilling?"

Her face softens. "I couldn't get ahold of you and got worried."

"That's sweet." I stand back up. "But no worries. I was there with Jonah and both Karl and Giuliana."

"Did you have fun?" But before I can answer, she adds, "Did you see Raul?"

I squint at her. "Raul?"

"Yes," she grinds out. "Raul. Tall, Spanish, hot?"

"I know who Raul is. And no, I didn't see him last night. Why?"

Her mouth tightens. "No reason." Eyes, eagle-sharp, focus on my hand. Hers snatches out and grabs mine. "What. Is. This?"

I try to tug my hand away, but she's abnormally strong for such a thin girl.

"This ring," she clarifies loudly. Several people nearby stare shamelessly. "And why is it on this finger of all fingers?"

"Stop," I hiss. "Let go before you have to fix whatever bruises you're creating."

Her grip lessens, but she doesn't let go.

"We can talk about this later, but not here at school."

"After school then," she insists, finally letting go.

"Can't," I say, rubbing my sore hand. "I have to go pick up Kellan from the airport."

She arches a perfectly groomed eyebrow. "Why isn't Giules getting him? Or Karl? Or his brother? Or father? Or anybody else who isn't you and likely to forget her pretty head when they see his sexy self?"

I blink. Praise for Kellan from Cora is . . . well, it just never happens. "You think Kellan is sexy?"

She grimaces, as if she's sucking on a lemon. "Duh. A corpse would find that guy hot." And then she leaves.

Kellan is already standing outside of the airport by the time I arrive, bag sitting at his feet, hands shoved in his pockets. He looks tired, stressed . . . sad, even. And my heart goes out to him, because somehow or other, Kellan always tugs at my deepest heartstrings.

Remember why you're here, the little voice orders. *Remember what's at stake.*

As if I couldn't. Jonah is back at my house, waiting with Karl and Giuliana. Goodness knows what he's thinking right now, or even worse, *imagining* might happen here with his brother. But he's put his trust in me, believes I'm here to break things off with Kellan so we can all start fresh on the correct paths we're supposed to be on. And I mean to prove that trust is well-deserved.

Once I'm standing in front of Kellan, though, I revert to the person he'd once talked to at a football game: a nervous, awkward girl whose heart is fluttering and finds it hard to breathe in his presence. "Hi there!" I practically yell, slapping the forced cheerleader smile on.

He's surprised and instantly wary. And then I stupidly remember that things like false smiles and cheery voices may work on everyone else I know, but not on an Emotional. He knows they aren't real.

And that makes it worse. Because now I'm grinning like an idiot with tears in my eyes. All I can think about is how I'm going to break his heart, how even though I love him, I'm going to tell him we can never be anything more than friends. Which I desperately want us to be, because something in me tells me I can't let him go—so if I have to torture myself by hanging onto him as a friend, I'll do it.

Even though I know he knows it's fake, I continue with the forced cheeriness. "How long have you been here? I hope I haven't kept you waiting!"

"Not long," he says, sounding so calm that I want to shake him.

"Did you have a good flight?"

"If by a good flight you mean having some old lady sleep on my shoulder and thereby restrict my movements out of fear of disturbing her, then yeah, it was great." He smiles when he says this, the self-deprecating one I adore so much.

"You should have taken the portal," I say, shivering in response. But Kellan misreads this, or at least pretends to, and says we ought to go sit in my car to get out of the cold. Once we're safely inside, with the heater on high, he tells me, in the same rational, calm voice he'd used before, that I should just say whatever it is I have to say.

Now I'm even more nervous, because of course Kellan *knows* something's wrong.

"Your trip? It was good?"

He sighs, leans his head back against the headrest, and stares at a family shoving their luggage in the back of their minivan a few cars across from where we're parked. He doesn't answer my question; instead, he says, "Thanks for the email, by the way," which is possibly one of the toughest things to hear him refer to. Because by acknowledging this, he's also acknowledging that he knows Jonah and I have, at the very least, been talking with one another in his absence.

"You asked me to do it, so I did." I hate myself for saying it, because it sounds like an accusation, or, at worst, a cop-out: *Me and Jonah, we're together because* you *told us to be!*

"Yeah, I guess I did, didn't I?"

Invisible hands are strangling me so tightly I can barely get coherent words out. "Kellan . . . I . . . I need you to know . . . that . . ."

His eyes do not stray from the family, now bickering about the weight of their bags. "Obviously, it went well. My brother is no longer angry and resentful."

It isn't enough, and I'd been doing it way too much lately, but I stammer out a heartfelt apology. He cuts me off, so calmly I want to scream at him, demand he sound anything *but* rational about the demise of our relationship: "Right. I figured this would be the case. I take it . . ." And then he pauses, searching for the right words. But he doesn't find them. Or, at least, he can't say them, calmly or not.

So I give him his confirmation, barely choking the word out he already knows and really doesn't need. "Yes."

His eyes close. The only sound between us is my tremulous breathing and the hiss of heat through the vents. Even the family outside has stopped yelling.

Why does this hurt so much? If this is how it's supposed to be, then why do I feel like I'm breaking apart? I mean, I don't doubt my love for Jonah, especially now. I don't doubt my future with him, either. We're Connected, and now that I know what it means, I absolutely see it and feel it with him. And that's an amazing thing, at seventeen, to be so sure of someone. To know that they will always be there for you, that they will always accept you as you are. So many people never find this, seventeen or seventy. So many people search their entire lives to find someone to share their existences with and fail. But not me—I've found my home. And I'm at peace with this.

So why then the crushing grief over having to let Kellan go? Why do I *know* that I love him, despite what everyone says about people with Connections only ever being capable of loving one person, and them alone? Why does it feel like my lungs are collapsing, my heart crumbling? Why these intense feelings of devastating loss, when I *know* Jonah is the one for me?

Even the little voice is muted. It has no more answers than I do.

"I . . . I wish . . ." I mumble, now on the verge of full-blown hysteria, "I wish I could explain all of . . . this . . ."

While still calm and measured, his words are also hollow. "You don't have to."

"But—"

He won't look at me. "Don't."

"Kellan—"

A muscle in his jaw twitches. "Look. You do not have to paint me a pretty picture of what you and Jonah have. I may be an idiot, but I'm not a masochist."

"No," I gasp quickly. "I wasn't—"

Finally, some heat fills his words. "You think I want to hear about how wonderful things are for you and him?"

"No! I just—"

"Honestly? There is nothing you can say right now that will . . ." He stops. Shakes his head. Runs his fingers through his dark hair. "I need to go."

Before I can even blink, he wrenches the door open and nearly hurls himself out of the car, slamming the door behind him.

I get out of the car, too. "Wait!"

But Kellan doesn't wait. He is striding away from me, without even his bag, which is still in the trunk of my car. I take off after him, jogging until I catch up. "Please," I say, grabbing his arm, "don't leave like—"

He jerks his arm out of my grasp. "Go back to the car and go home."

"Kellan, I want to—"

"What part of me telling you I didn't want to hear it did you not understand?"

I reach out for his arm again. "Please don't leave like—"

"You're the one leaving," he says dispassionately.

"You don't understand—"

He takes a step back, just out of my reach. "Oh, I understand, all right."

"Then you know—"

"Go *home,* Chloe."

"Goddammit!" I shriek. "Will you at least let me finish a sentence already?!"

But when silence and listening is offered, my words disappear. I stand there, staring at him, loving him, wanting him, wishing I could explain things in a way that wouldn't be more devastating, and loathing myself for bringing all of this pain and misery about because . . . because . . . well, I don't know exactly why. I wish so badly I did.

I say the one thing that comes to mind. The one thing I can offer to explain why I'd ever think of giving him up, which, in any other circumstance, I'd never do. "Jonah's . . . he's my Connection."

There is absolutely no reaction to this statement.

So I struggle to continue, to find more words to possibly explain away the madness of leaving him. "And . . . it's real. . . . I mean, I wouldn't have ever been able to do . . . what we're able to do . . . if it's not real, right?"

Now he speaks. "Do?"

"I . . . I don't know what you call it . . . but . . . I guess people with Connections do it? Because it shows that . . . they're supposed to . . ." I swallow a huge lump in my throat, "be . . . together?"

Kellan's eyes go huge and the little voice shouts, *Are you an IDIOT? Why would you TELL HIM THAT??*

Kellan may claim he's not a masochist, but clearly, I am. I drive the final nail in my coffin by crying, "I wouldn't even think of breaking up with you in any other circumstance . . ."

"Because," he snaps coldly, "you and my brother are able to merge together?"

He knows exactly what I'd meant. "No! I mean, because I *love* him, have loved him since I was little . . ."

He takes a step closer, looking, for once, dark and dangerous as opposed to beautiful and loving. And then, inexplicably, he pulls me up against him and kisses me hard. My mind, already on the verge of total meltdown, transitions into self-survival mode. There is nothing I can do except kiss him back like my very life depends on it. Like he's the air I need to breathe.

WHAT IN THE HELL?? the little voice screeches, but I ignore it, have to ignore it, because right here, right now, this is what matters.

Just as suddenly as he began, he stops, letting go of my arms and taking a step back. In that same frustratingly dispassionate voice from before he says, “Really? Because right there, you pretty much told me how much you love *me*.”

And then he turns on his heel and leaves.

chapter 35

When I get back to my still-running car, I let the anxiety attack take over. I came here to break up with Kellan and instead kissed him.

I'm not surprised when Caleb taps on the glass, insisting to be let in. I don't ask how he knew where I was, or how he knew I needed him. I simply sob as he sits nearby, murmuring soft words of comfort. He insists on coming home with me, and I don't argue. I only wish he was three feet taller so he could be the one driving. He flies me up to my door, reminds me that I'm seventeen and that I shouldn't be so hard on myself, and then leaves when I go in.

Jonah is slumped in one of the living room chairs, *Siddartha* open in his lap, eyes closed. I wonder if he knows it's my favorite book, that I've read it at least five times, and if it means something to him, too.

Even though I'm tempted to wake him and plead for forgiveness and understanding, I instead go into the kitchen to get myself a drink and take some aspirin for the headache intense sobbing has brought about.

Karl and Giuliana are sitting at the island, playing cards. "Is Kellan back at the house?" Giules asks me, checking her watch.

"I don't know."

Both Guard stop so they can stare at me. "Where is he?" she asks.

"I don't know," I repeat.

"Did he get off the *airplane*?" she stresses.

I nod, swallowing two aspirin. After much prompting, I let them know I last saw him in the airport parking lot. Giules mutters something in Italian under her breath. Then she grabs her keys, tells us she's going to go find Kellan, and leaves.

Karl pats the stool next to him, but I do not sit down. "So I take it things didn't go well?"

I let my sad eyes do the talking, terrified my voice might break.

And then Jonah's hand is on my shoulder. I turn around, shove my head against his neck, and cry in his arms. Karl discreetly exits the kitchen.

It amazes me that Jonah's here comforting me, especially since I'm crying because I feel like complete crap for hurting his brother. But he does it anyway, wordlessly until the tears dry up and my breathing returns to normal. And then he leads me up to my bedroom and shuts the door behind us.

"Do you want to talk about what happened?"

I drop onto my bed in a heap of quivering exhaustion. "I think it's safe to say I suck at this sort of thing."

"Breakups are never easy, Chloe."

"Yeah, but . . . I pretty much said the wrong thing at every opportunity. I only made the situation worse." I look down at my hands, still trembling. "He definitely hates me now."

Jonah sits down next to me. "He doesn't hate you. He's angry, and hurt, but he doesn't hate you."

"You don't know that."

"I actually do," he says, taking my hand.

I give him a wobbly smile. "I told him I love you."

Jonah doesn't say anything.

Our fingers look right together, like puzzle pieces that fit. I tell him the truth, because he deserves it. "And . . . he kissed me. After I said that."

Jonah sighs loudly, his fingers tightening against mine. I feel like a broken record tonight, apologizing over and over, but I do it again. Time inches by until he finally speaks. "Will you do me a favor?"

"Of course," I quickly say.

"Don't kiss him again."

My stomach twists as I promise him this. I insist it hadn't been part of the plan, and he knows this. He knows his brother, and he knows me—but even still, I can tell it hurts him more than he wants me to know.

"I love you," I tell him, crawling up on my knees so I can face him.

"I know. I love you, too, Chloe."

I lean against him, and he wraps his arms around my waist. "I *love* you." There is a small sigh of contentment from him. But I feel the need to drive the point home. "I love *you*."

And then I'm on my back, and Jonah is kissing me so fiercely that all traces of sadness or anxiety go flying straight out the window.

Much later, Jonah stands up and stretches. "I should probably go home so I can face the firing squad."

So not funny. I check the clock. "It's late."

"Time stands still for no Magical," he quips. "Except for possibly a Mover."

Still not funny. "You really want to go have an argument with him?"

“I never like fighting with Kellan,” he admits. “But I think tonight, it can’t be helped.”

I look at the clock again. “Don’t go home.”

Jonah merely raises an eyebrow.

Why hadn’t I thought of this before? It’s the *perfect* solution. “It’s late, and who knows? Karl may already be asleep.”

“Karl is one of the biggest night owls I know,” Jonah scoffs. “He’s not asleep. He’s probably video chatting with Moira.”

“All the more reason not to interrupt him. Stay here with me tonight.”

Now his eyes widen in surprise.

“Your dad is in Annar, right? So are my parents. Back at your house, you have an angry brother. Here, you have a loving girlfriend who wants you to stay. So . . . stay.”

“Chloe,” he says gently, sitting back down next to me on the bed, “I have to talk to him sooner or later.”

I reach out and run my fingers through his hair. “I know. And this isn’t about that. This is about me wanting you here tonight. With me.”

Convincing Jonah to stay, though, is far easier than convincing Karl, who, as predicted, is talking to Moira. His initial response is a firm, “No.”

This pisses me off, since we normally get along so well. “What’s your problem? It’s not like you get a vote anyway. I’m merely letting you know as a courtesy.”

He turns a dark red. “You are not having sex tonight!”

Jonah, for his part, says nothing. I, on the other hand, fly off the handle, because I haven’t even contemplated sex as being on the menu.

"Are you *serious*? Tell me you did not just say that. YOU! Who got married at nineteen!"

"You are seventeen!" Karl bellows. "There's a difference!"

Moira tries desperately on the computer to reason with him, but he's not having any of it.

"Look," Jonah says once Karl's eyes are about to explode out of their sockets, "calm down or I'll force you to. I'm staying over whether you like it or not. And frankly? If we have sex, it's none of your damn business."

And then he takes my hand and leads me out of Karl's room, leaving our friend sputtering in outrage.

Karl appears in my room ten minutes later, thrusting a T-shirt and flannel pants at Jonah, snarling something along the lines of, "You are not sleeping with her naked."

"He's very protective of you," Jonah says rather approvingly when he's gone.

I'm glad someone finds this a good thing, because I'm not right now. "I figured that's Karl's typical M.O."

He pulls his hooded sweatshirt off and drops it to the floor. My mouth goes dry in so many ways at the sight of his tanned, perfect chest. "No. I don't think that's it at all."

I am blatantly staring as he pulls Karl's T-shirt on, hoping I'll be lucky enough to see the pants exchange, too. But no—Jonah heads into my bathroom to change, leaving the door open to talk to me as I desperately try to get the sudden bursts of heat racing through me under control.

Which, of course, he senses, because when he comes back out in pants way too baggy and long, he flashes me a wicked grin. My cheeks are on fire when I escape into the same bathroom to change into my pajamas.

Despite being exhausted from an overly emotional evening, I'm not ready to go to sleep once we slip under the covers. Instead, I play twenty questions with Jonah, mostly wanting to hear his voice as I lie against his chest, but also because I'm curious about life back in Maine.

Midway through my questions about his old school, I wonder out loud if he's dated before. He's had to, right? Because, let's face it, he's Jonah, and he's gorgeous and smart and kind and girls would have to be blind, brain-dead morons to *not* want to date him. But then, he surprises me by tensing when I ask the question.

Which is not good. I try to act nonchalant. "Did you date as often as Kellan?" I know about these exploits over months of teasing from Karl and Raul.

"I don't think anyone's dated as much as my brother has," he says dryly.

Okay, I so did not want to hear *that*. "But you did, right? Date, I mean?"

"I guess." He rolls over on his side so he can see me better. "You don't really want to talk about this sort of stuff, do you?"

"Why not?"

"Seriously? Because it does no one any good. And I personally do not want to hear about you with any other guy other than me."

Aw! But I'm not letting him off the hook. "Jonah. Just spill already."

He shifts uncomfortably. “I dated as much as the next person—well, not Kellan, but . . . you know. The average guy, I guess.”

“What do you consider average?”

“I don’t know. Not a lot but not a little?”

It’s so cute that he’s flustered by this. “Did you date anyone at your old high school?”

“You,” he says, flashing me his brilliant, dimpled smile.

“Stop trying to distract me with this,” I say, touching his dimple. “You know I meant outside of dreams.”

His eyes suddenly find the ceiling very interesting. “Um . . . yes?”

“You’re asking?” I tease.

“Yes, then.” When he doesn’t continue, I prompt him for more information. He finally admits, “There was someone I dated at my old high school.”

“How many someones?”

His discomfort expands until it nearly fills the bed. “One.”

I scoff at this. He expects me to believe only one girl was ever interested in him? But I play along. “For how long?”

“Chloe. Really?”

I give him a big smile to assure him this is interesting, not torturous, at least for me. “Yes!”

“We started dating in the ninth grade and broke up about a month before I moved here.”

Wait. WAIT. I’m sorry, but did he just say that he dated someone for THREE YEARS? I jerk into a sitting position. “This,” he says, reaching out for me as I evade his grasp, “is exactly why I didn’t want to talk about it.”

THREE YEARS?

"Chloe—"

And they broke up, what, three, four MONTHS AGO?

He captures my wrists and tugs me closer. "It's over—completely, one hundred percent over."

I was missing him, so upset over losing him that I was a mess, and he was DATING SOMEONE ELSE?

"And it doesn't matter, anyway—"

"Hell yeah, it matters!" I bark. "You were dating this chick even *after* you found out I was real?"

"Do you really want to go there?"

"Well, if the shoe fits . . ."

Oops. That was the wrong thing to say. "You dated my brother for two months, even after you knew I was at your school for you! A couple additional months of trying to figure out how to let Callie down easy was *nothing*."

Callie.

Images of some faceless yet gorgeous, fabulous girl fill my mind. She had to be amazing, right? For him to date her for so long? What was she like? Sweet, sarcastic, smart, funny, witty, put-together? Sexy? Oh my gods, was she sexy? And if so, did they—

"Chloe, you need to calm down. That relationship was never going to go anywhere in the long run because she's a non. I always knew that and was reminded of it often by the Old Man."

I think I'm going to puke. "Do you miss her?"

The look on his face is clear as he lobs a silent question back at me: *Do you miss Kellan?*

I change tactics. "Do you still talk to her?"

He drops back down against the pillow. "Let it go, Chloe. This isn't doing either of us any good."

It's the oddest thing, because I know I should let this go. Jonah's proved himself to me—he found out I was real, manipulated his father into moving clear across the country so he could be near me, and has risked his relationship with his brother to be with me. But something in me—a deep, dark possessive streak I didn't even know I had—digs its heels in. I have to know who's shared his heart. "Please," I say more softly. "Just tell me."

He stares back up at the ceiling. "She's called a few times since I moved."

"Recently?"

"Two days ago," he admits after a beat.

Sunday. We'd spent all of Sunday together, which means she must've called late that night.

"I can't believe I even have to tell you this, because I'd figured you'd known by now that my feelings for you supersede anything and everyone. Including Callie. You have nothing to be jealous about."

Jealousy is such a foreign emotion for me when it comes to sharing someone I love. I've been jealous in the past, of Magicals who are knowledgeable and content with their paths, of people comfortable in their skins when I'm so often grossly uncomfortable in mine. But I've never before felt such strong pangs of jealousy toward another being for daring to love someone who is mine. Which is awful and possessive and radically immature, but for crying out loud, I'm only seventeen and far from perfect.

I ought to be focusing on important things, like honing my craft and finding out more about Annar and my job, but seventeen means still being held hostage by your emotions. And clearly, having a Connection with someone means my emotions won't even get a ransom request. They're permanently gone.

So, I persist even when I ought to drop the subject. "What about her? Is she jealous?"

"It doesn't matter whether or not she is."

"Did you love her?"

He sighs.

"You asked me the same question," I point out.

It takes him a long time before he says carefully, "I told you last night that you are the only person I've ever truly loved."

The way he phrases it stings.

"Listen to me," he says, once more reaching for me. I don't sidestep this time, nor do I resist when he tugs me back down on the bed. "I love you. I'm going to marry you. I intend to spend the rest of my existence with you. But there was a time in both of our lives, whether we like it or not, where we weren't sure whether each other was real. So in that time period, even though I was in love with you, I dated several girls. And I know it sounds crazy, but just because I dated them doesn't mean I ever stopped loving you. Now that I know you are real, and now that we're together, you have nothing to worry about. There will be no other girls, ever. You're the only one for me, Chloe."

Just like that, I'm able to relax against the pillows. "Okay."

"I think," he says, scooting closer to me so we're pressed up against each other, "we've talked enough tonight. Don't you?" He doesn't give me a chance to answer, because his lips are against mine, his hands are moving across my body, and words no longer exist in my mind.

chapter 36

Karl and Jonah are already in the kitchen when I make it downstairs. Karl is making French toast while Jonah sits at the island, nursing his coffee. I stand in the doorway, admiring him as neither guy notices my presence yet.

Karl dips a piece of bread into egg batter. “I got a call from Giules about a half-hour ago.”

Jonah props his head up with a hand. “Let me guess—last night was not pleasant at Chez Whitecomb.”

“You got it. She and Kel got into a screaming match of epic proportions. She was so frustrated she almost called down a thunder storm in your kitchen.”

“It surprises me,” Jonah muses, “that he let his guard down around her.”

“Agreed,” Karl says, laying the bread on a skillet. “Which tells me that the shit didn’t only hit the fan last night, but also exploded. You talk to him yet?”

“You must be kidding.”

“In a way, Chloe saved your ass last night by having you stay here.” Karl pauses, pushing down on the bread with a spatula. “But, dude, I’m telling you now. If I catch you two—”

"You'll what? Slap my hand and revoke my driving privileges? Karl. Butt out. I don't tell you what you can and can't do with Moira, do I?"

But Karl isn't insulted. "All I'm saying is that if Kel brought Giules down in hysterical tears last night, imagine what he would've done to you."

"Probably tried to beat the crap out of me," Jonah says calmly.

Karl sets the spatula down and leans against the island. "Look. I'm not taking sides—you know me better than that. That said, having a Connection myself, I'll admit that if *anyone* tried to come in between me and Moira, there'd be hell to pay. I'm just saying . . . I was around Kellan and Chloe a lot. He genuinely loves her. I've never seen him like this about a girl before. I feel bad for the guy."

It takes Jonah a long moment before answering. "I do feel guilty about that, because had I done things differently when I got here in the first place, none of this would be a problem now. Or if I'd actually told him the truth any one of the hundreds of times he'd asked what was going on with me over the last year. But it is what it is, and I won't back down. Chloe's my Connection, and I love her, and I'm not letting her go—not even for Kellan."

"She's probably dead to him now, anyway" Karl muses, turning back to the skillet.

A small, uncontrollable shudder runs through me at his words.

"She's not," Jonah says. "He's furious right now, but he still loves her. All of his anger right now is focused on me."

Karl stops. "He's not blocking you?"

"Nope. He wants me to know exactly what he thinks of me."

What's this? Jonah can tell what Kellan is feeling, even at a distance?

"Whoa," Karl says. And then—"You must be exhausted right now."

"It's certainly no picnic."

"Think you two can maintain civility at school?"

"Of course." Jonah appears mortally offended. "You know better than to ask that."

Karl flips the toast. "You going to shield Chloe from all of this?"

"As much as I can," Jonah says, and I take a step back into the hallway, stunned, because I stupidly never thought things would go this far. "She shouldn't have to suffer because my brother and I are about to go to war."

"Keep it that way," Karl says. "Because I'd hate to have to jump into the fray if it's not necessary."

This makes Jonah laugh. "Yeah? Think about the last time you tried to take one of us on." Then Karl laughs, too, and I turn away and head back to my room to hate myself some more over what I've done.

"Where's Cora?"

I look up from my notes to find Lizzie and Graham, giants blocking the sunlight from above. "I don't know," I say, shutting the binder. "I haven't seen her this morning."

"I've tried calling her three times." Lizzie holds out her cell phone, tapping on the keyboard as if it'll magically produce Cora's voice. "And she's not answering."

"Maybe she's with Meg and Alex?" I offer. I have yet to see them, either.

"Maybe," Lizzie murmurs. "It's just weird she's not here at school. She's never late."

"There's a first time for everything," Jonah says under his breath, and I laugh, remembering my own humiliating tardy fiasco a couple months prior.

Lizzie launches into a recap of some movie she and Graham saw, but I'm not listening because Giuliana's Hummer is pulling up in front of us. Karl and Jonah's conversation rears its head in my mind, forcing all kinds of uncomfortable feelings to spring forth.

"Please don't fight," I whisper urgently to Jonah. "Not over me."

He doesn't bother to look at the Hummer when he takes my hand and kisses it, the first bit of PDA we've risked at school so far. "It'll be okay. Trust me to handle this."

I do trust him, but it's hard to imagine reason trumping emotion in a situation like this, even from someone typically as level headed as Jonah. It's unfair to allow him to shoulder this burden, considering the two other players in this mess are his twin and his Connection, but it would be a lie to say I wasn't relieved to hear him offer to take charge of the situation.

I'm well aware of how cowardly that makes me sound.

I think back to all of the boys I've broken up with in the past—and while there aren't many, there are enough for me to feel familiar with the awkwardness of a breakup. I've never shied away from the role before, as I'd always known that these things happen and when it's wrong, it's best to cut ties before things get too serious. And none of these other boys *were* serious. All of them had been unfairly compared to Jonah and found lacking over the years, and therefore I'd never developed anything stronger than a mild crush on any of them. Breaking up was easy, even if it meant having to stand there the next day at school and face them down.

I'd always done it with a smile on my face, with the reassurance that this was best for everyone involved, and the ability to move on without any big struggle. Oh sure, there'd been a boy or two who'd resented this, but it'd never been a problem for me.

Not until now. Not until Kellan.

I figure, as I watch him slide out of the Hummer but then turn right back around to lean in and laugh at something Giuliana says to him, it's because if there was no Jonah, there never would've been a breakup. But there is a Jonah, and I don't doubt the wisdom of choosing him over Kellan, yet there is a great deal of unfamiliar, indefinable feelings raging around my stomach, making me want to run and hide instead of facing the problem headfirst like a normal person. Truth be told, the only thing tethering me to the spot is Jonah's grip on my hand.

"Listen," Jonah says quietly as Kellan begins his approach toward us, "I swear to you right now he won't make a scene here at school. I know you're freaking out—"

Of course he does.

"And you feel like running—"

Damn he's good.

"But as uncomfortable as this will be for you, I promise it'll be okay."

When we stand up, Lizzie and Graham suddenly find five convenient excuses as to why they need to be elsewhere. Kellan shakes his head when he stops in front of us. "Wow. Can I clear a crowd or what?"

I quickly interject, "I don't think that's—" But Jonah squeezes my hand and I stop talking.

"How was the trip?" he asks in a superbly mild voice.

Kellan answers, sounding exactly the same, “As well as can be expected.”

“Aunt Hannah?”

Kellan shrugs, still looking relaxed. “The Old Man has been dispatched.”

And then they fall maddeningly silent, both hiding behind dark sunglasses that make it impossible to determine if they’re even looking at one another.

I wait out the silence for a full minute, spending the bulk of my time shuffling from one foot to the other. It’s a painful silence, punctuated every so often by Jonah’s fingers tightening against mine and the occasional sigh from one or the other. Not able to deal with the vacuum, I tentatively offer, “Um, guys . . . ?” Jonah squeezes my hand again, this time purposefully. He’s asking me to not speak. I give it a good three minutes before I can’t help myself. “What’s going on right now?”

Kellan cracks the smallest of smiles. “And why wouldn’t I?”

But he’s not saying it to me . . . so . . . what does *that* mean?

Jonah snaps, “Leave her out of this.”

Her? Her who? Does he mean me? “What are you two talking about?” I demand.

The tiny smile slips off Kellan’s face. “Whatever.” When he finally acknowledges me, it’s only to say, “See you later, C,” before strolling off.

And Jonah is no help, refusing to explain what just happened.

Two periods later, I’m trying to shove books into my locker, but I pretty much only succeed at knocking them out. And when I bend down to pick one up that smashed my toes, another book falls, smacking me squarely on the head. I fear I'm about to set off a massive explosion when a hand reaches out to pick up the novel. Startled, I jerk up, slamming my head on the locker door.

Kellan is holding out my book. "Your head okay?"

No. It's stinging like bloody hell in two spots, which I'm certain he knows about because my pain levels are off the charts. I snatch the book. "It's fine."

He gingerly touches one of the rapidly growing welts, and the pain subsides. Despite so much in me wanting to step into that concern and allow it envelop me, I physically will myself to take a step back. He drops his hand, asking, "How are you today?"

I stop rubbing my head. "How am I today?"

His half grin appears. "If I'm not mistaken, that's usually an acceptable form of greeting between people nowadays, especially those who know each other well."

Ugh. I am so flustered. "What are you up to?" I accuse, shoving a book into my backpack. Getting my eyes off him is good, even though the pull toward him is as strong as ever. How can that be? I'd felt it this morning during the silent stare-off, but it didn't feel half as strong as it does at the moment.

"I was asking you how you're doing today."

I zip up the backpack. "Peachy, thanks."

"Good," he says, and it's done in such a way that I have no other choice than to meet him directly in his eyes.

He's so gorgeous today I can barely stand it. And that only confuses me more, and drives up the already sky-high levels of guilt. "I . . . uh . . . need to go to class now."

It takes a tremendous effort, but I manage to turn to leave. But two steps away, he grabs my arm and says in an achingly vulnerable voice, "Wait."

So, I wait.

"I'm sorry about the way I acted last night," he murmurs. "I really shouldn't have walked away like that."

"You don't have anything to apologize about." I'm ashamed when my voice cracks halfway through.

His voice drops even lower as he steers us back towards the lockers. "I expected bad news when I sensed Jonah wasn't angry anymore. I just . . . I guess I didn't expect to hear what you used to rationalize your choice."

I think back to the conversation, and the guilt flares brighter. "I'm so sorry—"

He winces. "Don't. I didn't say that to get an apology, Chloe."

I look up into his blue eyes, dark and troubled and so out of place on his otherwise calm face. "I didn't want to hurt you," I whisper hoarsely. "I'd give anything to make this painless for . . . for all of us."

He looks off into the distance. "I'm mad, Chloe. I'm so pissed off right now. And hurt. And a thousand other emotions I didn't ever think I'd feel."

Cue my tears. "I know. I'm so sorry, Kellan."

"I can't do this today, because I can barely think straight, but . . . I'd like it if we can talk later, because . . . I *know* how you feel. About me."

I nod, blinking back the tears. "Okay. Just . . . let me know when." And like a fool, I take a step closer, unable to resist the pull toward him any longer. He is confused, wary . . . and yet also unable to resist the pull, because he tentatively reaches out his hand and touches my face so lightly, I wonder if the fingers are even there or not. So I lean against his hand, allowing the tingle that always accompanies his touch to take root in my skin, proving there can be a very distinct disconnect between mind and body.

Because the little voice is shrieking at me to take a step back and run as fast as I can in the opposite direction, for Kellan is not my boyfriend any longer, and he shouldn't be allowed to touch me like this whether or not my body likes it.

His hand drops away. "You don't want to be late."

I slam head first into a wall of confusion.

Kellan bends down and picks up my backpack. He hands it over wordlessly before turning around and walking away.

In the seventeen years I've known Cora Carregreen, she's missed school exactly three times, and all three were in the last two months when we went to Annar and had to skip due to being chased by the Elders. During this time period, I've also learned that Cora never ignores her cell phone, not even in class, when she puts it on vibrate and finds ways to sneak peeks at texts and call logs. So, by lunchtime, when no one has been able to get ahold of her, I am officially worried.

"This isn't like her," Lizzie is saying. "Why isn't she calling back? Or answering in the first place?"

"Babe," Graham says soothingly, "are you sure you don't remember her saying she wasn't coming to school? Maybe she's gone off to that . . . er . . . place you guys go to?"

Innocent comments like this really stress Jonah out.

"No!" Lizzie practically wails. "I would remember her telling me that!" And then she holds the phone up and shows it to me. "Fifteen calls, Chloe. *Fifteen.*"

I pull out my own phone and set it on the table. "I've called five times myself."

"Graham," Lizzie says, her long ponytail whipping as she turns to him. "Call her. Now. Maybe she'll answer you."

Graham clearly doubts this wisdom, but does as he's asked.

Jonah, who has so far been silent through Lizzie's ravings, calls Giuliana, asking her to go to Cora's house to check on her. And then it hits me.

What Karl has warned me about.

Why Cora's been partially under his protection for the last two months, too.

"You don't think . . ." I say, panic rising, but Jonah cuts me off.

"We don't know anything yet," he says in a low voice. "She could be at home, asleep."

I can barely choke out, "They sometimes target the people closest to . . . to . . ."

Jonah pulls me close, kissing my temple. "Let's just wait until Giules calls before sounding the alarm, okay?"

I nod, having to bite on my lip to not say anything else.

Lizzie's knee begins bouncing up and down, jarring our lunches. "So," she says rather loudly. "So. What's new with all of us? Is anything new with you two? Graham bought a new shirt yesterday. I picked it out. It's nice."

"She rambles when she's upset," I tell Jonah quietly.

Graham strokes Lizzie's arm softly. "It's a good shirt," he says. "Plaid."

"Plaid's nice," Jonah offers.

"I thought so, too," Lizzie shrills. "It's red. Red plaid is nice, right?"

I cannot believe we are talking about plaid shirts as a way to alleviate our worries. So I try another tactic. I ask Lizzie about her upcoming appointment with the regional Seer.

She's still gripping her cell phone. "It's Friday. I'll have to miss the game. But it's important to go, right? Because my road is changing?"

I'm assuming she's referring to her relationship with a non. "I wish you luck," I tell her sincerely. "Be sure to ask specific questions. I learned that from my visit."

"Oh, that's right," Lizzie says. "I'd almost forgotten you saw one in Annar recently."

"Really?" Jonah asks. "Was it Astrid?"

"Actually, yes," I say, surprised. "Do you know her?"

"I do. She's my . . . a close family friend."

Lizzie leans in closer, intrigued and thankfully distracted enough her knee stills. "I've never met a Seer, except, of course, the day I was born. What's this Astrid like?"

"She was kind," I admit, wondering if I ought to admit she was also very unhelpful to Jonah, who's already made mention of knowing her well. I decide not to, instead adding, "She's an Elf."

"You know, I'd never even seen one before until the Storyteller." She turns to Jonah. "How do you know this Astrid?"

He shoves the French fries on his plate around. "Astrid lives on the same street I grew up on."

"But she's an Elf," Graham says, confused. "Don't they look different than . . . well, us?"

"Not really," Lizzie supplies. "They're somewhat taller, more elegant in a way. Their faces are a bit longer, their eyes a bit more slanted. But I can see how she'd blend in." To Jonah, she says, "Continue."

I nearly laugh, because I'm pretty positive Jonah hadn't the slightest intention after his first explanation to continue anything further. But he does, more to me than my friends. "After my mother died, Astrid sort of took pity on Kel and me. I guess you could say she's a surrogate mother of sorts."

Why don't I know this? "Do you still talk to her, despite moving?"

"She calls pretty much like clockwork every other day. And whenever I'm in Annar and she's there, too, we see each other."

I think back to the woman I'd met, and how I'd thought, when she'd hugged me, how warm and motherly she'd been. "She was really nice."

"She is," he agrees.

"Was Astrid the Seer you saw, the one who told you about me?"

"No. It would've been a conflict of interest having her view me." His cell phone goes off, prompting all of us to go silent. "It's not Giules," he reassures us. Then he stands up and kisses me on the head. "I'll be right back."

Of course, the moment he steps away is the moment Kellan enters the cafeteria with some pretty girl I don't know too well. She's flirting like crazy, her hand resting far too long on his arm or her hair brushing against his shoulder too often when she leans in to say something. I watch them in blatant perverse fascination until she touches his hair. The white-hot urge to tear her own shiny hair out by the roots rips through me like a wildfire. Kellan disentangles himself from the girl. He does not look in my direction.

You realize he felt that, the little voice grumbles. *Might as well have stood up and waved a red flag.*

Kellan excuses himself and then heads my direction. I hold my breath, wondering just what I can say to even explain that completely irrational moment just now, but he passes right by me without a single glance and exits the glass doors facing the courtyard. He goes directly to Jonah, who shoves his phone into his pocket.

"What happened this morning?" Lizzie demands.

I continue watching the twins as I answer her. "They stood staring at each other in silence for nearly five minutes. It was bizarre."

"Just staring?" Lizzie asks. "No talking?"

Jonah and Kellan are talking now, standing so close I can tell no one outside can hear a word they're saying. They appear to be simply having a normal conversation until Jonah raises a finger and points it at his brother. Kellan shrugs and stuffs his hands in his pockets. Jonah jabs the finger at Kellan a few more times, not speaking anymore, either. And then he takes three steps towards the cafeteria, stops, and turns back to Kellan. And then they just stare at each other for a long moment.

"I think I see what you mean about the no-talking thing," Lizzie says. "Graham? Is this normal male behavior?"

Startled to be lumped into the grouping, he asks, "What?"

"Never mind," she mutters.

The moment Jonah gets back to the table, his phone goes off again. "Oh, for the love of . . ." he swears softly under his breath. But once he sees the Caller ID, his entire expression changes. "It's Giuliana," he says, and we are all instantly alert.

"Hey, Giules—what? Was her mother there? How can she have no idea . . .?" Jonah pauses, listening intently. "No, we're all fine. Yes, Kellan is still here . . ." He pauses again, and when a fleeting look of concern races across his face, the panic in me doubles.

"Strategically, I don't think that's a good idea," Jonah says. "I think our chances are better here at school. I can't see them attacking us with such a huge crowd. It doesn't fit their profile."

Attacking? Oh. My. Gods. He's talking about the Elders.

"They went after you on the road," Lizzie whispers, obviously thinking the same thing I am. "There were cars and witnesses everywhere."

Kellan appears at our table, his hand stretched out. Jonah surprises me by placing the phone in it, no questions asked.

Okay, how did Kellan know about the phone call . . . ?

"What was the last time Cora was seen?" he asks Jonah before putting the phone to his ear.

"Seven," Jonah answers.

Kellan covers the phone and says flatly to his brother, "I don't give a shit if the sky is falling, next time you tell me right away."

Jonah levels a long, pointed look at Kellan.

"That's not an excuse," Kellan continues. "And you know it. May I point out how ballistic you would've been if it'd been me who neglected to tell you?"

"Just talk to her already," Jonah says, motioning toward the phone.

"What *was* that?" I ask Jonah while Kellan grills Giules. "Do you two speak in twin code?"

"Twin code?" Jonah repeats, eyes on his brother.

"You know," Lizzie interrupts. "Studies say some identical twins have their own languages."

"Uh, sure," Jonah says. Then he says to Graham, "Will you go and get Meg and Alex? They're in the library right now."

"How do you know this?" I ask as Graham bounds away.

"Alex is in Kellan's math class," Jonah says, as if this answers the question. "Honey, I'm sorry—but let me concentrate on the phone call right now."

Lizzie and I exchange a confused glance as Kellan is basically just mm-hmming now.

As soon as Kellan hangs up the phone, Jonah says, "I disagree."

Kellan sighs. "It's the best plan, and you know it."

Jonah shakes his head slowly, looking at his brother the entire time.

"It's you or me," Kellan says after a long moment. "And I'm assuming you'd rather let hell freeze over before letting me do it. But hey, I'm happy to—"

"You know that's not the issue," Jonah says tightly.

Kellan cracks a tiny smile. "Shall I remind you that you're also under an order of protection, too?"

"Oh, for gods' sakes," Jonah mutters. "Are you *serious*?"

Kellan merely looks at his brother for a long moment.

"Fine," Jonah grinds out.

"Hold on," I say, forcing myself in between the two of them. "I have no idea what you two are talking about, but can one of you fill me in on what's happening with Cora?"

"What she said," Lizzie seconds. Graham reappears with Alex and Meg.

"Chloe and Jonah are going to Annar as soon as Karl gets here," Kellan says.

I turn to Jonah. "Why?"

He tells me, "It's the safest place for you to be right now."

This is not good. "What are you not telling us?"

"Cora is officially missing," Kellan supplies. "She hasn't been seen since this morning when she left for school. Since there's also been an Elder sighting called in within the last three hours—"

"Why haven't we heard about this sooner?" Alex demands.

"Because," Kellan says, annoyed, "orders came down that it might be safer to keep Chloe inside the school."

"So what changed?" Alex presses. "Why the trip to Annar now?"

"Cora's missing," Jonah answers. "Keep up here, Alex."

"Are you going, too?" Meg asks Kellan. "Are you leaving us?"

"No," Kellan tells her. "I'm staying behind to make sure the rest of you stay safe here at school."

Meg sags in relief. Alex, on the other hand, looks put out by her lack of faith in his protective abilities.

"Raul is coming in," Kellan continues, more to the rest than to me. "He and Giules will start searching for Cora immediately. Karl and I will join up as soon as we can."

"Wouldn't it be smarter to use us to search for Cora, too?" I ask.

Apparently, I am the only one who thinks this a good idea, because every single person, including Graham—who, it ought to be pointed out, has no idea what's really going on—looks at me like I'm speaking in tongues.

"Chloe," Jonah says, "it's important you stay safe this time."

I try to argue, but Kellan cuts me off. “Don’t think we don’t remember what happened last time you tried to help.”

“I *did* help,” I snap. “I saved all of your asses and you know it!”

This doesn’t sway Kellan or Jonah, who both argue how ridiculous it is for me to risk myself needlessly. Karl arrives during this verbal beatdown, thankfully saving me from the Cousins joining in the fray.

“We’re leaving now.” Karl waves two pieces of paper. “I’ve already signed you two out, thanks to your parents calling in before I arrived.” Then, to Kellan, “I want the population locked down.”

“Fine,” Kellan tells Karl, but his eyes are on me.

“Maybe the rest of us ought to be looking, too,” Lizzie says hesitantly. “School seems irrelevant if Cora’s missing . . .”

“School,” Karl says firmly, “is the safest place for you to be.” He looks at me and Jonah. “Let’s go.”

Kellan reaches out and grabs Jonah’s arm. They stand there silently for a moment before Jonah says quietly, “I will.”

And then, before I can ask what that meant, Jonah puts his arm around my shoulders and leads me out of the cafeteria.

chapter 37

The Guard have a number of safe houses all throughout Annar for a variety of reasons, including, I suppose, hiding a Creator in a plane that has never been breached by Elders. The one we're taken to by Iolani, who took over for Karl when we reached the Transit Station, is in an ornate building which houses the main branch of Annar's bank. Which, to me, is pretty conspicuous, but Iolani insists it's one of the safest buildings in the city-state.

Outside the apartment, on the third floor, is a Goblin dressed entirely in black talking on his cell phone. He's quite tall and well built, with pale, matte pea-green skin; salt-and-peppered, closely cropped hair; a Romanesque nose; and piercing black eyes. The moment he sees us, he barks out an order on his phone and then hangs up. Just when I'm afraid he's going to start yelling at someone, his eyes crinkle at the corners and he smiles. "Jonah," he says in a low, gravelly voice with just the hint of an exotic accent. "It's good to see you, despite the circumstances."

Am I the only person who doesn't know *anyone* in this town?

"Zthane," Jonah says, "I don't think you've met Chloe in person yet. Chloe, this is Zthane Nightstorm—he's one of the best Guards we have."

"Please," Zthane grins. "Flattery will get you everywhere." To me, he extends a hand. His grip is strong and brief. "It's good to finally meet you, Chloe."

I find myself instinctively liking this guy. "You, too. Karl's said a lot of good things about you."

Zthane bursts out laughing. "I find that hard to believe." To Jonah, he says, "Once you get settled, call me, because we need to talk."

Jonah agrees, as if this is expected.

"I've decided to have your brother bring the . . ."—he looks down at his cell phone, scrolling through some notes he's made—"three additional teenage Magicals here to Annar for the night. Just in case."

"Just in case of what?" I ask.

"He's got the school done," Jonah says, ignoring my question. "He figures he'll have the rest of the city done in the next half-hour. He's been a bit distracted, as Megan Blueton has been . . ."—Jonah looks at me sympathetically—"somewhat hysterical and a bit difficult to deal with. She literally wasn't willing to let go of him."

Zthane nods, perusing his notes some more. "Joy, correct?"

"Yes," I answer for Jonah. "What does that mean? Is she freaking out?"

"Not anymore," Jonah assures me. "Kellan has her sedated with Alex back in the library."

Okay, wait a minute. "How do you know this?"

"All the more reason to bring them here," Zthane says, both of them ignoring another of my questions. "A panicky Joy does no one any good. You boys would have your work cut out for you if she began wreaking havoc on that school. What about the others? How are they dealing with the possibility of being targets?"

My stomach hits the floor as it sinks in that Cora is missing . . . because of *me.* My other Cousins are targets . . . because of *me.*

“Elizabeth Pinkston also had to be sedated,” Jonah continues, “yet Alexander Himura is fine. But then, he’s an Intellectual, so that’s no shock.”

“Lizzie panicked?” I whisper, horrified at the thought of my normally stalwart friend flying off the handle.

“Nothing like Meg,” Jonah assures me.

“Good, good.” Zthane’s fingers are flying over the phone’s keyboard. “Glad to hear it.” He pauses, then says, “You clear on everything, Jonah?”

Jonah simply sighs, exasperated.

The Goblin lays a hand on his shoulder. “You boys should stop expecting me to change.”

“You’re an ancient rock,” Iolani grins. “Who never changes despite the weathering of storms.”

“If thirty is ancient,” Jonah says, “I’d hate to think what he’ll be like at forty.”

“Decrepit,” Zthane says with a straight face. “Anyway, once Kellan rolls in, expect a meeting to go over some new intel we’ve acquired.”

“I won’t be leaving the apartment,” Jonah tells him.

“This is fine,” Zthane says, unbothered. He pats Jonah’s shoulder a couple times before telling Iolani the apartment has already been checked. “No one except the list I’ve sent is allowed in or out,” he adds. And then he walks away, phone back at his ear.

Iolani opens the door. “You heard the boss. Inside you go.”

“Why such scrutiny?” I ask once we’re inside and the door is locked. “I thought Annar is safe. Everyone’s acting like there are assassins outside the building with sniper guns trained on me.”

“It’s not too far from the truth,” she says before Jonah gives what appears to be a warning, to stop talking.

Asking them for clarification does no good. So I ask Jonah instead how well he knows Zthane. Iolani is surprised at the question, which irks me. Clearly she has no idea how much *I* don’t actually know.

“We’ve known him most of our lives,” Jonah tells me.

“I swear,” Iolani laughs, “he thinks the sun rises and sets on your brother.”

Jonah laughs, too. “I’m glad I don’t have to deal with all of the Guard expectations Kel is under.”

“C’mon,” she wheedles, “you must admit that the Council ones are just as bad.”

“Maybe I’ve just learned to tune them out.”

“Maybe,” Iolani grins, “it’s because Council members tend to have sticks up their asses and don’t know how to have fun. They’re easy to tune out with all their moaning and droning. The Guard, though . . .”

“Yeah,” Jonah concedes, smiling, “you guys are awful. Like a pack of sixth graders.” He sits on the couch and stretches his legs out.

Iolani appears to view this as a compliment. She bows to us with a grand flourish, grins, and then excuses herself to go make some phone calls.

I spend the next hour vacillating between specific panic over Cora and general panic over the rest of my friends. I’m also acutely uncomfortable knowing Kellan is out there, risking himself along with the rest of the Guard, while I'm stuck in some cushy, safe apartment on a completely different plane.

These feelings are only exacerbated when I learn about a rash of attacks on the other planes over the last month. There have been three deaths, all powerful Magicals, and five injuries. Talking about it only makes me more anxious, so Jonah suggests we table the subject until we have more concrete information to go on. "Good idea," I say, pacing restlessly through the living room as he flips through a newspaper. And then, I remember to ask, "Who called you earlier today while we were at lunch?"

The paper in his hand stills.

"Today at lunch. Before Giules called with the news about Cora. Who were you talking to on the phone? I mean, you got into a fight with Kellan over it."

The guarded look on his face melts into his typically even one. "It was nothing."

I roll my eyes. "I'm not an idiot, you know."

He sighs and sets the paper down. "It was Callie."

I stop pacing. "Ex-girlfriend Callie?"

A nod proceeds, "It's really nothing for you to worry about."

Oh, hell no. He is not going to get away with these sorts of answers. I mean, my boyfriend, no, my *Connection's* ex-girlfriend of *three stinking years* called him and got him upset enough to argue with his brother? Which, pardon me, doesn't make sense? Yeah, he's going to tell me about it starting right now. "Why was she calling, Jonah?"

"Chloe—"

"Look, I was honest with you about what happened between me and Kellan at the airport. I told you even though I knew it'd upset you, because I figured you have a right to know. So are you telling me I don't have a right to know why your ex-girlfriend is calling and upsetting you?"

He captures my waving arms and pulls me closer. "Of course you do. I just didn't want to upset you over a petty play at revenge my brother is enacting."

Again, this doesn't make sense. "Why'd she call?"

"Apparently she and Kellan had a long talk last night after he left you at the airport."

Wait a minute here. "Why would your brother and ex-girlfriend be talking?"

He sighs. "They're still really close."

"That's funny, because in the two months I dated him, he never mentioned her name once," I say flatly.

"I don't know what to tell you," Jonah says, "other than I happen to know they're still close."

This irrationally pisses me off. "Really."

"Well, yeah. The three of us did a lot together, considering we've known Callie most of our lives, so—"

"Most of your *lives*?"

Now he looks irritated, too. "Yes."

"How long?"

"Since second grade," he says.

The jealousy I'd felt the night before is nothing compared to the wicked flashes streaking through me now. Not only did Jonah date this chick for three years, but he's known her most of his life. Not quite as long as I've known him, but long enough to give her a genuine place to stake a claim in his life.

I've never met her, but I really think I hate her.

"Whoa," Jonah says, startled. "I don't know what you're thinking here, but . . . I thought we covered this last night. Things with Callie are over, Chloe."

"She's aware of this?"

"Yes." He looks oddly tired.

"So why'd she call?"

He meets my eyes right on. "Kellan told her the truth—that you were his girlfriend and while he was back East, I stole you away. How you and I have known each other our whole lives, and that I'd, for all intents and purposes," and here he sighs deeply, "used her during the time we were together as a replacement or holding place for you. Something along those lines. She was upset after hearing this. I don't like hurting her more than I already have, Chloe. She doesn't deserve that."

Rationally, I can understand why he doesn't want to hurt this girl. He's a good person, and at the time they'd dated, he hadn't known I really existed. But jealousy is an irrational, cruel creature who doesn't like to be reasoned with. And I really don't care if this Callie's feeling hurt or not. "You didn't steal me away."

"But that's how he sees it, and, you know what? I totally get that, because I felt the exact same thing during those months you two were dating. I was eaten alive with jealousy and anger every day. It was pretty hard to control myself at times."

Goodbye, jealousy. Hello, guilt! It's been a whopping two hours without you, and I was beginning to worry you'd forgotten me. "I'm so sorry," I whisper.

He shakes his head. "I don't want us to have to keep going over and over this, feeling like we have to apologize for all the mistakes we've made. It serves no purpose. What's done is done. We can only move forward, and that's what I want to do. But at the same time, I can't let Kellan drag Callie into this. He can be as pissed off at me as he wants and I know I've just got to take it, but she has nothing to do with what's going on between the three of us."

A horrible idea rears its head. "Is that what he's doing? Trying to bring her back around to . . . I don't know . . . tempt you away?"

"No. Kellan knows better than that, after I explained how you're my Connection. He knows there's nothing, and no one, who will ever be able to tempt me away from you again. I think, though, he sees it like stabbing me in a place that isn't fatal, just one that'll hurt like hell." Jonah's quiet for a long moment. "He's right, you know. I dated Callie, knowing I didn't love her the way she loved me. It wasn't fair to her, and I felt like a jerk for a long time for never being what she deserved. I think part of me used to hope I'd learn to love her, but the harder I tried, the harder I failed. So when Callie called, crying and accusing me of using her for years . . . I think it hit home a little too hard." He rubs at his forehead. "You're not the only one who's hurt somebody, Chloe."

I'm instantly contrite, babbling yet another round of apologies.

But he cuts me off. "I'm going to be honest here—I do love Callie; she's been a part of my life and a good friend for a very long time. I do miss her, but Chloe, I'm not *in* love with her. I've only ever been, only ever will be, in love with you."

Admitting you love someone else is not the best way to reassure a jealous girlfriend. So I snap, "Nice, Jonah. Any other girls you loved you want to tell me about?"

He lets me go and takes a step back. "Don't you think I felt—*feel*—that way about you and Kellan?"

What did you expect him to do, just roll over and let you throw your hypocrisy around with no ramifications? the little voice offers in regards to my inner outrage.

"The difference is," he says in a low voice bordering on anger, "that I actually had to watch it happen, not just hear about it. It was excruciating, Chloe. Every time he kissed you, I thought I was going to throw up. Every time he held you, it took every ounce of control I had—and by the end, there was very little left—to not beat the crap out of my own twin brother. So yeah, I understand jealousy, too."

The little voice murmurs, *Don't even bother trying to argue against this one.* And it's right. There's nothing I can say to excuse what I've done.

Zthane comes by later that evening, bringing with him bittersweet news. Cora's been found, but our worst fears are realized: she'd been attacked by the Elders.

"She's alive," Zthane is telling us, but I'm only catching some of his words. Is Cora in pain? Is she awake? "Karl and Kellan found her blahblah, roughly a mile blahblahblah. Blahblah way to school."

I let Jonah ask the questions as I stare down at my hands—they're shaking, and all I can do is wonder if her hands are okay. I can't focus. Why can't I focus? Oh, gods, is she all right?

"The car blahblahblah," Zthane is murmuring. "She tried escaping, but they blahblahblah . . ."

Can a Shaman heal herself?

"Blabblahblah hospital here in Annar—"

I jerk my head up. "She's here?"

“Yes,” Zthane says gently, as if he isn’t acutely aware I’ve been out of the conversation. “She’s in very good hands, Chloe. The best in all the worlds.”

“When can I see her?”

“Maybe tomorrow.” His phone is ringing again—but then, in the short time I’ve known him, it seems to ring constantly. “Maybe the day after that. She needs her rest.” And then the conversation between Zthane and Jonah falls back into the familiar buzzing of words that are just out of comprehension’s reach.

Cora is in a hospital, and it’s because of me.

Karl warned us early on that sometimes people close to powerful Magicals are targeted. Cora and I had laughed this off, saying just because she was my best friend, no one would want to go after her, because she’s not Council bound. We didn’t give his warnings credence, not even after I’d been attacked twice.

She’d been attacked, all alone. Had she tried to fight back? Defend herself with any of the multitude of diseases in her arsenal? It’s unbearable to imagine my Cousin going through this—Cora, who always tries to be so strong and flippant when it’s really a mask to hide her confused and sensitive soul.

I want to smash something, destroy it in ugly, permanent ways.

I’ve never felt so helpless in my life.

chapter 38

Karl and Iolani are sitting at the dining-room table, talking quietly while drinking tea. I join them, asking Karl, "When did you get here?"

He pours me a cup. "About a half-hour ago." He looks me up and down. "You're up early. Jonah still sleeping?"

I nod, taking the cup from him. "Any word on Cora?"

"Do you want me to sugarcoat it, or give it to you real?" I roll my eyes despite the seriousness of the situation. He knows better than to ask that. "The Elders took quite a bit of Cora's life force from her. By the time we found her, she had very little left."

I swallow hard. "Meaning?"

"Meaning it's a damn good thing we found her when we did. She's still at the hospital, and they're still working on her. Truth be told, we don't find a lot of survivors, especially at this level of . . ." He struggles to find the correct word. "Depravity, I suppose. Most survivors are usually only superficially hurt, like your father. Things Shamans can fix easily. But even the best don't have a lot of experience regenerating someone who is barely existing. I'm sorry to have to put it that way, Chloe."

She's strong, and she's a fighter, the little voice murmurs. *She'll pull through—just you wait and see.*

Tears flood my eyes. "Are they hopeful, though?"

He reaches out to squeeze my hand. "I think so."

Jonah wasn't joking when he said he wasn't a morning person. It's already after ten in the morning and he's still blissfully sleeping in the room we commandeered together. I don't bother waking him, as there's no reason to. I spend my time, instead, getting to know Iolani and listening to all the fun stories about the Guard she and Karl have to share in an effort to keep my mind off of Cora.

"Are you looking forward to moving here?" she asks me as she lounges on the floor, feet propped up on the coffee table.

When I say, "I think I finally am," Karl laughs.

"You must be excited that you get to Ascend so early," Iolani continues, picking at nonexistent split ends in her dark, lush hair. "That's already got a bunch of the Guard jealous as all hell."

Huh? "Ascend early?"

Karl groans. "She doesn't know yet, Lani."

"What don't I know now?" I demand, throwing visual daggers at Karl.

He holds his hands up. "Look. It wasn't my call. Your parents were informed and they specifically asked me not to tell you. They said they'd let you know when it was appropriate."

"And you believed them?" I yell.

"Here's the deal," he says, completely nonplussed. "The Council has decided you need to Ascend early, considering the threat against you. They know you're already powerful, but feel it will be prudent to allow you all your powers at the earliest convenience."

This is so typical of my parents! "And just when is my earliest convenience?"

"No Magical has ever Ascended before eighteen. Most have to wait a number of months afterwards, due to stability factors and whatnot, but they figure you'll be fine if you do it at the time of your birth."

The little voice and I both choke out, "*Fine?*" at the same time.

"Well," he clarifies, "sometimes people who are still unstable with their powers, or immature, have some trouble during Ascension . . ." He pauses. "How would you put it, Lani?"

She rolls over and sits up. "They crack like an egg. They can't deal with the influx of power." She holds her hands on the side of her head and makes an explosion noise as her fingers expand.

Actually, that's a good way to describe how my head feels with this piece of information. "Is this common?!"

She considers this. "Maybe ten percent."

"Maybe less," Karl argues.

I wheeze, "Could this happen to me?" The little voice urges me to calm down.

"No, no, of course not," they both say, as if in league with one another.

"And I've got to do this early?"

"You won't be alone," Iolani says in a soothing voice I imagine she'd use for a psycho she found on the street and was trying to get under control. "Jonah and Kellan will be Ascending early, too, for the same reasons."

I jab a finger at Karl. "Do *they* know?"

He scoots away from my finger. "I believe so, yes. But I don't think they know you will be. Frankly, I can't see Jonah approving of it, what with the odds and all . . . I mean, I think I'd have gone nuts if I knew Moira would've—"

"What odds?" I ask through clenched teeth.

Karl sighs. "This is why your parents should've been the ones telling you. See, it's like this: Ascending early increases the odds from ten to about forty percent."

I sort of choke as I draw my knees up to my chest. "I have a . . . forty-percent chance of . . . ?"

Iolani puts her hands by her head again and makes the same explosion sound.

"But you won't," Karl says quickly. "I have faith in you."

I sag back against the couch. "At least one of us does."

Iolani sits down in between me and Karl. "Enough talk of doom and gloom. Let's gossip instead. I hear you and Jonah have a Connection, Chloe. Spill."

I crane my neck so I can throw more daggers at Karl on the other side of her. "Look," he says, putting his hands up again. "The Guard is a vicious pit of gossip. Everyone knows everything about everyone. To be fair, I wasn't the one who spilled this bit of information."

"It doesn't matter who squealed," Iolani says. "I'm just looking for confirmation. Is it true? Did you snag yourself one of the über-hotties?"

I feel blindsided. "I . . . well . . . yes?"

"I could have sworn," she says to Karl, "that I remember hearing she was dating Kellan. Isn't that funny?"

"Hilarious," he says flatly.

"Jonah's so awesome," Iolani says, leaning back so she can stretch her feet out on the coffee table. I notice, as she wiggles her toes, that her nails have flowers on them. She sighs loudly. "I wish I had a Connection. Fricking Fate. But no—I have to schlep through bad date after bad date in my eternal quest to find Mr. Right."

"She does date a lot," Karl tells me.

"I mean," Iolani continues, "how fabulous is a Connection? You're guaranteed to always be loved, always be accepted. It'll never break, so heartbreak is totally avoidable. Who wouldn't want one of those?"

"Some people who have Connections never find each other. It does happen sometimes," Karl offers.

"If I had a Connection," she orates, holding out a finger, "I would never rest until I found him. I would move heaven and earth to be with the person I was meant for." She sighs again. "Karl here is so lucky. He and Moira had their little doorway and never had to work at finding each other. Bastards."

"Go ahead and send some of that bitterness Chloe's way," Karl grins. "She and Jonah did the whole dream thing, too."

"Seriously?" Iolani asks, eyes wide. Then she looks me up and down. "Bee-yatch."

Should I be flattered or insulted? "Er . . . thanks?"

"Tell me you two have already merged together, and I may puke," she says bitterly.

"Uh . . . okay?"

Karl jerks forward. "What?"

"Is this bad?" I ask, confused, because I'm pretty sure there's no way such a thing could be bad. In fact, it's pretty awesome, if I may say so myself, and something I really look forward to doing with Jonah when we're alone.

"Was it good?" Iolani asks, practically salivating over this bit of gossip. "I hear it's amazing. Better than sex—well, almost, I suppose. I hear that if it happens at the same time you're having sex, then it's mind blowing, but in a good way, not like what we were talking about earlier, and man . . . with Jonah? It's got to be—"

"When was this?" Karl booms, cutting her off.

"Dude, calm down," Iolani laughs. "Like you have a leg to stand on, what with you and Moira getting caught doing nookie all over Guard Headquarters."

"ARE YOU SAYING THEY'RE HAVING SEX, TOO?" he roars as he stands up.

"Whoa," I say nervously. "No one is talking about sex. At least, I'm not talking about it. She said *you* are having sex—"

"I'M MARRIED AND OLDER THAN YOU."

"Yeah, by like three years!"

Karl's eyes are bugging out so far I worry they might hit me when they explode. But then, after grinding his teeth for a good five seconds and balling his fists up over and over, he takes a deep breath and sits back down. "Leave it to Jonah to go and do that right away."

"Hel-*lo*," Iolani says. "If it'd been me, I'd have done it two seconds after finding my Connection. And according to Moira—"

"We're not talking about me and Moira," Karl snaps, and then Iolani and I laugh, because he plays the role of angry protector so well.

Jonah appears in the doorway, still sleepy and utterly adorable with rumpled hair. "What's all the yelling about?"

Iolani grins slyly. "Yes, Karl. What were you yelling about?"

He mutters something under his breath and stands back up, pointing a finger at Jonah. "You're lucky I like you so much."

Jonah blinks. "Huh?"

Karl looks back down at me and Iolani and then back to Jonah. "I'm going to go call my wife now." And then he exits the room swiftly, prompting me and Iolani to burst into laughter once more, and Jonah to watch his friend retreat in confusion.

Lizzie, Alex, and Meg show up later that night, along with Kellan, who appears completely at ease with being in the same room as me and Jonah. I am not at ease, though. I am grossly uncomfortable to the point my palms sweat at the same time my mouth goes dry. It always amazes me when that happens—it's like all the moisture in my mouth leeches out through my palms.

I listen to Lizzie's recollections of what happened back home before they came here—how, admittedly, she and Meg both flew off the handle and how they'd freaked out when Kellan left them at Graham's house so he could go look for Cora. Graham is still in California, worried sick about Lizzie, making her wonder how she can get around the whole "Don't tell" rule so he can come to Annar, too. She ends up calling him twice during our conversation.

Bored, Alex flips through television channels while Meg squeals at every other stop, declaring her love of each show and lamenting each time he skips past her choices. "I love these two," Lizzie says quietly, "but they are driving me bonkers. Thank gods I had Kellan to talk to for part of the day, when he wasn't off doing Guard stuff."

I slide my eyes over to where Kellan and Jonah are talking with Karl and Iolani. They seem completely comfortable around each other, as if nothing has happened at all over the last few months.

I wonder if I ought to go over there, too. I want to, because I want to be in the loop. But I also don't want to highlight my awkwardness for all to see—or rather, feel. I wish I could control my emotions as easily as they do, that I could pretend everything is peachy and manage to do what's needed without obsessing over the smallest details. But I can't. So I stay where I am, sitting with my equally clueless Cousin, watching our two even more clueless Cousins squabble about what to watch on TV. This goes on for at least twenty more minutes before Zthane comes crashing through the door.

Everyone stops talking as he surveys the room. His eyes settle on me. "Lilywhite. Good. Still here."

It's Raul's turn to burst into the room. "They're five minutes out," he yells, charging to the windows.

"Who's five minutes out?" Karl demands.

Zthane joins Raul at the windows. "Annar's boundaries have finally been breached, my friend. The Elders are here, and they're on the warpath!"

Chaos breaks out in the room. Meg goes hysterical. Lizzie is shaking in her boots. Everyone begins yelling, even Alex—everyone but me. There are a thousand questions floating above us, but the only answer that really matters is that the Elders are here, and it's believed they are specifically here for *me*.

This declaration from Zthane has Jonah by my side in a split second. "Come with me," he says, and while everyone else is arguing, I'm taken down the hallway into a windowless room. Within two seconds, the Cousins run in, all three exhibiting terror in different stages. Finally, Kellan saunters in, locking the door behind him.

"Meg," he says gently, "I'm sorry to have to do this again." And the next thing I know, Alex barely catches her as she slumps to the ground. Kellan gives Lizzie a meaningful look, but she holds out her hands.

"I'm okay this time. I swear. I can keep it in."

He looks doubtful, but leaves her alone.

“Will the lock hold?” I ask no one in particular.

“No,” Jonah says. “But it’d be a small roadblock that could give us a few seconds to counter-attack.”

Feeling utterly useless and helpless, I ask, “What can I do?”

“Nothing,” he says. “Right now, I just need you to focus on making sure our friends stay safe and comfortable. Trust me and Kellan to take care of the logistics for everything else.”

I am not a damsel in distress. It goes against me in so many ways to just sit back. “What logistics?”

He says quietly in my ear, “Do you trust me to deal with this? To keep you safe?”

He plays dirty. “You know I do.”

“Jonah,” Kellan says calmly. “They’re here.”

Jonah’s head cocks to the side. “There are . . . fifteen, maybe?”

Kellan nods. “Fifteen severely pissed off Elders. Good times ahead, don’t you think?”

The screaming begins, the same awful keening that accompanied the other two times I’d been chased by these things. It’s almost deafening, and clearly too much for Lizzie. She hysterically babbles about the end of the world while nearly pulling her hair out. My own nerves go raw.

Since Jonah is closer, he’s the one to calm Lizzie down. She sinks down next to where Alex is holding Meg. “Alex?” Kellan calls out from across the room. “You okay there?”

“Somebody has to watch over the girls,” Alex murmurs, his face a weird green shade that might indicate he’s on the verge of puking. I take a gigantic step backwards from where he’s propping up both girls.

The sound of winds whipping feverishly rises up outside, howling in fury as the building rocks. My ears pop from the pressure. Both Jonah and Kellan are silent, listening from their respective places on opposite sides of the room. "Do you think the building will hold?" I yell at Jonah.

He yells back, "I'm not sure," but I'm pretty sure the answer is a resounding *no.* The Elders were able to attack cars with little to no difficulty. What would stop them from attacking a building?

I lean against the same wall Jonah is against and I have my answer. Each time the building rocks, it's because something is hitting it from outside.

I turn to Jonah, to tell him my fears, but he's looking at his brother. His forehead is furrowed when he shakes his head very, very softly.

My eyes track across the room to Kellan, who is rolling his own eyes. He leans his head back against the door and nods. I switch my focus back to Jonah, who is also leaning his head against the door, nodding as well.

They are communicating. Wordlessly. How in the worlds . . .?

Before I can ask about this, the building is rocked hard by another blast. Jonah grabs me to keep me on my feet. The screaming reaches such a fevered pitch that my ears ring painfully. And then the ground groans and rumbles in wide, rippling waves. All of the pictures in the room jump off the walls, shattering down around us. Jonah has to steady me again as I nearly slip on pieces of glass while finding my footing.

"It's only Karl," he tells me, as if this makes things less terrifying. Like strong earthquakes are so much better than buildings being attacked. Then Jonah looks back at his brother and nods. "Can you make us something? Some kind of screen which would let us see and hear what's going on outside?" he yells, coming up right to my ear.

Grateful that I've finally been asked to do something, even if it's to make a glorified security camera, I get straight to work. I construct a massive screen out of the plaster on a now pictureless wall, stretching from one side of the room to the other. I don't bother with volume controls or an on/off button—I simply will the screen to show me what I need and make whatever sound there is loud enough to be heard over the screaming. Large as life, we get a front-row view of what's going on beyond the walls. The streets below are chaos, with people running every direction. There are three thin twisters in the vicinity, striking out toward the black shape-shifters throwing themselves at the building.

Zthane is hard at work casting lightning bolts down at the Elders, but they streak in and out of the twisters and bolts, deftly avoiding any strikes. "Karl!" the Goblin yells, his voice echoing off the winds, "I want that hole bigger!"

Karl is bent to one knee nearby in front of a thick crack running through the street. His fist slams into the pavement fast and hard, making the ground roll so strongly people all around him fall, hands over their heads. The crack widens, groaning so loudly it almost overcomes the screaming.

Raul steps into view, angling his twisters towards the Elders. Zthane shouts, "Again, Karl! It's got to be deeper," shoving two more bolts simultaneously toward the shapes. Karl hammers his fist down again, widening the crack significantly. Most of the people scramble to get away, leaving only the Guard left standing their ground.

The black shapes shift direction and zero in on Karl. We watch helplessly as they attack him. And, just like with Jonah months before, one twists itself into a whip and lashes out at Karl's arm. The crunch of bones is sickeningly loud even over the din outside. When Karl roars and falls over, Kellan grabs the doorknob.

"Not yet!" Jonah barks.

Now that Karl is down and his fist useless, the Elders turn toward Zthane. Two Blazes are running nearby, shooting fireballs at them, but they are no match for the agile shape shifters. They whiz in and out of the explosions, dart clean by the lightning strikes, and hurl themselves directly at the Goblin. He doesn't run, though—he keeps reaching up and pulling down more lightning. Benches are destroyed, trees are exploding, and yet nothing seems to connect with the Elders.

"I slowed them down before!" I yell at Jonah. "I should be out there!"

But he grabs my arm to stop me from running to the door. "You are not leaving this room unless absolutely necessary, Chloe! They are out there protecting *you* right now! Don't make it more difficult on them!"

I turn back to the screen just in time to see an Elder strike Zthane from behind. He flies forward, slamming his head against a light post.

It's Alex's turn to become hysterical. He's raving about how we're screwed, how there's no way the Elders won't make it into the building if they keep taking down some of the strongest Guard we have. But Jonah and Kellan are so focused on watching what's going on outside, they don't bother sedating him.

Zthane staggers briefly to his feet, just long enough to drop another round of bolts. Then he slumps back to the ground, bleeding profusely from a gash on his forehead. Kellan turns to Jonah, eyes wide. He no longer looks calm—in fact, he's vibrating in anger. Jonah is the same, hands gripping in and out of fists.

Raul races over to Zthane, screaming his name. The Blazes are trying their best to bomb the Elders, but the shifters are still moving too fast to pin down. Raul's tornadoes are barely faring better; with his attention diverted, they're doing more damage to the buildings across the street.

A Tide comes into view, wrenching a tunnel of water out of the crack Karl had been working on. He angles the sharp geyser directly at the Elders, but as with everything else, they evade easily.

Then an Electric tries his hand, ripping currents from all of the lampposts nearby, exploding the glass shells on top. Crackling bits of blue electricity race directly into the shape shifters—finally, something strong enough that momentarily causes retreat. But just as I'm about to breathe a sigh of relief, a stray Elder appears from behind and slams the Electric to the ground.

Alex's ravings finally come to Kellan's attention. He barely flicks his hand toward my Cousin, but it's enough to silence him.

"Will they be safe, out like this?" I yell.

"They're fine," Jonah assures me. "None of them are targets."

I look at the pile of friends in the middle of the room and think of Cora, who is in a hospital nearby due to her proximity to me. "Are you sure?"

"Yes," Jonah says. And then all of a sudden, he shoves me toward his brother. Kellan catches me at the same time the entire wall Jonah and I had been standing next to collapses, knocking Jonah to the ground. I attempt to run to his aid, but Kellan's grip turns vise-like as he hauls me backwards.

Jonah rolls over and pushes himself up to his knees. Before him, and us, is the bedroom Iolani had been sleeping in. Beyond that is a huge hole leading straight outside.

And beyond *that* is a mass of Elders.

I am nearly overtaken by fear, despite the little voice urging me to remain calm. Jonah takes a huge breath and then staggers to his feet. His eyes connect with mine. "Go with Kellan!"

Wait. *Wait*. WAIT.

Jonah's hand swings out in an arc. All of the Elders in the hole back up, squealing in agony. "We need to go now, Chloe," Kellan is saying in my ear, but I am flailing against him, gripping onto a desk as he tries to drag me closer to the door.

"Jonah!" I scream, hysterical now. "Jonah!"

Jonah pushes himself off the wall and runs directly toward the hole leading outside. And just when I think he's going to stop, skid to a halt to oversee what's outside, his feet move faster to launch his body directly out of what used to be a fourth-story window and out of my view.

The desk below my hands explodes, nearly knocking me and Kellan down. This cannot be happening! He did not just do that! I squirm enough to face the screen I created, but Jonah is not in its line of view. As if it knew it'd failed me, the screen melts down, popping and hissing. "Get ahold of yourself!" Kellan yells in my ear. "We need to get out of here now!"

I begin sobbing. "No, Jonah . . . he . . . he . . ."

"I know exactly what he did! And he specifically requested that you get out of this room, so that's exactly what we're going to do right now! Do not make me sedate you, too, Chloe."

His words stun me enough that my muscles lock, facilitating Kellan's attempts at extracting me from the room.

Once outside the door, though, the hysteria returns. "He jumped out . . . he just jumped out! Oh my gods, what if . . . ?"

Kellan's grip doesn't loosen one iota. "Raul caught him."

"C-caught him? From four stories up?"

"With a tornado. Now listen to me—I'll answer all your questions *after* we get to safety. But I need you to stop talking and let me get you to the basement."

But I can't do it. All I can think is that Jonah is out there, Jonah—all of seventeen, and not Ascended. Strong Guards have fallen outside. I've watched them go down. What's to stop the Elders from getting to Jonah? Who's strong enough outside right now to protect him? What if something worse than driving off a cliff happens? What if more than an arm is broken?

I can't take the risk. If something were to happen to Jonah now that we've finally found our way back to each another, I don't think I'll maintain sanity. I need to get out there, find him, and make sure he's okay. My mini suns could work. They worked before.

We are in the stairwell of the second floor when another blast rocks the building. It's strong enough that Kellan finally stumbles, just enough that his grip on me loosens. I wrench myself free and sprint as fast as I can into the hallway, stumbling over chunks of downed walls and plaster, before I reach the stairwell on the opposite side of the building.

Kellan is behind me; I know any minute he's going to zap me with something. I don't put it beyond him for one second to tranquilize me and carry me over his shoulder like a sack of potatoes out of here. And normally, I'd be thankful he'd do that for me, that he'd risk my anger just to keep me safe. But not today. Not with Jonah outside for who knows how long now.

I throw my hand out and the wall before us disappears. I can practically feel Kellan's fingers ready to scrape at my back, so I pick up speed. I made a life raft on the way down from the Bay Bridge. I can do something like that again, right? I'm just about to jump through the hole I've created when Kellan catches me. He rolls to the side just before we tumble out, slamming us against the remaining bits of wall left behind.

"Are you insane?" he growls in my ear.

I squirm frantically, trying to break free again, but this time, he's got a lock on me. The roaring of the winds, the screaming filling the air are too much to bear. Jonah is out there, he's a target, too, and I've got to do something.

I change tactics and shove my feet against a slab of concrete nearby. I push off, attempting to wrench my arms wide, hoping to confuse him as to which ploy to counter. But it doesn't work. His arms clamp down harder, his legs twist until they're around mine.

"You're not going to win," he hisses in my ear. "Because I will do anything to make sure you stay alive today. Including knocking your ass out until I have you hidden."

I duck my head and kick again, rolling us over until I'm on my stomach. I manage to pry one arm out long enough to grip the open edge of where wall meets sky. Concrete and stone crumble beneath my fingers, cutting into the soft flesh of my palm, but the pain is irrelevant. I try to dig my fingers in long enough to pull myself, but Kellan is extremely strong. Kicking does no good any longer—and even though my adrenaline is off the charts, I know he won't give.

I sob helplessly. "Would everything just *stop*?"

"Chloe, I know you're frustrated—"

"It just needs to stop," I cry. "I need it all to just *stop*."

And just like that, everything does.

chapter 39

The screaming has stopped. But it's more than that—there are no roaring winds, no lightning, no smashing against buildings. The air around us is oppressive, so thick, so still it doesn't feel right. Kellan lets go of me and rolls away; while this is what I've been fighting for, I still reach out and grab his arm as he leans toward the ledge. He looks down below and pauses, lips parting in surprise. I scramble forward to see what he sees.

Nothing is moving. The winds have frozen in the sky, the black shapes dangle like grotesque mobiles over the fallen Guard below, tornadoes hang like pictures in a diorama. Every last person is contorted mid-motion, like statues caught by Medusa's stare. There is no sound. There is nothing but stillness.

Kellan rocks back on his heels, stumbling over pieces of concrete. Whereas the rubble had skidded around like marbles ready to cause falls mere minutes ago, now they're firmly glued in place, refusing to budge even a millimeter. I try to pick up a rock, but nothing gives way.

I am so taken aback that I nearly fall back over again. My toes slam against a rather large chunk of debris nearby when I try to right myself, but when I open my mouth to yelp, nothing comes out.

No sound. No movement—nothing but me and Kellan.

He grabs my arm, steadying me. And then he brings me close—my heart goes berserk being in such proximity—and mouths slowly: *Can you make us talk?*

It hits me then: *I've* done this. I made everything still. I've created a world where everything has stopped.

Panic shoots sky high in my chest, but he grips me tighter. *Focus,* he mouths to me.

I close my eyes and concentrate. When nothing happens, I put a hand on both of our throats. *Talk,* I will myself. *We can talk. If we can move, we can talk.*

"Okay," he says, his voice echoing dully in the vacuum, "this is good." He grabs my face so he can look into my eyes. "Are you okay?"

My throat feels like it's been dry and unused for centuries. "I did this."

"Why do you sound so surprised?"

I look around at the world I've created and then down at my fingers. They should be shaking, but they're not. "I guess I never thought I could do this."

He lets go of my face. "You're a Creator. You can do almost anything." He takes a few steps back toward the ledge and looks out, surveying the scene I'd frozen.

"If you jump out, I will kill you," I threaten.

"That's rich, coming from you. Weren't you the one ready to do just the same thing?"

"It's different!"

"How so?"

"As you said," I say through my teeth, "I'm a Creator. I would've made something to stop my fall. What was your big plan? Hope fuzzy feelings will lessen the impact?"

Eye rolling proceeds, "I wasn't going to jump."

My silence indicates my disbelief. So he turns around and says evenly, "Sometimes we have to do things we don't want to do, Chloe."

I join him at the ledge. "Why did your brother jump out of that window?"

"He was told to." After I make a few choking sounds, he clarifies, "Well, he wasn't told to jump out of the window, per se, but he had orders that if the walls were breached, he was to join the fray."

I press the palms of my hands against my forehead. "And you?"

"The same. One of us had to get you to safety first, though. I was closest to the door."

Now I'm glaring.

He turns his focus back below us. "We're not going to argue about this. Besides, I think this may work to our advantage."

I nearly laugh. "You're kidding, right?"

"How long can this hold?"

I hold my hands out and shrug.

"Do you think you can wake select people up? Allow them to function, like we can function?"

"I guess." I stare at the statues below me. "Why?"

He leads me away from the edge and out of the building. "Because we're going to go kick some ass, and not even get dirty doing it."

Minutes later, I tell him, "I want to find Jonah first."

Kellan stops in the middle of the street. "I want to make sure he's safe, too, but I think—"

"You want my help? You play by my rules."

He sighs, giving me a look I can't quite decipher. I resist the urge to tell him that if it'd been him out there, I'd have done the same thing to get to him, too.

"And," I add, pointing to a clock tower nearby, "we have all the time in the worlds right now."

"The clock might simply be frozen." He doesn't even bother to look at it.

"Or," I counter, "time might have stopped, too."

"We have all the time in the worlds," he says, beginning to walk once more, "as long as you focus and keep this thing stable."

I hurry to catch up. "Meaning?"

"Meaning you're extremely emotional right now, and I've seen your Magic go wonky when you're upset."

"You have *not*!"

He stops again and raises an eyebrow.

Okay, so he's right. "As long as I know it matters, I can keep it together. We find Jonah first and then the three of us will go with your plan." I pause. "Can you feel him right now?"

Kellan starts walking. "No."

"Can you feel any of these people?"

"No."

"Can you feel *me*?"

He sighs. "Yes."

"So . . . how are we going to find Jonah?"

"We are going to start in the direction where I felt him last," Kellan says, stepping around two people cringing on the ground. "And then we'll work from there."

I think it takes us nearly forty-five minutes to find Jonah, but I can't be sure since I don't have anything accurate to judge time. He's in an alley with three other Guards and, much to my terror, two Elders.

Jonah is down on the ground, one arm stretched toward the sky. The Elders are above him, hovering about an inch above his fingertips. This isn't what has me panicked, though—no, while that is horrifying in itself, it's the deep gash on his left temple and the dark red matting his black hair.

I whimper his name and crouch down so I can look at his head. Before my hands make contact, though, Kellan pulls me back.

"Make it so I can sense him."

"What?"

"I can't feel my brother," he grinds out, "and I'm not going to let you wake him up if it's only going to make him worse. Make it so I can sense him."

I have no idea how to do this, of course. I didn't even know I could. I attempt to do what he's asked by visualizing the link between the brothers, and then imagining clearing the debris blocking it.

It must be enough, because Kellan sinks down and lays his hands on either side of Jonah's face. He closes his eyes and presses his forehead against Jonah's bleeding one. After an agonizingly long time, he opens his eyes and says quietly, "Don't wake him up yet."

I am fully aware of how shrill my voice is. "Why?"

He lets go of Jonah's face. "Because he was right on the verge of blacking out." Kellan then moves over to one of the other Guards lying on the ground. "This guy . . . he was out when Jonah found him." Another Guard looks as if his leg is broken, as it's angled in a weird direction. The third's hand is out, inches from an Elder's whipping tail.

But as much as I ought to care about the others, I really can only focus on Jonah. "Is he okay, though?"

"I'm not a Shaman. I can't diagnose anything."

"But you know what's going on with him. Just tell me, Kellan. And don't try to sugarcoat it."

He rubs at his hair. "There's something wrong with his left leg. And what they did to his arm before, they tried to do to his head when he was helping one of those guys over there. They caught him off guard—he thought he had more time before they struck. So, he's barely hanging onto consciousness, and I'm no Shaman, but the way his thoughts are distorted, I'm thinking something's wrong with his head."

I don't even know how to process these words. I want to touch Jonah, soothe him, hold on and make sure he doesn't let go, but I don't, out of fear of possibly waking him up and making it worse. And that is impossible to accept, because I should be able to help him. I'm his Connection. It's my duty to keep him safe.

Kellan slides down the wall until he's sitting on the ground next to his brother. He reaches out and touches Jonah's hair. I envy Kellan this luxury, this touch. "I know it's asking a lot of you right now. I know you're scared. I know you're so worried about him you can barely think straight. But I need you to focus. We need to get this done, get rid of these things, and then we can get someone here to take care of Jonah."

It goes against every molecule in my body to even contemplate leaving Jonah in such a situation. "Can you promise me he'll be fine?"

Kellan leans his head back against the wall. "You know I can't. But we still have to try."

I sit next to him and stare at the blood in Jonah's hair. "A lot of people are hurt," I whisper.

"Yes."

"They're hurt because of me."

"No."

"He's hurt," I cry quietly, "because of me. He was trying to protect me."

Hesitantly, ever so gently, Kellan puts an arm around my shoulders. "We're going to fix this, Chloe. We're going to stand up, wake our friends, and fix this."

I don't ask for his promise this time, because I know Kellan. I trust him to help me fix this.

Our preferred choices over who to wake up first are technically both knocked out, so it's sort of a crap shoot.

"It doesn't make sense to wake up Karl first," Kellan says, giving me a no-nonsense look I'm not quite familiar with. "We need Zthane."

"Why? I trust Karl—"

"I'm not saying you shouldn't. But Zthane is lead out here right now, so Zthane is the one we go to with the plan first."

I have to jog to keep up with him and his frustratingly long strides. "Are you sure about the plan?"

"We've gone over this already. It's the same one we were working under before you froze time—entrap the Elders in a hole beneath Annar's streets. It'll just be easier this time to complete, now that we don't have to actively battle these things."

"Didn't seem to be going so well before," I throw out, winded from six blocks of jogging.

He glares at me.

"Just saying. Don't you think it'll piss them off, being stuffed back into a hole?"

He stops. "Do you think I give a rat's ass if it does?"

"No, of course not," I say, glad to stop and catch my breath. "I'm just saying, if they were able to break free of a hole before, what's to stop them from doing it again?"

"The first hole was disrupted because of an earthquake. There are no earthquakes in Annar." I merely lift my eyebrows. "Normally," he clarifies. "Outside of Elder attacks. Besides, we're going to have you seal the hole up along with Iolani, so it shouldn't be a problem."

"Funny how I'm allowed to do something now," I mutter, "besides cower inside a building and pray that everyone around me doesn't die."

He takes a step back, but I don't think it's because he's worried I'll smack him or anything. "Let's put it this way: Did you like it when Jonah jumped out of that window?"

"What kind of stupid question is that?"

"How did it make you feel, seeing him in that alley, bleeding, on the verge of gods know what?"

Like he doesn't know. "What's your point?"

"My point," he says, walking again, "is that you have to think of how people would feel if you were out there fighting, too. What if that'd been *you* out there? Would you have wanted to do that to him? Worry him like that?"

"Concern about worrying me didn't stop him, did it?"

Kellan shakes his head. "For someone who has a Connection to him, you really don't know Jonah at all, do you?"

I relent and give into waking up Zthane first. It's an easy process—all I do is lay a hand on his chest and order him to wake up. Which, of course, he doesn't—I mean, his heart is beating, and he's breathing, but considering he'd been unconscious when I'd frozen Annar, that's how he's returned to us.

It doesn't faze Kellan, though. He simply touches his mentor's head and wills him to feel lucid and relatively pain free. It takes a minute or so, but Zthane eventually opens his dilated eyes. Confusion, then anger, fills them as Kellan helps him sit up. "Why is Lilywhite out here? Orders were to take her to one of the panic rooms below the building!"

"I tried," Kellan says, squatting down next to the Elemental. "But she decided to do something else."

"Chloe, don't you know how dangerous it is out here?" Zthane asks, rubbing at his heavily bruised forehead. "Good gods, girl, are you trying to get yourself killed?"

"Uh," I say, looking around. "Are you referring to you or Kellan doing the killing?"

Zthane then has a look around himself, mouth open so wide that I'm sure I could see his tonsils if I looked. And then Kellan explains to him what's happened, and the anger in his eyes fades to begrudging appreciation.

I'm overruled again when it comes time to wake up the next person. Zthane insists on another Goblin named Sjharn Thunderbridge, the Guard's best Shaman. He's huddled over another fallen Guard across the plaza, and Zthane reasons that if we're going to wake up so many injured people, we might as well get them into fighting condition before asking them to do anything, plenty of time or no.

After Sjharn finally comes Karl, which makes me feel a bit better. His arm looks worse upon inspection; in fact, if I were a betting woman, I'd say every bone had been broken. It takes Sjharn a long time to fix all the bones, and Kellan has to help by upping Karl's endorphin levels until he's nearly drugged out of his mind. Karl is giggling like a schoolgirl while rambling on about things I can't even begin to understand. During this process, Zthane goes over the plan with us. Karl will work on the hole while we wake up the rest of the Guard. Then I'm to solidify the ground, making it impenetrable. Iolani will create a lid of sorts, which I'm to also make permanent. And then I'm to will it so nothing but a Creator can ever open this patch of land again.

"Best to keep your enemies close," Zthane is saying. "Will be much easier on us if we always know where they are."

I'm exhausted by the time Kellan and I wake up the thirty Guards around the plaza, not including the ones with Jonah. Everyone has already insisted that we do them last—I think, especially with the way a now-lucid Karl is watching me, that they're all worried I won't be able to focus if I have to watch Jonah go through a painful healing process.

They're probably right. I can barely focus as it is, wondering how he's doing. And that's ridiculous, really, because I know nothing can happen to him as long as he's not moving. But it feels wrong to have him like that, even more wrong to know it's me who has taken life away from him, even if it's only in a temporary stasis.

Karl pounds away at the hole after I will the ground below us to react to his fist, shaping it in ways I didn't know was possible for a Quake. Now that he has the time, he's able to smooth the crack until it's roughly circular, rather than a jagged edge. He makes it deep by extending certain fingers during each of his fist poundings—so subtle and nuanced that it's really a marvel to watch. During this time, I sit on a partially broken bench and observe him and Iolani, who is mixing the rock with magma she's moving and pulling upward, while the rest of the Guards discuss the situation.

This part of Annar is devastated. The other Creator will be asked, apparently kicking and screaming, to come and rebuild before the week is out. When I offer to do it myself, I'm told no—not that they don't trust me, but that sometimes things like this take a seasoned, Ascended Creator, instead of a wild card who flies off the handle and freezes time and whatnot.

Well, they didn't actually say that last part, but I know it's what they're thinking.

Once the hole meets Karl's standards, I'm called over to tighten and make the walls permanent. I throw a bit of class to the joint, making the surrounding walls reflective so it doesn't seem so oppressive once sealed.

"You know," Iolani says, amused, "they won't have any light down there to throw reflections off of."

I dust my knees off. "It's the thought that counts."

Jump-starting the tornadoes already hanging in the sky is a bit tricky, especially since I keep remembering how it felt to actually be in one of them. I end up creating little balls of my willed thoughts to hand over to Raul to toss into his winds. He has no fear of one-hundred-and-fifty-mile-per-hour winds, so I let him deal with them.

Rustling up the Elders takes an excruciatingly long time. Raul is the only Cyclone around, and since the other Elementals deal more with other weather aspects, they are not much use. Like a cowboy, he uses his twisters to rope and herd the Elders toward the hole. He goes after one at a time, making sure it's safely ensconced before heading out toward another. I'm not allowed to go with him when he goes to fetch the two hovering over Jonah, but Kellan is, and I know—as pissed as he is at his brother—he'll never let anything happen to Jonah. Even still, I find it hard to breathe until those last two Elders are in the hole and I've been promised that everything is exactly as I left it in that alley.

Iolani uses more lava to create a thick lid to the hole. It amazes me how, in the face of such heat, she doesn't manage to sweat one single drop. I'm fifty feet away and ready to pass out from the extreme temperatures, especially since there are no more winds to move the stifling, thick air. The two Blazes stand next to her, also apparently impervious to such high temperatures. Their arms, I'd noticed, are covered in bumpy, distorted scars, making me wonder if they began playing with matches at a very early age.

Once the lava lid is finished, I'm called back over to make it permanent. During this process, Iolani gets more lava to fill the rest of the cracks in the streets around us. While not pretty, it's at least safe now to walk without fear of dropping dozens of feet down.

And then, just when I'm about to go crazy that we're not already with Jonah, Zthane tells us, "I'm afraid to tell you all that this isn't all of them."

"Who'd I miss?" Raul demands. "We scoured the entire city."

"You misunderstand," Zthane says. "You did get all in Annar. But shortly before I got knocked out, I got a call from the Dwarven plane. There was a sighting of Elders there. It appears they split up to attack two spots at once."

"Fantastic," Karl mutters. "Do you know if any were captured there?"

"No," Zthane says. "I'm afraid cell phones don't work in Chloe's no-time zone. But, I'm doubting it. In fact, after today, I'm doubting any of our tactics. It appears most of our skills don't seem to work on them too well. We know that Emotionals, Electrics, and a Creator are effective. The rest of us unfortunately are flying blind when it comes to controlling them."

This is not what any of us want to hear.

It isn't an easy thing to listen to a Shaman tick off the things wrong with the person you love. *It could be worse,* I'm told, *a broken leg is nothing*. Sjharn claims he fixes those all the time. The Guard goes off and gets legs messed up on missions frequently. But it's the head injury that has me freaked out. The Elders managed to crack Jonah's skull, and there is significant swelling of the brain.

I can create a city on the turn of a dime, I can destroy it with the blink of an eye, but I cannot do anything to help fix Jonah. All I can do is sit nearby and watch and wait and remind myself that I need to breathe, because when he wakes up, and I know he will, he'll need me.

So this is what I do while he lies in a bed in yet another safe house. I hold his hand, stroke his hair, and talk to him as if nothing's wrong. And I wait when waiting is not easy.

chapter 40

In the past day, I've gotten used to the sounds of different knocks on the door. Lizzie's are soft, fingernails against wood. Meg's come in short bursts, like flits of unrestrained chunks of excitement. Alex's are measured and come in threes, Iolani's a shave and a haircut. Karl doesn't knock—his fist would shake the entire building—so he bellows from outside the door. Kellan simply enters whenever he wants. And when he comes, it's not to talk to me—never to me. He checks on his brother, and then leaves.

Lizzie's latest round of soft tapping comes nearly twenty-four hours after Sjharn brought Jonah here. "Cora's awake," she informs me. "I just talked to her on the phone."

A set of weights rise off of my shoulders.

"I'm going to go over to the hospital to see her," Lizzie continues. "Meg and Alex, too. We were wondering if you wanted to come with."

I hate the thought of being *that girl*, the one who, when she gets a boyfriend, disappears from her friends' lives. I don't think I'm that girl, but I can see how it'll be interpreted as such when I say I don't believe it's a good idea if I leave just yet.

I know he'll wake up. Sjharn says he has no worries about Jonah right now. Jonah will wake up, and he'll be fine, albeit tired and possibly prone to headaches for a few days. But I want to be here when he does; I want to be the first person he sees. I want him to know he's not alone, that I'm not leaving. We've spent far too much time apart as it is.

Lizzie accepts this, and is kind enough not to voice any judgments she may have about my clinginess. I ask her to give Cora my love and tell her that I'm so, so glad she's safe.

I'll save my apologies for when I see her.

The Cousins leave, and eventually, so do Karl and Kellan. They're off to some kind of Guard meeting. Now that Annar's shields have been reinforced and the other Creator has gone round to solidify them (based on what I'd done in California—apparently he'd never thought to do such a thing before), no one seems to think we need babysitting.

My mother calls a little while later, to tell me she and my dad are going back to the Human plane. I wait for her to mention the attack, so when she doesn't, I am hurt enough that I bring it up.

"Yes, well," she says, sounding bored, "everything turned out for the best, didn't it?"

What the hell? I look at the receiver as if it's alien technology. I'm done with her lack of caring. "I could've been killed! Doesn't that mean anything to you?"

"Of course it does. But, Chloe, you're alive and well. The Guard did their job and protected you."

"Is that what you've heard?" I ask incredulously.

"Is it a lie?"

I think of all the times she's lectured me about needing to fulfill my duties, to live up to expectations and to make the family proud. I may've broken rank, gone rogue with the whole time-freezing bit, but it ended up being the right thing to do. A number of Elders are now safely secured under Guard supervision. Nobody died, and thanks to being petrified in the midst of injuries, everyone had ample time to be taken care of by Shamans before anything too serious took hold. I don't want to toot my own horn, but this is pretty much thanks to me.

But I know better. I simply wish her and my father a safe journey and say, not hesitantly but almost wistfully, that I hope to see them soon.

Jonah's father calls, too; it's the first time since the party earlier in the fall that I've spoken to him. His call is also brief—he asks how Jonah is doing, but needs no details, as he's been apprised on the situation. He doesn't ask why I'm with Jonah, or why I'm the one answering the phone. He doesn't ask where Kellan is. In fact, he doesn't ask much at all—just how Jonah is. When I answer the question, he mumbles something along the lines of, "Good. Well, give him my regards," and then clicks off the line.

The one bright call comes from the Seer Astrid Lotus, who I now know is Jonah's surrogate mother. She spends nearly ten minutes with me on the phone, both asking questions and giving me information she's learned from the Shaman. She is kind. Comforting. Before she hangs up, she tells me, "I'm so glad you're there with my boy, Chloe."

It's sweet enough to bring tears to my eyes. Maybe Jonah's right. Maybe there are Magicals out there who make excellent parents, even if they come in the form of surrogate mothers.

"I have the *worst* headache."

He's awake! I nearly throw down the book I've been reading and turn to face Jonah. He's rubbing at his forehead, adorably confused and tired. I lean in, saying, "Let me kiss that and make it better. Any other pains?"

There aren't, which relieves me. Not that I didn't trust Sjharn, who everyone claims is a miracle worker, but I needed to hear it from Jonah. We talk about what happened—I don't gloss over anything, because I've decided that, being tired of always being kept in the dark, I want us to have the truth always, even if it's tough at times to hear.

Which I'm assuming is the case for him when I lecture for a good five minutes on how he's never allowed to pull such a stunt again. He merely laughs at this, unbothered by my growling, and subdues me quickly by yanking me back down in bed so we can lie together.

"You can't do this again," I whisper against his neck. "You can't leave me again."

"I didn't leave you. I was protecting you. There's a difference."

"Why you, though? With all the Guard around, why did you have to go out there?"

"Because I love you, and I'll always do everything I can to make sure you stay safe."

He's smooth, but I'm not swayed. "Getting yourself killed is not a good way to keep me safe," I mutter. "That would, in fact, probably cause me to blow up a number of buildings."

"I'm sorry for worrying you," he says sincerely. "Forgive me?"

When he says it like that, there's no way I can deny him anything.

"So, I have a question for you."

Jonah opens his eyes and squints up at me. We're out on the couch, watching a movie. The apartment is empty—the Cousins have gone back to the Human plane, Kellan is out with Guard friends, and Karl is having dinner with his wife. "I'm not paying attention to the movie, so if you're wondering about the plotline, you're out of luck."

His head in on my lap and I am running my fingers through his silky hair. "Are you able to talk to me in my mind?"

He moves his head so my fingers can reach new pieces of hair to play with. "No."

"But you talk to your brother like that."

"Yes."

Even though I'd suspected this, I'm still surprised to get an actual confirmation. For one thing, I've never heard of anyone, Magical or not, being able to do this. Secondly, when we surge, only memories and the feelings associated with them are accessible, never interactive language. Still, wondering about how much the two of them are able to communicate with one another, and potentially about me, has been gnawing at me ever since their bizarre silent exchange before school a few days before.

"So," I say, "all those times you two are silent with each other, you're talking?"

"Not always. Sometimes it's just silence."

"Does he have to be in the room?"

Jonah is unbothered by my questions. "No."

"Could you talk to him now?"

"If I had something to say," he admits, moving his head again.

"How?"

"I don't know. We've always been able to do it. It's a twin thing, I guess."

I think about this as he relaxes against me once more. Right before he's on the verge of sleep, I say, "Explain it to me. Does this mean that whatever you say or do, he automatically knows about it?"

Jonah must sense my uneasiness, because he sits up. "No, of course not."

Even the little voice in my mind is curious about all this. "Then how does it work?"

"Well, he and I are connected together in a lot of ways because we're twins. We can surge, like normal Magicals. So obviously we can see each other's memories and all that. We can talk by reaching out our minds to each other. And we can sense how the other person is feeling without having to be within a certain distance like Emotionals normally need to be."

"Can he hear what we're saying right now?"

"No." His eyes search my face. "Chloe, why are you so troubled about this?"

"It's bad enough that you can read me like a book at all times," I say quietly. "It's another thing if someone who isn't even in the room can do it, too. And . . . it freaks me out to think that you two might've been talking about me, or worse, fighting when I had no idea."

He takes my hands in his. "Kellan would be able to hear what's going on if I specifically let him. But that's not going on right now. He has no idea what we're talking about, I swear."

"Does he know what you're feeling?"

"You mean right now?"

I nod.

"Probably, but I doubt he's paying attention."

"Do you know what *he's* feeling?"

"Yes, but only because you asked me to focus."

I mull this over, uncomfortable. "Can he tell when we're . . . you know . . . making out? Or . . . merging?" My face burns.

The little voice practically cackles at my smoothness.

Jonah turns red, too. "NO. Listen—I get that you are weirded out about all of this. But I promise you there's nothing to worry about. For your information, there are times I always block him, and vice versa. What you and I do is none of his business. And frankly, I highly doubt he'd want to know."

Thank. Gods.

"Besides," he adds, "we've always agreed that relationships are off limits. Blocking this sort of stuff from one another is routine."

"Why'd you hide this from me?" I ask, not so much accusing, but genuinely curious.

"I didn't hide it from you, Chloe . . . At least, if I did, it wasn't purposeful." He sighs, rubbing at his forehead. I worry he might be getting another migraine. "Maybe it's the curse of being an Emotional. We're just not able to express as much as we inspire in others." He laughs quietly. "Ironic, right?"

I mull this over. "Do a lot of people know that you two can communicate like this?"

"I think some people suspect it; there are a select few who know simply because they've known us, as a unit, for a very long time." He suddenly looks vulnerable. "I've never been very good about opening up often. I guess it's a self-defense mechanism I've built up over the years. I don't let a lot of people in. But," he adds, when I try to apologize for being nosy, "you are not everybody. You are the person I love, and the person I'm going to spend my life with. You have every right to ask me these things and, in turn, expect to hear whatever it is you want to know about me, without hesitation. I know you're worried right now that I'm upset you're asking, but I'm not. I think . . . sometimes there are things I don't actively tell you, but it's more because I don't think they're worthy of being discussed. I'll never hide anything from you, though. If you were to ever ask, I would never lie or deny the truth."

Jonah's cell phone goes off later that night while he's sleeping. Normally, I'd ignore it, because I wouldn't want to be nosy (despite Jonah's arguments earlier), but a picture flashes across the screen, of someone blonde.

While I can't see it too well, since it's on the coffee table and I'm still on the couch, I have no doubt who it is.

A minute after it stops ringing, the voice-mail beep sounds. And then, a couple minutes after that, a text appears. I debate whether or not to read it, because it's not my phone, but the green-eyed monster lurking inside demands to know what it says. So I gingerly slide the phone closer until I can see it.

Please call me. I'm freaking out not knowing how you are.

The little voice tries to rationalize with me, saying that just because Callie has texted Jonah, it doesn't mean anything. But then, how does she know he's been hurt? He'd said she's a non, and since it's forbidden to tell . . .

Remember, the little voice offers, *Kellan told her about the dreams. So she knows something, right?*

Which only confuses me more. I mean, both Jonah and Kellan had been pissed off at Lizzie telling Graham about our kind. Was it because they'd told once, too?

Later the next morning, I watch Jonah check his phone. He reads the text silently before setting the phone back down. But, when he turns around, he knows that I know.

I do not apologize for having read it. Instead, I ask, "Are you going to call her back?"

He comes over to where I'm standing. "No."

I try to play it cool, as if I'm totally unaffected by his ex-girlfriend of three years texting him. "Why not?"

He looks at me like I'm speaking Swahili. "Because it would upset you."

"No it wouldn't," I lie.

"It's okay that it does." He's serious. "It bothers me when you talk to my brother. But that," he adds, "is unavoidable, due to our circumstances. It is very avoidable to just not call her back."

Oh great. He had to play the generous card. I offer hesitantly, "She's worried about you."

"I'm sure she already knows that I'm awake and fine. Besides, the last time we spoke, I told her I didn't want her to call me anymore. Not just because of you, but because I thought it makes things worse for her, too."

Which makes me wonder just how hard things are for Callie.

chapter 41

Karl has a number of things to tell me once we get back to California. Due to the most recent attacks and despite the latest occurring in Annar, the Council has decided I'm to spend most of my free time on the Magicals' plane, including, but not limited to, all weekends and many afternoons directly after school. Jonah and Kellan are also under said order, but I have my doubts that it's because the Council believes they truly need protection. But there is enough fear of another attack that I'm to be constantly surrounded by as many Guard as possible, including, I suppose, my boyfriend and ex-boyfriend, who are, I'm discovering, virtually already members of the Guard in their own rights.

In addition to this, I'll be expected to move, along with the twins, to Annar within five days of graduation. Apparently, the Council wanted us there the very next day, but a few members (with kids) argued we deserved the bare minimum of fun before being sent off to the gallows—I mean, work.

And that's the final nail in the coffin. On the first day I move to Annar, I'll be inducted into the Council. No internship first, which freaks me out. I'd been looking forward to that, considering my general lack of knowledge about what it takes to be a fully-functioning Creator on the Council. But Kleeshawell Rushfire, the current Creator, is really old, Karl says, and pretty much stays in grumpy self-appointed time-outs. In fact, he adds, all of the things Rushfire had done in Annar to help fix the breached shields were done under protest. His power is waning, and he doesn't like being put into a position to possibly fail. He's apparently eager to hand the reins over to me as quickly as possible.

So there it is. I don't get a summer vacation. I don't get to hang out at the beach before moving. I don't get three years of school and internship before assuming my chair on the Council. Come June fifteenth, I'll be doing what I've been born to do.

I'll be a Council member, first tier, with six worlds' worth of expectations weighing down on my shoulders. And boy, do I feel like running.

Cora's back to fighting form, waving off any concern anyone has about her attack like it'd been a minor fender bender. Trying to talk to her about it does no good; all she'll say to me about it is that she expects me to listen to Karl from here on out. It's like she's aged ten years.

She makes a lot of secretive phone calls lately, yet I can never figure out to whom. She's constantly texting someone, and when she receives one, she smiles like she's won the lottery. Asking about this, too, is pointless, because her lips are zipped tight. I don't bother surging, because I figure if she wanted me to know, she'd tell.

A month after the attack, Alex and Meg blow my mind by admitting they've been secretly dating for several months. This revelation prompts Lizzie to quietly beg Alex for help finding some kind of loophole for her and Graham. She insists that she doesn't think she can go through with her commitments if she's not allowed to love who she wants. It takes some convincing, but Alex agrees, and the two of them, along with

Graham and Meg, spend countless hours after school researching in my dad's library.

Kellan's mostly kept his distance from me, but over the last week or so, he's slowly begun to come around and slide back into the group, albeit on the fringes. He eats with us at lunch, although on the opposite end of the table from me and Jonah, and even spends some time with his brother, outside of my presence. They are, according to Jonah, in an uneasy truce.

I hate the distance between them and that it's because of me. I want to do something to fix it, but any attempt at communication with Kellan is rebuffed, even in emails and texts. The truth is, I miss talking to him, miss his wisdom and advice and, even more importantly, just his sheer presence in my life, even if only as a friend. I think Jonah knows this, and even hints at it at times, claiming he knows his brother, and figures, with enough time, he'll come around. But I can't help but wonder if I've done such irreparable damage that I've lost Kellan for good.

So I'm stuck watching him from a distance, like I did with Jonah all those months ago. I watch him and worry about him and miss him so much it aches. And, as with Jonah before, I can tell Kellan isn't happy: the smiles he gives others aren't the ones I know to be real. They're too bright, strained from trying too hard.

Three days before Jonah and Kellan's eighteenth birthday and nearly a month before mine, I find Kellan at my locker during a passing period. It's the first time he's sought me out in months, and my heart goes berserk in so many conflicted, confused ways.

There is the obligatory small chitchat which has lately defined our relationship before he leans back against the lockers and stares straight ahead. "I was wondering if we maybe could talk about what's happened." He clears his throat uncomfortably. "Between us, I mean."

I want to, desperately. I want answers probably just as much as he does. But, I'm also terrified of being alone with him. Being together during the Annar battle was one thing, especially since we had a common goal of ensuring Jonah's safety. But here . . . now? What's to stop me from doing something unbelievably stupid? I mean, something about this boy encouraged me to betray Jonah for a little over two months.

Even so, I agree to have the talk, because no matter what, I need this attempt at closure, too. But I still say to him, half-heartedly, "Are you sure you want to go through this again?"

He gives me a sad, rueful smile, not the beautiful, sarcastic one I've long loved. "Stupid, isn't it?" He taps his forehead. "I get it, I really do—I mean, every day, I see you and Jonah and know, logically, how things are." He looks away, tearing my heart away with his gaze. "But my heart hasn't quite figured it out yet."

Ohh . . .

"I just think, maybe . . . if we really *talked* about it, maybe my heart will finally catch up with my mind. I figure it's worth a chance. I mean, what else can I lose?"

I want to cry, admit to him that he hasn't lost me—not entirely, at least. I may not be able to give him the relationship we once had, but I still need him. Want him. But I keep those messy thoughts and feelings in, even if he can sense them. Because we are in a crowded high-school hallway, and my boyfriend—his twin brother—is somewhere on the grounds nearby, and neither of us are willing to risk hurting him again.

“You know,” Cora says to me later, her phone out in her hands but tilted just enough away from me so I can’t see the screen, “I’m glad to report that Kellan is finally over you.”

We are standing in the same place where Kellan unequivocally told me a mere hour before that he is most definitely not over me. I shut my locker and turn to her. “Oh?”

She waits until she’s finished typing a message before answering. “Yeah. This past weekend, when I was in Annar—”

“Wait,” I say, holding a hand up. “You were in Annar this weekend? Why didn’t you come see me?” Me, who was also in Annar, trapped in some random, albeit swank, safe house. It doesn’t matter that Caleb and Jonah were with me—she should have called.

“I figured you and Jonah wanted time to yourselves. Anyway, the point is, I saw Kellan with some girl.”

“Some girl,” I repeat slowly.

“Yeah,” she says, eyes back down on her phone. She blushes and types out a message. I wait impatiently, tapping my foot before she glances back up. “As I was saying, he was with some girl. And they were, you know, *friendly*.”

I try not to grind my teeth. Which startles me, because, HELLO, this is actually good news, right?

“And I was told it’s not the first time, or first girl. He’s playing the field, and having a swell time doing it, I guess.”

And yet, I’ve begun to see red. “Why are you telling me this?”

“I thought you’d be happy. I mean, less guilt now, right?”

I want to strangle her. Truthfully, anyone would do, but I’d prefer it to be her. Rather than screaming at her for her oblivious idiocy, I instead demand shrilly, “Who in the hell are you texting so much lately, Cora?”

She doesn't look up. Instead, a small, sly smile curves her lips. "Secrets are fun, aren't they?"

"I think Cora has a secret boyfriend," I grumble to Jonah as we get into the Hummer.

"And this pisses you off why?"

"Because she won't tell me who it is!"

Karl and Jonah exchange an amused glance, which only further irritates me. I sulk in petulant silence for the next two miles before Jonah says, "So. You and Kellan are going to have a talk this afternoon."

This snaps me to attention. "How'd you know?"

"He told me a little while ago. I think it's a good idea."

"I was going to tell you," I whisper as Karl conveniently turns up the volume on the radio. "Just as soon as we got to my house."

Jonah looks out of the window on his side. "I know."

It's at times like this I resent his ability to read my emotions when I have to fight to figure out what he's feeling. His face is neutral, his body fairly relaxed. But I know he can't be happy about this. "He thinks it'll help," I whisper.

"He can think that," Jonah says, so softly that I can't even be sure these are the right words.

Kellan is already at the beach in his wetsuit, sitting in the sand and staring at the ocean. It's bitterly cold outside; just to stay moderately warm, I'm forced to wear a knit hat and gloves as well as Jonah's wool pea coat and my Uggs. I sit down next to him in the sand and together we watch the waves crash in front of us.

After a long while, he murmurs, "So."

"So," I repeat just as quietly.

Sand shifts through his fingers. "I've been really angry at you and Jonah for awhile now."

"You have every right to be angry at me," I say, even though it hurts to hear this. "But please—don't be mad at Jonah. He's not at fault for any of this, and you know it."

"Oh, Chloe," Kellan says, laughing softly. "Don't you understand? He had every opportunity for a year to tell me what was going on, and he didn't. So yeah, I have every right to be mad at him, too."

I sigh and pull my knees up under my chin. Rehashing the bad choices Jonah and I made will do none of us any good. I'm here to listen, the little voice sternly reminds me, to answer what Kellan asks, and to accept what he has to give, even if it ends up being nothing.

It takes him another few minutes to continue. "You know about Callie, right?"

I nod warily.

"I watched him with her for years. Until a few months ago, I'd thought I knew what Jonah was like with someone he loves. But . . . what he feels for you . . ." More sand trickles through his fingers. "Let's just say that I am very clear on what you two mean to each other. You are the most important person in his life, and not in just a typical high-school-crush sort of way, either. So, believe me when I say I *get* that. What I don't get is how I can't seem to let go of the feelings I have for you. But I'm trying, I want you to know that."

It's impossible to feel worse at this moment. I apologize, but he cuts me off. "I know, and to be fair, you've been pretty upfront about your feelings ever since you and Jonah got back together. I know it's not like you two did this to hurt me." He scoops big chunks of sand up in both hands and squeezes. “But . . . I thought that, given time, I’d move on. And it’s not happening, not like I want it to. So . . . I think maybe once we get to Annar, it’d be best if we just weren’t around each other anymore. It’s a little hard in high school, but maybe there, with you two on track for Council, and me for the Guard, there’s more room for space.”

I drop my head onto my knees so I don’t have to watch him tell me this. “You know I have to work with the Guard, too.”

“I know. But it’s logical that you’ll be paired up with Jonah.”

The little voice in the back of my mind is relieved. I’m not, though. I’m devastated by such a request. But I know I have to give this to him, because he’s asking, and because I love him enough to give him what he wants and needs. And if he needs me gone, if he wants the distance . . . I’d hoped we’d be friends. I hoped I could have that small bit.

“Can I ask you one thing, though?” he says.

I don’t look up, because breaking down while Giuliana is watching from her car in the parking lot would be a very bad thing. I’ve been around the Guard enough to know that this bit of juicy gossip would spread like wildfire within twenty-four hours. I mumble miserably, “Sure.”

“Is there anything left that you might have once felt for me? A part that belonged to *me*, if it ever did really exist?”

I’ve also been around two Emotionals long enough to know that he knows exactly how I’m feeling at the moment, and whether or not I still love him. He knows I do. I don’t get why he wants to hear it, though. Maybe to torture me . . . ?

Sometimes words are nice, the little voice begrudgingly offers. *Words are tangible things to hold onto, even when a person is long gone.*

"You know there is," I finally tell him.

We sit in uncomfortable silence for another few minutes, Kellan continuing to sift sand slowly through his fingers, me gripping onto my knees in an effort to stay sane. When I can't handle the hush any longer, I ask, in an effort to shift the conversation toward something not so painful, "Are you looking forward to Ascending in a few days on your birthday?"

He offers a humorless laugh. "I guess."

I roll my head to the side so I can see him. "Jonah won't let me get him a present. He says you guys never celebrate your birthday."

"It's hard to celebrate a day like that."

"Your birthday?"

He gives me a confused look.

"Because . . . birthdays are . . . bad?"

"Hasn't Jonah talked to you about this?"

It's my turn to be confused.

Kellan shakes his head and looks away. "Our mom died on our fifth birthday."

Whaaat? I knew she'd died when he was young, but on his birthday? "Jonah never told me this," I finally manage. And just why hadn't he? "Is it a secret?"

Kellan gives a short laugh. "If the Old Man had his way, it would be."

"Meaning?"

"He blames us. Still."

I can't help but scoot closer. "That's ridiculous. Why would he?"

"Maybe you should ask J," Kellan offers.

"I'm asking *you.*"

He lets go of the sand and rubs his hands together. "My mother had taken us to the grocery store to buy stuff to make cakes. She always made each one of us a cake . . . just a little one, you know—that way, she said, we'd each have our own and not have to share."

"That was very thoughtful," I say, resisting the urge to put my arms around him in comfort.

His lower lip trembles for just a second. "She was really great, Chloe."

"Of course she was," I say, completely believing this. I mean, look at how wonderful her sons are. How could she not have been?

He smiles just a little, and I urge him to continue. "We were playing in the parking lot, like idiots, not really paying attention—and I guess a car was coming toward us that we didn't see. She pushed us out of the way just in time, but it hit her. There were no Shamans in the area, my father was in Annar at the time, and I guess . . . I guess her injuries were enough to kill her."

I don't try to hide the tears this time.

He says, very, very softly, "We knew better than to play like that."

"You were five," I say, no longer resisting the urge to touch him. I lay a hand, just one, on his arm and squeeze gently. "It wasn't your fault. It wasn't either of your faults."

There's another short, sad laugh before he takes a shuddery breath. "I'm going to have to concur with J on the no-birthday thing. Just let him have the day without making a big deal out of it." He then sighs and moves his arm away from mine. "It's too bad you can't be there for Ascension; he'd probably really appreciate having you around."

I quickly lace my fingers back together in front of me. "Will you be there for each other?"

"Sure. We'll always have each other, especially on that day each year."

chapter 42

Jonah and Kellan will have each other during Ascension, whether or not they're angry with one another. I, like everyone else who isn't a twin, will have no one. Ascending is a solitary process that pushes a Magical to their boundaries. If you bounce back, you're good to go. If you crack . . .

Well, I don't really know what happens to those who crack, and Karl won't tell me when I ask, since no one is allowed to talk about their Ascension experience. Each Ascension is unique and tailored specifically for the person going through the change.

It's safe to say that I've begun praying that I won't be part of the forty percent who cannot deal with their influx of power.

Karl was right—Jonah was upset when he initially heard I'd be Ascending early, which was ironic, as he's set to do the same. He apparently already knew about the odds, which made it all the worse for him when it came to me. I listened to him and Karl argue about it, and then him and Zthane on the phone, but the decision was already made so there was nothing he could do to change it.

"It'll be okay," I tell him, right before he's to leave for Annar for his own Ascension. "We're going to be okay. Ascending will be a piece of cake. Just watch."

He holds me closer, and I close my eyes when he presses his lips against my forehead. "I know."

"Are you scared about tomorrow?" I feel his head turn against mine. "It's ridiculous they won't let me come, even if it's to hang out in some safe house. I'd feel easier being close by, if something . . . if . . ."

"I wish you could be nearby, too," he murmurs. "But nothing will happen. It's like you said: We're going to be okay."

A brief, horrible image flashes through my mind, of what would happen if something were to happen to him tomorrow morning. It would be bad, very bad . . . because I don't know if I'd be able to control the grief. "Tell me what time again?"

"Two thirty-two in the morning." The exact time of his birth—the very earliest second he can Ascend. "Promise me you won't stay up all night worrying."

Silly boy. "How long will it take?"

I love the scrape of his stubble against my cheek. "I don't know. I wish I did."

I drill Karl later that night. "You know I can't talk about this stuff," he says. "You might as well give up now."

"Forty percent," I stress angrily.

"Them be crummy odds," he agrees. We are in the backyard, along with Caleb, once more working on my skills. They think this will better prepare me for Ascension, even though there is no empirical evidence to support such a belief. "Now, I want you to create a striated layer of rock."

Annoyed, I flick my hand out and a small slab of brightly striped rock appears on the table in front of him. He picks it up and frowns. "What's with the amethyst layer?"

I roll my eyes. As a Quake, he knows far too much about rocks. "Can we get back to—"

He pushes it back toward me. "That's a gemstone."

"So?"

"Give me a genuinely striated rock, Chloe. One found in nature."

"Is that even a genuine geological term?" Caleb muses.

I laugh and produce another small slab, this time with the requisite layers. And then I sit down on the bench, folding my hands in front of me. "No more parlor tricks until you spill the beans, Karl." I look at my Faerie friend. "Or Caleb."

"Oh, I think I'm going to stay quiet and let the big guy do the explaining here." Caleb gives me a wink. "If he can."

Karl glares at him, but it's just for show. He and Caleb are actually pretty good friends nowadays. "Look. It's not that I'm banned from talking, it's that we physically aren't able to. Protection of the species and whatnot."

"Then tell me what you can."

He struggles for a good minute. "All right. I can tell you this: you have approximately fifteen percent of your powers right now. Once you Ascend, you will automatically be pushed to one hundred percent—that's a big difference, right? Imagine what it'll be like—you'll be saturated in power. It's difficult to contain immediately, and would be destructive if let loose on society. So, you're given time and a way to contain it. That's something only you can learn to do—no one can teach you that."

"So, it's like . . . solitary confinement?"

Caleb says, "That's an interesting but valid way to see it."

I think about this. "Jonah and Kellan will be in the same room, sequestered together?"

"Is that what he told you?" Karl says, surprised. "Because if that's the case, it's a lousy idea." Caleb agrees wholeheartedly.

"Jonah says his dad told him that's how it would be."

Karl laughs under his breath. "Don't be surprised if they both come back with black eyes."

So not what I was expecting. "Why?"

"Two Emotionals, already powerful, coming into full power in the same room? It's going to be a fricking tidal wave of strong feelings. Everything will be exacerbated. All this stuff going on between them? *Ka-boom!*"

"Oh, to be a fly on that wall," Caleb murmurs, shaking his head.

I stand up, startled, but Karl reaches across the table and motions me to sit back down. "There's nothing you can do about it."

"But—"

"But what? You gonna storm Karnach, insist on playing referee? Please. Now, let's get back to work. Make me a diamond. I have a lot of kissing up to do to my wife lately."

I sigh, but do as he asks.

Karl is a slave-driver for the next two days, forcing me over and over to hone my craft. We work in the backyard, in the woods, at the beach, in downtown . . . even in the parking lot of the high school. I build and destroy, over and over again, while philosophizing with him about the morality behind my creations. We talk about right and wrong, and why the Council sometimes decides what they do.

“All the worlds have to be balanced,” he says as I shiver on the beach, having built and destroyed a mini-coral reef half a mile off shore. “Thus the reason for so many of the dual edges in our crafts. Bettering civilizations is a good thing, but sometimes they have to be struck down in order to advance. Does that make sense?”

I sink down to sit in the sand. “Like a fire in a forest.”

He sits down next to me. “Exactly. Sometimes fire is what a forest needs in order to clear out the old so the new can spring forth.”

“How many earthquakes have you caused?”

A sort of uneasiness settles over him. “More than you’d like to know.”

I ask, as gently as I can, “Has anyone ever died because of one of your quakes?”

He flinches, just a little. “Sure.”

“I may be asked to do something like that, and it scares the crap out of me, Karl.”

“I know,” he sighs. “And it always will.”

“How do you deal with it? What you’ve done?”

Karl stares out at the water for a long moment. “I try to remind myself that I’m not doing it because I enjoy devastation and death. I do it because it’s necessary, and that sometimes, good can come from it, too.” He clears his throat. “Ecologically, you know?”

“Do you ever wish you were another craft?”

There’s no hesitation. “No. This is what I am. This is what I’m capable of.” He holds his hand out and makes a fist. “And, honestly, I’d rather it be me than some sick freak who gets a kick out of it. Does that make sense?”

The funny thing is I’m starting to think it does.

Jonah comes home three days after his birthday. I'm not sure what I expected to see, or how he might have changed, but tired wouldn't have been at the top of my list. He has dark circles under his eyes—thankfully due to exhaustion and not his brother's fists—and messy hair that tells me he's been overly preoccupied.

I try to pump him for information, but as Karl warned, there's very little Jonah can tell me other than a) it didn't hurt (an irrational fear I've developed), and b) you don't notice the time it takes to recover.

"Do you feel differently?" I ask, smoothing his hair down as we snuggle in a large chair in my living room.

"Yeah," he admits. "I didn't think I would, but I do."

"Different bad, or different good?"

He thinks about this. "Different *complete.* It's like . . . a balloon, I guess. When air is added, it becomes something more. But, other than air, the composition is the same."

"Do your powers feel different?"

He flexes his fingers. "Yeah. Clearer. Stronger."

"Do something to me."

His hands drop. "What?"

"You never work on me—"

"Because you're my *Connection.*"

I laugh. "Yeah, yeah. You don't want to work on people and wonder why they're around you. Ethics and whatnot. But this time, why not? You've got all these great, new powers. Test them out on me." When he hesitates, I wheedle, "Just this one time. C'mon. It'll be fun. Make me feel something special."

An eyebrow lifts. “Are you saying I need to use my mojo to get you to feel something special around me?”

I give him a sly grin. “Of course not. You’re quite talented at that sort of stuff all by yourself.”

He laughs and caves in. “Alright. What do you want to feel?”

I close my eyes. “Surprise me.”

His breath is soft against my face. Tingles deliciously zap up and down my body. “This is good,” I murmur.

“I haven’t done anything yet.” I shiver contentedly anyway. “Are you ready?”

“Yes,” I whisper.

And then, the most incredible sensation of pure bliss sweeps through me. It starts slowly, a series of goose bumps rippling alongside my arms in union, and then inside me. Once it convenes where my heart is, it alters, infused now with the sensations of first and true love—all tingly and breathless and exciting at the same time.

I know this feeling. I’ve felt it a million times with Jonah over the years.

“This is how I’ll always feel about you,” he whispers, feather soft, against my ear.

The love I have for him violently expands beyond the limits of my heart. I do not know how my rib cage manages to hold it in.

chapter 43

I am being hugged by Karl's wife, Moira, as we stand in their living room. It's nice to be in a real home and not one of the many safe houses I'm normally sequestered in during my weekends in Annar. Karl had offered to see if I could stay at with my dad, but I dismissed that ridiculous idea right away. So here we are, in the Graystones' apartment, and everything is safe, friendly, and welcoming. The only thing missing is Jonah, who, like me before, isn't permitted to come to Annar while I Ascend.

Moira is very short, with a wide, pretty face; skin the color of coffee mixed heavily with milk; a pert nose sprinkled with freckles and dark curly hair. She's also so pregnant she can barely stand up without teetering. Karl notices this right away, practically peeling her away from me so he can usher her to a chair by a fireplace. When he goes to get her something to drink, it gives us a chance to catch up, face to face.

"I've been wanting to thank you for some time now," I say, sitting down in the chair opposite her. "I know it can't be easy to have Karl gone, especially with the baby due soon."

"As you and Jonah have a Connection," she smiles, "I'm sure you are well aware what it's like to be away from your significant other. So yes, it's hard. But it's for a good reason, and therefore, we deal."

"Karl's been good to me," I admit.

Her eyes sparkle. "Shh! You'll ruin his reputation. He rarely tolerates most people's crap, but he's gotten all squishy about you, like you're his sister or something. It's very sweet."

"I bring with me a lot of crap," I say solemnly.

"Who doesn't?"

Karl re-enters the room, carrying a cup of juice and a snack for his wife. It's the first time I've gotten to watch them interact in person, and the only time I've witnessed another couple with a Connection together. They seem to be constantly aware of each other's presences in the room and move, therefore, in tandem. She leans toward him, he leans toward her, as if they are magnets that can't be away from one another. He's no longer "serious Guard extraordinaire," but a man hopelessly in love and unafraid to let anyone see it. And she's just as obvious, with every look, touch, and word filled with love for him.

It is a beautiful thing to witness.

"I've been thinking a lot," I murmur, "about the baby."

"Our baby?" Moira asks. Karl instinctively puts his hand on her tummy; she wraps her hand around his.

Honestly, as I know no other pregnant couples, who do they think I'm talking about? "I'm moving here in a few months, you know."

"And this has to do with our baby, how . . . ?" Karl asks, forehead scrunching.

"Once she's born, you should stay here and assign someone else to me."

You'd have thought I'd just asked them to cut off each other's arms by the way they're glaring at me.

"I mean," I clarify, "I'm moving here soon, anyway, right? Within five days of graduation? And if I'm one of the lucky sixty percent whose head doesn't explode upon early Ascension—"

"What kind of fool are you to have told her that?" Moira snaps incredulously.

"Then," I continue, "I'll have my full power load. And Jonah's Ascended now, too. So, you could stay here, with Moira and the baby."

After a long silence, in which I genuinely worry they've lost the ability to speak, Karl manages, "I have orders, Chloe. I'm to oversee you until you graduate and move here."

"I just explained that. Your baby will need you more than me."

Moira turns to her husband. "I think I can understand what you mean about her now."

He rolls his eyes. "I know. And when she and Jonah get together, it's like there isn't a single ear between them."

"Hey," I protest. "I'm trying to help here."

"Don't help," Karl says. "And don't worry about us. We're good. We'll always be good."

There is a special place in Annar meant exclusively for Ascension. It's located a half-mile below the surface, accessible by a singular elevator which can only be manipulated by a Mover. As I have no idea what a Mover does, I have to rely on Karl to explain how Kiellee, a rather plain-looking Faerie on the Guard, can shift the space continuum and make doorways appear where they normally are not.

I'm not sure what I expected the place where Magicals Ascend to look like, but it certainly wasn't what I'm faced with. Everything is opulent—all silks and velvets, gorgeous antique furniture made of exotic woods and metals, and museum-worthy artwork.

"What's this place called?" I ask Karl.

"Valhalla."

"Like the Norse legends?"

He smirks at me. "As you well know, most legends have some basis in fact."

I think about this. "Valhalla was filled with Valkyries. Warriors Odin stockpiled."

"Well," Karl muses, "I suppose it's sort of like that. Only we *make* the warriors here." He winks. "As for Odin, he was one of the early Magicals."

Sitting at one of the most ornate desks I've ever seen is a cheerful Elf, his white-blonde hair twisted up in odd knots across his head. He has only two things adorning his spotless desk: a sheet of thin gold and a name placard that says: *Quincey Buttercup, Master Secretary.*

"Is that a craft?" I whisper to Karl as we approach the desk.

"You mean Secretary?"

I nod.

"Nope," he says, trying to hide his smile. "Although Quince here probably wishes it were. He's a Smith." When I cock an eyebrow, he clarifies, "He works with metals."

"Good morning!" Quincey chirps loudly. His voice echoes off the heavily wallpapered walls. "What a gorgeous day to Ascend!"

I look around; there are no windows, and on our walk over this morning, it'd rained on us. Quincey's hand whips out and grabs mine, even though it was hanging by my side. I try not to wince as he pumps it up and down like he's putting air in a bike tire. "Look at you! All adorable and eighteen! I could just pinch your cheeks!"

"Simmer down, Quincey," Karl says. "There'll be no cheek-pinching this time."

"Right!" Quincey says, mercifully letting go of my hand. "Well, I suppose Lilywhite here is an eager beaver to get this over with. Shall we?" He motions to the two chairs sitting in front of his desk. I sit down, but Karl remains standing.

"Smashing," Quincey says, sliding the sheet of gold in between us. "First, the logistics. Name? Age? Birthday? Craft? Current location?" He drills me, rapid-fire, question after question, yet doesn't write down a single answer. Once done, he smiles so brightly that I'm blinded by his white teeth. "Put your left hand on the gold, please. And do not move until I tell you to."

Karl nods encouragingly, so I lay my hand onto the sheet. Within seconds, it grows scalding hot. Just as I'm about to rip my hand away, Quincey barks, "I said no moving!"

Had he grown fangs, I would not have been more surprised. I keep my hand where it is.

The metal grows hotter and liquefies under my skin. I have to bite my lip from screaming out in pain, but just as I'm about to tell Quincey what he can do with his gold, it cools. "You may remove your hand now," he says, smiling brightly once more. I rub my red palm, scowling; Quincey, on the other hand, admires the sheet of gold. There is a perfect imprint of my hand in it, every last line present.

I motion toward it with my wounded hand. "If you don't mind me asking, what's that for?"

"Your file," the Smith says. "We must be able to always accurately identify you, no matter your state. As long as you have your hand, we'll be able to do that."

"And if I don't have my hand?"

He titters nervously. "Oh, well—in that case, we have your blood from the oath-binding ceremony."

What's this? EWW.

He runs his hands over the gold, smoothing out the edges as if they're made of putty. "And . . . if I'm not mistaken, you're Connected to Jonah Whitecomb, correct?"

"Uh . . ." Is this common knowledge?

"Connected pairs are always able to identify their mates, even if the body is badly mangled," Quincey continues, sounding like he's describing his favorite kind of cotton candy. "So if need be, Whitecomb would be able to ID you, even if it was just a small piece left. If he was still alive, of course."

I nearly choke on my tongue. Karl hauls me up out of the chair and says, "Keep working on those people skills, Quincey."

"Always!" the Elf chirps. "I'm doing a hell of a lot better lately, aren't I?"

"I can't . . . I can't believe . . ." I gurgle as Karl tugs me down a hallway. "He just . . . is he . . . ?"

"Stupid?" Karl offers. "No. Actually, Buttercup is pretty smart. But he's got no idea how to interact with people. He's been down here working with the Medium for most of his life, making rare one-day-a-month trips to the surface."

He definitely needs more time up there.

The Medium, the person in charge of helping Magicals go through Ascension, is an extremely old Gnome dressed entirely in white. He moves slowly with a cane, his bare feet covered with grass stains. "Well, well," he says, his voice surprisingly youthful for a face so craggy with years, "if it isn't the notorious Creator."

"Uh . . . yes?" Karl has already left, not being allowed in the Medium's office. Which is, in itself, a misnomer, because the room is huge, at least twice the size of the room Quincey rules, and more like a hotel lobby than any office I've ever seen before. It's circular, with doors spaced roughly ten feet apart lining the walls. Each door is made of a different wood, each door handle a different metal. Some doors look new, some old. None are marked.

"You aren't sure?" he asks, lifting a very hairy eyebrow up. The hairs are so long that they brush down and threaten to scrape his eyeballs.

"Yes," I say more firmly. "I'm the Creator. My name is—"

"Frankly, child," he interrupts, tapping the cane on the ground next to him, "I do not care what your name is. It is irrelevant."

Oo-kay?

"You are aware of the risks?" he asks, leading us to sit down on the only two uncomfortable chairs in the entire room. There are plush couches and loveseats everywhere, yet he chooses two small, wooden stools.

"That come with Ascending early?"

"It is not normally recommended," the Medium continues. "And the truth is I dislike having to clean up the mess afterward."

Flashes of blood-splattered walls pockmarked with gray matter fill my mind. "I thought the whole head-exploding thing was metaphor-ical—"

"Sometimes," he says, not smiling. "Sometimes not. Did anyone explain how a Creator's chances are even higher of becoming unstable during the process?"

NO, NO THEY DIDN'T.

"I'd say they hover more around seventy percent of failure. Creators are tricky creatures; your sort have more power than the others. Many bodies don't deal well with Ascension even at the appropriate time."

Seventy percent?! WHAT. THE. HELL?! I close my eyes and count to twenty. Slowly. Then I pinch the bridge of my nose. "If I choose not to Ascend today?"

"There is no more choice. Your handprint has already been collected."

You can do this, the little voice says. *Trust that the odds are in your favor.*

I am an overthinker. Typically, when it comes to the big stuff, I think and think until I make myself sick. All those weeks fretting over what Jonah was thinking and feeling when he'd moved to town. All these past weeks worrying about how Kellan is dealing with things, if I'm failing my parents, of what expectations are on my shoulders, of what I'll be doing in Council chambers, of what I'll be asked to do. Of what it'd be like to run, of where I'd go and who I'd become. I've thought of all of these things. In great detail.

If I were to contemplate how small my chances are of surviving Ascension, I'd go mad. So I stand up and smack my hands together. "Tell me what I need to do."

"Pick a door." His cane swings around in an arc. "And then go through it."

"Are all the rooms the same?"

He's amused. "No."

I close my eyes and turn my body round and round, like a kid at a birthday party, getting ready to hit a piñata. When I open my eyes, I walk directly to the door in front of me. It's a pale wood—blonde, really—with a sapphire doorknob surrounded in platinum.

Behind me: "I wish you luck, Creator."

Blinding light assails me, so much so that I stumble forward for a good few minutes before it begins to fade. Once it does, I halt in my tracks at what I see in front of me.

It's the exact setting where I'd met Jonah for the very first time—a dappled riverbank, complete with the small, stone bench he'd once sat on. I'd perched in the tree above, watching him night after night. I know this spot. I know the tree hanging over the river. I know this bench like the back of my hand.

What I don't know is why I'm here, or how the door I just entered, half a mile below Annar's surface, could lead to someplace from my dreams. Or, perhaps most importantly, just what I'm supposed to do here. The Medium gave no specifics, let alone helpful hints.

I wander around, rediscovering places I'd believed long lost. Eventually, I shuck off my shoes and wade into the water. I bend down to run my fingers through the inky darkness. It doesn't feel like water. It's more . . . dense. Soft. When I pull my hand out, no droplets fall. It's oddly warm, soothing, and far more sparkly than I remember.

I don't know how to explain it, but I suddenly know what to do. I back out of the water and climb the tree hanging over the river. It's the same tree Jonah first kissed me in. I take my time moving across the branch, smoothing my hands across the worn bark, remembering how beautiful and magical it'd been up here.

So it makes sense that this is the place I launch into my new life. It's where I knew, for certain, I was in love. To move into my new life, I want these pieces, these reminders of who I am, what I have, and what I stand to gain.

I pull myself into a standing position, grabbing onto the branches above me. I creak and sway, but I have no fear. I will survive—not because of the expectations on my shoulders, or the ones from my family, but because I simply know I will. I will not be part of the seventy percent who fail.

I close my eyes, take a deep breath, and let myself fall forward.

chapter 44

Darkness is the first sensation—not uncomfortable or terrifying, but safe and enveloping. It pushes against me, seeps into every pore until I am heavy. Sated. And then, just when I feel as if existence is a pleasant, distant memory, the darkness evolves into sunlight—still warm, still comforting, yet exciting now. The darkness flattens, then twists into strands of yellow light, escaping through the same pores it'd once sought refuge in.

When there is nothing left, no darkness, no light, no nothing, and I'm floating high and weightless, something rushes into me. Something so sharp, I'm knocked breathless—not in pain, but surprise.

The unknown pulls toward my center, sucking every last molecule of air with it. And then it explodes until everything is glitter, all blues and silvers and golds, and it's beautiful, amazing—like the birth and death of the universe all at once. I become a part of the iridescence, a free-floating consciousness no longer attached to anything tangible at all.

And then consciousness floats away, leaving nothing at all behind.

The room I'm standing in is nondescript. Plain off-white walls, scuffed hardwood floors, no windows, no door, one singular cot-like bed with a white sheet and a flat pillow. I do not know how long I've been here or how I even got here in the first place.

What I do know is that my body is thrumming with so much power that I can't believe my skin hasn't split open yet. It races through every vein, every pump of my heart, every firing of a synapse in my brain. I'm crackling with energy, so much so that I have no doubt that if I were to toss a single strand of hair at the bed in the corner of the room, I'd blow it up.

It's then I realize this is the whole point of being in this room. I've got . . . well, who knows how long, to get myself under control. I can only hope that the room can keep me from destroying everything in the process. But a small victory is that my brain seems to still be functioning, that my thoughts are fairly coherent and rational.

I spend the next hours (days?) honing my craft. Building and destroying things I've never done before, just to see if I can—things I expect to be asked to Create in the coming years. Miniature planets. Miniature cities. Doorways leading to very specific places I don't dare to tread through until I know my powers are stable. Complete books down to the last word, written by authors I love and authors I don't even know. I move through subject after subject, building, tweaking, and then erasing, until I can barely see straight. And then, exhausted, I intuitively build more. I push myself to the point of nearly passing out, still Creating, knowing that there might come a point in time in which I'll have to work under such conditions, and I want to make sure that I'm good with it all.

Every so often, a plate of food and a glass of water appear on the floor next to the cot. I know it's not me making it—I may be able to make many things, but not those. I eat, but do not sleep. I push myself until the power in me no longer feels like it's going to leak out. It's still humming throughout me, but it's beginning to assimilate rather than overtake.

And finally, when I cannot build another thing without my eyes drooping, a door appears on the wall opposite the cot. The Medium steps through. "Congratulations," he says. "You have successfully Ascended. You may leave now."

I struggle to stand up. "Just like that?"

"It's been a week. I assumed you'd want to go home."

Whoa. "I've been in here a week?"

"Creators always take longer than the rest," he says. "Frankly, I'm surprised you didn't take two."

part III

chapter 45

I feel like a rock star with no band, no fans, and no stage to play on. But so goes life for someone who's beaten crappy odds, come out for the better on the other side, and lived to tell the tale to . . . well, almost no one, because I'm not even allowed to tell the stinkin' tale. But still! Woot! Go, me!

The Cousins pummel me with questions, but much like Karl did when I quizzed him, I find it impossible to answer. Jonah simply tells me he can feel the difference in me—not that it's bad or good, but that it's simply now part of who Chloe Lilywhite is. And he accepts it, which is a comforting thing. "This is part of what's awesome about Connections," I tell him one afternoon as we stand at his locker. "Unconditional acceptance and love."

He puts one of his books into the locker and slides out one of mine. I've been using his most of the time nowadays. Then he gives me one of his smiles, one that makes me feel all tingly and warm and uncomfortable about being in public because there are so many things I want to do to him—with him—that I can't, thanks to all the people around us.

"Stop that," I laugh.

He says, "What am I doing?" but he knows exactly what he's up to.

I slide my fingers under his shirt between button holes. This is something I shouldn't be doing, especially since there's a pair of teachers across the hallway talking, but I like touching him and knowing that these small grazes against his bare skin have a huge effect on his control. "You know."

I watch his control waver, how the heat in his eyes flares to the point that I'm thinking we ought to just ditch school to go have a marathon make-out session, and it makes me even more excited. Getting Jonah out of his comfort zone in public is always such a rush. He makes this tiny groaning sound and then kisses me—*really* kisses me—making the two teachers across the hall issue a series of disappointed sounds until we pull apart.

In my ear, Jonah laughs quietly, "They're such hypocrites, considering they're trying hard not to give into sex right now, too."

The teachers continue to stare at us. The woman, a science teacher who's normally straight-laced and boring, flushes bright red, like she knows we know what's going on. And it's weird, but rather than being embarrassed about being caught by the teachers, I'm okay with it. Because I know that when it comes to Jonah, I never have anything to be embarrassed about.

A couple months after my Ascension, Lizzie announces, "I love summer," as we head toward our history class.

Graham rolls his eyes. "May is still technically spring."

"And," I add, "sixty degrees is hardly warm."

Kellan, who is walking with us, doesn't say anything. In fact, he doesn't say anything at all to me anymore. The closer I get to Jonah, the further Kellan retreats. And it sucks, because he interacts with everyone else—well, not Cora—but me? It's like he has the ability to look right through me.

I'm about to throw caution to the wind and attempt a conversation with Kellan when my phone beeps. Jonah's sent a text, saying he has to leave school early and that he'll call later tonight.

As we walk into our history class, I tentatively say to Kellan, loathing every second of unease between us, "Jonah's left school."

He studies me wordlessly before turning toward his seat. I contemplate following, but one rejection per day from Kellan is painful enough. So I head to my own seat and get out my textbook.

It takes nearly a half-hour of arguing, pleading, threatening, and wheedling before Karl caves in and agrees to let me drive over to Jonah's. He initially balked at going due to a mandatory check-in phone call with Zthane to report this week's activities. So, allowing me to go comes only after a promise to do all of Karl's laundry and dishes for the next several days.

I do not relish the prospect of handling his underwear and sweaty workout clothes, but as Jonah still isn't answering his phone and all Giules will tell us is that he's busy, I figure it's worth it to set my mind at ease.

Which is silly, but there's the crux of the situation: I feel severely uneasy at the moment, not knowing what Jonah's up to. Karl says this is ridiculous and that I'm bordering on stalker-girlfriend behavior, but the urge to go find Jonah as soon as possible is overwhelming.

There is no answer when I knock on the Whitecombs' door, which is weird, since Jonah and Giuliana must both be home. Both of their cars are in the driveway. Knowing that the back door is often unlocked, I loop around the gate on the side of the house.

The uneasy feeling expands, pricking more and more places on my spine. And then, I spot Jonah in the backyard. He's talking to someone nearby in a low voice, so low I can't make out distinct words. Whoever it is has his complete and undivided attention, though. I'm just about to make myself known when the other person steps into my line of sight.

My body turns to stone.

The girl talking—no, arguing?—with Jonah is possibly the most gorgeous I've ever seen. She's very slender, so pale she's almost translucent, with long, silvery-blonde hair. It's starkly obvious she's an Elf, or at the very least, part Elf.

I just know. It's a no-brainer. The girl before me, the impossibly gorgeous Elvin girl, is none other than Callie. Jonah's Callie. Ex-girlfriend Callie. Three-years-together Callie. Callie-who-lives-across-the-entirety-of-the-continent-and-was-told-never-to-contact-Jonah-again Callie.

My heart smacks the inside of my chest like one of those huge drums in a marching band. Somewhere in my mind, I realize I ought not to spy on them, that I should say something right away, but my feet refuse to move, my mouth is unable to open. So I continue to watch, even though everything in me is screaming for me to run, because I know I shouldn't be here. I shouldn't see this. Something bad is happening here.

She's crying, which makes her look—unlike my own ugly brand of messy tears—like a delicate porcelain doll. It's the kind of crying that instills immediate pity and a maternal urge to take care of her. And Jonah

. . . he looks like someone cut off his right arm, like he's in agonizing pain.

He says something that brings her closer. She tugs at her hair and asks a question, exotic eyes pleading. He nods slowly, and the pain so clear on his face doubles. It devastates me to see him look like this. And it's all the worse because his pain comes from this girl.

Jonah says something else, something which softens her crying. Nearly his height, she looks right into his eyes and presses her long, graceful hands on his chest.

He does not move away.

Get the hell out of there. Right now, the little voice suddenly commands.

But I don't. I can't.

Her head drops onto his shoulder. As her eyes drift close, a small, contented smile forms across her perfect lips. His head dips until it rests against hers. And then he lifts a hand and strokes her hair in a very intimate gesture that I suddenly can imagine happening hundreds of times in the past.

She has to be Callie. There's no one else she can be.

Her hands snake around his back, sliding under his T-shirt to skim the top of his jeans. I wait for him to flinch, to move away, but he doesn't. And then, when she says something, his face turns just enough so it's now resting in her hair, and even though I can't see it, I know he's kissing her, just a small one, right there on her head. In a place that he kisses me all the time, like it's second nature. He's kissing her the same way.

Please leave, the little voice urges. *You should not be seeing this.*

After what feels like forever, she pulls her head away to look him in his eyes. They don't say anything—not a single word.

They don't need to talk, because they are kissing.

And my heart stops beating.

It starts small, just a brush really, but then it's like something inside them switches on. He's kissing her like he kisses me, with his heart, and each millisecond takes me closer to hell.

This is my Jonah, the person I'd given my love and hopes of a future to, the person I'd literally dreamed of since I was a little girl.

And he's kissing *her*.

Like a supercomputer, I calculate all possible scenarios of why my boyfriend, my Connection, my frigging *fiancé*, is kissing his ex-girlfriend, but all the answers come back to the simple fact that Callie, impossibly gorgeous and elegant Callie, is in Jonah's arms, looking for all intents and purposes as if she belongs there. Like I've been the momentary interloper, not the other way around.

They are beautiful together.

My breath finally returns, only to disappear again as the distinct feeling of being kicked in my stomach strikes me strong and hard. And then I drag in a long gasp as I continue to stare in disbelief.

It's loud enough for them to hear, though. Callie finds me first, eyes widening in surprise. And then it's Jonah's turn to notice me.

His arms drop from her like she's on fire. His mouth opens, to say something—what exactly, I have no idea, but what can he say? What can he possibly ever say that would explain what I've just seen? And then I realize I can't take hearing his voice, can't handle any kind of explanation.

“Don’t,” I gasp, my hand reaching out to steady myself on a tree as I stumble. The bark shudders below my fingers and then the tree explodes, sending branches and leaves in every direction.

I trip over a chunk of bark behind me before catching myself. Jonah’s only a few steps away, frantic, saying something as he reaches for me. But I don’t want his words, so I shut them out.

His hand comes within a half inch of mine before the fence next to us explodes. A large piece shoots toward him, startling him enough that he has to recoil in order to knock the slat down.

I bolt.

Giuliana is jogging down the front steps as I’m throwing open my car door. “Chloe! When did you get here?”

I slam the door and peel out of the driveway. Everything in me, every last piece of dying matter, tells me to run.

So I do.

chapter 46

I find myself at the beach, parked next to Kellan's car. I have no idea how he's here when Giuliana is back at his house. And, frankly, I have no idea how I'm here, either, because the last half-hour is a blur.

When I'd fled, something in me kept insisting that I needed to be with Kellan. Not the little voice—no, that kept telling me to go home and call Jonah to discuss what I'd just seen—but something infinitely deeper and more primal in me insisted that it was Kellan I needed to go to.

For a half-hour, I'd resisted. But then flashes of all the times in the past I'd felt safe with him hammered at me. So, despite all of the progress I'd made in terms of my feelings for him over the last number of months, my body craves his presence and touch like a drug addict searching for relapse. It's the worst idea ever, but I gave in and ran straight to my ex.

My cell phone rings again for the zillionth time since I left Jonah's house. I know it's him—the one time I'd stupidly looked at the Caller ID, it'd said his name and showed his picture—but I cannot talk to him, cannot see him anymore, because parts of me are collapsing in on themselves.

I throw the phone back into the car, slam the door, and lock it, as if this will keep Jonah at bay. Then I scramble down the cliffs, scraping my palms to the point where blood bubbles out in ragged paths. Not caring, not even fully feeling the sting as I clench my fists over and over again, I make my way to the water where he is surfing.

I wait until I'm hip-high in the water before I scream Kellan's name. It takes a few times before he notices me, and when he does, he's so startled that he flips and crashes, disappearing under a break. Just when I'm tempted to do something incredibly stupid, like drain the ocean, his head bobs to the surface, eyes wide with surprise. He grabs his board and paddles closer until he can stand in the water.

I'm at an absolute loss at what to say. I gasp like a fish drowning, wondering why it has to hurt so goddamn much to do basic things like breathing.

"What are you doing out here?" he demands, but then pauses, close enough in range that I'm sure my emotions hit him as hard as a trailer truck going full speed into a brick wall. He grabs my arm with his free hand. "What's going on?"

I can't answer. Instead, I sob uncontrollably. He leads me back to shore; my teeth chatter so hard I fear my jaw will crack. He tries to let go of me in order to get his towel, but I clutch at him so tightly he gives up trying. After a moment where I cry and chatter against his shoulder, he manages to grab the towel with one hand and then wrap it around me. Then he pulls me close, allowing me to soak in his body warmth. He doesn't say anything for a good ten minutes; he simply holds me, allows me to weep, and gives me the safety and comfort I so desperately need.

Finally, when the tears subside to dull, numbing lethargy, I ask in a surprisingly even yet hollow voice, "Tell me everything you know about Callie."

He is genuinely surprised at this first question. "You mean Callie Lotus?"

I blink a couple of times, the supercomputer in my mind no longer working in overdrive. It has time to consider this bit of data. Lotus. Lotus.

Click. An association is made. Oh my gods. "As in . . . Astrid Lotus?"

"You ought to ask Jonah about her. I'm sure he'd be more than willing to tell you anything you'd like to know."

I refuse to meet his eyes. "Please, Kellan."

"Can we at least go to the car? You're soaking wet and it's freezing out here."

I shake my head and burrow closer. Despite the numbness, I fear I'm going to fall apart at any second. I just want to hold off long enough to get the data I need from him.

He sighs but doesn't force the issue. "Then, yes. Astrid is her mother."

The computer in my mind whirls slowly, taking in this latest piece of information. And then, I'm back in Astrid's office, asking her about the relationships before me. Had she known who I was when she'd seen me? Who I was to her daughter's boyfriend?

Slowly, I whisper, licking my salty lips, "What else?"

"What is it specifically you want to know?" he asks softly.

Ha. Is Callie sleeping with my boyfriend? "She's an Elf?"

"Yes."

I'm not embarrassed when my voice cracks. I'm beyond embarrassment. "So, she's a Magical?"

He answers hesitantly. "No."

"How is that possible, with a Magical for a parent?"

He pauses. "Callie is adopted. Look, Chloe—this really is a conversation you should be having with Jonah."

I flinch at his brother's name; this only adds to Kellan's confusion. I ignore his suggestion, instead asking, "How serious are she and Jonah?"

"Not at all, considering they broke up."

A hysterical laugh burbles past my lips. Did they ever really break up?

"Why are you asking these things, C?"

Although I knew it's irrational and unfair to even think of asking him, I do so anyway. "Show me something. Anything that was theirs."

He practically recoils. "Are you insane?"

So I beg him. And then I force the issue by surging into his mind. He reluctantly hands over a memory of a day when he and Jonah were at the beach, smiling as Callie called out to them to say some ridiculous word for the camera. Afterwards, she pressed many lingering kisses against Jonah's lips, forcing Kellan to jokingly order them to knock it off.

I pull out of his mind, even more numb than before.

He then surges into me and I allow it, too shell-shocked to care about blocking anything. He flips through the last hour or so before I'd arrived at the beach, glancing through a scene of me standing at his door knocking, the wild flight of a drive to the bluffs, my series of near crashes, the revelation that I'd instinctively sought him out, and finally, of seeing his brother and Callie kissing passionately in his backyard.

I close my own eyes against the memory. It wavers and then disappears, but he's seen enough of it to get the general gist of the situation.

Kellan pulls out and surprises me by holding me even closer. "I see," he says gently.

My mind teeters on the brink of blackness.

After I'm buckled into his car and the heat is turned up to high, he says, "I need to go get my stuff, but I'll be right back. I promise."

I stare out ahead of me, but my eyes and mind do not connect any dots. I have no idea what I'm seeing anymore.Worse, I don't care.

Kellan climbs back into the car, shutting the door. I hear the motion, but it's so impossibly far away. I try to shift my eyes toward him, but they slide, no longer focusing on any particular objects. I think he's worried—somewhere in my mind, it tells me that. *He's so scared for you,* the little voice frets, but it's fading.

I want to reach out and grab Kellan, to hold on, but I'm no longer able to control any actions at all. All I see and feel is impenetrable blackness, and I when I let go, I gratefully welcome it, letting myself fall into a vast abyss of nothing.

chapter 47

Although my bedroom is mostly dark, I can make out Kellan in a chair by the window. He's sleeping, legs kicked up on my desk. But when I sit up and the bed creaks, he jerks awake. I apologize, voice hoarse, but he waves this off and comes over to sit next to me. And then he allows me to hold his hands: warm and calloused and comforting.

"Did you drive me here?"

"We took a magic carpet," he teases, squeezing my fingers. My mouth cracks slightly upwards and he rolls his eyes. "Of course. Don't you remember?"

I search through only the freshest of memories—yes, I vaguely recall being led to his car. I nod and then think some more. "My car?"

"Lizzie and Graham went to get it for me. It's in your driveway."

"Did you . . . go with them?"

"No, hon. I stayed here with you."

Despite everything, despite knowing my heart had been shattered by his brother that afternoon, he allows me to crawl into his arms without hesitation or question. "Thank you. For everything."

"Chloe," he says gently against my hair, "like I was going to leave you. You are so dense sometimes."

"You saw . . ." I shake my head. "You *stayed.*"

Beneath my ear, his heartbeat speeds up. Finally, "If you need me, I will always be here for you."

These words mean more to me than he'll ever know. I press my face harder against him, clutch at his shirt tighter. He is my anchor. He is my strength. He is here, for me, and even though I don't deserve it, I take it.

When my cell phone rings an hour later, it doesn't take a rocket scientist to know who's calling. I try my best to ignore it, to talk right over the distinctive ringtone or to burrow my head closer to Kellan's chest and focus on his heartbeat, but it's persistent.

Ring after ring, minute after minute, pausing only to start a new cycle. When I can't take another ring, I take the coward's way out: I ask Kellan to answer it.

I feel, rather than see, his surprise. But he disentangles himself from me and goes over to where my phone is. He lays his hand on it and gives me a long look, one that demands absolute certainty.

I know what this means, how it's the equivalent of throwing a match into a barrel of gunpowder. And selfishly, horribly, I kind of delight in wondering how Jonah will feel discovering I'm with his brother. But then, it's not like he has a leg to stand on, right? Considering he was making out with *his* ex-girlfriend just hours before?

"Just don't leave," I say when Kellan moves toward the door. Because I don't think I can handle being alone yet.

He nods and rubs at his forehead. The phone goes silent for a good ten seconds before starting again. He waits until the third ring in this cycle before answering with a curt, "Yes?"

I lay back down, stiff with tension, even as I inappropriately and gleefully find pleasure in knowing that Kellan is standing up to his brother for me. "You think I stole her phone or something? That that's why she won't answer? You're such a dumbass sometimes, Jonah. She's not answering because she doesn't want to talk to you. And gee, I wonder why." There's a long pause before Kellan snaps, "You don't need to fill me in on all the gory details. I've already seen them. How is Cal, by the way? She still there with you at the house?"

Is there a way to block a name, like unwanted email from the confines of my mind? Because if there is, I definitely want to do it. I never want to hear Callie Lotus' name ever again.

Kellan's quiet again, but the faint sound of Jonah's voice on the other side of the phone carries through. It hurts, it hurts so, so much to hear his voice, even when it's this soft and far away. "Frankly," Kellan growls, "I really don't care what your excuses are. As you've long told me, they're none of my damn business."

My stomach flip-flops, sending a nasty gust of bile up to burn the back of my throat.

"No, you may not come over." Kellan pauses, his breath coming out harder. "I think it ought to be pretty clear that if she's ignored your last ninety calls, it's because she wants nothing to do with you right now. If you come over, you'll have to come through me *and* Karl."

The urge to puke is so strong that I debate briefly whether or not to get up and flee to the bathroom or merely use my bedroom trash can.

Jonah is yelling now, and his words, his voice, even as far away as they are on the other end of the phone, are too much for me. So I escape to the bathroom and throw up every last bit in my stomach. And then, I throw up some more, dry heaving until I sob from the intense pain. I hug the porcelain, gagging and wishing that I'd just wake up from this nightmare.

Yesterday, I was in love. How did this happen? How did I get here?

The doorknob jiggles, but a quick glance shows I'd instinctively locked it when I ran in. Then come the knocks. "Chloe? Are you all right? Please let one of us in."

It's Caleb. When did he get here?

"Chloe?" It's now Karl. "I will kick this door down if you do not open it for us immediately. I will give you to the count of three—"

Caleb cuts him off. "Are you crazy? Why would you threaten her? Kellan! Give this man some compassion!"

"Compassion!" Karl bellows. "I have plenty of it! It's the only reason I didn't kick Jonah's ass this afternoon!"

Hearing his name only triggers another series of gags.

"Would you prefer to be left alone?" Kellan asks through the door. His voice is gentle. Loving. Worried. It nearly breaks me. "We could leave, if that's what you want . . ."

"Leave her alone?" Karl yells, but he's muffled quickly.

I absolutely do not want Kellan to leave, but every time my mouth opens to tell him this, I feel like puking again.

Caleb says, "Kellan, maybe you should go home . . ."

This gives me my voice. "Kellan, don't you leave me!"

The door swings open—I'm not sure if it's because I willed it so or because Karl finally had his way. But it's Kellan through first, and I collapse in his arms.

"I won't leave if you don't want me to," he assures me. "I'll stay as long as you like."

I cry again, clutching at him like the life raft he is.

"Will one of you call Giules and tell her I won't be coming home tonight?" he asks our friends quietly.

I'm not stupid. I see how both of their foreheads furrow, but Karl nods, just once, and then they leave, which is what I'd wanted them to do anyway.

I am nearly asleep when Kellan says gently, "I think it only fair to let you know that Jonah is going absolutely insane not being able to talk to you."

Maybe he should've thought of that first before playing tonsil hockey with Callie Lotus.

"Do you maybe want to talk to him, hear his side of the story?"

Oh, HELL no. "What possible side can he offer?"

He strokes my hair softly. "I'm not excusing what he did, C. I just know how you work, how you like to talk things out."

"No," I snarl. "I do not want to talk to him. He has nothing to say that I want to hear. Nothing!"

"Alright," he says soothingly. "No calls until you're ready."

I crumple against such tenderness. "Don't leave me tonight. Promise."

"I won't." I feel his words, sincere and comforting, against my ear. "Whatever you need, I will do it."

I'm so selfish. But, I need him. I *need* him so acutely that my body is screaming out for him, craving his touch so badly that I can't even begin to fathom the thought of sending him away like I should. So I scoot as close as possible, breathing him in like he, himself, is the tranquilizer, the cure I require.

He may be working his mojo on me again or not, I have no idea. But a small sense of peace finally settles over me as I pull his scent in, hording it like a greedy drug addict intent on messing everything up despite knowing better. And when the black abyss blessedly surfaces below me once more, I stand on its edge and swan-dive in, plummeting into the pool of sedation, relieved to once again no longer have to be thinking or feeling anything at all.

chapter 48

The next morning sucks. Because reality, that pesky, unhelpful slap in the face, forces me to wake up and face facts.

And oh, how I wish I could blame all of this on a bad dream.

Kellan comes in to check on me around noon. I'm still in bed, picking at a stray string on my quilt. He has dark circles under his eyes, but gives me a smile, and it's real. He sits down next to me on the bed. "How long have you been awake?"

Does it matter? I motion to the clock on my nightstand, as if it'll answer his question. Then I clear my throat, sandpaper rough against delicate skin. "You didn't leave."

My non-sequitur doesn't throw him. "Of course I didn't."

I rip the string off of the quilt. There's a hole now, the edges jagged. I've had this since I was ten, a gift from my mom back when I used to believe we could and would be close. And now it's got a hole. I focus on that small space and the slice of blanket below it when I ask where Karl is.

Me and this quilt. We both have holes now where no holes used to be.

"Downstairs with Caleb." He smoothes back stray strands of my hair, tucking them behind my ears. "They'll take you to Annar this afternoon."

Anywhere is better than here right now.

"You should take a shower," Kellan continues. "It'll make you feel better."

I personally doubt this, but I do feel pretty uncomfortable in my skin. And that's frankly a pathetic thing to feel, since the rational part of my brain tells me so many people have it worse off than me. People who do not fall apart and disintegrate into abysses simply because their boyfriends cheat on them. And yet the hole inside, the one in my heart, grows bigger.

I listlessly roam around my room, picking out multiple pairs of jeans and T-shirts before arbitrarily selecting a set. The rejected pairs litter the floor. But then, I laugh at the ridiculousness of the situation. Why should I care about what I'm going to wear? What does the perfect pair of jeans and T-shirt have to do with anything, anyway?

Rather than a shower, I draw myself an extremely hot bath, pushing the water way past the typical stopping point. My head drops below the water line, so that only my nose and eyes peep out. I like it this way. All sounds are muted, making it a good place to think, to figure out things without all of the extraneous crap that can confuse matters.

Because I'm already confused, horribly so.

Jonah said he loves me.

That he wants to spend his whole life with me.

That I'm the only person he's ever been in love with.

So much ache and sadness fill me. Anger, too. I'd believed him when he'd said these things. I'd never questioned them.

My whole life, I've idealized Jonah. I've always believed him. He was the person I could always count on, even when I was breaking his heart by being with his brother. He'd protected me even then.

But, I'd been wrong. I'd been fooling myself, because if he'd been sincere about all these things, he wouldn't have been with Callie yesterday. He wouldn't have kissed her.

It is a horrible thing, realizing that the person you love has feelings for someone else. It's almost impossible, really. It hurts to breathe—my lungs shrink up, making it difficult to get air into my body.

Jonah isn't some random high-school crush to me. I haven't counted our days on a calendar, celebrating each week together as a victory in terms of status and achievement. This is the person I fell in love with before I could read. My best friend. The person I've trusted with my tragedies and victories. The person who knows all of my deep, dark secrets.

He is my heart.

I thought I was his, but I was wrong.

My cell phone is on my dresser. I'm still not ready to talk to Jonah—not sure if I ever will be—but I'm masochistically intrigued by exactly how many times he's tried to get ahold of me. And if *she* knows he's called me. Is he upset? If so, does she know? Not that the call log will tell me or anything, but it's still a pleasant, petty thought to hold onto.

I delete the multiple messages from the Cousins and the one from my mother without bothering to listen. And why should I? I can guess what they say. Cora and Lizzie probably said something like: *Are you okay? Call us so we can talk*. My mother, oblivious to the fact that my life has shattered into a million pieces, probably said something stupid like: *Make sure you're doing your homework.*

There's also a voicemail from Karl. I choose to listen to this one, even though he's downstairs now. *Where the hell are you? I just got off the phone with Jonah and could hardly understand him! Where are you? CALL ME NOW!!!*

Two voicemails left. Two from Jonah. What would he say? Would it make a difference?

Maybe it'd be: *Chloe, sorry you had to see that, but I just can't get Callie out of my mind. You and I may have dreamed about each other forever, but . . . did you check her out? She's a gorgeous, sexy Elf! You can't blame me for wanting that, can you?*

Or, maybe: *Hey Chloe, what was up with you and that fence? Are you even going to come over and fix it? Technically, it was the neighbor's. And don't even get me started on the tree. That's it. WE'RE DONE.*

I don't want to talk to him, but listening to his voicemails . . . well, it seems safer this way, because it's already been said and done. So, I press play and raise the phone to my ear.

The time and date are given first. Then his voice, still so dear to me, appears: *Chloe, oh gods, I can't even imagine what you think you just saw. No, I can imagine, but please, just let me explain it to you.* Giuliana says something, in the background. His answer is muffled, but I can still make out: *I said I'm fine! Leave me alone!* Then he continues: *Please, just . . . just call me back, all right? Just call me and I will come over and we will talk about this. Chloe, I love you. Do you hear me? I LOVE YOU. You are my everything.*

Why would he insist so forcibly that he loves me when he was kissing someone else? And not just any old kiss—I mean, they were really going at it.

Gods. I hate them both.

The second message is all of twenty minutes old. *Chloe, I . . . I would really . . . I would like to see you, please, as soon as you want me to. This is . . . I feel . . . like it's an insane nightmare I can't wake up from. They tell me you're going to Annar but . . . no one will let me come over again, not after what happened last night. I suppose that's fair . . . but . . . I really want to see you, just . . . I'm not allowed to go there this weekend, so . . . Please don't leave without letting me talk to you first. I'm begging you.*

He sounds as listless as I feel. I slide down the front of the dresser until I'm hunched on the floor, gripping the phone like my life depends on it. My mind flatlines.

The door opens and Karl steps in. "I wanted to see . . ." But he stops when he notices me rocking on the ground, sobbing.

I wave at him to pay me no mind. Karl squats down and waits for me to stop crying, but it's hard. And then, somehow or other, the crying transitions to laughter. Karl just watches me, growing more and more concerned until I finally stop laughing. And then I start to cry again. Dammit, where's the anger? Why does it have to be pain rather than anger?

I wave the phone around. "Why do you always have to be so mad when you leave me messages?"

He puts an awkward arm around me. "I didn't know where you were. Jonah wasn't being very helpful, and I got worried."

This only makes me cry harder. "He called me."

Karl pauses. "He came over late last night, too, but we made him leave."

I'm blubbering now.

"Do you want me to call Jonah? Go get him? Take you there?"

Everything in me tenses, becomes a wire stretched taut on the verge of snapping. "No. I can't. Please, no." Footsteps sound behind us, and then a familiar hand reaches down and touches my back.

"She listened to her voicemail," Karl explains as I dissolve in Kellan's arms.

"Oh," Kellan sighs. "I should've taken the phone out of here."

Karl hesitates before saying, "Did you . . . ?"

"Yeah. He won't be coming over again, nor will he be doing anything stupid like trying to meet you at the portal."

"Good. We'll be leaving in about an hour. I've asked Cora to drive us, as I thought it'd be best if . . . you know . . ." Karl trails off uncomfortably. Kellan has no response.

The door clicks shut behind Karl before I formulate any thoughts. "You're not coming to Annar?"

He's oddly resigned. "It's best I stay back."

It's the worst idea I've ever heard. "You need to come!"

"Chloe," he says quietly, "you'll be staying with Karl and Moira. You'll be in good hands."

It's completely unfair of me to demand that he come with, but I can't help myself. I do it anyway. I tell him I need him. I have to have *him*.

Ever so slowly, "You need some time to—"

I cut him off, nearly hysterical. "You promised you wouldn't leave me!"

His eyes close and his face opens up, showing the struggle he's fighting inside. But I have faith that he will come through for me. Because it's Kellan, and that's how he is.

And he does. "If that's what you want, I'll come, too. But . . ." He hesitates, his words twisting slowly away. What he's not telling me, and what I know he means, is that if he comes, it pretty much means the same thing as the two of us slapping his brother right across the face. And then thumbing our noses at him afterwards.

"Good," I say without the slightest hesitation.

Kellan is subdued. "Well. I need to . . . um . . . go tell Karl about the change of plans and see about how things can be switched around." He looks back down at me hesitantly, rubbing at his hair. Then he says to himself, almost inaudibly, "Alright. Fine," as he walks out the door.

chapter 49

I am sitting on a step halfway down the staircase, leaning against the wooden railing. There's this poem I'd read when I was little, about how the middle of a staircase is a safe place. Neither up nor down. A decision-free zone. And this is how it feels as I sit here. Upstairs, in my bedroom, there is the agony of tears and abysses. Downstairs and out the door is the reality of Jonah's betrayal. Here on the stairs, there is nothing but me.

Somewhere nearby, Karl and Caleb question Kellan about the reasoning behind his change of heart about Annar.

"She begged me to come," Kellan answers, his voice far too vulnerable.

The guilt in me grows. The safety of the stairs is disappearing.

"Just keep it in the forefront of your mind that she's just had her heart literally blown to smithereens by Jonah," Caleb says.

"Believe me, I know," Kellan says so quietly that I can barely make out his words. "I saw it in every last detail."

"She needs to talk to him," Karl says.

"She doesn't want to," Kellan counters. "And, I'm not going to push it just because you think they should talk."

"They're Connected!" Karl snaps. "You think this distance will make things easier on her? Them? Think again. Speaking from experience, I can assure you the best thing they can do right now is work this out as quickly as possible."

Stony silence fills the house before Karl adds, "You going with her to Annar is only going to make things worse, Kellan."

Anger envelopes me with a vengeance.

The wooden railing cracks loudly under my fingers, a sharp fissure racing the length of the banister. I jerk back, startled. The movement is enough, though. A ripple shudders throughout the wood as it splits entirely in half, crashing to the ground with a deafening thud.

Horrified, I recoil back against the wall. Oh my gods, I've destroyed something again, and like with the tree and fence, I hadn't even been aware of doing it. Which makes it all the more terrifying, because it's exactly what I've been frightened of for years.

I am not in control of my powers. Maybe I'm exactly what my mom accused me of being: a scared girl who doesn't know what she's doing. And that thought nearly pushes me over the edge of sanity.

The little voice argues with me, insists this is not the case, that there's a very real and valid reason why I'm falling apart, but just then, Karl, Kellan, and Caleb dart into the living room. All three come to a halt, gaping at the mutilated railing at their feet. I don't even know what to say.

It takes a minute, but Kellan eventually steps over the railing and makes his way up the steps to me. "Don't worry about this," he says calmly, taking my hands in his. "It's nothing."

"I'll . . . I'll fix it," I manage hoarsely.

"Later," Caleb gently insists, and then he and Karl retreat back into the kitchen. Kellan slouches on the step below me, stretching out his long legs against what is left of the railing. He waits until our friends are gone before asking quietly, “Do you maybe want to talk to my brother on the phone? You wouldn’t have to see him . . . just talk. Or not even talk, just hear what he has to say.”

The pictures on the wall behind us begin to vibrate. I have to focus to get the hysteria under control. “No.”

“I know it doesn’t seem like it right now, but it might help to hear from him.”

I stare off into the distance and try to piece together my reasons. But all I can come up with is, “It’s too much.”

He sighs, but doesn’t push. “Did Karl tell you J came here last night?”

I nod.

“He’s so pissed at me right now since I wouldn’t let him in.” Our hands find each other.

My eyes narrow in on the tiny cut above Kellan’s lip. How did I miss that this morning? Did Jonah hit him? How dare Jonah even remotely think about getting mad at his brother! Wasn’t *he* the one who’d wronged *me*?

Kellan continues, “Didn’t you hear anything? I could’ve sworn we woke up the entire neighborhood.”

“No. No sounds. Nothing but black.” I think about the abyss and ask, “Was that you?”

“Was what me?” he asks, running his thumb up and down mine. It feels good. Beyond good, actually.

I struggle to focus on what we’re talking about. “The black. The abyss.”

“No, C. I can do deep depression, enough to create an abyss and more, but I would never do that to you.”

"And the numbness?"

"Oh, well . . . that's me. I thought numb would be better than hysterical. Do you want me to stop?"

I shake my head. Numb is definitely better than having to feel anything acutely. "Kellan?"

"Yeah?"

"Am I overreacting?"

He studies me quietly.

"I mean," I clarify, "you obviously know a lot more about emotions than I do. Is this . . . normal? Freaking out like I am. Shutting down. All over something like seeing my . . ." I have to swallow first. "Jonah . . . kissing someone?"

"I think that if this is the reaction your heart gives you, then you are not overreacting. Hearts don't lie."

"What about 'mind over matter'—"

He cuts me off. "Our minds do not rule our emotions. Our hearts do. Chloe, listen to me . . . If this is how you feel, then it is how it is." He pauses, looks away. "Besides, it's the Connection. People who have Connections and are separated from each other don't deal with it well."

A car door slams outside and I nearly jerk out of my skin.

"It'll just be Cora," he says flatly.

And he's right. She strolls into the house without bothering to knock. "Ready to go?"

Kellan doesn't say anything to her. He merely regards my Cousin with narrowed eyes. Then he squeezes my hand and leaves.

Cora sits down in his spot. She nods at the twisted half-sticks before us. "What happened?"

I murmur, embarrassed, "I guess I got upset."

She nods, as if this was expected. "Look. I need to talk to you about some stuff before you leave. Let's go sit on the porch."

We settle on a comfortable bench that my mother has fitted with an overstuffed pad. Cora looks out at the front yard and says, "I brought your homework, just in case."

Like that's even on my radar at the moment.

She smiles and rolls her eyes. "Yeah, I know." Then she takes a deep breath, blowing the air out hard and loud. She nods once, twice, before turning to face me. "What are you playing at?"

I am stunned, not prepared in the slightest for this particular question. "What?"

"Kellan was going to stay behind, so, I'm assuming it was at your request that he changed his mind and is now going to Annar." She sighs loudly through her nose. "Why would you do that?"

Blink. Blink. *Huh?* I tell her, "I need him." It's the honest truth. I don't care if she understands it or not. She doesn't have to.

"You do not *need* Kellan. What you need to do is to go and talk to Jonah." I flinch at his name but she doesn't seem to notice. "Just a couple of days ago, you were engaged to Jonah! And now you're, what, running away with Kellan? What the hell?"

I can't believe this is Cora, that she's saying these things. "You didn't see what I saw!"

"You mean the kiss?" The grass in front of me blurs slowly before coming back into focus. "He showed me." Her face remains calm—how is she doing that? How can her voice and words contradict so much with how her face looks?

Confused, I ask, "Kellan?"

"*Jonah,*" Cora stresses, grabbing my hand. Her fingers are like hot pokers: judgmental and painful.

And then what she'd said finally hits me. She's seen Jonah, she had to have been with him to see something like that. Oh, oh, what did she see, what did he say, was he missing me, was he okay, was he sad, was he happy I was gone, is he happy with Callie, is she still with him?

The little voice urges me to focus. "I'm . . . surprised he would show you that."

"He didn't purposely show me! I surged, and he was so off his game at the moment, I was able to see bits and pieces. I want you to know it took me a good couple minutes to calm him down before we could even talk, not to mention fix the damage you did when you decided to attack him with twenty tons of fencing material."

FIX. THE DAMAGE. I'D DONE?

Black spots appear and grow before my eyes. I've hurt him, and there's nothing to ever excuse this. Not even his cheating and lying.

"You could've killed him, Chloe. What were you thinking?"

Everything just sort of splinters in my mind. The black now encompasses half of my eyesight. "I . . . I didn't . . ."

She stands up. "Do you remember when they first got here, and you knew who he was, and yet you decided to throw yourself at Kellan? And Jonah actually forgave you, which still beats the shit out of me, because I sure as heck wouldn't have. I mean, you dated his *brother*. That's just . . ." She shakes her head, disgusted. "Yet, he makes one tiny mistake, and you won't even give him the opportunity to tell you his side of the story? You're a hypocrite, Chloe."

This is my best friend, my Cousin, and she is taking his side. My boyfriend cheats on me, and Cora defends it, calling it a *tiny mistake*.

“Do you even know what things are like for him right now? Are any of his so-called friends telling you?” she asks angrily, but she doesn’t wait for me to answer. “No? Well, let me fill you in. His emotions are so out of control that when I stepped into his house, I felt like I was on a rollercoaster. And now, with what you’re doing to Kellan . . .”

Kellan? I blink at her, trying to hold on. The black doesn’t clear, though. It’s only getting worse.

“Have you even stopped to think what insisting on him going to Annar with you will do to *their* relationship?”

“Stop,” I whisper, blinking furiously.

She doesn’t hear me. “They are twins, and you are hacking at their bond with an ax! Even worse, it is almost like you’re doing it with a grin on your face!”

The blackness is so overwhelming now that I know it’s only moments before I’m gone. Even still, I manage to shriek, “Do I look like I am *smiling*?”

Caleb’s voice suddenly barks, “Enough Cora!” He hovers in the air next to her, anger practically steaming off his body. When did he come out here? Has he been here the whole time?

My hands shake as the tears I’ve tried so hard to hold back finally fall. I break down and start sobbing again. “He . . . he . . . How can you take *his* side?”

And now Kellan’s outside, the door slamming behind him. “Cora, what the hell are you doing?”

“She needs to hear the truth, Kellan,” my Cousin says defiantly.

“Yeah, you are so good with the *truth,*” he spits back.

She jabs a finger in his direction. “Why aren’t you letting him talk to her? He’s her Connection, Kellan, not you! Why are you even here?”

“Stop it, stop it,” I weakly cry out, but their voices are much louder than mine.

“Stay out of this, Cora. It’s none of your business,” Kellan growls.

“It’s just as much my business as it is yours. I can’t believe you. Are you so ready to throw away your brother for a girl that—”

“ENOUGH!” Caleb roars, flying in between them. “You go too far, Cora. Kellan’s right—this doesn’t concern you, so shut up!”

She’s stunned momentarily into silence—Caleb has never yelled at her before. I throw him the best weak, but grateful, smile I can muster. But then the defiance comes back as Cora swivels her focus back to Kellan. “Did any of you bother to try to tell Chloe what Jonah is saying?”

“She made it clear to me that she didn’t want to talk about it. I’m respecting her wishes. Are you?”

“If you guys stopped indulging her—”

“NO!” I scream, shoving my hands over my ears. “Stop it! I DON’T WANT TO TALK ABOUT THIS ANYMORE! I DON’T WANT TO HEAR ANYTHING ABOUT HIM!”

Cora’s mouth snaps shut as Kellan says, “Point made.”

I sag, and before I know it, dark hands pull me back under the oily waters of the abyss.

chapter 50

I wake up in Karl and Moira's apartment early in the morning, well before sunrise. The entire house is quiet, but, somehow or other, I know I'm not the only one up. I wander the house until I find him sitting out on a huge balcony, overlooking Karnach.

"She's alive!" I joke weakly, hands held up like Frankenstein's monster.

Kellan smiles and I sit down next to him. He hands me his mug of tea and I curl my hands around the warmth. "Why are you up?" I ask.

Instead of answering, he looks out at Karnach. "It's very pretty at night, isn't it? They keep it lit up at all hours. Karnach never goes dark."

But I did. And it turns out, after asking him what day it is, that I've been asleep on and off for three days. Which is terrifying and, if I'm being honest, more than a bit embarrassing.

Kellan is gentle with his questions. "Do you remember anything from those days? Did you dream?"

No, there were no dreams—just the all-encompassing blackness. I tell him this and he nods as if he already knows. So I ask him, once more, if this is a normal reaction, because I'm thinking it isn't.

He chooses his words carefully. "Sjharn visited yesterday, if that's what you're asking. He expected you'd wake up soon enough on your own, though. That was reassuring."

But Kellan himself doesn't look reassured. Not really.

Karl and Moira are the epitome of gracious hosts. I can barely lift a finger before Moira appears with a cup of tea or a new blanket for me to snuggle under. Karl attributes this to nesting, since the baby is due any day. I hope she'll come while I'm in Annar so Karl will be present at the birth. Maybe if he sees his little girl he'll finally agree to assign someone else to me and stick closer to home. I'd miss Karl, having come to rely on him a lot over the last year, but this is where he really belongs.

No one brings up what happened back home with Jonah, which I'm grateful for. And, for the most part, I've been able to keep the memories at bay since waking up from the last trip to the abyss. It's like I'm aware they're there but they are locked up tight enough I don't have to relive any part in detail if I don't have to.

And I absolutely do not want to.

Friday evening, after dinner, Kellan suggests we take a walk around the neighborhood, something Moira and Karl insist is a good idea. I don't really want to, but I consent when I realize it's something everyone believes I *ought* to do.

A lot of people are out and about on the streets when we exit the building. "There's this Guard party tomorrow night, and me, Karl, and Moira are expected to go," Kellan says as we linger at a stoplight. "I was thinking . . . maybe you'd like to come with? As a distraction of sorts?"

The last thing I want to do is go to a party, but as the alternative is to stay home alone, I agree. And me saying I'll go seems to relieve Kellan some, so I figure it's the right answer.

After we've walked several blocks, he pulls me into a chocolate shop, explaining, "I'm told this is one of the best places in the city for desserts, and I know how much you love your chocolate. Besides, Moira's craving some, and Karl said we couldn't come back without a box for her."

He's so sweet to bring me here. I am not surprised, though. This is the sort of person Kellan is.

We've just begun perusing the different offerings when the door opens, bringing with it an extremely beautiful, dark-haired girl. "Kellan Whitecomb," she purrs. "I thought that was you! I was across the way at a café with some friends and had to dash over, since you're so hard to pin down nowadays."

Kellan's discomfort is palpable. But he manages a smile, and while I can tell it's forced, one of inconvenience rather than insincerity, she doesn't appear to be able to tell the difference. She continues to bat her thick black eyelashes at him so hard I wonder if she's got something in her eyes. "Gina. What are you doing in Annar? Last I heard, you were in Greece."

"You could've come," she drawls. "You were invited."

"Yes, well," he says, hooking his fingers in his back pockets, "I've been very busy."

She flicks a look toward me. "Who's this?" The way she says this is distinctly insulting, especially since she asked him rather than me. But then I catch a brief glance of myself in one of the windows and realize, with a sinking heart, that I look like the wreck I feel I am.

"I'm Chloe," I answer, attempting a smile. "You're a friend of Kellan's?"

"I suppose you could say we're . . . *friends.*" She studies me carefully, her dark-brown eyes narrowing. "Chloe . . . Where do I know that name?"

Kellan yawns. "You didn't answer me, Gina. What are you doing in Annar?"

"Other than wanting to hook up with you again?" She licks her lips in this really sexy, forward way. *This* is the sort of girl he's been dating? "I'm here for the party tomorrow night. I wouldn't dream of missing it, not when I figure you'll be there, too."

"Yeah, we'll be there," Kellan answers, sounding bored.

Yeah, Gina. *We*. "How do you two know each other?" I interrupt, forcing her to reluctantly turn her attention back to me.

"Kellan and I, we've had some fun, haven't we?" She smirks again, twisting a strand of hair around her fingers. I try not to think about what she's insinuating.

Because I think I could hate her. Between her and Callie, I ought to just start a list to keep track of girls I can't stand.

"Kellan, is this your latest conquest? Please say no, because . . ." She pauses. Laughs. "She's not quite your style, is she?"

Okay. Now I *know* I hate her. I've never really wanted to claw another girl's eyes out, but Gina seems like a pretty good candidate for my first try. I don't know if this is because she's such a troll or if it's because Kellan is mine and she needs to back off.

Wait. That isn't right. *Jonah* is mine, not Kellan.

My heart sinks. That's not right anymore, either.

"We go to school together," Kellan says, looking at his watch.

"Lucky girl," Gina says, clearly not catching on.

He puts an arm around my shoulders, and she frowns. "Greece was beautiful," she says, returning to the subject. "I got to sunbathe on daddy's yacht in the Aegean all day long. It was sumptuous. I know there's precious little surfing there to tempt you, but perhaps you'll still find reason to go."

"Maybe," Kellan says, eyes focusing on the doorway and not her. It's amusing that she really can't tell just how completely disinterested he is with this conversation. "It all depends on where the Guard sends me."

"I keep forgetting you've already Ascended, you sexy creature you."

Is she for real? I mean, he's standing here, with his arm around me! My hands itch to slap her.

"So did Chloe," Kellan offers.

Gina regards me as if I am a bug to be squashed. That's right, Gina. Suck on that. "Chloe . . . Lilywhite, correct?" Her kohl-lined eyes narrow at me. She looks like frigging Cleopatra. "The great Creator, hmm?" She definitely has a knack for making anything sound insulting. "I suppose I thought you would be . . . *different,"* Gina continues. "Such stories about you here in Annar already. Word is that you are a force of nature."

Obvious translation: *Force of nature? More like disappointment.*

"Well, I don't know about stories . . ." I murmur, at the same time that Kellan says, "Chloe definitely lives up to the hype."

"Oh, enough of this modesty," Gina slyly coos. "We should all be so fortunate to have such a reputation." She shifts her attention back toward Kellan. "Like this one. What a reputation he already has."

Kellan has absolutely no reaction to this.

Gina snaps her fingers. "Oh, I remember *now*. Chloe—she's your brother's girlfriend, right? Where is Jonah, anyway?"

His name, coming from her, hits me out of left field. I'm not sure if my gasp is audible or not, but Kellan's grip on me tightens significantly.

"He's back home," Kellan answers smoothly. "He wasn't able to come out this weekend."

Gina notices the change in my demeanor, of this I am sure. "What a good brother you are, taking *such* care of his girlfriend while he's gone."

Her malice is beyond nauseating. The little voice is encouraging me to tell her off, to not put up with her crap, but I can't. Because there's this horrible, suffocating feeling in me. Jonah smashed my heart to pieces, and now I find myself put out and jealous over a girl I know I have no right to be jealous of. It shouldn't matter if Kellan has dated her. It really shouldn't, but it does.

I am so messed up.

Misery and pain suck into me and spread out until I ache. It's like I've run ten miles and can barely stand anymore. Every part of my body is weary.

Cora said I'd hurt Jonah. I can barely breathe now, remembering this.

chapter 51

Gina finally sashays out of the store after Kellan blatantly rejects her repeated suggestions to go out together. He waits until she's gone before turning me to face him. "Talk to me, C. What's going on?"

And then I break down. My fingers dig into his arms as I struggle to get air into my lungs. "I *hurt* him."

His brows furrow. "What?"

"Cora said—"

"Ignore her! Cora knows shit, Chloe."

"She said," I continue more forcefully, "I physically *hurt* Jonah. Did I? Do you know?"

He drags me to a corner of the store, since the man behind the counter is totally staring. "Don't worry about this, C."

"Did I?"

"He's okay," Kellan says quietly. "He's fine."

So it's true. "How can you stand being here with me, knowing I hurt your twin like that?"

"You didn't mean it," Kellan insists. "He knows you didn't. I know you didn't."

"I . . . hurt . . . him . . ." I gasp. The urge to throw up is irresistible.

"He's fine. Do you hear me? *Fine.*"

"How do you know?"

Kellan forces me to look in his face. "Because I saw him when he came over that night. Cora fixed everything that needed to be fixed. He also told me he was fine. And before you go believing you smashed his head in, there were only three bones in two fingers broken. They didn't even hurt him."

I'm going to be sick right here in the middle of the store. I'd broken three of Jonah's bones. Anything Jonah had done, anything at all could never warrant such retaliation on my behalf.

"It was an accident, Chloe," Kellan tells me, but self-loathing infects every cell in my body. I hurt him, I hurt him, I broke Jonah's fingers— "Let me call him," Kellan insists. "That way you can hear for yourself that he's okay."

"No!" Then I cry harder, wildly accusing, "I'm sure Callie is making sure that he's fine!"

"I don't think—"

"She's . . . She's . . ." I can barely get the words out. "Your friend, right?"

He sighs deeply. "Yeah, she is."

"Is she still there with him?"

"I don't know if she is or not, C."

He's not lying. I can tell. When I don't say anything, he adds, "I realize I sound like a broken record player, but you really need to talk to Jonah. I mean, look at what this is doing to you. You were . . ."

More than just sleeping. *Catatonic*. I am beyond ashamed.

"You need to hear how things went down. From his side. Whether it's to resolve things between you two or find closure, you need to have that conversation."

I'm fully aware what it must be costing Kellan to even say such things to me. "Did what I saw . . . happen? Between them?"

He sighs again. "Yes."

I squeeze my eyes shut. "And . . . she loves him?"

"Yes, but—"

"I'm so dumb! I really believed him. I mean, all those years. All my life."

"I think you should—" he tries again, but I stop him.

"Isn't it enough that I lost him? Do I really have to hear it straight from his mouth, too?"

A hand clamps over my lips. "Karl said that you listened to his messages on your phone. Did Jonah say those words to you?"

I blink, confused.

Kellan tries again. "Did he say, *Chloe, it's over*?" When I don't answer, Kellan moves his hand away. "Look, I need to make a few things clear, okay? Because it's the fair thing to do."

I merely look up at him.

He takes a deep breath. "Jonah tried talking to me about this before you and I left to come here. Never once did he say those words to me. But he is very scared right now that *he's* losing *you.*"

"Why are you being so nice about this?" I accuse irrationally. "How can you defend him?"

He leads us out the door without making any purchases for Moira. "I'm not excusing what he did. I would never do that. I know what it did to you, what it's still doing. I told him as much. All I think is that you two need to talk."

"I'm sure he had a very good excuse as to why he was practically having sex with his ex-girlfriend in your backyard," I say bitterly.

"Kissing is not the same thing as having sex, and you know it. If you want to be pissed off at him for that, then by all means, be pissed off. But he didn't have sex then and you know it."

"Then," I say, jabbing a finger at him. "The key word is *then!*"

He starts to roll his eyes, but apparently thinks better of it. "You need to be able to ask him all the questions you have, Chloe. And he deserves the opportunity to answer them."

We are halfway to Karl's when I say, "There can be no explanation that is satisfactory."

"You'll never know until you hear it."

"You showed me how they were—"

"I wish I hadn't. It was stupid of me. I regret that more than you know."

"You like her." But it isn't an accusation.

"Yeah. She's a good girl."

"Is she . . . nice?" I hate asking, but I just have to know. If I'm honest, though, of course I know the answer. Because Jonah isn't the sort of guy who would date a bitch. Kellan, yes, as Gina is a perfect example. But Jonah . . . No, Callie must be something special. Three-years Callie.

"I think you would really like her under different circumstances."

I decide to completely wallow in pity. "She's *perfect*."

"No, not perfect. No one is perfect, least of all Callie. She'd be the first to admit that."

Please. "She's like the most beautiful thing ever. How could I even possibly compete with that?"

Kellan stops us on the sidewalk. He says, so seriously that it makes me shiver, "Nobody can hold a candle to you, Chloe. No one."

Something like this should make me feel better. And it does, which then automatically makes me feel worse, because, holy moly, are my priorities out of whack.

I think back to the look Gina gave me in the chocolate shop, the look of pity and condescension. I guess I can see why Kellan had been attracted to someone gorgeous like her. And why Jonah would be to Callie. "Did you date her?"

"I told you—Cal and I are just friends."

"No. The one who followed you into the store. Gina."

Kellan coughs and looks away. "I wouldn't call it dating. She can be fun, believe it or not."

I do not believe it. "I don't like her."

At this, his eyebrows rise silently.

"Why would you date someone like that?" I demand.

"I think you know why, C," he says softly.

I back up against the building behind us. The surface is rough and textured, prickly against my back. Yeah, I know why. I wish I could pretend that I don't, but I do. And once again, I hate myself because I still care about this guy, still love him, and here I am, dying because his brother broke my heart, wishing that I could get into a time machine and make this last week disappear, but at the same time, glad that I'm finally with Kellan again, too.

Like I said: priorities WAY out of whack.

"Kellan," I say, but I really don't even know how to start this conversation, let alone apologize for all the crap I've put him through.

"We should get back to Karl's—"

"No," I say, grabbing him. "I need . . . just hear me out, okay?" He nods, and I continue, my voice tiny. "I don't know what's going on. I don't know why I'm blacking out and finding it hard to breathe because Jonah cheated on me, and still finding time to be jealous of Gina."

"I swear, Chloe, there's no reason at all to be jealous of her."

"I mean, something's wrong with me, right? I shouldn't feel like this. I knew asking you to come to Annar with me was wrong. But I did it anyway. I knew it would hurt Jonah, and I did it anyway, would do it again, and I . . . I had to have you, because you're the only one who makes me feel . . . anything, really, and . . . and . . ." I swallow back the massive clumps of tears clogging my throat. "Something's wrong with me."

He studies me for a long moment, eyes so solemn. "Nothing's wrong with you," he finally says.

"Maybe Jonah has the right idea," I sob. "Maybe you both ought to get away from me."

"No," he murmurs, leaning closer. "Listen to me—I came willingly, okay? I know the situation. I know you're still in love with Jonah. Why do you think I keep pressuring you to call him? It's because I know it's what's best for *you.* I took that risk when you came running to me. It's worth it. Chloe, *you're* worth it."

I transform into an even more pathetic, weepy mess.

Karl and Moira meet us at the door, concerned over my hysterical state. When Kellan tries to pass me off to one of them, the hysteria ratchets up so badly that no one can pry me away from him. Eventually he takes me to my room and lies down with me, silently stroking my hair as I cling to him, still sobbing.

I doze fitfully, waking up when Karl come in the room. I listen with closed eyes.

"What happened? She seemed to be doing better," he whispers.

"Cora had told her about J's hand," Kellan says. "When I confirmed it, she lost it."

"You assured her he was fine, right?"

"Yeah, but it didn't matter. She's completely convinced everything is done and over. I couldn't reason with her, Karl. I tried."

It takes Karl a moment before saying, "I don't know how you do it."

"I love her," Kellan admits quietly. "She's my . . ." He stops, shakes his head against mine. "It doesn't matter what the reason is. Stupid Connection. How I wish it didn't exist."

"Maybe you should go home. We'll take care of her, you know that."

NO. I am just about to start screaming this when Kellan answers him. "I can't, Karl. She asked me to stay." He shifts under me. I have a feeling he knows I'm listening, awake, but he doesn't say one way or another. He must sense my panic over him leaving. "Have you heard from Giules?"

"I talked to her briefly this evening, while you two were out."

"Chloe wants to know whether or not Cal is still at the house."

"Yeah. She is."

Of course she is.

chapter 52

Moira bought me a dress for the party tonight. It's red and flirty and sassy and so not what I am feeling on the inside.

"You'll have fun," they've been telling me all day. "The Guard throws the best parties."

But I don't feel like partying. Or having fun. I feel like crumpling up in a ball and crying my eyes out, which is pretty much what I've already been doing lately every time I think about what's happened.

But I've also been thinking about what Kellan said to me.

He's right, you know. You need to talk to Jonah, the little voice urges. *Even if you don't like what he has to say, you still need to hear it.*

Logically, this makes sense. But the pain over his betrayal is incredibly tangible, like it's venom pulsing through my veins and mixing with my blood. It's hard to imagine talking to him right now.

Don't you want to know how he's doing, though?

Karl had told Kellan that Callie was still there. Didn't that answer everything?

But, technically you're with Kellan. Does that mean you're dating again?

No—it's entirely different.

How do you think Jonah would react if he knew you and Kellan slept together in the same bed all last night?

Hold on a sec. That didn't count. He was comforting me—

Would Jonah see it that way? And if you knew he'd slept with Callie?

I'LL RIP HER HAIR OUT.

You've been in love with Jonah your whole life. Are you really ready to let go without even a goodbye? You're smarter than that. One conversation. He deserves that, but more importantly, so do you. Call him.

I have no idea where my phone is.

Use the phone by your bed.

Yet I still hesitate.

C'mon. What's the worst that can happen? Can anything be worse than what you've already gone through?

Um, YES. Let's see, off the top of my still exploding head, I can come up with Jonah and Callie getting married and producing a slew of hateful, part-Elf babies. They'd be beautiful and—

Oh, for crying out loud! Will you just CALL HIM?

It is with great trepidation, but I do it. There are several rings, and then a voice: "Hello?"

But it's not him. It's *her*.

"Karl?" Callie asks. Her voice is sultry. Exotic. "Is that you? I'm so glad you called . . ."

I do not correct her assumptions.

"Karl?" Callie asks again. "Kel?" And then . . . "Chloe?"

I hang up. It rings not two seconds later—once, twice, three times before going silent.

I scoot away from the phone, sliding off the bed and onto the floor. Black dots dance before my eyes and I debate briefly whether or not to let them take me.

She has his phone. She knows Karl.

Next thing I know, Kellan is squatting down next to me. Very gently, like he's comforting a scared kid, he says, "Did you just try to call my brother?"

I sort of issue a cross between a gurgle and a laugh.

"Callie just called. Caller ID, you know."

Somebody get the girl a prize for being resourceful.

His hand comes to rest on my arm. "If you want, we can call back, and I can assure you that Jonah will answer this time."

I swallow and tell him, "No."

"But, you obviously wanted—"

"It was a mistake."

He studies me. "It must have taken a lot of courage to do what you just did."

Courage? Try stupidity. "It just proved my point."

"No, I don't—"

"*She* answered."

"Well, to be fair, I could have just easily have answered your phone. Do you even know where yours is?" I shake my head and he smiles. "That's because I have it. So, let's just say that if J had called, I would've been the one to answer it."

Hope, albeit unwanted, sprouts. "Has he called?"

"No, hon . . . but he was warned to stop calling you and wait for when you were ready."

And . . . the hope dies. If he'd really wanted to talk to me, he would've called. Of this I'm sure. And it only serves to spiral me deeper into self-pity.

My chest feels vacant. It's an eerie sensation. I don't cry anymore, which is a relief, because there's precious little liquid left in my body to generate tears. It's rather ironic that the mighty Creator is nothing more than a silly, overemotional girl. My mother has been right about me all along.

I'm numb, and I don't think Kellan has anything to do with it anymore.

The hotel ballroom is packed, making it hard to move. But Moira commandeers a loveseat for me and her to sit on while the guys prop themselves on the arms. It's hard to hear anyone's conversation over the music playing at full blast and the sounds of hundreds of people talking. It doesn't matter, though. I'm in no mood to chat, and they must sense this because, for the most part, they leave me alone.

A Dwarf walks by, carrying a tray of saké. The drinking age in Annar is eighteen, so I figure what the hell. I grab myself a tall, fluted glass and chug the golden liquid.

Karl gives me a long, hard look as everyone but Moira also takes a glass. I level a good, long look back and place my empty glass back on the tray. And then I pick another one up and drink it just as fast as the first.

Kellan says something to me, but I refuse to look at him to confirm this. I simply shrug and set the glass to the side. Things began to blur and buzz.

A bunch of people I know from the Guard come over to talk. Everyone is polite enough, but they all have this horrible hint of pity in their eyes.

And the pity only pisses me off. I refuse to talk to anyone, and eventually, everyone just gives up. I spend my time focusing on my growing collection of glasses on the table next to the couch.

I excuse myself awhile later, mumbling *"Bathroom"* to no one in particular. Halfway through the crowded room, a server with a tray materializes. I grab another glass, downing it quickly before handing it back. That tramp Gina magically appears nearby, and the moment she spots me, she scans the room for Kellan. Upon finding him, she winks at me.

Winks!

Bitch. My fingers curl into tight balls. I'll deal with her later.

Zthane finds me as I push my way towards the patios. I think he asks how I'm doing. Like he doesn't already know, frigging gossip machine.

"Good, good," I yell exuberantly. That'll show them, right?

He is concerned, but some hot Elf comes up to him, leaning in to whisper something into his ear. He is completely distracted by her, which gives me the opportunity to slip by.

I make my way to the railing, leaning over to look down. We're on the . . . Huh. I don't even know which floor. High up. Annar is sparkling all around me, romantic-like. The bitterness in me is lethal by this point.

"Chloe?"

I turn to find Kiah. Concern is practically etched onto her face. Gods. How pitiable am I, anyway? I've never been that sort of girl before. I hate that I'm her now. I don't want Kiah's pity. I don't want anyone's. Although, come to think of it, Kiah would understand pretty damn well, wouldn't she?

"Are you okay?" she asks.

"Better than ever," I snort. "That's what you want to hear, right?"

I can practically smell the Eau de Pity wafting off of her. "I called a few times," she says, "but I always seem to catch you when you're sleeping."

Sleeping. Right. I giggle—is this how they're referring to what I've been doing?

"Where's Karl? Kellan?" she asks, frowning at my continued giggling. And then, tentatively, "Moira?"

UGH. Like I'd send her over to deal with the guy and girl who broke *her* heart. "I'm fine, Kiah. Honestly."

But she doesn't buy this. "I should go get Kellan for you . . ."

"No, that's okay. He's . . . busy." I laugh even harder. I can see Kellan from where we're standing. He's talking to Gina. The laughter dies, replaced with anger.

She says gently, "I should stay with you."

But I can't deal with her pity. I want her gone. I want them all gone. "I said I'm fine! What's it going to take for you all to get the hell off my back and leave me alone?"

Apparently . . . say that, because, stung, Kiah finally retreats.

A tray is presented to me. "Drink?"

I two fist it. "Hell yeah. Keep 'em coming."

chapter 53

Kellan is shirtless, a Greek god with beautifully sculpted, golden skin. One of his arms drapes across me, his chin rests on top of my head. He is asleep, still oblivious to the fact I am lying in his arms.

I wrack my brain, but cannot, for the life of me, remember how we got *here*, let alone this hotel room. Or *why*, although a peek at the floor shows an array of discarded clothing items. But staring at his shirt jars a memory: pale and feminine fingers had worked at those buttons.

Shaking, I slide out from underneath him and stumble into an unfamiliar bathroom. Dull pain hammers at my skull with every small movement. I lean back against the door, dizzy. All memories of the night before are hazy at best. Even still, I catalogue what I do remember.

One: holy hell, did I drink a lot.

There's a very good reason that on your plane, the legal drinking age is twenty-one, the little voice snarls.

So not helpful, thank you very much.

Two: Kellan and I fought.

Three: Fighting must've been brief, because we'd been laughing uncontrollably, too.

Four: I yelled at that girl Gina.

Five: I yelled at Callie Lotus.

Wait.

Had Callie really been there last night? Or am I hallucinating?

But that isn't the biggest surprise. That would be six: Kellan and I kissed. Actually, it was more than just plain kissing. It'd been the meaningful kind. The hungry kind. The falling-onto-the-bed kind. Kisses filled with promises and wishes and of wanting more.

Washing my face does not remove this memory like it does my smeared make-up.

I kissed Kellan.

After a bout of hyperventilation, I slink back into the room. Kellan is still sleeping, and, coward that I am, I'm glad for it. Because . . . because . . .

Because maybe if he's still asleep then none of this is real. Which doesn't make any sense, and I realize that, but I am so blown away by all of this that I simply don't know what to do, let alone think or say.

Petrified, I don't move for a couple of minutes. But then I spot Kellan's cell phone on the ground by the door. And for some inexplicable reason, I decide to check his messages. There are two: one from Karl, one from Callie.

Just seeing her name makes me want to incinerate the entire building.

Knowing Kellan won't mind, I listen to Karl's message. Unsurprisingly, our friend is both pissed and worried: *Where the hell are you two? We couldn't find you guys at all last night when we had to leave. Moira's water broke around one-thirty. I know you're not at home—I was there twenty minutes ago. So, again—where the hell are you two? CALL ME NOW.*

It's comforting to know it's not just me he threatens at the end of calls.

The news about the baby is great, exciting even, if anything could be exciting in the midst of a hangover and the possibility of . . . well, too many things, really.

Kellan shifts, and I quickly slap the phone down on a table. It's loud enough to wake him.

Predictably, the hand wringing begins. What should I say? *Hello?* Is that what one says when they find themselves partially undressed and in bed with a boy the morning after drinking heavily? Or maybe a more mundane *good morning*, even though, in no way, shape or form, does it feel like a good morning?

He squints in the mild, filtered light. Then he pushes himself up on his elbows, twisting his head to look around the room. "Um . . . where are we?"

He sounds so adorably husky and confused that I find myself swaying a bit closer. Goodness, is he gorgeous.

"Chloe," he says when it's apparent I'm not going to answer, since I'm too busy ogling him and his perfect chest, "where are we?"

My hands are so sweaty already, my throat so tight. I have to clear it just to say, "A hotel." Then I wait quietly, desperately, for him to remember anything at all that will absolve us of any crime. Because from my standpoint, things are looking like we've . . . No. *No*. Don't rush to assumptions.

"I have a hangover," he finally offers, groaning.

"Me, too." I lick my dry lips, resisting the urge to touch him. "Do you remember anything about last night?"

I try not to stare as he puts on his shirt, but it's a lost cause. He doesn't look at me, though, when he says, "We had our first fight, if you don't count when you dumped me."

Ah, there's my trusty friend guilt. I knew it couldn't leave me alone for too long.

"I think," he continues, "it was because you were drinking too much."

I briefly close my eyes in shame.

He's not done, though. "But then, after fighting . . . I drank way too much, too." He gives a short, ugly laugh. "With you, no less."

Must find rock to crawl under.

He gives me a tiny grin before letting it fade away. "I remember Cal. She was there."

Everything in me deflates even further, which is a miracle, because I'm already feeling as crummy as one can possibly feel. "Maybe," I choke, on the verge of tears, "we were fighting and drinking because she and . . . and . . . Jonah were there, just . . . doing whatever disgusting things they do with one another."

"Jonah wasn't there," Kellan says tiredly, fingers rubbing at his hairline.

"You don't know that—"

"Yeah, actually, I do." And then, "Want to tell me what's going through that head of yours?"

I whisper, after an excruciatingly long moment during which I debate a million different times whether or not to broach this potentially explosive topic, "We're in a hotel room."

Is ignorance better than knowing if something between us had really happened? And is hypocrisy always such a bitter pill to swallow? After it becomes obvious he's not going to be the one to willingly continue the conversation, I stammer something lame like, "We . . . uh . . . were here . . . you know, together?" I tap the bed a few times. "And . . . there was alcohol involved . . . ?"

I think he'd have laughed at me had we not been discussing whether or not we'd had sex and didn't both have wretched hangovers.

And oh, good lords. SEX. How pathetic would it be if it'd happened while drunk, even if with someone I love? And then don't remember it? I've always assumed—at least once I'd gotten back together with Jonah—that my first time would be with him, when the time was right. Which, despite temptations, never seemed to happen considering a) we've been chased around by vengeful quasi-Magicals and b) we've both been babysat by nosy, gossipy Guards who wouldn't think twice of spreading our news to the greater masses. And then, of course, there's c) the core belief I've always had that having sex for the first time ought to be romantic and for all the right reasons and with the right person during the right time. Not that I don't love Kellan, and not that I haven't secretly fantasized doing such things with him over the course of the last school year, but *still*.

This is not what should have happened.

"So . . ." I trail slowly, stymied by his lack of participation in the conversation, "any . . . thoughts about any of this?"

His face shifts into neutrality. "We didn't have sex, Chloe."

I blink. Twice. "Are you sure?"

He laughs under his breath. "Yeah."

"But . . . I remember us . . . ?" I say, waving a hand between our bodies.

He lifts one eyebrow and waits.

I've got to be fire-engine red by now. "We did a lot of kissing."

"I remember." But he looks away.

I let a breath out. "You remember it all?"

"I didn't say that. I simply said I didn't think we had sex."

"How . . . uh . . . would you . . . know?"

"I'd know," he says, rubbing at his forehead some more. "If it was with you, I'd know."

Even still, something happened. Something strong, something meaningful, and something wanted—even without the alcohol. And this makes me cry, because it's a million times worse than what Jonah and Callie have done. As far as I know, all they did was kiss. What Kellan and I did . . .

It's unforgivable, sex or not.

His voice is devoid of emotion when he says, "You love my brother. You picked him."

Huh? "That doesn't mean we didn't—"

"In our case, I think it does."

I grip tight red bunches of my dress. "Because I love him?"

He nods.

When it comes to Kellan, I continuously do the stupid, wrong things. So, in the worst, most ill-opportune moment, I choose to finally verbalize what he already knows. "I love you, too."

Now he stands up, shoves his hands in his pockets. "You love him more."

Even though I know, if I peeked, his face would be impassive, calm even, I can't look at Kellan. So I evade in the worst sort of way. "I checked your phone this morning. Karl called—Moira had the baby."

"That's great news," is Kellan's response, although it doesn't sound great coming from him at all. And I know it's not how he must really feel, because he loves his friends, and I'm sure he's happy for them.

I admit reluctantly, "*She* called, too."

"What did she say?"

It's my turn to laugh bitterly. "Like I'd listen to her message."

He sighs. "I should probably go call her back."

I leap into his path to the phone. "Wait."

He stops and gives me a sad smile. "I know you're freaking out about what may or may not have happened. And while I can't one-hundred-percent guarantee nothing did, I can assure you that I honestly believe I would know if it had. As would you."

"But . . . we were drunk," I say, shamed to my core.

"Let's try a little experiment." He leads me over to a pair of chairs nearby. "One that might set your mind at ease. Do you trust me?"

I don't hesitate. "Always."

"As you and my brother have found fit to point out to me in the past, you two have such a strong Connection you've been able to merge your minds. Correct?"

He doesn't really expect me to talk to him about *that*, does he?

"And . . . it's said that people who are able to do this typically do not find themselves . . ." He struggles for the correct word. "Capable, I suppose, of becoming . . . *intimate* with someone else. Does that make sense?"

Yes, even though this is the first I've heard about it. But I also know people who have Connections aren't supposed to be able to fall in love with someone else. So if this is Kellan's theory, it's riddled with holes and is leaking like a sieve.

"But—" I try, and he silences me with a finger over my lips.

"Your Connection with my brother is strong. Strong enough I don't think, despite our . . ." He pauses, shakes his head. "What you may . . .

feel for me . . . That anything happened last night. So, I'll surge first. And then you can try next. Okay?"

I can't believe he's asking me to do this. That *he's* willing to do this.

He surges into me before I can protest, pressing his forehead against mine, eyes closed. He doesn't look for anything in particular, just stays in the moment with me. It feels so sweet, so lovely to have him in my mind. But I'm terrified of what will happen if we connect, what it'll mean. So when I tentatively stretch my mind out to his, I'm physically shaking. I'm just about to reach the very outer edge of his mind before the link snaps back.

I try again, anxiety nearly out of control, but the same thing happens.

He pulls back out, and in that frustratingly rational, calm voice of his, says, "See? I think had we been able to connect on this level, it might have meant . . ." He swallows. "Well, it doesn't really matter, does it? It only confirms what I said. Nothing happened between us. Your consummated Connection with my brother never would've allowed it."

I nearly choke. "Consummated?"

He smiles. Just a little. "You know what I mean."

And then he pulls away. I want to touch him, but I don't—not because it's wrong, but because it'll make things worse for him. "Please promise me," I beg, "that someday you and I will be . . ."

He waits for me to finish.

"Just, *anything* important to one another."

"You are important to me," he murmurs. "I don't think that can change, no matter how much I wish differently. And there's nothing to forgive. I came here on my own accord. I knew what I was doing."

My heart breaks again over this man.

He takes a deep breath. “You need to talk to Jonah.”

I don’t know why, but I still stonewall. “He’ll never forgive this.”

“He will.”

“You don’t know that. I can barely imagine forgiving him for kissing Callie.”

“You will.”

“Kellan, Kellan, I can’t . . .”

“You can.”

And when he says it like that, I want to believe him.

chapter 54

An hour later we are nursing our hangovers at a small café a few blocks from the hotel. Kellan has procured us aspirin, which, along with dark sunglasses, are the only things that save me from fleeing back into the dark.

“Did you get ahold of Karl?” I ask as he sips his coffee. I’m drinking water, afraid anything else will threaten my perilously fragile stomach.

“I did,” Kellan tells me. “His temper was waylaid by the fact that he’s got a very healthy daughter who, apparently, is the most perfect child ever to be born.”

I have no doubt she is. “Can we go and see them?”

He sets his cup down. “I’m sure they’d appreciate that.” Then more hesitantly, “While you were getting ready this morning, I called Callie back.”

I stiffen at her name.

“And,” he adds, “I invited her here to talk to you.”

When I go to stand up, he grabs my arm gently. “Chloe, she came to the party last night to try to talk to you—”

“Probably gloat,” I choke out.

“No. But it’s been five days since you’ve last spoken to Jonah. I think—”

I ignore the curious stares from the people around us as I start yelling. "Why would you do this? You know I'd rather cut myself than talk to her!"

He squeezes his eyes shut for a moment and takes a deep breath. Then his hand slides down my arm to rest on my hand. "I will always want what's best for you. And this, believe it or not, is best right now. Besides, she's already here, about twenty feet away, looking as if she's ready to bolt, too. Hear her out?"

I turn around just enough to see Callie Lotus, gorgeous as a runway model, evil villain of my imagination, picking at a piece of peeling paint on a newspaper box.

"Will you at least stay?" I whisper frantically.

He shakes his head. "This is a conversation for the two of you."

As if she can hear these words, Callie comes over to our table. She and Kellan hug, which sets off yet another round of uncomfortable, ugly feelings in me.

"Thanks for agreeing to meet this morning, Kel," she says, her voice better suited to a sexpot diva than a girl of seventeen. Then her eyes settle on me. "Hello, Chloe."

Like I'm going to volunteer a greeting. I think I end up snarling at her.

Nothing further is said until the server takes her order for chamomile tea. Once that's done, she says to Kellan, "Give Karl and Moira my best when you go to the hospital."

"Don't leave," I hiss. Callie shrinks back in her chair, no doubt remembering exploding trees and fences, but Kellan is unfazed by this.

"Karl probably needs to be calmed down," he jokes to me. "For Moira's sake."

Uncaring about what little bit of pride I have left, I plead, "Please don't leave me here with her."

He turns in his chair so he's facing me. "Chloe, you know I'd never purposely put you in a position where you'd get hurt, right?"

"Then don't leave—"

"You trust me, right?"

I nod helplessly.

To Callie, he says, "Remember what we agreed on?"

Callie sighs, sipping her tea. "Yeah, yeah. You aren't the only one who has conditions. My mother, when she found out I was coming . . ."

Kellan laughs. "Astrid not approving of interference? Shocking." As Callie gives him a rueful smile, he stands up.

"Please don't go," I beg again. And then, unfairly, to myself: *If you truly love me, you won't go.*

"I have to," he says, voice oddly strained. He leans down, kisses the top of my head, and extracts his hand from mine. And then he leaves. He actually leaves me alone with Callie Lotus.

Who is all calm and grace, sipping her tea like we're in a swank restaurant, friends rather than enemies. But then, maybe she doesn't see me as an enemy or even a rival, since she's won Jonah back.

She leans back in the chair and tilts her face to the sun. Her sunglasses are on the table—she doesn't have a raging hangover, after all—but when her eyes train on me, I'm startled to see that they are almost my shade of green. "Do you remember anything about last night, Chloe?"

My eyes narrow behind the dark plastic. "Why?"

"We had a bit of a conversation," she says, "or rather, I attempted a conversation. You slapped my face, called me a whore, and tossed your drink all over my shirt."

I'm sorry, but—*what*?

"Not that I'm blaming you." She pours a bit of honey in her tea. "I mean, I knew you and Kel were blitzed by the amount of empty glasses on the table in front of you two, but I thought, what did I have to lose?"

I dislike her, this is true, but I am not a violent person by nature, nor am I typically someone who'd be so crass to actually slur somebody, even her, in public like that. "Um . . . I don't remember any of that . . ."

"I figured you wouldn't. Thus the call to Kel. You and I, Chloe, need to have a talk. And now that you're sober," she looks me up and down, frowning, "this'll be a bit more civil." She pauses, fingering her cup. "Hopefully."

"You have nothing to say that I want to hear."

"Look," she says, hands flat against the white tablecloth. "This isn't easy for me, either. You think I want to take on the girl who blows stuff up and then smacks me, calls me names, and ruins one of my favorite shirts? Heck no. But I'm here, because I care about Jonah."

"*Love* him," I growl.

She's unapologetic. "This is true. And an even better reason to be here." She motions for the waiter to bring another pot of tea. "Before I tell you what happened last week between me and Jonah, I'd like to go back to the beginning, so maybe you can understand where I'm coming from."

The nerve! She steals my boyfriend and then has the audacity to come and brag about it?

"I met Jonah and Kellan Whitecomb when we were seven." She smiles as the waiter sets the pot down. "I had a really lousy childhood. My parents had been murdered the year before—"

"What?" I say, taken aback by how calmly she's telling me this.

"My biological parents had been murdered," she repeats, like I'm an idiot, "and I'd been living in an orphanage until adopted by Astrid. She happened to live a couple of houses down from the Whitecombs, so I got to know the boys pretty quickly. They were over at Astrid's a lot, what with their mother dead and their father mostly absent. They were my best friends."

It takes quite a bit of control not to demand her to get to the point, and she must see it from my face.

"Well, anyway—I won't lie, I loved Jonah from the moment I met him. He was so intensely loyal, so incredibly kind to everyone, even me. I was an outcast—outside of our little group, that is. Being . . . well, what I am, many adult Magicals shunned me and refused to have anything to do with Astrid through association. I mean . . . I really shouldn't even exist."

Stupidly, I'm intrigued now, when I really ought to be leaving. "Meaning?"

"One of my biological parents was a Magical—an Elf . . ." she motions up and down her body. "But my mother was a Human non. I think that's why they were murdered. I mean, it's all well and good for the different Magical races to mate together, but gods forbid, a Magical and a non? It's forbidden, you know."

Uh, I didn't know. I worry even more for Lizzie and Graham.

"So lame," she mutters, pouring herself another cup of tea. "Anyway, Jonah always accepted me from day one. I mean, so did

Kellan, but it just wasn't the same. And everyone knew I crushed on him—even him, although we'd pretend I didn't. Then in ninth grade, I finally worked up the courage to say something to him." She laughs ruefully. "He was so surprised. I don't think he'd ever considered me as an option. Why would he? I'm some weird half-breed, not even Magical. But somehow or other, we started dating.

"My mother warned me repeatedly that Jonah and I would never work out, not with him being all Council bound and me being a non. He even alluded to this a number of times. I always just assumed he was saying it because he heard it from his father, but, upon reflection . . ." Callie shifts her eyes away from me. "But I didn't care. Star-crossed lovers and all, right? And then he went to see some local Seer. Came back restless, distracted . . . and eventually more and more distant. And then came the kicker,"—her voice drops to a pretty fair approximation of Jonah's—"'*We're moving to California, and I'm really sorry, but it's best to break up now.*'"

Good lords, why do I feel sorry for this girl? How is she doing this?

"It was awful. I initially blamed his father—the Old Man always disapproved of me. And Jonah wouldn't talk about it, wouldn't elaborate." She takes a long sip of her tea. "Kellan didn't know what was going on, because Jonah wouldn't talk to him, either. Let's just say I had a really hard time when they left. I called him, of course. All the time. I cried and cried, and he was so apologetic. But when push came to shove, all he'd say was that things had changed, that it wasn't me, that he did love me, but he knew his heart belonged elsewhere. I'm sure I don't have to explain to you how impossible that sounds when you love someone so completely."

I don't answer, mostly because I'm still focusing on the whole *love* bit.

"And then came the day he told me he was dating someone. Claimed he'd found the love of his life, and then apologized again for hurting me. Man, I was so pissed off. How was it possible that he'd found the love of his life in such a short time, when I'd been there, more than willing to be such a thing for so many years? What made it worse was when Kellan called, more upset than I've ever heard him, claiming J swept in while he was with me in Maine and stole his girlfriend away. That same weekend J had told me about you."

So many pieces of the puzzle start to fall into place now.

"I was furious," she continues, "just really heartbroken, thinking that Jonah would ever do that to anyone, let alone his best friend and brother. But, of course, there was also Kellan's claim that you and Jonah had known each other even before I'd even met him, and that Jonah insisted he'd been in love with you his entire life." She sets her cup down and gives me a look—it's a combination of many things, but the most obvious is scorn. "I'm sure it's not beyond your scope of imagination to guess how I reacted. And Jonah didn't deny anything. I became a masochist of the worst kind. I would call Kellan and demand to know what was going on. Poor Kel, he really struggled. . . . I at least had the gift of distance. I never had to see you and Jonah together. But he did." Now she gives me a look of abject disapproval.

I merely stare back, refusing to give her a peek of the shame I'm actually feeling.

"When Kel told me he'd finally come to grips about you and Jonah, he urged me to also accept there was no changing the situation. I couldn't. I thought maybe if I showed up and reminded J of what we'd once had, things could go back to the way they once were. So, I came to California. Jonah was stunned, to say the least, when I called to tell him I was in town. He tried explaining how I'd wasted my time coming, that things were never going to change between us, but I didn't want to listen. Who does when the person they love says stuff like that? And, by this point, I had very little pride left—I mean, I'd basically thrown myself at him—so begging and pleading weren't beneath me. But nothing would sway him. He was sad, I think, knowing he was hurting me again with his refusals. I mean, I know the guy. He doesn't get off on hurting people. But, I was being pigheaded and he had to basically slap me in the face—"

"He *slapped* you?" I interrupt, aghast.

She rolls her eyes. "No, Chloe. Not literally. He laid down the law, hard. And then, finally . . ." She looks down at her teacup, but not quickly enough to hide the unshed tears in her eyes, "I began to comprehend what he was saying. Really accept it. My heart, I think, died a little at that moment." Then she picks the cup up and busies herself with drinking.

I don't know what to think. Here she is, telling me that Jonah forcefully told her it was over, that he's in love with me, and yet . . . I *saw* them kissing.

"Do you know what it's like," she says quietly, after clearing her throat a few times, "what it feels like to have to *hear*, to *accept* that there is no hope to ever be with the person you're in love with? It pretty much sucks, Chloe. Because it's not like I have an on/off switch when it comes to my feelings. I can't just say, 'Oh, well, okay then. You don't love me, so I don't love you.' That's not how I work. See, I love him. I'm in love with Jonah still."

Well, *duh*.

She shoves her sunglasses on and levels me with a look I wish I could decode. "He knew, of course. He felt all that stuff in me. And . . . I think he took pity on me."

Pity. Right. How stupid of me. When one pities another, the obvious solution is to kiss that person senseless.

If she's bothered by my lack of participation in this conversation, she doesn't show it. "He was my boyfriend for three years, Chloe. He may've been in love with you all those years, and you two may have some kind of super-Magical Connection that makes you soul mates or whatever, but I've known and loved the guy my whole life. So yeah, I asked for one last kiss. And, I'm gonna be selfish and say I'm not sorry for doing so. Because no matter what you may think or feel, you're not the only person out there who loves him. I just had no idea that it'd be the equivalent of World War III when it came to you, him, and his brother."

I have to clear my throat to speak. "You didn't think that this might upset me?"

"Frankly, Chloe, you were at the bottom of my care list that afternoon."

I jerk into a standing position, having heard more than enough.

"Oh, sit down," she snaps. "I'm not done. Gods."

"Look, you don't get to just order me around—"

"Do you want to hear the rest, or what?"

Is she for real? "If you mean how you two kissing made him remember what a great thing he had in you, then—"

She has the audacity to laugh. A nice, long, loud laugh that makes the people around us stare. "Is that what you think happened?"

I'm taken aback enough I sit back down.

"I may've put my heart and soul into that kiss, but he sure didn't. In fact, I was just about to break away, because I'd realized that he really wasn't, and never had been, mine, when we noticed you."

"You expect me to believe this?" I ask, hating the fact that it's done shrilly.

"Yes," she says flatly.

That's enough. "Why are you here, Callie?"

"Because," she says fiercely, "I love him. He's so miserable right now, and it's partially my fault. And while I'd be the happiest girl in all the worlds if you two were really done and over, I'm not a completely selfish bitch who'll manipulate things so the person I love is in pain."

Great. Now I'm crying in front of *her*. And blubbering about how, if he was truly upset, he'd have gotten ahold of me by now.

"Hasn't anybody told you what's been going on with him?" she demands incredulously.

I can't believe I just broke down in front of her. My spiral into breakup hell knows no boundaries, apparently. I shake my head and wipe at my nose.

"After you blew all that shit up and nearly killed him," she says, her voice cold, "and then ran to his brother and refused to speak to him, Jonah lost it. And girl, I've never, *ever* seen Jonah lose it—not during the entire time we've known each other. A nuclear war could break out and he'd be just as calm as could be. But when you caught us kissing and then disappeared? It was . . ."

As she *tsks-tsks* at me, my lungs tighten. I can't breathe. I grip the table so tightly I worry I might break it in half. Because . . . if she's telling me the truth . . .

"You were gone, and you took his heart with you. He was . . . I don't even know how to describe it. Inconsolable, frantic, angry at himself, devastated, and in the end, I think, numb. When Kellan answered your phone . . . it was like watching him talk to a complete stranger. I don't think you understand how hard those two work at containing their personal feelings. Being Emotionals, they have to if they ever have any hope at using their craft effectively in the worlds. But Jonah . . . it was like there was a large crack in the wall, and the emotions were seeping out without rhyme or reason. The whole area around him was chaotic; any person who came near was an emotional wreck."

That's . . . that's not Jonah. He's always so in control. Everything in me is screaming that I need to get to him as quickly as possible.

"Giuliana finally called Cora over to attempt to help. She had to sedate him."

"She was there because I broke his fingers," I croak, the tablecloth tearing under my grip.

"Yeah," Callie says, her lip curling in a sneer. "You *did.*"

I can't breathe. I just can't. "You stayed with him," I rasp.

"Why should I apologize for that? He's messed up right now, and somehow or other, you got his brother and one of his best friends threatening to kick his ass, and he's emotionally alone—so yeah, I stayed. Because even if he doesn't want me that way, I will still be there for him when needed."

The little voice murmurs, *I know it sounds ludicrous, but you ought to thank her for being there for him when no one else was.*

"By the way. When you had Kellan come with to Annar? Wow. If things had been bad for Jonah, knowing you'd run to Kellan afterwards, they went straight to worse when he found out you two were together here. Me and Giules, Cora even, tried to rationalize with him—telling him you needed time and space to deal with things—but nothing helped. It was like someone sucked the life and soul out of him. We took his phone away—he wanted to call you, you know, despite what he'd been warned, but we all thought it'd only make things worse. And I'm sorry, but I didn't believe Jonah needed worse." She sighs through her nose. "When you called yesterday, I answered, because he was asleep. He's been sleeping a lot, which has me really worried. It's like he's here one moment and then gone for hours and hours, sleeping. Cora told me yesterday that you were doing the same thing. She said it was some kind of stupid Connection thing."

Wait. Jonah's going through it, too?

"I realized I needed to talk to you, to explain how things went down. So I called my mom, had her override Karl's orders, and we brought Jonah to Annar."

"He's . . . here?" I manage to whisper.

She nods, back to drinking tea.

"Was he there . . . last night?"

"No," she says. "He was at my mom's, asleep. And thank gods for that, because if he'd seen how you and Kellan were acting . . ."

I swallow the rather large lump in my throat.

Her voice drops and wobbles a little. "Jonah and I are not together, and even if you kick him to the curb like he fears you've done, he will never give me a shot again, because he's in love with you."

I desperately want to believe her.

"If you're stupid enough to give him up, then you don't deserve him in the first place. But it's up to you. I'm telling you where he is, and I'm strongly suggesting you go talk to him."

"Why?" I ask quietly, wiping at my tears.

"Why am I helping?" she clarifies. When I nod, she says, "I already told you. I love him. And sometimes, when you love someone, you have to think beyond yourself. He needs you right now." She clears her throat. "Not . . . me. So, yeah. We kissed. And maybe I should apologize, but I'm not going to. I've apologized to Jonah, though, for messing things up for *him.* You, me . . . that's different. Because I think you know exactly where I'm coming from."

There is so much swirling around my head, so many questions, fears, and hopes. But ultimately, Callie and Kellan are right. Only Jonah is going to have the answers I need.

Right or wrong, we need to talk.

I'm finally ready for that conversation.

chapter 55

Forgiveness is a tricky thing. There are those who say it's easy—to hold onto wrongs is tiring, so forgiveness is a natural thing. And then there are those who think forgiveness is a sign of weakness, that once a wrong has happened, to let that person back in is only asking for more hurt.

Jonah hurt me by kissing his ex-girlfriend. Was it cheating? Probably. Callie makes it sound like no—but then, there are those who'd say kissing is kissing, and therefore cheating.

But then, I kissed someone, too—not first, but does that matter? And can alcohol be an excuse? Should it be?

These are the things I consider as I stand outside of Jonah's bedroom in Astrid's luxurious apartment. Giuliana is out in the living room; she'd insisted on being here for Jonah even though Astrid outranks her in every way, shape and form. She's watching trashy Faerie soap operas, which are thirty times hokier than anything the Human plane has to offer. They're addictive and ought to keep her thoroughly distracted while Jonah and I have our chance to talk things through.

We've both wronged each other. And forgiveness—something so alluring and yet frightening at the same time—isn't a guarantee, even with a Connection. Because sometimes pain is searing and imprints itself, whether you want it or not, on your soul.

It could be worse. There are women out there, and men, who have been wronged far worse than I. A kiss, to these people, may be nothing. And I know this—but it doesn't stop the feelings of betrayal. Knowledge is power, but sometimes, even when you *know* something, it doesn't change anything.

Will things change between me and Jonah today? Do I want them to?

He is asleep, as I've been warned, in the middle of a huge bed decorated exclusively in white linens, making his messy black hair a stark, beautiful contrast. There are worry lines on his forehead, a tightness around his eyes that make me wonder if he's in an abyss like I'd been or in the midst of a nightmare. And even though I'd believed he'd ripped my heart out and damaged it beyond repair this last week, I feel it twinge in sadness at this sight, yearn for him in ways that are incomprehensible, because I shouldn't want him, shouldn't crave him when he's hurt me like he has.

But I do. Because the heart wants what it wants.

I sit down next to him and reach out, not hesitantly, but assuredly, to stroke his hair. He instinctively moves toward me, still asleep, and I suddenly know that forgiveness, as impossibly far away as it can feel, is within my grasp.

Not because I'd kissed Kellan, and therefore am as guilty as him, but because this man here is my love. And that means a lot, and is worth even more, considering how much he's hurt me. But I know I can forgive him, even if he doesn't ask, because sometimes that's what love does. Love isn't always clean and pretty—sometimes it's messy, cruel, and confusing. And sometimes, it doesn't turn out the way you want it to. But then, the beauty of love is that it's very strong, and when it's real, it's worth it.

I don't know what's going to happen in our future, long or short as it may be, but it feels right being here with him right now. I'm still angry, still so hurt I want to rage at him and let him know what he's done, but I'm also more balanced than I have been in almost a week. So I slide into the bed and he turns in his sleep toward me. And this small movement makes me realize that this is just how it is, this is love—this is us knowing, even asleep, that we are Connected.

When I wake up, he's the one watching me, still so tired and sad looking. I reach out and touch his face gently; he closes his eyes and shifts his head so it's closer to me. There are no words between us for a long time; we just slowly move until we're pressed up against each other.

I don't know how much time passes before he says, his voice barely above a whisper, "I am so sorry, Chloe. Hurting you . . . it makes me sick to my stomach. I can't believe . . . Gods. I'm so sorry. So, so sorry."

And, I know he is. I just do. I can feel it in him—not as a Magical, certainly not as an Emotional, but as someone who knows and loves him. "Callie came and saw me today," I tell him in a rather calm voice, which impresses the hell out of me. I figured I'd probably be raging by this point, but I'm not. At least, not yet.

I can't exactly see his face, not that it'd matter, because he'd probably look calm anyway, but I do feel his muscles tighten in stress.

"I didn't want to talk to her," I continue, still amazed by my control, "but apparently, she likes to get her way. So I heard her out. She told me what went down, at least from her perspective. Care to share?"

He struggles with this, searches for the right words—not so much, I think, for exoneration, but to accurately explain himself to me. I do pull away now, just a little, so I can see his face. And, to my surprise, he doesn't look calm. He looks, as Callie put it, like he's losing it. Like he's ready to cry, which is impossible for me to accept, because Jonah doesn't cry. "She . . . Callie, I mean . . . called me last week, saying she was in town. And . . . it surprised me, but I thought . . . I thought I could take care of it, just maybe . . . if she heard things, face to face, she'd finally accept that she and I are done. I don't know why, but I thought . . . I could convince her to go home . . . and then . . ."

Despite knowing I'll forgive him, there are still things I want—no, *need*—to know. "Would you have told me?"

"Yes," he says quickly, and I believe him. "But I didn't want to worry you . . . so that's why I didn't tell you beforehand. I was going to tell you afterwards, later that night, because I really believed she'd leave once I . . ." He trails off, his hands curling against our chests. "I guess I underestimated her, which . . . which is stupid, because I know how she works, but she . . ." He gives me a look, a supremely sad one, which makes me realize the level of guilt he has toward this girl. "She started talking about things from our past, and . . . and it's no excuse, none at all, but . . . it made me remember that, even though I've never been in love with her, I do have a lot of feelings that are . . . are . . ."

"Real," I offer. "She's been your friend for a long time."

He nods, biting his lower lip. "And . . . like I said, it's no excuse, I just . . . I guess I got carried away with the memories. So, when she asked me to kiss her one last time, I . . . I figured . . ." He shakes his head. "It didn't really matter, not when it came to me and you because I knew it would never change how I feel about you. I know that doesn't make sense . . ."

"It does," I say, "in a really odd, sick way." His eyes widen at my assumed easy acquiescence. But even though I'm fairly calm, I'm not ready to let him off the hook quite so quickly. "But what if I hadn't been there? How far would things have gone?"

He is genuinely flustered by this question. "I don't know . . . I'd like to say nowhere, not any further than where we were."

At least he's being honest with me. So now it's my turn. I let him know, both calmly and at times angrily, just how it made me feel, finding him with his ex-girlfriend. He listens to me, genuinely contrite, and when I'm done, and he's apologized again, forgiveness fills me up.

But this is not the end of our talk, because I have my own confessions I don't look forward to laying bare for him to see. And he knows there's something more, because the tension hasn't left him. I wonder how much Kellan and he have already shared, if they've had a talk, too, or if things have remained quiet between them like I'd believed. So I ask the question, and he says, "We didn't talk for the first twenty-four hours, except by phone and when I came over that night . . . but yeah. We've been talking every day since then—at least, when I was awake."

"Has he told you anything?" I ask, glad that we are now sitting and not lying down anymore. Somehow sitting feels safer, a better position to defend.

"About you?" When I nod, he adds, "No. He said it was your choice whether or not to let me know how things were." I watch him close his eyes, at how the breath in his chest just barely shudders. "I was so scared, Chloe. I kept hoping that you'd give me a chance to explain, but . . . I hated knowing you were with him. I hated that you went to him. I think it was even worse than when you two were dating. Maybe it's because our Connection is stronger now . . ."

I want to remind him that, strong Connection or no, he still managed to kiss his ex-girlfriend, but harping on that particular issue now will get us nowhere. So I tell him, as calmly as I can, which is difficult at best, what happened the night before. "We were drunk," I conclude. "And that's not an excuse. But it's the truth."

You'd think by his reaction that he hadn't kissed his ex, because he leaps off the bed, furious. "You did *what*?!"

"Hey now," I say, on my feet, too. "Don't you go getting on your high horse, here, Jonah!"

"You . . . you . . ." He points at me. "You and my brother found yourselves in a hotel room, *together*, remembering that just hours before you'd been . . ." He chokes on the words.

"How dare you," I hiss. "Hypocrite, much?"

He flinches as if I'd slapped him.

"I was hurt," I continue hotly, "and I'd been teetering between blacking out and crying so much that people probably thought I ought to be stuck in a padded room, and *yeah*, I got drunk, and your brother was with me, and we ended up kissing. And you know what? I have no idea if we were waxing nostalgic like you and your girlfriend—"

"*Ex*," he snaps.

"Or," I continue, nearly shouting now, "if it just happened, but it did. And notice that I'm not hiding it from you! I'm telling you about it!"

"Oh, that's all well and good," he shouts back, "considering it comes after the fact!"

"Are you forgetting why I ended up here in the first place?" I shriek. "You kissed someone *first*!"

"Someone," he seethes, "that I am not in love with. Can you claim the same?"

I am breathing hard now, so furious that the knick-knacks on the dresser are trembling. *You need to calm down,* the little voice urges. *Blowing up this apartment will NOT make things better.* I clamp my hands down by my sides. "I forgave you."

"I did not end up in bed with someone," Jonah counters, just as angry.

At the little voice's urging, I count to ten—and then to twenty—before answering. "Callie loves you. And you, yourself, just admitted to having feelings for her. Bed or no, you were kissing her like your life depended on it!"

"I told you the difference! Gods, Chloe! How many times do I have to say it? I am not in love with Callie! But *you* can't give me that assurance, can you? Don't bother lying! I can feel it in you!"

"The difference," I say, fists clinched, "is that I am *here,* with *you.*"

He blinks a few times and then takes a step back. A myriad of rare, visible emotions flash across his face—rage, confusion, shame, and then understanding.

"I am here," I say again, not so angrily now. "Not with him. Here. With you."

Jonah falters in his anger. And then forgiveness fills him up, just as it did for me.

Just like his brother predicted.

We spend the next few hours talking about what's happened between us over the last week. We take turns telling the other exactly what we went through, leaving nothing out. He admits everything to me. I admit everything to him. We leave out no gory details. It is a contest to see who was worse off.

We tie.

We make promises to one another, ones we mean to keep. Apparently, the reason both of us had fallen into such dark places, succumbed to abysses, is because of our Connection. It's Fate's twisted way of letting soul mates know how impossible it is to be away from each other. Astrid explained this to Jonah the night before, telling him that all of the aches, the wild mood swings, the difficulty breathing—they're all signs a body is in withdrawal from their Connection. Which is troubling and difficult to accept, because it appears it's yet another way Fate controls me. It's chosen my vocation and my love, and although I would never give Jonah up, it's disheartening to learn that I'd never really have a choice if I ever wanted to.

"It's a good thing I love you," I tell him as we pack his things up. It's been decided that he will not stay at Astrid's for the night, even though she's his surrogate mother. Because Callie will be here, too, and our wounds are too fresh.

He loops an arm around me and pulls me close. I take a moment to breathe his scent in, to relax in his arms and know that I'm home. "You don't know how thankful I am for that fact," he says, kissing me. "Because I am hopelessly, endlessly in love with you."

This is enough. I'm scarred and bruised, but sometimes, when you're in love, there are risks you have to take. It's not all sunshine and roses. Gods know how great everything would be, how the worlds would function, if love was that easy. But it's not. Because there are times when it's hard, and others when it's scary. Risk is like that. When you take a gamble, and love is always a gamble, there are two outcomes: fulfillment or heartbreak.

Sometimes all you can do is pray for the best and hope it turns out.

chapter 56

Life can be funny. Sometimes things go as planned, exactly the way you expect. This is the normal path for a Magical. At birth, a Seer tells you who you are, where you're going, what you're going to do. And you live your life accordingly.

Then there are the events and experiences that go so against expectations that they alter your road, deviate you off course and into a different direction. Sometimes it's a good thing. Sometimes it's bad. But it's really all in the perspective you choose to take.

You finally are starting to get it, the little voice calls out. *I think you're ready to learn the truth about who I am.*

I pause, the cup of tea I've been drinking on Karl's balcony halfway to my lips. Aren't I . . . me?

Absolutely. See . . . Huh. This is harder than I thought it would be. Maybe I ought to just use my real voice with you. I think you can handle it now. The little voice deepens, alters from my familiar tones into something else familiar: *Hey there, Chloe.*

I blink a few times, the cup still halfway up. Caleb?

Yeah, babe. It's me.

WHAT?!

Calm down, will ya? Let me explain this to you.

The cup shakes in my hand. Is this like what Jonah and Kellan can do? How can you be in my head?

I said, calm down! Let. Me. Explain.

I've been to hell and back in the course of a week. Yet this seems like the biggest shock of all. MY FRIEND CALEB IS IN MY HEAD.

First off, set that cup down. We don't want you breaking anything, right?

I am so blown away. How are you here, Caleb?

Well, for all intents and purposes, I'm your Conscience. With a capital C. It's a Magical craft. I'm not actually a Watcher, like I've told you all these years.

Why is this the first time I've ever heard of a Conscience?

Because no one with a Conscience is allowed to tell anyone else that they have one. We are assigned to certain people at the time of our birth, even if that person isn't born yet. So, it's like we wait our lives until you come around. That's why I moved to the Human plane—you knew I wasn't born there, right?

I guess I've never thought about that before. Does everyone have a Conscience?

I have no idea since we're not allowed to talk about it with others, but I'm thinking no. But what I do know is that we're able to link minds with our wards.

Okay . . . and the point of all this . . . ?

I'm your sounding board. DUH. What have we always done? I talk to you, you talk to me. We ask each other questions, get you thinking about things. I point out the big stuff you sometimes overlook. Stuff like that. We've always been good friends—why do you think that is? You've always instinctively known I was your buddy, that I would be your confidant. Even when we go days—weeks—without physically seeing each other, our friendship is always tight.

I can't believe this. It's just . . . crazy! Do you know everything in my mind?

Ummm . . . he murmurs. And then I hear a little sigh. *Yeah. I pretty much know everything there is to know about Chloe Lilywhite.*

Are you telling me that all these years, you've been able to hear what I'm thinking? Every time that little voice perked up in my mind, bossed me around, that was *you*?

That's about the gist of it, yes.

So, what—am I able to get ahold of you whenever I want?

Yeah. But Chloe, don't you go abusing that privilege. Faeries have to sleep, too! Man, all of those years of Jonah dreams. I know it sounds rotten of me to admit, but I was glad when the door was lost. I was tired of not getting a lot of sleep. You two used to be so cheesy to watch. Oh, look, the perfect guy, the perfect girl, can you believe they're so meant for each other that they meet in their dreams? Please.

Wait. You *saw* all those?

Sure did.

Did you know he was real?

Yeah, I knew. I also knew you two had to figure it out on your own. Figures that he did first. He always has been a little more aware of things than you.

I take a deep breath and then laugh. Yet another thing Fate has mapped out for me. My conscience isn't even my own. Granted, it's one of my best friends, who's always understood me, but still . . .

Yeah, I know, he says, sympathetic. *But, Chloe— you don't have to let all of these define you. They're like . . . jewelry, really. All of these things just add embellishment to who Chloe Lilywhite really is.*

I laugh. I don't wear jewelry much, remember?

Caleb laughs, too. *Poor analogy, I guess. But the point is—it's all up to you over who you're going to be. Who you are now. No one has say over that, not Fate, not me, not Jonah, not anyone. Just you. By the way, I've been so proud of you this last year. You've really grown up, taken ownership of your craft and your direction.*

Jonah comes out onto the patio, sits down next to me. "Mind if I ask what you're thinking about?" he asks, pulling a blanket over my lap. "Something has you pretty surprised right now."

I'm unable to tell him about my most recent revelation concerning Caleb. So instead, I tell him how I've been thinking about Karl and Moira's little girl. Her name is Emily, and it turns out, as a Faith, she's not being slated for either the Guard or the Council, much to the surprise of everyone involved. At first, I thought both Moira and Karl would be disappointed their little girl wasn't going to be a warrior like they are, but they surprised me. They're thrilled, ecstatic even. And as I've watched these young parents adore their baby, I can't help but think this is the right way to think about things.

Take the punches and roll with them. Because honestly, sometimes you don't have a choice.

When I'd finally come back to Karl's apartment, I found a note waiting for me:

C -

I'm heading back home – and by home, I mean Maine. There are a lot of things that I need to figure out for myself, by myself, and I won't be able to do it in California. Know that I don't regret coming here for one second. I'd do it again, no questions asked. I will always be here for you if you need me—please remember that. But if it's okay, I'd like to try for that space we talked about before. I know I said I'd like it to start when we moved to Annar, but I'm thinking now is a good time. It's best for everyone.

You asked if we would be something important to one another. I want that. I expect it. It's just going to take some time. I can't give you a timeline, because I'm not there yet.

Take care of yourself -

Kellan

I read it twice before handing it over to Jonah. After reading it, he said, "I'm glad Kel was here for you this week."

I'd sighed and sat down on the bed. "I owe him a lot of apologies."

"He won't want to hear them," Jonah said, sitting down next to me. "Just give him the space he's asking for, because that's what he needs."

"What will happen between the two of you?" I asked, staring down at the note. It was just a piece of white paper, the message written in plain black ink. It could've been anything, really. But it wasn't—it was something more. It was Kellan finally doing what I hadn't been able to.

And it made—makes—me so *sad*.

"Things will be fine between us," Jonah had said. "He's my twin and my best friend. We need each other no matter how much we may fight."

"Are you still mad at him?"

"No. I was—I was really angry, so much so that I even wished our link together would break at one crazy point. But that's gone now. I rationally know that, despite everything, his heart was in the right place. I can't be mad at him for that. I love him. He's my other half."

When it comes time to go back to California, Jonah and I face a few uphill battles based on some agreements we'd come to. The first is with Karl when I tell him I don't want him to follow.

"School is out in about a month, and then I'll be moving here," I inform him and Moira. "I think . . . a month is a long time to be away from your daughter. What if she smiles and you miss that?"

Emily is in my arms, all sleepy and perfect. They'd surprised me this morning by asking me if I'd like to be her godmother. Heck yeah, I would. And I'm going to do everything I can to look out for this little girl, including, if need be, going to war with her dad to make sure he's around for all her firsts.

Because these are new parents, barely adults themselves. And maybe Karl has too many responsibilities on his plate at way too early of an age, but I know he and Moira will be truly involved in Emily's life, more than my parents have been in mine. Karl's shown me that over the last year with just how well he's taken care of me, an ignorant girl who is now much more comfortable with her craft and mindset thanks to his guidance.

He's going to be the best kind of dad.

And then Jonah and I call Giuliana and dismiss her in a similar way. The Council and the Guard argue vehemently, even haul us in one of their closed-door sessions, but we stand our ground. One month—that's all we're asking for. In a little over a month, we're going to have to give our lives over completely to Annar and its expectations. I want this last month. We *both* do—our equivalent of a summer, to enjoy the last fleeting moments of freedom, of feeling like the kids we've never really gotten to be.

The Elders have been silent since the attack on Annar. I know that doesn't mean anything. They'll come for me sooner or later. And I'll have to be ready for them.

In the end, we manage to convince the Council that we've proven, over the course of the year, that we're capable of taking care of matters ourselves. Reckless as some of our decisions may be, both of us helped ensure the safety of others. And this ends up being enough to grant us thirty days' reprieve.

I deviate from my expectations, from the requirements and plans that everyone else has for me. I alter my road.

Cora comes alone, as requested, to pick us up at the entrance of the woods. Halfway home, she tries to apologize to me for our fight the day I left.

"I get where you were coming from," I tell her, and the thing is, I do. It's all about risks when it comes to love. And Cora loves me. She really does. She'd done what she thought was best. It wasn't, though, but I won't hold it against her. Because when push comes to shove, I'll be there for her, too, trying to do what I think is best.

She surprises us by admitting she and Raul Mesaverde are dating. I'm ashamed that I've been so self-absorbed these last few months to not have figured this out. Cora shrugs it off, happily explaining how their awkward, if not endearing, courtship occurred, starting with his first initial visit as my personal Guard to where he babied her back to health in the hospital following her attack to where they decided, while Jonah and I were imploding over the last week, that time is short and love is great. And they took a risk, and now my Cousin is acting like a fool in love, and it's a beautiful thing to see. I don't point out that he's older, or how I've been told repeatedly that he's a player, because none of these things matter, not when you're in love.

chapter 57

I begin to think about the links people have, the ones I have, and of how they tie us together even when the entire concept of the bonds are inexplicable. The four of us—me, Jonah, Kellan, and Callie—are linked together by a series of complex threads which are utterly confusing and heartbreaking all at the same time.

Over the last year, I'd repeatedly hurt both Jonah and Kellan with the feelings I have toward the other. They've hurt me. Jonah had hurt Callie, and Callie, in turn, had hurt him. I can't wrap my mind around any of this—and, in order to move forward, I need to know *why*.

So I break down and place a phone call one afternoon to the regional Seer, one who has nothing to do with any of us. I'm not going back to Astrid; it wouldn't be fair.

Ronald Violethill is an eccentric hippie who lives about an hour south. I meet him outside his small cottage, surrounded by riotous roses and camellia buses. He's on his front porch, wearing rainbow suspenders, a carrot-colored beard, and smudged glasses. He smells like patchouli incense.

"Chloe Lilywhite," he drawls, sticking a pudgy hand out for me to shake. It's a firm grasp, confident. He motions for me to have a seat next to him. "I have to admit I was a little surprised at getting your call. Lemonade?" he asks, pointing to a glass pitcher sitting on a white wicker table in front of us. I glance out into the yard and spot a lemon tree. He notices this. “I cheat,” he admits. “I get a Nymph friend of mine to occasionally come and coax the tree to be happy in this climate. Northern California—not the most favored location for citrus, you know, especially this close to the coast.”

I smile and sip my drink. It’s delicious—tart and sweet at the same time.

“Summer’s my favorite time of year,” he says, settling back on the wide, comfortable bench. “There’s a lot of opportunity for escape, for those moments where life just lets you coast along the river, free in your inner tube.”

I swirl my glass so the ice cubes clink together. “Is there ever really a moment where a Magical gets to do that?”

“Sure there is. I know it’s standard issue to say our lives are just a series of set expectations, but I don’t buy that crap. We’ve got our roads, and there is a start and a stop that everyone shares: birth and death. But in between . . . Yeah, there are lots of things for us to stop and see. Lots of little places to wander off the path and experience something new. We always keep going forward, though, because the end destination is the same. But it doesn’t mean you have to do it in linearly. Who’s to say the road can’t be crooked? You’ll come to that end no matter which way you head—we all die, just the same.”

I laugh quietly. “My parents would definitely disagree with that.”

“I wouldn’t be surprised. See, it’s been indoctrinated into us that this is the way it has to be. But it’s not. You even just sitting here with me right now, when the expectations on you are so heavy and great—well, I think it shows how you’re going to be an exception yourself.”

“Yeah?”

“Hey, look. I’m no dummy. I know you’ve already seen Astrid Lotus. I mean, that’s big time—people who go to see her? They’re big-time path followers. Me? I’m just an old hippie, ready to tell everyone that life is what we make it. That even though you’re a Creator and Council bound, and you’ve got the Connections you have, it doesn’t mean you can’t stop and see those sights. So, I’m thinking, because you’re sitting here, maybe you’re ready to do things a little differently. Cool. Now—you’ve got some questions about those things, those paths.”

Already, I feel less suffocated. “I do.”

“And you’re specifically looking at the Connections you have to the loves of your life.”

“Yeah,” I sigh quietly.

Loves. Plural. I know enough from my recent experiences to now accept this as truth.

And he tells me. Sitting on that porch, smelling those roses and drinking that lemonade, he finally explains to me why things are the way they are.

I don’t go straight home. Instead, I head to the nearest beach and lounge in the sand, watching the local surfers cut through the waves. I call Jonah, telling him I’d be home late. And then I dial another number.

It takes seven rings before being answered. And just the sound of his voice makes my heart twist, especially with all the new knowledge Ronald has just given me. “I know you want space,” I tell Kellan, “and I want to give you that—but do you maybe have a few minutes to talk to me?”

There’s a pause, and then the sound of a door closing. “I never could say no to you, C. I probably won’t start now. Where are you?”

"I'm at a beach, watching the surfing." I am ridiculously nervous all of a sudden. So I find myself babbling a bit. "I went to the regional Seer—he lives down the coast a little bit. There's a really nice sunny beach here, sort of warmer than the one locally. Some people even dare to go without wetsuits."

"Sounds nice."

"You been surfing at all lately?"

"Yeah, went today. Thinking about maybe going on a trip soon, somewhere even sunnier than where you are now. Maybe try some really big waves, the tow-in kind, right out in the middle of the ocean. Would be a good experience, a good place to lose myself."

Or find himself. It makes me think of the deviations that Ronald talked about, how these little experiences can alter us in small ways.

"You should do it," I tell him.

There's a pause. "So. Why the trip to the Seer?"

The moment of truth. No turning back now. "I asked him to have a look at some things, maybe help me understand why things are the way they are. And—I think you should hear what he had to say."

"So I'm assuming I was part of the conversation."

"Kellan," I murmur. "Like you could ever doubt you wouldn't be part of a conversation about my life."

He sighs a little. "Let me hear it."

"There's a reason why we feel the way we do about each other, why you can't break your feelings for me and why I'm always inexplicably drawn to you. I think . . . well, I think things will finally make a little more sense after you hear what Ronald thinks."

"That the Seer?"

"Yeah. He's this free spirit. I like him."

"A free spirit," he muses. "Almost contradictory when it comes to describing a Magical." But then, more quietly, "You said you have some answers?"

"Yeah, I think I finally do. You may or may not like what Ronald had to say. But, I believe him. It feels right."

"Go for it then."

You can do this, Caleb encourages softly, warm support filling me up.

I think the point is, I *have* to do this. For me and for Kellan. So I state the obvious. "You and Jonah are identical twins."

I can practically see his smirk across the miles. "That I already knew."

"Did you know that there have only been between ten and fifteen sets of Magical twins throughout all of history?"

"Actually, I didn't know that. I know we're a rare breed, though."

"According to Ronald, Magical twins tend to have very strong bonds, stronger than the ones nons have. There have been a lot of studies done on normal twins, how they can know what the other is thinking, feeling . . . you know, the weird links they share."

"Yeah, I've heard of those."

"And you two—well, it's like you said. You were once one." I gather my courage. "You two have a Connection, a bond between you no other living Magicals have. One that allows you two to stay linked, no matter what the distance or situation is. It's like . . . when the egg split in two, it kept a cord between your souls, tethering you permanently together."

Kellan stays quiet, just listening to me now.

"And . . . obviously, you two can talk to each other when none of the rest of us can. You've always been able to know how your brother feels, what he thinks, more than just surging. You knew the entire time we were in Annar how he was, didn't you? Outside of phone calls."

"Yeah, I knew," he murmurs. "It killed me to know he was like that, but . . . I guess that's how it goes. I also know he's happy now."

Which is how I wish Kellan could feel, but what I have to say will surely make that impossible. "It's that link you have, that permanent Connection," I say softly. "That bond, the genuine remnant connecting two halves that were once whole, does more than allow you two to communicate without really every having to say a single word." I close my eyes and order myself to stay strong. "My Connection with your brother is unbreakable. It's one of those things that neither of us really ever had a choice about. It was created pretty much when we were born. And you . . . you're Connected to *him*, permanently. Which means you also have a permanent Connection to *me*." My heart is beating hard. "You knew me that day in our history class because of that Connection. *Our* Connection. You would've always known me, no matter what. And vice versa. It's why I'm in love with you, too."

Kellan's silent for so long, I wonder if he's still on the phone. But he finally speaks, telling me, "I've also got a confession to make. I already knew about our Connection."

My eyes fly open. "What?"

"I went to a Seer, too, Chloe. When I couldn't figure out why I couldn't get over you. She saw our Connection—I mean, she didn't explain it to me like your guy did. I didn't know it was some kind of sick twist Fate had thanks to being a twin and all, but I knew I had a Connection. And I knew it was to you."

“When was this?” I ask, barely breathing.

“When you were Ascending.”

I am blown away by this. “So you knew? The whole time I was falling apart, you knew the reason I was with you, that I needed you, was because we’re Connected?”

“I knew,” he says.

And he stayed with me, even though it must have hurt like hell to see me crushed over the Connection with his brother, because he really didn’t have a choice. Because his love for me, like mine for him, is a forever sort of thing.

Sometimes I think it would be a good thing to kick Fate in its ass.

“I’m so sorry—” I begin, but he cuts me off.

“I’m sorry, too, because I can’t really deal with this right now. I’m having a lot of trouble processing what’s going on, dealing with how I’m never going to be with the person I’m meant to be with. And,” he adds, when I try to apologize again, “yeah. It fucking sucks and hurts like hell. But I’ve got to find a way to deal, Chloe. And you need to let me, because if I don’t, I’m going to go crazy since the pain is so acute, it’s all I think about.”

I can’t help it—I start to cry. “Does your brother know?”

“Not yet.” He laughs quietly. Bitterly. “I never knew how to bring that one up. Things are already tenuous between us—I worry how this might make things worse. I mean . . .” He pauses. “You’re his Connection, Chloe. And to find out you’re mine, too? I can barely process it. I can’t imagine how Jonah is going to take it.” There’s another pause, during which a few of my sobs are stifled. And then, from him, “I should go . . .”

“Wait,” I say, struggling to get myself back under control. I wipe at my tears with my sleeve. “There’s one more thing I need to tell you.” When he doesn’t answer, I plow forward. “Remember how . . . that first day? There were three shifts?”

“I remember,” he says so quietly I have to press the phone close to hear him.

“Those weren’t all because of Jonah. That last one? It was me finding you.”

When I get back, Jonah is in his backyard, reading a book in a hammock. I crawl in next to him, my heart a hammer in my chest. He senses this immediately. But, as nervous as I am, I don’t hesitate to tell him about my trip to see Ronald, and my subsequent call to Kellan. He deserves to hear this, and he deserves to hear it from me. I leave nothing out . . . except the truth about the third shift.

Somehow . . . that’s just mine and Kellan’s to know. It’s hard to explain, but I want to keep that one to myself, to symbolize the bond I have with Jonah’s brother. My Connection to Kellan is strong—there’s no doubt about this at all. But the one with Jonah is stronger.

It just *is*.

Jonah listens to everything without comment, taking it all in to process before saying anything. “I can feel how this is hard for my brother, and I feel guilty that I’ve resented his feelings for you,” he says. “But now I can see he never had any control over it at all.”

He sounds so rational about the whole thing, I begin to worry. “Are you angry? About me having two Connections? One to him, too?”

“I’m not thrilled about it,” he says slowly, “and . . . I’m upset, yeah. It’s going to take some time to wrap my mind around all of this. But I finally understand why you two have had a hard time turning away from each other. That it wasn't because you were trying to hurt me—"

Startled, I say, "I would never purposely try to hurt you!"

"I know." His head comes to rest against my shoulder. "I mean, I never really thought you did. But I had a really hard time accepting why you two just wouldn't let go of each other. It makes sense now. It's . . ." He trembles, just a little bit. "So screwed up."

"Fate sucks," I say, trying hard not to cry. Which is stupid, because he knows I'm upset, and even worse because he knows it's over his brother.

"Yeah," he says quietly. "Sometimes, it really does."

chapter 58

Cora isn't the only person delirious in love. The coming of summer and warm weather seems to trigger a wild rash of pheromones amongst our loved ones. Meg and Alex are inseparable, even nauseating, with their frequent displays of PDA. I never thought I'd ever accuse Alex of being overly affectionate in public, but man, is he ever.

Lizzie and Graham fall deeper in love every day. Inspired, Jonah and I decide to help them, as they haven't yet found a way around the Council's rules. Despite everything that's happened recently, I don't mind when Jonah calls Astrid for advice. He tells me how Lizzie and Graham's situation hits close to home for Astrid, how it reminds her of Callie's parents, and how, just maybe, if someone had been there to help them, they might not have died.

I don't know how she does it, but Jonah gets news one afternoon telling us that as long as Graham will consent to taking the blood oath as soon as possible, things might very well work out for my friend and her boyfriend. Sharing this good news with them is magic in itself—I've never seen Lizzie so happy. They leave right away for Annar, where one of Astrid's assistants will be waiting to take them to Karnach for the oath ceremony.

"That," I tell Jonah as I watch Lizzie and Graham leave, hand in hand, "was incredibly awesome of you."

He watches them, too, as our fingers entwine together. “She’s your family,” he says. “And that means she’s mine, too.”

This is who Jonah is. He is generosity, love, and loyalty all wrapped in one. Fate may suck sometimes, but in other instances, it can be so wonderful that I would get down on my knees and offer thanks if I could.

Another person Jonah welcomes into his life without reservations is Caleb. He’d met my friend and Conscience a number of times over the last half-year but had never gotten the opportunity to grow closer. But now, in our month of freedom, he and Caleb have the chance to get to truly know one another, outside of my head and my viewpoints. And Caleb genuinely likes him, which means the worlds to me.

All this makes me think a little more about how I need to pay more attention to those around me. That even though I’ve been consumed by my own personal soap opera dramas, the people around me keep moving forward with life, and if I want to remain relevant in their spheres, I better make myself worthy.

Every so often, I ask Jonah questions about his brother and how he’s doing. Jonah says Kellan’s already talked to the Guard, delaying his move until a month after ours. He’s going to take that trip after all, to go out and find those monstrous waves to conquer.

“Are you jealous?” I ask while we’re at the beach one afternoon, two days before we’re set to move to Annar. Jonah’s been attempting to teach me to surf, as Kellan had never gotten around to showing me since Karl and Giuliana left little time for us to even try something like this. I’m horrible at it, barely able to stand up even in baby waves, but it’s still something that I like doing because we can do it together.

“A little,” he admits. “I mean, I’d like to try that someday, too. But, I’d rather be here with you.”

He's sincere—and things are good between us now. Better than ever, actually. We don't have the distractions of the Guard watching our every move. We now have the luxury of hanging out with the Cousins after school, going to movies, on dates, hanging out at the beach . . . all of the good stuff, because, finally, it's just him and me, eighteen and pretending the weight of the worlds aren't resting on our shoulders.

At first, our parents had all been furious at our decision to dismiss the Guard, but they've mostly come around. Jonah's dad eventually just ignored the issue—he's now spending all his time in Annar. And with Kellan and Giuliana both gone, that left Jonah alone in his huge house, despite Astrid's urging to come and live with her. My parents surprisingly felt bad about that, insisting he move into our spare bedroom for the time being after they discovered he's my Connection. It's not like we've begun doing family things—that'll never change, but even still . . . I take it as a good sign from them, that they know he's a permanent presence in all our lives. At lunch one Saturday, my mother even, in passing, refers to our future marriage and questions us on our upcoming move to Annar. I'm told my grandmother set aside a trust for me, one that'll help me find an apartment when I move there. I've already decided to not live with my parents. Instead, Jonah and I will move into apartments next door to one another so we can be close at all times.

My mother and I have even started to talk to each other a little. It isn't warm and loving as many mother-daughter talks, but it's something.

It's a start.

"You may not feel the same once I'm out there," I laugh, in answer to what Jonah said.

He merely smiles, letting me know he'll be happy to be with me there, whether or not I'll ever get the hang of it.

And then I ask him how Kellan is dealing with things lately.

"I think this trip is his way of figuring stuff out," he says, shoving long, black locks out of his eyes. "Did he ever really explain to you what happens when we're surfing?"

"I'd rather hear it from you," I say, and it's the truth.

This makes him smile. "When we finally find ourselves as part of the whole, then our minds sort of expand into everything, as well, to find clarity. Any answer we want is there, no matter the difficulty. You may not like what you find, but it's there all the same. Our uncle told us of a place where he was able to finally find the inner peace he'd always been seeking. He had a lot of inner demons, things I won't go into here, but . . . when he came back from there, he seemed more at peace with himself. Kellan recently found a letter he'd written to us before his death, detailing where this break is. That's where he's going."

"He said it was in the ocean, far from the shore . . ."

"Yes. He'll have to take a boat to the spot."

"Is it dangerous?"

Jonah doesn't lie to me. "He sees the payoff as worth the risk."

"Will he be safe?"

The questions don't bother Jonah, because he accepts now that, despite everything, I'm always going to love and worry about Kellan. "I hope so," he admits. "He's a good surfer—he's strong. Our uncle taught us well."

We stand up and grab our boards. Just as we're about to walk to the water, I ask, "Do you think I'll find any answers out there?"

"Are there things you want to know right now?"

For once, at least for today, I find myself question free. Because I'm good—I'm here with my Connection, the sun is shining, and I'm at peace with who I am. I'm not worrying about the future or the piles of expectations waiting for me on another plane. The only thing I really have to worry about in this moment is standing up on my board. If I don't, it's no skin off my nose, because I can try again. And if I do stand up, it's sweet icing on the cake.

"Nope," I tell him.

He kisses me, and I shiver, because even now, after so many years together, he still has this power over me. "You ready for this?" he asks, and I know he means more than just surfing.

Can anybody be truly ready for their future? We can only do what we can. Someday soon, there's going to be a lot expected of me. I'm going to be asked to influence all of the worlds. I may be asked to destroy things. There are so many ifs, so many maybes that a person can go crazy thinking about them all.

But today is all about *this* moment. Because that's what life is really all about. A series of moments strung together. We do our best to deal with what we have at any given second.

Today is a good day. Today is filled with love and acceptance. I turn my face toward the water, feeling the salty air against my cheeks. I close my eyes, savoring it all, and smile.

There are no guarantees, except as Ronald says, birth and death. So I guess I'm as ready as I ever can be.

acknowledgments

To my fabulous editors, Sarah Cloots and Rekha Radhakrishnan, THANK YOU. Without your guidance and ideas, this book wouldn't be what it is today.

Tracy Cooper, this book would not be much without your support. Thank you, my friend, for being one of Chloe & Co.'s biggest fans. Your feedback and critiques have been invaluable from the first version to this last one. I am lucky to count you in my corner. Erika Treller, the same goes to you. Thanks for always being willing to listen to me talk out plot points. To my friends who took the time to read early versions and offer input as well as support, I am grateful for you.

To my peeps at the Coffee House Writer's Group, your support and encouragement of my writing has meant more to me than you will probably ever know. I value your insight and the ability to share my stories with you.

Carly Stevens, your cover rocks. I am so grateful to have one that I love. Thank you, thank you!

Nicole Friedrich, thank you for taking an amazing author photo. You and your camera work magic.

To my parents, thank you for believing in my writing. It is a really lovely thing, knowing your parents will be there to support you with your dreams. I am a fortunate girl, indeed.

To my boys—thanks for sharing your mommy with these characters. Especially you, Mr. K. I will never be able to think of this book without thinking of you, since you were conceived and growing at the same time it was.

And finally, massive thanks go out to Jon Lyons. Your belief in me has been one of the best gifts I've ever had the honor of receiving. Thank you for stepping up and being super dad so I could find bits of writing time during the craziness of our lives. I love you. If Connections were real, you'd be mine for sure.

Made in the USA
Middletown, DE
01 June 2015